Island of Fog, Book 10

Forest
of Souls

Forest of Souls

by Keith Robinson

Printed in the United States of America
Published by Unearthly Tales on July 20th, 2018
ISBN-13 978-1723447204

Visit www.unearthlytales.com

Island of Fog, Book 10

Forest of Souls

a novel by
KEITH ROBINSON

Meet the Shapeshifters

In this story there are nine thirteen-year-old children, each able to transform into a creature of myth and legend . . .

Hal Franklin *(dragon)* – Thanks to a werewolf bite, Hal had to be cleansed of his original dragon shapeshifter blood, rendering him ordinary. But the new and improved Shapeshifter Program allowed him to become a much bigger, adult dragon.

Robbie Strickland *(ogre)* – At three times his normal height, and with long, powerful arms, Robbie is a mass of shaggy hair and muscle.

Abigail Porter *(faerie)* – She often sprouts insect-like wings and buzzes around. She can shrink to six inches tall but usually stays at normal human size.

Dewey Morgan *(centaur)* – Although impressive in his half-equine form, this small, shy boy is ashamed of his roots after discovering what some of the centaurs had done to humankind many years ago.

Lauren Hunter *(harpy)* – With enormous owl-like wings, yellow eyes, and powerful talons for feet, this beautiful white-feathered human-creature soars and swoops like a bird of prey.

Fenton Bridges *(rare lizard monster)* – Able to spit a stream of water that turns to glue, Fenton is black and reptilian with an impossibly long tail. Though tentatively dubbed an 'ouroboros,' he's still compared to a gargoyle.

Darcy O'Tanner *(dryad)* – As a wood nymph, she has the ability to blend into the background like a chameleon, allowing her to sneak around unseen.

Emily Stanton *(naga)* – Part human, part serpent, the naga come in three different forms, only two of which Emily has explored.

Thomas Patten *(manticore)* – The redheaded boy spent six years in the form of a vicious, red-furred, blue-eyed lion creature with a scorpion's tail. Now he's struggling to adjust to human life.

Miss Simone is the resident mermaid shapeshifter and respected scientist. She's in charge of the Shapeshifter Program and everything else at the science laboratory. Others of her generation have either moved away or are currently on missions.

It's been three months since the young shapeshifters dealt with a hostage situation and fought a battle on the beach of Brodon. Things have settled down, and life is quiet. But something is afoot in the woods . . .

Chapter One
Steamer Dragon

"Has anybody seen Hal Franklin?"

The sound of his name being shouted across the market square caused Hal's ears to prick up. He stepped back from the dizzying collection of brooches, pendants, and necklaces and squinted into the morning sun, looking across the bustling Sunday market toward the east.

"You gonna buy that, sweetie?" the lady behind the stall asked.

Hal blinked at her, then realized he still held two pendants that he couldn't decide between. They were both tiny wooden carvings no bigger than his thumb, one of a dragon, the other a faerie, dangling from delicate leather straps. "I can't figure out which would be best," he admitted. "Abi's a faerie shapeshifter, but . . ."

"She's a faerie, you're a dragon," the lady said with a smile. "I know. Everybody knows. So which would she most like to have around her neck? Something that reminds her of what she is, like she doesn't know already? Or . . ." She tilted her head. "Or would she prefer *you* close to her heart?"

Hal felt his face heating up. "It's a birthday gift," he explained. "She'll be thirteen soon."

The lady nodded. "If you want my opinion, and if I were the lucky girl, I would like the dragon better. A constant reminder of her handsome and heroic friend."

"Hal Franklin!" the voice yelled, closer now.

He turned and scanned the crowd. Quite a few had stopped to look in the direction of the yelling. Something was brewing.

"I guess I'll choose the dragon, then," Hal said hurriedly, patting his pocket for some money.

A middle-aged woman stepped out of the crowd and touched his shoulder. "Someone's calling for you, son," she said. Then she turned and hollered. "He's over here!"

The lady behind the stall deftly wrapped the dragon pendant and took Hal's handful of coins. She also took the faerie pendant back, probably to save him from figuring out where he'd picked it up. "I'm sure she'll be pleased," she said with a wink. "Now, go see what all this fuss is about."

It seemed the entire market crowd was catching on to his whereabouts now, and as if by magic, an aisle formed directly across the square to where a messenger boy came running. "Hal Franklin!" the boy shouted, spotting him. "You need to hurry! A dragon is attacking!"

Hal instantly went cold. He stuffed the cloth-wrapped pendant in his pocket and ran to meet the messenger boy. The boy stopped, spun around, and started running the other way, glancing back over his shoulder like a dog checking that his master was following. A few hands reached out to pat Hal's shoulder or touch his arm as he hurried through the now-silent crowd.

"Go, kid," a burly man said.

"Send it packing!" another shouted.

More words of encouragement filled the air, but the faces blurred together. Hal could have transformed and launched into the sky if everyone had cleared a large space instead of pressing closer. As it was, he and the messenger boy ran from the square and tore down one street after another.

The breathless boy drip-fed him bits of information as they dashed through the village of Carter. "Don't know what its problem is, but it's tearing into the wall," he said halfway along one street. It wasn't until they were around the corner that he added, "The teacher tried to lead the class outside, but the dragon snapped at them and nearly bit someone's head off."

"Teacher?" Hal panted. "On a Sunday?"

Weaving around a small group of people that had clustered on a doorstep, the boy glanced back again and said, "Mrs. Hunter's Sunday School. They're just small kids."

Hal felt a stab of fear. He knew exactly which school building that was. If he could have transformed earlier, he'd have been there in a flash. "Why didn't you say so?" he complained.

Sunday School was something Lauren Hunter's mom had been involved with back on Old Earth in her earlier years, and she was keen to introduce the idea to New Earth. Each week she discussed a few different ways life on Earth might have been established—the Big Bang Theory, Creationism, or Magic—and the children loved it.

Hal shifted into dragon form while running, something he'd been practicing a lot lately. Abigail kept telling him he was pushing himself too hard, but he wanted to be at the top of his game whenever needed. He wished he could speed up the morphing process, too. While it had always seemed rapid, he now realized there was an important difference between *rapid* and *instantaneous*, a difference that could get him killed in certain situations.

He felt that clumsy, awkward moment when his human legs thickened into stomping claws and his upper body toppled forward under a thousand pounds of extra weight. *Too slow*, he chided himself as his smart clothes rearranged themselves around his expanding mass. He spread his wings in the half-second they were still forming and launched the moment the leathery webbing caught the air.

The narrow streets threatened to cripple him before he got off the ground, but he was prepared for tight spots and curled his wings a little on the downward stroke while springing upward with his legs. It only took one beat to clear the gutters, and a second beat to scramble and soar above the rooftops. A few slate tiles came loose in the process, but he doubted anyone would mind in an emergency like this.

A few beats later, Hal descended on the school building where Mrs. Hunter taught on Sundays. It galled him to see a dragon right there inside the fenced-in courtyard tearing into the stone wall of the school. The dragon had ripped great chunks out already, widening a window to almost double the original size, and now it was trying to clamber through the opening. Its wings caught and held it back, and the monster seemed too stupid and impatient to try and wriggle through, and instead resumed its frantic clawing.

Hal landed directly behind, aware that anxious faces peered from neighboring windows. He reached out and yanked hard on the dragon's tail.

The thing swung around with a snarl.

It was a female, far smaller than Hal, and much younger. That meant her mother or father had to be close by. She was a forest dweller, her scaly hide awash with a pattern of vibrant greens rather than the dull, darker greens he was used to. These dragons were slender, too, better suited for slipping between trees and curling around shrubs to sleep. Hal always ended up crashing through forests and leaving a flattened path.

To his relief, this little dragon had no fire-breathing capability—no doubt nature's way of saving its trees. She puffed hot steam, but that was all. She steamed up even now while he stood his ground and glared at the troublemaker.

"Stop that," he warned in a low, rumbling growl.

Stay away from me, the small dragon hissed back at him.

It never ceased to amaze Hal how he could understand dragonspeak. He clearly heard the growls and clicks and roars and hisses coming from the creature's throat, yet something in his mind translated the noise with ease. And though he'd tried his hardest to form human words with his stiff, reptilian, dragon mouth, the result was always the same—a lot of meaningless rumbles that apparently other dragons understood just fine.

"You're destroying a nice building and scaring my friends," he said calmly. Through the hole in the wall, he thought he detected movement in the darkness as Mrs. Hunter or some of the children made a sudden break for freedom or moved to a safer spot. "Why are you doing this?"

A human stole from me.

Hal paused a moment. The dragon seemed angry rather than downright mean. She had obviously been steaming quite a bit judging by the smell of smoke and a touch of carbon monoxide.

"What did this human steal?"

A gemstone. I felt its absence during the night, and I traced it here. I want it back.

Hal advanced, ignoring how the steamer instantly spread her wings, lowered her head, and began clawing at the ground. She had a lot of spirit and backbone, that much was clear. But she was still young. An older, wiser, even bigger steamer dragon might balk at a showdown with a fire-breather.

"Relax," Hal said. "I'm going to get your gemstone back."

He stopped mere feet from the steamer and waited while she sized him up.

You're going to burn this place down? My gemstone will not be harmed in the fire, but it will be difficult to retrieve in the flames and debris. If you could help me widen the hole—

"I have a better way. But I'm going to trust you not to hurt me. Okay?"

4

The steamer narrowed her yellow eyes.

Before she could answer one way or the other, Hal steeled himself and reverted to human form. The transformation took a couple of seconds, and he was aware of his magical smart clothes reforming around his body. Right after the morphing was complete, he patted his pocket and had a moment of panic—but then he found Abigail's pendant in the *other* pocket where it had somehow ended up.

The steamer dragon reared back, her eyes wide, pressing against the damaged wall as if wishing she could ghost through to the other side and flee.

"It's okay," Hal said softly, knowing his words were meaningless but hoping the tone soothed the skittish creature. Boldly, he stalked past the dragon and leaned into the gaping window opening.

The mess was appalling—chunks of stone and dust everywhere, the nearest desks turned on their sides, glass sprinkled about. In the background, Mrs. Hunter and her entire class crouched behind the desks near the wall. As the messenger boy had said, they had likely run for the exit earlier, but it let out into the courtyard where the dragon had landed. The only other exit was a doorway that seemed free and clear . . . but also in the line of fire if the dragon had blasted hot steam into the room. It had intended to keep them trapped until it could climb inside.

"Are you okay, Mrs. Hunter?" Hal called.

"We're fine," she called back, making herself visible above the desktops. She looked dishevelled and scared. "Did you send it away?"

"Uh . . . well, not yet."

He glanced sideways, trying not to think about the danger he was in. One quick snap of those jaws, a single blast of steam, a savage swipe of the claws, a flick of that tail . . . He would be dead in a second.

"One of your class found something," he said carefully. A kid might not own up to stealing, and things could quickly turn far worse. This called for tact. "This poor dragon lost a gemstone, but it's here somewhere. Could she please have it?"

A long silence followed.

Hal swallowed. Everything could go very, very wrong if the child failed to produce the stolen gemstone. He felt the warmth of steam on his right side as the dragon nudged closer to peer over his shoulder.

Classmates gasped and hunkered lower. Mrs. Hunter's eyes widened. "Hal—"

"Just need that gemstone," he said, trying to keep his voice from wavering. "*Now*, please."

He heard a shout from the street behind him. Not wanting to make any sudden moves, he casually and slowly turned his head. He spotted something in the sky—two dots, rapidly approaching.

The parents.

Hal leaned into the window again. "Guys, I'm not kidding. I need that gemstone, or we'll probably all end up steamed to death." He regretted his harsh words, but the time for gentle persuasion was over. "Whoever found it, give it to me—now."

"Do as he says," Mrs. Hunter urged, looking around at the class.

After an agonizing pause, a small blond-headed girl stood up and tiptoed out from behind the desks, reaching into a small pouch that she carried around her neck. Rather than look scared, she had an expression of misery. Tears welled up as she said, "But it's mine. I found it in a cave by a waterfall yesterday. It's *mine*."

"I know," Hal said softly.

He glanced over his shoulder and saw the clear outlines of two adult forest dragons descending toward the village. More shouts of alarm went up, and someone screamed in the distance.

Hal focused on the girl as she shuffled toward him. He reached out his hand and leaned over the enlarged windowsill. "Let me have it, please."

Still she delayed, her bottom lip trembling.

"Sarah!" Mrs. Hunter snapped suddenly. "Hand it over!" She started to rise.

Many of the other children chimed in. "Yeah, Sarah, hand it over!" they said in hushed, scared voices.

Seeing more tears welling up, Hal glanced outside, sucked in a breath at the sight of the mother and father dragons swooping closer, and then stared into the face of the young, female creature by his side. Steam curled from her nostrils, and Hal could sense her muscles bunching as though preparing to launch herself at the window opening and snatch the girl up in her jaws.

He reached into his own pocket and pulled out the cloth-wrapped pendant he'd bought for Abigail. "Sarah, look—you can have this instead. Take it."

Hal had no more time. He almost fell inside the window onto the rubble in his effort to grasp the pouch from around Sarah's neck. The clasp came free when he yanked on it, and he shoved the pendant into her hands before she could start wailing.

"Get back out of the way," he told her.

He swung around to face the steamer dragon and hurriedly opened the pouch. The gemstone—bright blue and beautiful but only the size of a walnut—almost slipped from his grasp, but he caught it and held it out.

The steamer dragon's eyes widened. Then she snapped her jaws to grab it, and a second later launched herself into the sky to join the adults.

Screams turned to cries of relief, and before long a cheer went up. "They're going!" someone shouted.

Mrs. Hunter came to the window, saw him, let out a shout of alarm, and hurried outside. She was with him in seconds, catching him as he stumbled and sank to his knees on the rubble.

"Hal, Hal—Oh my goodness, you poor boy!"

"I think they're gone," he muttered.

"Yes, they're gone, thank you—but never mind that now. Let me see."

The pain hit him then. He held up his bloody right hand and stared in utter shock. All four fingers missing, bitten off down to the knuckles. He fell back on the grass and moaned as a wave of agony swept up his arm.

Mrs. Hunter's face swirled around and around along with the puffy white clouds in the blue sky. He dimly heard her saying something, but she sounded far away.

Then he blacked out.

Chapter Two
Healing

Hal woke to the sight of Abigail's lightly freckled face close to his, her minty breath on his cheek. Her dark-brown hair hung messily over her face. Just for once, she had no scrunchie tying it back.

He smiled at her and mumbled, "Hey."

She didn't smile back. Her eyes were shadowed and red from crying. "Why do you always have to be the hero?" she demanded.

"Uh . . ."

He recognized the room as part of the laboratory building just outside Carter. Miss Simone spent most of her time in this place, working on one scientific project or another, performing minor procedures on patients, often experimenting with ideas and new medicines. The door had a glass panel, and he could see his parents out in the corridor talking to the lady herself.

"Do you have any idea how close you came to dying?" Abigail grumbled. "That dragon might have bitten your head off! You were twice its size—you could have shooed it away, or roasted its backside, or worse, but instead you stood right next to it *in human form* and politely asked a stubborn little girl to return a gemstone—who by the way doesn't seem even the tiniest bit sorry that she caused so much trouble and doesn't even seem to care that—"

"Abi, Abi, stop," Hal interrupted, holding up a hand in an effort to block the verbal attack. "It's okay, really. Everything turned out . . . uh . . ."

He trailed off as a terrible memory surfaced. He gasped and held up his *other* hand. It was heavily bandaged, and he could tell at first glance that something was wrong.

His fingers!

"Did I—?" he started. "My hand—tell me I didn't—"

"Lose your fingers?" Abigail said, her voice breaking. Her lower lip and chin trembled as she nodded. "Yes. You lost your fingers. Way to go, you idiot." Despite her harsh words, tears began flowing. Wiping them away and blinking, she batted at his shoulder. "Miss Simone said you *might* grow them back, but that's a big might. Shapeshifters can heal, but growing new fingers . . . ? That's a bit iffy."

Hal sat up, staring in horror at his stump. He still had most of his hand, and a thumb stuck out of the bandages like he was perpetually signalling that everything was okay. He felt no pain, thankfully. "I can't be like this forever. I just can't. It's my right hand, and I'm right-handed! I have to transform and fix this."

He started to climb out of bed, but Abigail planted her own hands on his shoulders and stopped him. "You will. But first, you should rest. Miss Simone pumped you full of painkillers earlier, and they're probably going to make you feel woozy for a while. You don't want to stagger about in dragon form."

"If I wait," he argued, "then the painkillers will wear off, and it'll hurt like crazy, and then I'll be an *angry* dragon staggering about. Let me up. I want to take care of this right now."

She huffed and shook her head. "Hal, you just had your fingers bitten off!"

"Yeah, but lying here isn't going to help me." He pushed past her and stood up. He did indeed feel woozy, but he tried to not to show it. Still, he planted his left hand on her shoulder for balance. "Let's get out of here."

Abigail opened the door for him, and they squeezed through the doorway together. Miss Simone spotted them instantly and narrowed her eyes. She said nothing, but Hal's parents spun around and immediately started fussing.

"Back in bed!" his mom ordered.

"You need to rest, son," his dad said.

Hal looked pleadingly at Miss Simone. "The best thing I can do is transform. Just let me outside."

The enchanting blonde pierced him with her blue eyes . . . and nodded. "I agree, Hal."

"You do?"

Both parents started complaining. Like Hal, his mom had sandy-colored hair, though flecked with grey, and it wouldn't be long before he was taller than her. His dad was broad, black-haired, olive-skinned, and bearded. He cut an imposing figure.

Miss Simone quickly interrupted them. "He's had some rest, I've given him antibiotics and painkillers, and the rest is up to him.

Honestly, the quicker he goes outside and transforms, the more chance of a successful healing." She raised her eyebrows. "It's not like that steamer dragon left his fingers behind for us to sew back on. Hal's only chance is to grow new ones."

"We know that," Hal's mom said, "but don't you think he should rest some more first?"

Abigail spoke up. "He's been out of it for hours. He fainted, and then he woke yelling, and then the painkillers sent him off again, and that was hours ago . . . I guess he's had all the rest he can take for now."

Hal blinked at her. He didn't remember waking.

His dad sighed and nodded. "Then let's go."

The group headed outside. It had been sunny that morning, but now rain clouds had moved in, and Hal felt a light drizzle on his face as he moved to a clear area on the grass. The sprawling laboratory building was nestled among the trees on the fringes of the woods, the path meandering between them, so he had to pick his spot carefully to avoid getting snarled up in low-hanging branches.

Hal studied his tightly wrapped bandages. "I guess I should peel these off first."

He grimaced at the thought. The last thing he wanted to see was nasty, freshly chomped finger stubs. But he didn't want to be constricted by the bandages, either. The thought of transforming inside a confined space had always bothered him, and though he didn't think a few bandages would prevent his hand from expanding into a dragon's paw, there might be a moment of pain as it strained against the fabric.

"Allow me," Miss Simone said, approaching.

She began fiddling with the bandage, and Hal peered off into the distance, trying to look nonchalant and bored. He gave Abigail a grin, and she managed to return a semblance of a smile before her gaze moved to his injury.

He could see out of the corner of his eye that Miss Simone had now fully unwrapped the bandage. It trailed on the grass, seemingly yards of the stuff. She quickly wound the bandage around her own hand, presumably to dispose of it later.

"Okay," Hal said, "stand back. Let's see if this works."

He transformed. As he came down on all four paws, something felt off with his injured hand. One shift wasn't likely to fix anything, of course. It would take several transformations back and forth before he noticed an improvement to anything as traumatic as missing fingers.

So he spent the next minute switching from human to dragon and back again, over and over. It must have been a weird sight for passers-by, as though a shapeshifter were on the fritz, unable to stick in one form. He paced his shifting, leaving ten seconds between each. He felt like it might be possible to wear out the ability if he wasn't careful, though the worst he'd ever suffered was fatigue.

After the first couple of shifts, he watched to see if his missing fingers grew back. He remained on hands and knees on the grass while in human form, so his hand changed into a dark-green reptilian paw and back again without moving—and the nubs of his digits extended bit by bit. Relief flooded through him. It was working, though slowly. He grew tired after ten shifts—five times a dragon, five times back to human—and his wooziness increased.

He paused to rest. "I think I need a drink."

His mom raced off to fetch him something.

"It's working, right?" his dad asked.

"I think so, Dad."

Miss Simone knelt and lifted his hand to examine the injury. Hal didn't mind looking now that his shifting had done some healing. The fingers were still missing, but the wounds were clean and smooth, the skin pinker than the rest of his hand.

"It's certainly an improvement," she said. "I prescribe a regimen of transformations, ten at a time every fifteen minutes until fully healed." She gave a wink. "You're young enough to heal terrible wounds like this. Wait until you're older, though; then something as simple as a scratch will be difficult to remove."

Hal remembered her brother, Felipe, otherwise known as Burnflank the dragon. He had terrible burns from a dragon attack. Of course, he'd chosen to avoid shifting and leave the scars alone, otherwise his cover as 'just another regular dragon' would have been blown . . . but he'd probably left it too long anyway, and those scars were now permanent. Best to fix the problem while it was fresh.

His mom brought him some water, and he drank thirstily before resuming his transformations. His fingers grew a little more. The process was slow but promising. Still, the dizzy feeling stopped him from continuing past eight shifts. "I'll have to do some more later," he said with a shaky voice.

"Just whenever you feel up to it," Miss Simone agreed. She turned to his parents. "Take him home. He has no need to be here anymore."

Hal started feeling a little better as he walked the streets with Abigail and his parents. She stayed on his left, holding that hand while he studied the other. He had no need for bandages anymore, so his weird finger-nubs were on full display. He marveled at the shiny white skin and the smooth, rounded tips. They were each no longer than half an inch, so they had a way to go yet. How exactly would his body know when they'd reached full length? And would his fingernails sprout as a finishing touch?

"At least you can still give a thumbs-up," Abigail said.

He realized he'd been too distracted to make conversation. He let his arm fall to his side and smiled at her. "Yeah. That's important."

His parents walked just ahead, but they kept twisting around to make sure he was okay. Passers-by glanced at him, too, some offering nods and grins. Once again, the village hailed him a hero—this time for saving a teacher and her class from an angry steamer dragon. He didn't mind the praise, but it embarrassed him a little that his friends rarely got a mention even though they did equally brave things in their roles as shapeshifters.

"Where is everyone?" he asked. "I'm surprised Robbie didn't come and visit."

"Well, Hal, it's not like anything major happened. All you did was lose a few fingers."

He chuckled.

Abigail nudged him. "Actually, he did stop by. So did Emily. The others might not have heard the news yet. Everyone's busy at the moment, doing their shapeshifter thing just like you were this morning, only safely."

He ignored the slur. "Can you imagine how bad things must have been around here before we came along?" Realizing that sounded conceited, he added, "I mean before *any* shapeshifters came along. Look what Felipe did for the town of Louis. He got those dragons in the Labyrinth of Fire under control, sneaking in there like he was a regular dragon and ending up the emperor's favorite. Now he's pretty much the leader, and he can make sure they don't go feeding on humans."

"Same with the harpies when they were swooping in and stealing things," Abigail agreed. "Lauren solved that problem. Now they actually work for food. Oh, and there's Emily and the naga, Canaan and the elves, Robbie and the ogres ... They're all friendly neighbors thanks to us. Even the manticores can be reasoned with now because of Thomas. We have Charlie Duggan, who can deal with griffins. Bo and Astrid are sphinxes, Orson's a pegasus, Molly's a gorgon ..."

"And look at the giant monster-lizards. Fenton rides those things and steers them away from villages so nobody gets trampled."

They looked at one another. "Yeah, we're pretty useful around here," Abigail said. "People are safer because of us."

"And Darcy," Hal went on. "She's actually out in the forest talking to dryads and learning how to make all kinds of natural medicines, which is amazing."

"Poor Dewey is stuck with the centaurs, though," Abigail said. "He pretty much uncovered the entire virus plot, and thanks to him they're pretty meek these days, so they don't complain whenever we step on their turf or knock down a tree somewhere."

Hal wrinkled his nose. "Who else? Oh, Miss Simone, of course. Well, I guess we're safe from mermaids because of her. And then there's Jolie and the miengu."

They both fell silent at the mention of her.

"She never healed," Abigail said. "I mean, she never grew her legs back. I guess being sliced in half is a little worse than getting some fingers chomped."

"A little worse, yeah."

They had cut through the village by now. They exited through a gate in the perimeter fence and took the woodland path.

"And then there's me," Abigail murmured. "I like being a faerie, but I'm not exactly useful."

Hal stopped and swung around. "That's not true!"

She smiled. "You're sweet to say so, but seriously, what have I done that's useful around here?"

"You gave us one of those tiny faerie balls. It let us see deep into our own minds and uncovered a few truths. You basically saved Thomas with that thing."

"And?"

Hal thought hard. "Oh! And you got us out of the Prison of Despair."

She sighed. "You're reaching now. Let's face it—being a faerie shapeshifter isn't much help to humankind."

"We don't all have to be saving people from dragons and monsters," Hal told her. "Learning is just as important. Don't be so hard on yourself."

As they approached the fork where Abigail would normally turn off for her own home, they paused and waited until Hal's parents had gone on ahead. Then Abigail whispered, "Do you think we'll ever have children of our own?"

Hal sucked in a breath. "What? Hey, hang on a minute. We're only thirteen—well, I'm thirteen, and you're still twelve. It's a bit early to be going on about stuff like that!"

She laughed softly. "Keep your hair on. I was just wondering what our kids would be like. Shapeshifters, do you think? Would we have a boy or a girl, or both?"

Swallowing, Hal shuffled awkwardly and glanced off into the woods. "Sure, whatever, yeah. Hey, speaking of being thirteen—"

He remembered the pendant he'd bought her and given away, and he sighed. Now he'd have to go and buy her something else.

"What about being thirteen?" Abigail prompted.

He shrugged. "It's your birthday in two days."

"I know. Did you get me something nice?"

She had that little twinkle in her eye, the sign of a new round of teasing banter. He played along. "How about a blue gemstone? I know where I can get one."

Her eyes opened wide, and she clasped her hands together. "Really? I always wanted one! Oh, *please* get me a gemstone!"

"Shouldn't be difficult. I doubt the steamer dragon will mind. I might even find some more jewels if I look hard enough."

She poked him in the chest, stomped a foot, and put on a spoiled-brat voice. "I won't be happy unless you bring me a stolen gemstone!"

Hal laughed.

After promising to keep working on his healing process, the two of them parted ways, Hal felt good enough by now to try a few transformations, but the overhanging trees were in the way, so he waited until he was outside his house before shifting back and forth another ten times.

His fingers grew another half-inch, forming a set of joints. He sighed with relief. Part of him had feared his regeneration would somehow forget that important detail and leave him with four stiff digits that didn't bend. How pointless would that be?

"They're getting there," he said, walking into the kitchen where his dad had seated himself at the table and his mom was busy filling a pot of water to boil over the fire. They enjoyed *coffee* these days, shipped in from Old Earth. Hal couldn't stand the stuff. He kind of liked the smell, but he thought the taste was bitter and nasty.

He wiggled his short fingers at her.

"Thank goodness!" she exclaimed, her face lighting up. "Oh, Hal, you came *so close* this morning. Please try to be safer in future, okay? You could have run that dragon off quite easily if you'd stayed in your own form."

"Yeah, but then her parents might have had a thing to say about it."

His dad nodded at her. "He's right. Still, sauntering over to stand next to the thing? That wasn't your smartest move, son."

Hal shrugged. He wasn't sure he could have done anything else, but he didn't feel like arguing the point. He retired to his room for a while, finding himself a little weary again. It wasn't just the transformations; it was the actual healing process. His body had a lot of work to do, and he was feeling it.

An idea occurred to him. His best friend Robbie was the master of *partial* transformations; he could grow as little or as much as he liked into his ogre form, even limiting his change to one arm if he wanted. Hal had done similar things, though he found it difficult. He could breathe fire if he was really careful.

He concentrated all his energy into his stubby fingers. He didn't need a surge of magic to shift into a dragon. He just needed to heal his injury. As he stared at his hand and channeled his power, his fingers twitched as though fine muscles were spasming beneath the skin. His hand turned dark-green and scaly, and it grew to twice the size. His thumb thickened, and a savage claw sprouted. All four fingers morphed, lengthening just a fraction.

Then, two seconds later, he reverted to human form again and wiggled his pink, ever-so-slightly longer fingers. So, no more effective that a normal transformation, but at least he could shift while lying on his bed in comfort.

He soon dozed off, though. At some point, his mom popped her head into the room and called him, and he woke just enough to say he was asleep. She murmured an apology and backed out again, closing the door softly.

When he next woke, it was dark outside.

He sat up, amazed. He'd slept all afternoon? His wind-up clock suggested midnight was only twenty minutes away.

Climbing to his feet, he gazed out the open window at the night sky and crescent moon. The air was warm but dry, a typical summer evening in New Earth. He felt like a walk, but he had nowhere in particular to go. The market would be shut down, and he doubted any of his friends were still up.

He paced his room for a while, checking his fingers for growth and managing a few controlled shifts that affected only his hand. It helped a little, but he decided full-blown transformations were better.

Suddenly making up his mind, he headed out the door. Wide awake, restless, bored, and in need of some shapeshifter healing—what better time for a midnight flight in the starry sky?

Chapter Three
A Cry for Help

Hal transformed on his front lawn close to the gate leading to the woodland trail. It felt good to be out at night when everyone else was asleep. His parents had probably gone to bed an hour ago like everyone else. There was very little nightlife in the village of Carter. The place was full of people who had no reason to stay up late and every reason to be up at the crack of dawn.

He launched into the air. *Fly first, then transform a bunch of times when I'm done. That'll wear me out, and I can go back to bed and sleep until morning. Sounds like a plan.*

Staying away from the village in case a nightwatch goblin saw him and raised the alarm, he flew low over the trees, heading west for a while before veering north. He'd turn again and head east shortly.

In the meantime, he inhaled deeply and enjoyed the air. Cruising like this always filled him with joy. The novelty of being a dragon had never worn off, nor the feeling that some of his friends envied him for it. Sure, Dewey probably loved galloping about in centaur form, and no doubt Emily found the naga fascinating, and he knew for a fact Robbie enjoyed the sheer strength of his ogre form . . . but nothing beat flying. Lauren knew it, and so did Abigail. For that reason, he was careful not to brag about having wings in front of those who didn't.

He breathed fire, a long and powerful stream that arced downward and flared wide as the wind got hold of the flames. Not surprisingly, it always gave him a warm feeling inside to let loose like that. The treetops stood out clear as day as he sailed overhead with his fiery breath, and he aimed upward a little to avoid setting branches alight. Sleeping birds in nests woke and chirped in alarm, and he heard the howl of an animal somewhere far below.

Don't worry, I'm just a random dragon passing by, he thought with an inward chuckle.

He veered east and practiced slowing his cruising speed to a crawl without having to flap like crazy to stay airborne. It was all about

17

angling the wings *just so*. Much easier for birds, though; they were light enough to bob and hover on a small gust. Dragons weighed thousands of pounds and, according to Old Earth scientists, shouldn't be able to fly at all. That was where a healthy dose of magic came in. Still, magic alone wasn't enough; a dragon had to learn some basic techniques as well.

When he began to plummet, he beat his wings to regain height and momentum. Flying at a slow pace was *hard*.

Angling to the south, he looked ahead and scoured the darkness for Carter. It was there somewhere, beyond the blanket of treetops. The village lay in a bowl-shaped depression in the countryside, making use of the rivers that flowed through it. The terrain made it hard to spot the village from the air.

He heard something to his right, a scream that pierced the night and caused him to jerk in surprise. Craning his neck, he peered down at the forest, looking for torchlight or campfires, something to pinpoint the source of the high-pitched noise. He had a horrible vision of a traveler being devoured by a manticore . . .

The scream came again, and this time he twisted around and flapped toward the chilling sound. It was a woman, clearly terrified. Then her shriek cut off, and suddenly all was quiet.

Hal searched the trees, but it was hopeless. A daytime search would be difficult enough; in the night, all he saw was blackness beyond the uppermost branches.

"Hello!" he yelled.

His dragon roar could probably be heard a mile away, but what use was it? Who in their right mind would answer the call of a dragon? Not even a terrified woman in the woods . . . unless of course she knew it was Hal, in which case she'd try to get his attention. He listened carefully but heard nothing, not even a pitiful moan.

Even if he could pinpoint her whereabouts, it would be almost impossible to crash down through the trees without seriously damaging his wings. He huffed with frustration. Sometimes, being a dragon was more of a hindrance than a help. Lauren could make it safely to the forest floor without injury. Abigail certainly could.

Reluctantly, he came to the decision he'd have to leave the woman behind and come back with help, though he feared it might not be until the morning.

He circled the area, looking for telltale markers that would allow him and others to return in the daytime for a proper search. He could guide a team of goblins on foot, but they'd need something to aim for.

Seeing nothing that stood out, he made up his mind to create a marker of his own. Lighting up the treetops with a blast of fire ensured that any animals residing in the branches had a chance to scamper to safety or take flight. Then he got serious and started burning.

It took a few minutes to scorch the tops of the trees in a fairly neat circle. In the morning, they'd stand out nice and black as he flew overhead. With a lot of roaring and fire-breathing, he could lead the goblins to the general area, and then they could do a thorough search.

Unhappy about leaving the screaming woman behind, he lingered a while longer above the forest just in case a campfire lit up, or something made a noise, or a flock of birds rose into the sky in panic—anything at all. He'd be willing to crash down through the branches if it meant he could swoop in and save someone. But it wasn't worth the risk when the chances of finding the poor woman were so slim.

He flew home, hoping this was just a simple case of a person getting lost in the woods and freaking out at the creepy nightlife.

But something told him it was more than that.

* * *

Hal thumped on the door again, louder this time.

Finally, a light came on inside. He stepped back and waited.

When the door opened, Miss Simone stood there in a nightgown, squinting at him. "Hal? What on earth—?"

"I heard a scream in the woods," he said. "North of my house. I marked the spot by burning the tops of some trees. She screamed twice, but then it all went quiet, so I don't know what happened. I don't know if she's still in trouble and needs help or . . . well, she might have been attacked by something. She might be dead."

Miss Simone took everything in and nodded. "Then we should investigate."

He felt a surge of gratitude for her. Not only did she refrain from asking stupid questions like "Why are you up at this time of night?" but she also got straight down to business without questioning whether he could be mistaken or not. She trusted his word as a shapeshifter.

"I can fly above the trees," he suggested. "When I see the burned treetops, I can make a lot of noise and guide you through the woods."

To his surprise, she shook her head. "And how will you see these burned treetops in the middle of the night?"

"Uh . . ."

She considered for a moment. "It's just five hours or so until dawn. I'll organize a group in a short while, and we'll set out before the sun's up. We'll be deep in the forest by the time your burned treetops become visible. You just make sure to be there."

"But Miss Simone," he protested, "the woman might be hurt! She could be lying there waiting for help to show up. She might not make it until morning!"

"Or she might be dead already. Or she might not be hurt at all and is a prisoner somewhere, in which case it won't hurt to wait until dawn. Or she might simply be wandering around lost, and therefore she'll be nowhere near your burned treetops by now."

"Abigail can see in the dark," he argued. "She can ride on my back and yell when she sees—"

"Go home, Hal." Miss Simone said, offering him a smile. "I'll be up in a few hours to organize a group. Go. See you at dawn."

She softly closed the door, and her light went out.

Hal couldn't believe she would allow a possibly injured woman to go without help for five hours. But, as he turned away, he realized she was probably right. If she wasn't dead already, she'd just have to survive until dawn.

He flew home. Thumping down on his lawn, he reverted to human form, waited a few seconds, and transformed again. He did this over and over . . .

* * *

When Hal woke the next morning with the sunlight streaming in, he lay there a moment staring at the ceiling. Remembering that he'd taken a midnight flight and managed eight full transformations and back again before he'd grown weary, he snatched his hand out from under the covers and wiggled the fresh-skinned, half-length fingers of his right hand. "Getting there," he said with a grin. "Being a shapeshifter is awesome."

Then he bolted upright as the memory of the woman's scream came back to him.

He was late!

When he rushed into the kitchen, his mom was seated at the table with her hands wrapped around a mug of coffee. It had to be nearly seven o'clock, then. The sun had been up for a while.

She smiled at him and pointed to the stove where scrambled egg sizzled in the pan. "Your timing is impeccable," she said. "I guess you smelled the—"

"Can't stop now, Mom," Hal interrupted. "I heard a scream in the woods last night. I think someone's hurt. Miss Simone is organizing a search party this morning."

She rose from her seat. "That's awful. But why—"

"I went for a quick midnight flight," he explained, rushing to the stove. He *was* hungry, despite his haste. "Couldn't sleep." He grabbed a fork and shoveled the egg straight from the pan into his mouth, then panted and gasped and almost spat it out on his hand. "It's hot!"

"It's still in the pan, sweetie. Of course it's hot. So you went on a midnight—"

"I'll grab something later," Hal said, throwing the fork into the sink.

"Have you remembered it's Monday? It's a school day, dear."

He stopped at the doorway. So it was. He groaned, wishing he could just take the day off. "Shapeshifter business," he stated. "Miss Simone's waiting."

"I realize that," his mom said with a smile. She came to him and settled her hands on his shoulders. "But you've obviously talked to her about it already, and she's got it all under control. So let her deal with it."

"It's not that simple. I had to burn some trees so I could find them in the daytime. Otherwise, nobody will find anything at all."

She opened her mouth, frowned, looked skyward for a moment, pursed her lips, and opened her mouth again. "Well—"

"I have to go, Mom," Hal interrupted yet again. "Love you, bye!"

He knew his mom stood on the doorstep watching him as he transformed and flew away. He knew she was annoyed by his hasty departure and vague-at-best intentions about going to school that day, but Miss Simone had always said shapeshifter business took priority over class. Attacks by harpies or rocs could happen at any time.

Potentially deadly disputes with their naga neighbors couldn't be put on hold until after school finished for the day. And the screaming woman in the forest needed help *now*, not sometime later in the afternoon.

Abigail would be getting ready for school right about now, and he would normally meet her at the fork. She'd just have to go to school on her own. He wished he could take her with him to the woods, but the shapeshifters had strict orders not to skip school unless absolutely necessary. Hal was needed; she was not.

He beat his wings as hard as he could and tore through the sky, annoyed at himself for being late. Miss Simone would be out in the woods already, waiting for his direction. He could imagine her standing there with a scowl on her face, arms crossed, tapping her foot and huffing.

Rising high above the trees, he looked for his marker. The endless treetops basked in the early-morning sunlight, dew dripping from their branches as birds and critters began another day's hunting and gathering. The sky couldn't be any clearer.

It took longer than expected to find the patch of blackened treetops. He began roaring as he circled around, hoping Miss Simone would hear him and follow the sound of his voice. There was no way to know for sure. All he could do was keep up the racket until somebody sent him a signal to stop.

After a few minutes of circling, he broke off from his constant roaring and let out a cry of surprise at the sight of a clearing. It was probably a five-minute walk from his charred marker—well, ten in such a dense forest—but a clearing like this meant an easy, safe way down.

He descended with anticipation, glad for the change of scenery. Now he could join in the search.

Thumping down, he surveyed the area. A stream ran down the slopes into a pool surrounded by smooth, moss-covered boulders. The clear water overflowed on the opposite side and continued down the gentle slopes, disappearing into the bushes deeper in the woods. This entire area was rocky, which explained the absence of trees; they had nothing to worm their roots into. Hal glanced up and around. Six or seven dragons could probably land here all at once.

Remaining in dragon form, he set off in the direction of his charred treetops. If only he'd spotted this clearing last night! Things looked a lot different in the daytime.

Letting out a roar every minute or so—dragonspeak for "Over here!"—he weaved between the pines looking for a sign of the missing woman. Several rodents and an ugly, orange-furred squonk scampered away as he stomped along. He was pretty sure he glimpsed a dryad out of the corner of his eye, but when he spun around, he saw only trees.

A whistle sounded right after he let out another roar. Pricking up his reptilian ears, he paused and listened hard. He roared again. An answering whistle pierced the trees, long and shrill.

"Over here!" Hal yelled again.

He heard the distant sounds of twigs cracking, followed by muffled voices. Then a woman called, "Hal!"

"Miss Simone!" Hal shouted.

Enough with the roaring, he thought. He reverted to human form and cupped his hands around his mouth.

"Miss Simone!" he shouted again. "Over here!"

His natural voice sounded weak and feeble in comparison. Still, at least the search party had pinpointed him.

He continued his scouting, absently glancing at his right hand to see if his fingers were any longer. They were just past halfway, almost to the final joints. After that, his fingernails would start appearing.

The search party caught up to him at almost the exact time he spotted an item of clothing in the bushes ahead. Fearing the worst, he dutifully waited until Miss Simone stepped into view from the trees, her silky green robe hanging to her ankles. She was followed by six stout goblins wearing armor and carrying flaming, smoking torches. Their piglike faces were set in perpetual grimaces as though everything in life irritated them.

"Hal," she said, "is this about where you—"

"There," Hal said, pointing.

Miss Simone looked. Then, silently, she headed that way while the goblins spread out in a wide arc.

Hal followed in Miss Simone's footsteps.

She bent over the dull-yellow material, studied it for a moment, then picked it up. "A man's shirt," she muttered.

That surprised him. "I swear I heard a woman screaming, not a man."

"The woman might have been watching while he was . . . taken."

Goblins exclaimed from nearby. One held a pair of brown pants, the other a single boot. "Scattered all over," a goblin snarled. "There's underwear over that way, and a knapsack yonder. A traveler passing through. Manticore?"

Hal shuddered. He'd feared that very thing.

Miss Simone shook her head. "A manticore would have eaten the clothes as well."

That was true, Hal realized. Manticores were notorious for devouring every tiny morsel of their victims including their clothes and belongings, leaving no trace of their existence. Scattering clothes and things around made no sense.

They continued searching and found more of the man's things—his other boot, a hunting knife that must have fallen from his belt, and a half-full leather water pouch. Everything was spread over an area the size of a small house. "Within throwing distance," Miss Simone suggested.

A goblin shook his head. "Why would anyone sling their stuff around?"

Miss Simone could only shrug. "Collect everything up. And look carefully for signs of . . ." She glanced at Hal, then lowered her voice. "Look for signs of blood."

Hal looked, too. And just for a while, he switched to dragon form and sniffed around, knowing his dragon senses were far superior to a human's. But he smelled nothing out of the ordinary.

Except . . .

He sniffed the air, searching. A hint of . . . what? Fear? Sweat? He advanced a few steps toward a clump of bushes and paused again.

Then he reverted to human form and turned to Miss Simone, who was watching him closely. "I think there's someone there," he whispered.

Goblins immediately marched over, spreading out around the bushes. One peered closer . . . then bent and disappeared from view. A moment later, a woman cried out, a brief struggle ensued, and the goblin backed out, dragging her with him.

"She was sound asleep," he grunted. "But all twitchy-like, having a nightmare."

Her white face, wide and red-rimmed eyes, tangled hair, and filthy clothing suggested she'd had a rough night. She wore pants and boots like the man's, and a pale-blue long-sleeved shirt, clearly a traveler with her own hunting knife and water pouch. She had a knapsack, too.

"Who are you?" Miss Simone asked, kneeling in front of her. "What happened here?"

She weeped and covered her face. "He's dead, isn't he? My Derek. He's dead."

Miss Simone reached out to touch her shoulder. "We haven't found him. Please—what's your name?"

"Matilda," she said with a sob.

"All right, Matilda, tell me what happened."

She let out a wail. "That . . . that *creature* did it. She cast a spell, and blue mist appeared, and Derek just . . . *disintegrated*. His clothes flew everywhere, and he . . . he blew apart like fine dust, swirling around on a breeze that wasn't there. It was terrible magic—*black* magic." Matilda's face contorted into a rage. "She's evil. She's a witch. She's a demon!"

Chapter Four
Hunting the Creature

As Matilda continued sobbing, and the goblins stood around awkwardly offering their support with occasional pats on the shoulder or a muttered platitude, Miss Simone pulled Hal aside.

"Go fetch the others," she urged. "I'm sending Matilda home with a couple of goblins, and they'll organize a larger search party. But I want you, Hal, to fetch your shapeshifter friends."

"All of them?"

"Those who will be useful." Miss Simone looked sideways for a moment, frowning. "Dewey, Emily, and Lauren. A centaur, naga, and harpy will be the best suited for the task of hunting down this witch creature. The rest can stay in school."

"And Abigail," Hal added. "A tiny faerie buzzing around . . . She can zip about faster than anyone."

Miss Simone nodded. "Yes, her too."

"And Robbie? Just in case we need his ogre strength?"

"And Robbie, yes, I suppose so. That should be all we need."

Hal gave a thumbs-up—something his short-fingered right hand was still good for. "Definitely. Plus Fenton. You never know when a glue-spitting reptile might come in handy."

"Well, maybe so . . ."

"Darcy as well, obviously," Hal said. "*Someone* in our group needs to be invisible. Not even a witch can spot a dryad."

Miss Simone said nothing this time.

Hal took that as agreement. "So everyone except Thomas—but you didn't mean to leave him out, because he's a manticore, and nobody knows the woods better than a manticore. Right?"

She sighed and closed her eyes. "Just go fetch everybody. Hurry."

Hal dashed back to the rocky clearing and launched into the sky, his dragon wings pumping so hard that he shot out of the forest like a projectile fired from a giant cannon. Excitement coursed through his veins at the prospect of gathering forces to hunt down a villainous witch, but that excitement was mixed with a great deal of trepidation, too. A creature that could cast a spell and turn people into dust?

He flew into Carter and almost skimmed the rooftops on his way to his familiar school building, which stood a few streets away from Mrs. Hunter's damaged Sunday classroom. He landed in the street, reverted to human form, and dashed inside to find a classroom full of friends already seated with pencils in hands.

Mrs. Hunter looked up from some papers. "You're thirty minutes late," she said mildly. "I'll forgive you, though, after yesterday's incident. How are your fingers?"

Hal held up his hand. "Mostly grown back. But I'm not here for class. I'm here to fetch everyone."

His friends stared at him in silence—Thomas, Dewey, and Abigail at the back; Fenton and Robbie in the middle row; Emily, Lauren, and Darcy in the front. Hal's own seat dead center of the nine-desk group was of course empty.

Fenton shoved back his chair and stood up. "Consider us fetched. Where're we going?"

Before Hal could answer, Mrs. Hunter put down her papers and approached him. "What's going on, Hal?"

"Somebody killed someone in the woods last night and turned to dust. A creature of some kind, probably a witch."

After a pause, Emily spoke up. "Somebody killed a witch and then turned to dust?"

Lauren reached over and batted at her. "No, silly. The *witch* turned to dust."

"No, that's not—" Hal started.

Robbie jumped up. "So somebody killed a witch, and then the witch turned to dust?"

"That's what I just said," Lauren griped.

"You morons," Fenton said, rolling his eyes. "Why don't you listen? He said the witch killed somebody and then turned to dust."

Emily folded her arms. "So who reported this? If somebody was killed, and the witch turned to dust, who saw it happen?"

Fenton frowned.

Darcy threw up her hands in exasperation. "Let Hal finish!"

Suddenly, everybody's attention was on Hal, and the room fell silent. "You all done?" he said. "Okay, listen. We need to go out to the forest and help in the search. Miss Simone's there right now with some goblins trying to find the witch. The witch is a creature of some sort. I don't know the details. Matilda was kind of upset about Derek."

"Wait, what?" Lauren said. "Who's Matilda? Who's Derek?"

"Derek was the one who was killed."

Silence.

Robbie pinched the bridge of his nose. "So was Matilda the witch? And who turned to dust?"

"Listen!" Hal shouted. "Never mind all this. Just get up and head out to the woods. It's somewhere north of my house. I can take a few on my back—Abi, Robbie, and one other—maybe Darcy—"

"Not Darcy," Abigail said with a sweet but meaningful smile. "Emily."

Hal sighed inwardly. Ever since his birthday three months ago, when Darcy had *almost* kissed him on the cheek, some kind of polite feud had arisen between her and Abigail. "Whatever. But let's go."

Mrs. Hunter cleared her throat. "Am I to assume this is shapeshifter business? That supersedes my class? And am I to assume each and every one of you is required for this hunt?"

"Yes, ma'am," Hal said, turning to her. "Sorry."

As chairs scraped and papers rustled, Mrs. Hunter approached him. "I have something for you, Hal." She pulled something from a pocket and, grasping it tight in her hands, placed it into the open palm of his left hand. "Sarah says she is very sorry for everything—for taking the gemstone, for making the dragon angry, and for refusing to hand it over until you offered her something in return. Oh, and she's sorry you had your fingers bitten off."

Hal stared at the wood-carved dragon pendant in the palm of his hand. Tomorrow was Abigail's birthday. He smiled and glanced over at her. She was filing out of the room with everybody else, poking Dewey in the back as she went.

"Thanks," he whispered.

"Go," Mrs. Hunter said.

Outside, Hal's friends quickly prepared for the short journey to the woods. In centaur form, Dewey clip-clopped around in circles on restless hooves with Darcy seated on his back. Fenton and Thomas set off without saying another word. It probably didn't matter to them what kind of task they had; just getting out of school for the day was all they cared about. They'd catch up eventually. Lauren transformed and, with her bright-white harpy feathers and yellow eyes, strutted around on powerful talons waiting for Hal to lead the way.

Abigail, Robbie, and Emily trailed after Hal as he moved out into the middle of the street. He switched to dragon form and hunkered down as low as possible so Robbie and Emily could climb aboard. Abigail sprouted her insectoid faerie wings and buzzed into the air. Perhaps because of the extra weight on Hal's back, she shrank down and alighted on his shoulder like a glimmering dragonfly.

He took off and led the way with his passengers on board. Lauren flew alongside, waving at them—or more likely at Robbie. Below, Dewey trotted through the streets, easily passing Thomas and Fenton.

It was good to be back together as a group. The last time they'd worked as a single unit was—well, on Brodon beach three months ago, when Queen Bee had taken over the castle and created scrag shapeshifters. She was dead now, and the scrags either imprisoned or working for a good cause.

Hal smiled. As grim as the situation might be, being together again was just like the old days. They'd soon find this mysterious witch-creature and lock her up. A few weeks in the Prison of Despair would make her realize the error of her ways.

Must look after Abi's gift, he thought, hoping the pendant was still safe in his pocket. As usual, the silky fabric had rearranged itself into a sash around his neck, but when he switched back to human form, his clothes would reassemble themselves, and his pendant should miraculously show up in his pocket again—or perhaps the opposite pocket!

He found the clearing in the woods without too much effort. Making sure Lauren was following, he descended and landed on the smooth rock surrounding the overflowing pool. Robbie and Emily climbed off while Abigail rose into the air with a buzzing sound. Hal could always tell when she was human- or faerie-sized just by the pitch of her buzzing, and right now she was a mere six inches tall and emitting a gentle, whispery whine.

She grew rapidly in mid-air, the pitch deepening and the volume increasing. Back at full human size, she dropped lightly onto the rock and stilled her wings. "Are we splitting up?"

Hal felt his heart skip a beat. "Splitting up? Why? Don't you—" Then it dawned. "Oh, you mean for the search?"

She giggled. "Did you think I meant *us*? No, we're still good."

Emily laughed, too. "Hal's eyes went big and round then. He looked heartbroken!"

Lauren landed at that moment. She kept her white-feathered wings spread a moment longer and gave them a flutter, then folded them and jumped down from the rocks. Hal had always thought her oversized feet—the powerful talons of a bird—looked clumsy, but she hopped about with confidence. She remained in harpy form, glaring around at the trees with yellow eyes.

"Okay, guys," Robbie said. "Let's get on with this. Where do we start?"

Hal led them through the trees to where he'd found Derek's clothing. It was all gone now, picked up and taken away by Miss Simone or the goblins, none of whom were present. Still, Hal had a feeling he knew where she'd be. He looked off into the trees. He couldn't see her, but something drew him in that direction . . .

"Where are we going?" Abigail asked, buzzing after him.

"This way."

"I see that. But why?"

Robbie came hurrying past them both. "Quit asking questions, Abi. This is obviously the way we need to go."

Lauren clicked her tongue. "Robbie, wait for us!"

Hal vied to keep up with Robbie. Glancing back, he saw the three girls looking perplexed. "I can't explain it," he called to them. "We just need to go this way."

Hal and Robbie came across Miss Simone shortly afterward. She was creeping about in the trees. Hal felt a curious sense of relief at the sight of her. "Find anything else?" he asked.

"Not a thing," she said with a sigh.

Though her silky cloak and knee-length dress were as pristine as always, her seemingly bare feet were dirty. Hal and his friends wore the newer-style smart shoes, more encompassing and offering better protection for the toes and around the sides of the feet. Miss Simone stuck with the original style, which somehow suited her better.

She pulled a dry leaf from her golden hair and stared at it, her blue eyes surprisingly bright in the gloom of the forest. "I have the goblins spread far and wide, but the wider they go, the thinner the search. Get to work, shapeshifters." She peered around. "Only the two of you? Where are the rest?"

The moment she asked, Abigail buzzed into view followed by Emily and Lauren, both out of breath from jogging.

"And the rest are on their way as well," Hal said. "Dewey's bringing Darcy, and they won't be long, but Thomas and Fenton . . . well, they'll get here when they get here."

"Why didn't *you* bring them?"

Hal frowned. "Well, I brought three on my back. That's about all I can manage."

"Nonsense," Miss Simone said. "Are you forgetting you're a much bigger adult dragon now?"

Hal paused. He *had* forgotten. "Um, well, anyway, the others will be here soon." Except he had no idea how any of them would find this remote spot in the woods. "Can we light a fire or something to lead the way?"

"No need," Miss Simone said shortly. "Go on, start looking. Remain in pairs or small groups, please. Find me something—a sign that a witch was here, evidence of foul play, anything at all."

It was clear she had no idea what to look for.

"Did Matilda say what kind of creature it was?" Abigail asked.

Miss Simone frowned. "A faun, perhaps. Goat legs, cloven hooves, upper human body, female, horns sticking out of her head . . ."

Abigail nodded. "Definitely sounds like a faun."

"Yet I've never known a faun to dabble in magic, let alone cause harm to a person." She waved them away. "Go now. Make this morning off school worthwhile."

She headed away through the bushes. Hal found himself trailing after her, but he stopped when Abigail planted a hand on his shoulder. Turning, he found Robbie by his side, equally drawn to Miss Simone's whereabouts.

"Quit staring, boys," Abigail said, rolling her eyes. "She's working some magic of her own at the moment, cranking the mermaid enchantment spell up to full volume. I'm sure boys will drift toward her from miles away without even knowing why. Dewey, Thomas, and Fenton—they'll be here soon enough. Darcy will probably wonder how they found this remote spot in the woods."

"That's ridiculous," Hal scoffed.

"Is it?" Lauren murmured. "Explains a lot."

Emily snorted. "Yeah. Explains your goofy expressions. It's exactly like when Jolie the jengu first came out of the lake."

Hal sucked in a breath. "It's not like that at all!"

But he had to admit he had an inexplicable crush on Miss Simone right now, just as he and all the boys had turned their gazes toward Jolie when the seventeen-year-old had first arrived on the scene. She, of course, had used her mermaid-like power of enchantment for nefarious purposes, whereas Miss Simone probably felt it was the most practical thing to do, an expedient way to bring search parties out to a certain remote spot in the woods. She'd turned her enchantment up to full volume to broadcast her whereabouts, and it was working. What a neat trick, a kind of walking beacon.

Like sirens luring ships onto the rocks . . .

Hal and Robbie stared into the woods as Miss Simone disappeared from view. Hal felt a blanket of dejection settle over him. He *so* wanted to go after her.

He shook his head. "Let's get to work."

Abigail buzzed off the ground. "We're here because we're shapeshifters. Let's use our talents."

Shrinking down small, she zipped off through the trees.

Hal would have preferred to stick close to her, but he couldn't fault her logic. His dragon sense of smell was superior, of that he had no doubt.

Setting off in a different direction, Robbie switched to ogre form and grew to three times his normal height and twice his width, towering above the foliage and having to squeeze between tree trunks. Lauren, still in harpy form, remained on the ground, her wings tightly folded. Emily seemed to melt into her serpentine naga form, her clothes reshaping and changing color so they looked rather like a dried-up skin about to be shucked loose.

Hal transformed and instantly filled the space between clumps of bushes. From here on out, he would have to trample the undergrowth flat to get anywhere. His nostrils instantly started twitching as he caught the scent of *something* . . . though he couldn't decide what.

Snuffling around, he forgot all about his friends and followed the trail. He detected . . . what? A kind of musky odor. It wasn't human. Neither were all the mouse droppings, the dead thing somewhere off to his right, the splashes of urine on all the tree trunks, the damp earth and pine needles, honeysuckle and swaths of moss, stagnant pools and more animal dung . . .

But the musky odor held his attention. Many larger animals had the same smell, but this one had an overlying hint of *human* on it.

He could tell without looking that Robbie was a little way to his left. The crashing sounds made it obvious, too, but the smell of ogre was overpowering. He kind of wished Robbie would turn around and go someplace else for a minute.

But there it was again. That musky odor tainted with human. He shook his head. Funny how a smell could be *tainted* with human. He viewed things differently when in dragon form. Sometimes he had to catch himself before taking a bite out of an annoying person.

He caught a whiff of strawberry-scented perfume or shampoo. That was Abigail. He usually liked the smell, but right now it was kind of sickly.

Another scent floated across his path. He stopped dead, trying to pinpoint it. Unlike the musky odor, which had rubbed off on the leaves of bushes and the pine needles coating the forest floor, this new scent had a definite source. It was eye-watering and vile, some kind of chemical nastiness, foreign to nature.

He found a small, opaque, rounded bottle with a long neck lodged in the crumbling bark of a rotting tree trunk that lay across the path. It had been placed there, perhaps put down for a minute and forgotten. Was it the witch's? It had a small plug, but it wasn't inserted; instead, it hung on a short piece of string, which was tied around the neck.

Hal gently nudged the bottle with an extended claw. He couldn't see inside it, and he couldn't pick it up. And the smell revolted him. He reverted to human form and shook his head to clear the myriad of scents that seemed to cling to his nostrils.

The bottle was half full. Maybe enough for Miss Simone to analyze? It could be some kind of liquor, perhaps? He doubted it. Even with his vastly inferior nose, it smelled like chemicals.

"A clue?" he muttered.

He didn't want to break it, so he inserted the plug, set the bottle down where he'd found it, and switched back to dragon form. The musky odor filled his nostrils once more, and he turned slowly, trying to find the trail.

That way.

He crashed past a surprised goblin, causing the stout fellow to stumble backward in a hurry. The goblin might have picked up a trail, but it probably wasn't the musky smell. Maybe no trail at all; it could be coincidence that the goblin was shuffling about right here.

Hal stomped on and on, excited that the odor strengthened bit by bit. So, too, did the hint of human. *What's musky and a little bit human?* he wondered. *A faun—half human, half goat.*

He quickened his pace. The source lurked just ahead, he was sure of it. He felt his chest heating up, instinct taking over and readying his fire glands for a roasting. His muscles bunched, and his claws dug deeper into the earth as he pushed through the thinning woods.

A cave appeared just ahead.

Hal would have punched the air in triumph if he'd been in human form. *This* had to be where the creature lived. He'd found its lair in record time thanks to his acute dragon senses. And now he'd capture the faun and hand her over to Miss Simone.

Darkness awaited him inside the mouth of the cave. It was big enough to stick his head into but too small to fit anything else. Still, it lit up well when he breathed fire, shadows dancing. A cloud of bats screeched and poured out in a frenzy, and he ducked to allow their escape.

"Sorry," he rumbled.

He spotted movement in the far left corner of the cave. When he breathed fire again, he spotted a figure scrambling to safety—a slender human woman with thick horns on her bald head, wearing nothing but a weird skin-colored fabric across her front and dark-grey furry pants. A second glance revealed they weren't pants at all; the distinctive shape of goat legs and cloven hooves told him he'd found the faun.

Then she was gone. He crammed into the cave as far as he could go, but his wings pressed against the roof. He reverted to human form before he could think too much about the risk he was taking.

Dashing inside, he raced after the faun and found a tunnel in the darkest corner. With his heart thumping and adrenaline flowing, he plunged into the shadows and managed to belch up a sheet of flame from his human throat, a trick he was most proud of. Orange light flickered across the walls and rounded ceiling.

Directly ahead, caught in the flash of firelight, the faun stopped and turned toward him, her eyes blazing. He had just a split-second to see that she raised her hands in a twisted gesture, long fingers stretched out—and then he ran out of breath and the fire went out.

He breathed fire again. It was much harder to maintain a steady flow in human form, but he kept it going long enough to see that the faun was gone. In her wake, a cloud of blue mist drifted outward, spreading and thickening, rolling toward him.

Hal stood still.

The fire went out, and he took another deep breath and blew out the steadiest stream he could muster. *Oh, for a flashlight!*

The blue mist drifted closer. He watched it with growing concern. It seemed to reach for him, hungry, possibly deadly . . .

He remembered how Derek had supposedly disintegrated. His nerve broke, and he turned and bolted for the exit.

Chapter Five
The Elusive Faun

"Blue mist?" Miss Simone asked, looking sideways at him.

Hal stood with her and a group of goblins outside the cave entrance. They held torches aloft, the flames twisting and flickering. Abigail, Emily, Robbie, and Lauren had been told to stay back, though they edged closer every chance they got, all in human form now.

"She made blue mist, yes," Hal said again. "Just waved her hands around and . . ." He shrugged. "Like magic."

Miss Simone stared into the darkness. "And did the blue mist follow you out?"

"No."

"Good. We shouldn't take any chances. Whatever it is, it might be deadly."

A goblin sighed. "Ma'am, we can take care of this."

He marched toward the cave, and the other goblins crowded along with him, apparently eager to get the job done with.

"It might not be safe, Gristletooth!" Miss Simone snapped. "Wait until we—"

"If we wait," the goblin interrupted with a snarl, "then the faun'll get away. Might already be long gone if there's another exit."

She protested some more, but the goblins were unfazed and stomped into the cave anyway, their armor jangling, torches burning, and swords drawn. Their sounds faded into the darkness.

Hal turned to find Abigail standing right behind him. Emily, Robbie, and Lauren had crept within a few feet of Miss Simone, who hadn't yet noticed.

"This is a shapeshifter's job," Hal muttered.

"Let the goblins deal with it," Abigail whispered back. "You know they want to."

The wait was silent and tense. In the distance, faint voices floated through the woods. Hal looked that way, seeing nothing but certain he'd heard Fenton laughing about something.

"The others are here," he said.

Miss Simone didn't respond. She just watched the cave mouth without uttering a word.

Several minutes later, as the voices in the woods grew louder, the goblins returned. Hal breathed a sigh of relief. He'd half expected one or two to be missing, and the rest badly injured and stumbling clear with panicked expressions on their faces. But no, they walked out calmly, looking bored.

"Nothing," Gristletooth grumbled. "Place was full of blue mist. Walked into it before we knew it, but nothing happened, so we kept going. Didn't see no faun. Probably went out a back way, but couldn't find that neither. Came across 'er stuff, though. Definitely her lair."

"She won't be back anytime soon," Miss Simone said with a sigh. "She could be anywhere by now.

"Why didn't yer stop her?" the goblin complained, turning to grimace at Hal. "She wouldn't have stood a chance against no dragon."

"There wasn't room to be a dragon," Hal said, suddenly feeling a wave of guilt. If the faun hurt anyone else because he'd let her get away . . .

Miss Simone patted him on the shoulder. "We'll resume the search. Everyone spread out and look for other caves and tunnel entrances on the slopes, perhaps in the rocky hillsides somewhere over that way. I expect the tunnels stretch a long way underground."

"I'm going to find some snakes!" Emily exclaimed, dashing away and transforming as she went. Her long, black tail was the last thing to vanish into the trees.

Hal had to admit that talking to snakes might be helpful. Maybe they'd know of some underground passages. Probably far more useful than Robbie stomping about in his giant ogre form, and Lauren shuffling around like a bird with broken wings.

The sound of hooves drew his attention. Dewey the centaur trotted up with Darcy clinging to his back. His face lit up when he saw Miss Simone. "I knew she was here somewhere," he whispered to Hal.

"See?" Abigail piped up. "Like moths to a flame."

A few paces behind, Thomas the manticore padded lightly from the trees with Fenton walking alongside. They both glanced about, eagerness in their eyes.

Darcy climbed off Dewey's back with a scowl on her face. "Wow, I'm sore from riding. So what's happening, guys?"

While Abigail filled them all in, Hal shuffled away. Guilt had settled over him, and he felt a need to track down that faun and actually capture her this time. If she'd truly escaped from the cave and tunnels and was wandering about in the woods, then he'd be able to confront her in dragon form.

He shifted and resumed his tracking, crashing through the undergrowth, uncaring of the thorns and jagged branches that scraped at his reptilian hide. As he crossed the path his friends had taken, his nostrils twitched at the plethora of fresh scents, especially the whiff of centaur dung. *Really*, Dewey? He caught the unmistakable hint of blood on manticore claws. Thomas must have been hungry on the way here. He detected human tracks, too. Fenton, probably, since Darcy had ridden the whole way.

He heard a distant buzzing and chuckled to himself, thinking of Abigail nipping under bushes and through tight spaces.

Foraging on his own for the next fifteen minutes enabled him to master his search technique. He stalked back and forth in long stretches, covering a lot of ground but never the same area twice. Whenever he picked up on something interesting—a possible musky faun smell—he triangulated and honed in, and after discovering it was likely just a deer or goat, he backtracked and continued where he'd left off earlier.

Voices drifted through the trees. He paused to listen. The quiet chatter of humans ... and lots of deep, guttural muttering and grumbling. Goblins! A band of men and a few women filed through the woods, at least a dozen of them, followed by another dozen of the stout, pig-faced goblins. Interesting how a male human led the way, Hal mused. The man—indeed, all the men—looked eager to get where they were going. Miss Simone's beacon was still at work.

"I'm telling you, it's this way," the one in the lead said at that moment.

"He's right," another man said, turning to speak to the woman behind him. "I can sense it. This is where Lady Simone needs us."

"Keep yer eyes peeled, then," a goblin grunted from the rear. "We're looking for a faun."

News travels fast, Hal thought. Matilda and her escorts had made it back to Carter already and dispatched a mob of eager, angry villagers on the warpath.

He glimpsed movement high above and looked up in time to see a white shape flitting about above the treetops. Lauren had taken to the air on the off-chance a valuable clue was only visible from above. At the same time, a series of crashes and crunches sounded off to Hal's right. He heard Robbie's distinctive ogreish grunts as his friend fought his way through a dense patch.

Hal resumed his work, nose down and trying to shut out the distractions. He just *had* to find—

At that very moment, he picked up a strong musky scent. It drifted by him on an errant gust of wind, and he spun to latch on. There! He started after it, then paused again. How could he know which way the smell, and therefore the faun, was traveling? He turned all the way around and decided the smell was stronger and fresher *this* way. He forged ahead, finding that the gust carrying the scent was really more like a continuous, meandering, and distinctly smelly airstream, strengthening as he went.

Oddly, it led him in a circle and ended up crossing the path of the newly arrived search party. He had to work hard to block out all the new smells—a dozen humans, a dozen goblins, and all the other aromas they'd brought from the village—but the faun's trail continued beyond, leading a zigzagging path through the undergrowth . . . and then doubling back once more to where the search party had blundered past.

Hal's heart began to thump hard. The faun was scouting around, spying on the new arrivals. She was right here somewhere, probably watching from the trees. He hunkered low, suddenly remembering how large he was. Full-sized dragons couldn't exactly sneak about, but he felt he'd been pretty stealthy all the same. Or had he? Maybe not. She was probably aware of him, too.

He followed her scent, putting on a burst of speed. If he couldn't take her by surprise, he could still catch up and overpower her.

The trail strengthened, her odor almost tangible. The faun had been here less than a few minutes ago. She led him around in a large circle, and where she'd squeezed through tight gaps, he simply pushed through and uprooted everything in his path. The scent faded briefly when he arrived in a rocky area, but he had plenty to go on and scrabbled over large boulders toward a craggy slope. His heart leapt at the sight of a crevice. Another entrance to the tunnels!

This was where the faun had escaped the tunnels earlier. Had she come back, hoping to give him the slip? The opening was too small for his dragon form, so he'd have to be human again if he wanted to chase after her.

But as he sniffed around, he realized the faun's trail bent sharply and led away into the woods again. She hadn't gone back into the tunnels at all. She was toying with him, or trying to trick him. He turned his back on the cave entrance, gave a roar, and crashed after her through the trees.

As he forged ahead, a tiny Abigail appeared out of nowhere. She quickly grew to full human size so she could be heard. "What's up, Hal? Are you onto something?"

He grunted "Yes" and concentrated on his task, aware that she buzzed alongside with her pleasant but obtrusive strawberry shampoo scent.

Dewey appeared ahead, angling toward him, his hooves picking up clods of dirt as he trotted. "Hal?" he called.

Centaurs were pretty smelly. Hal grunted with annoyance, wishing he could tell his friends to back off and leave him alone. The faun's trail bent to the right, and he dove through a thicket almost in an attempt to shake off his companions. They, of course, quickly circled the obstruction and caught up.

"Did she come this way?" Abigail whispered, zooming closer.

Dewey flanked his other side, bringing the smell of sweat and equine rear end with him. "We're with you, Hal."

I wish you weren't.

The faun's scent was so strong now, though, that it probably didn't matter if his friends hung close.

Almost there, almost there . . .

To his horror, he saw the search party directly ahead—over two dozen humans and goblins in all, standing around talking to Miss Simone and a few shapeshifters. The faun's trail led directly toward the large group. But had she already passed this way earlier and moved on . . . or was she there right now?

An overpowering blast of fresh smells washed over him, drowning out the faun's. Maybe that had been her plan—to lead him to a place where her own trail would be masked. If so, her plan had worked.

Hal burst out of the bushes onto the search party. Some of them had already swung around at the noise he'd made. Though they probably guessed he was just the friendly shapeshifter, for that first second or two, the sight of a dragon leaping out of the trees caused everyone to yelp in fright and skedaddle. Even Fenton and Thomas scuttled out of the way, though Fenton instantly feigned nonchalance the moment he realized who the dragon was.

"Where is she?" Abigail yelled. "She's here somewhere! Hal's tracking her smell!"

Goblins and humans alike immediately forged into the nearest bushes with hunting in mind, a collection of meager weapons raised—a few short swords, pitchforks, a spear or two, even a wooden stick. One woman had an small ax.

"Find her!" Miss Simone demanded. "Don't let that faun get away!" Then, like an afterthought: "But be careful—she's dangerous."

Hal sniffed around, furious that the faun's scent had been completely washed out by everyone else's. He plunged deeper into the trees, trying to find it again. She could be anywhere now. She might not have crossed the path of the search party at all; she might have doubled back once more.

He turned around, snout to the ground, dimly aware of people running about and Dewey trotting closer. "What's—?" the centaur started to say, but Hal ignored him, trying again to pick up the faun's musky smell.

"She's here!" a man yelled.

"Got her!" a woman screeched.

The next half-minute was a frenzy of activity as Hal, Dewey, Fenton, Thomas, Abigail, Miss Simone, more than a dozen goblins, and a whole mob of villagers stormed through the trees to where the faun had been spotted. Hal found himself side by side with humans, goblins, a manticore, and a centaur, with a faerie buzzing overhead, and he had to slow down just to avoid stomping on anyone or causing injury with his wings or tail.

Way too crowded around here, he thought angrily.

A scream filled the air, then several shouts and a man's strangled hollering. Abruptly, several voices cut off, which led to others starting up.

Then a stampede as people and goblins turned and dashed to safety, bumping into those who had faltered behind them.

"What's going on?" Miss Simone demanded, nearly being bowled over by a couple of terrified men carrying pitchforks.

A woman ran past, sobbing, "She killed them!"

It was clear now that the search party—the mob of angry villagers and goblins who had taken on the job of faun hunters—had turned and fled. Hal still couldn't see the faun, but he saw where she had to be— behind a clump of dense brambles from which people darted in fear. And he saw a cloud of blue mist drifting out from around it, creeping through the air like a couple of smoky tendrils sniffing out their next victims.

"Stay back!" he roared to Abigail as she buzzed closer.

She didn't understand his words, but his dragon roar made her jump anyway; she got the message and zipped away.

Hal had a moment of foolish bravado and, uncaring of the blue mist, leapt straight between the creeping tendrils and pounced on the brambles. He squashed the thicket flat under his tough chest and belly, and as he thudded down on the soft, squishy earth, he finally came face to face with the elusive faun.

He glimpsed her dark, coppery skin and splashes of what looked like gold paint on her arms and shoulders. What she wore around her torso looked rather like a vest made up of wet leaves, covering her chest but riding low on her sides and back, the whole thing painted to match her skin and daubed with gold. Her curled horns looked like they might do some damage if she dipped her head and charged, and her goatlike furry legs suggested she could spring away at any moment.

Instead, she snarled and crouched, waving her hands about in circular, twisting motions. The blue mist emanating from her hands thickened and billowed outward, engulfing Hal's face and momentarily blinding him. Feeling nothing, he roared and leapt through the mist, intending to pin the faun to the ground—but, just as he'd feared, she'd already sprung away in powerful leaps and bounds.

Aware of Dewey galloping into view, Hal spotted a number of discarded items of clothes—a shirt here, two pairs of pants there, a few boots, another shirt, a long skirt . . . all of it scattered randomly, some snagged on branches and others lying in the dirt.

What the heck—? Hal thought. *That's at least three more people gone!*

He went after her, wishing he could take to the air and fly instead of having to crash through the undergrowth. It was getting tiresome having no space to stretch out.

A manticore raced past him. Thomas panted hungrily as he sped past, his scorpion tail raised, the ball of quills puffed out.

Abigail shot past, too, a high-pitched whine as she shrank to her six-inch faerie height.

Dewey was hot on Hal's tail, following his trail of destruction through the woods. He thought he heard Robbie's ogreish grumbles, too, somewhere back there. And overhead, he caught a flash of white as Lauren joined in the chase.

As Hal thundered onward, keeping the springing faun in sight just ahead, he struggled to understand the significance of the blue mist. It didn't seem deadly at all, though it had temporarily distracted him. Still, Derek and now three more people were apparently dead, with nothing left but scattered clothing.

No more, he thought as he veered to the right where the faun was headed. *She's not getting away this time.*

With a snarl, Thomas leapt at her. Hal saw the flash of red manticore fur, and then the faun went down. The roars and screeches that followed chilled Hal's blood, but by the time he got there, the faun was on her cloven feet and kicking at Thomas's face. She had vivid claw marks across one shoulder, and several poison-tipped quills stuck out of her neck, but she seemed driven by fear and anger.

Seeing Hal, she snarled, spat, and sprang away again.

He gasped at her agility. She must have jumped ten feet high and double the length, easily clearing some brightly colored thorny shrubs. Thomas shook his head, scowled, and tore after her again.

Abigail buzzed into view, then zipped away.

Lauren came hurtling down through the trees, her wings spread wide and barely missing the close-set trees. "She's headed for the river! No trees, Hal! I'll see you there."

He understood exactly what she meant. No trees on the riverbank meant no restrictions—he could fly! He forged onward through the woods, focused on the distant figure springing this way and that.

Man, she's fast!

Dewey overtook him, galloping now that the woods had thinned somewhat.

And then Emily appeared out of nowhere, slithering at a terrifying speed with her head low, proving what a formidable force the naga could be.

Everyone else had been left far behind.

Hal arrived at a clearing before the forest ended at the river. Without hesitation, he spread his wings wide and launched skyward. He cleared the treetops in seconds, then pumped his wings hard to get some real speed going. A few beats later, a telltale gap in the forest came into view—a long, twisting, hundred-foot gap where a substantial river flowed from east to west.

If the faun emerged from the woods onto the grassy banks, she would be vulnerable to an attack from the sky. And she couldn't go back without running into Thomas again, not to mention Dewey and Emily.

Hal spotted Lauren circling like a vulture waiting for her prey. He joined her, adding his ominous shadow to the grassy banks below. The river flowed fast here, the water churning and frothing over rocks.

The faun appeared, leaping out of the woods. Hal dive-bombed, wings back and neck stretched out, fire forming in his throat. At this point, roasting her didn't seem too harsh. She'd killed four already. She could *not* be allowed to escape.

The faun looked up at him and stood perfectly still.

Lauren swooped in from the side, equally intent on dive-bombing her prey.

Thomas charged from the trees followed by Dewey and Emily.

She's trapped! Hal thought with glee.

But the faun didn't seem too perturbed. She looked around, snarled, then sprang into the river. She went in with a small splash and never resurfaced.

Hal came out of his dive with a roar of disappointment and thudded down on the grassy bank alongside Thomas and Dewey. Abigail zipped into view. Lauren flapped down, too, but she hovered in place, waiting.

Emily shot into the water. Her long black tail disappeared, and she vanished from sight amid the frothing, churning water. She, like the faun, never resurfaced—or not for a long while, anyway. She came up eventually, swimming back upstream to join them, disappointment on her face.

"No sign of her," she gasped as she slithered out onto the grassy bank, her serpent body slick and her smart clothes hanging like shreds of skin. "I don't know how she could—I mean, she's a faun! Can fauns even swim? Can they breathe underwater?"

A lot of crashing from the trees suggested the search party was on its way. Not that they could do anything now. Hal sat and panted alongside his friends, stunned that the faun had escaped again. He was tempted to fly off downriver and wait for her to emerge, as she surely would, but he suspected she could swim as fast as she could leap through the woods. She could be miles away already. Or she might have gone upriver. That wouldn't surprise him, either.

Miss Simone was the first of the search party to arrive. The moment Emily explained where the faun had gone, Miss Simone threw off her silky cloak and leapt into the water herself, diving gracefully. Her legs morphed, fusing together to form a mermaid tail before she submerged.

Then she, too, was gone.

Chapter Six
Blue Mist

"We need a full-time vigil," Miss Simone said, looking around at the group of shapeshifters. They shuffled with uncertainty, all in human form now.

She stood on the edge of the grassy bank, barely wet despite her recent dive. She'd hunted around, returned fifteen minutes later, and had climbed out dripping—but her hair had instantly dried in a sudden and mysterious gust of wind. Her simple knee-length dress seemed to repel moisture in such a way that the river water sluiced off her in a rush. All the shapeshifters and some of the villagers and goblins had arrived at the river by then, and they'd been awed at the rare sight of Miss Simone's 'instant-dry' magic. Mermaids possessed a number of weird and wonderful tricks.

"You mean stay here?" Emily asked. "For how long?"

Miss Simone scowled over her shoulder at the river. "Until you find that faun."

The local men and women muttered to each other. Then a man spoke up. "Lady Simone, we need reinforcements. We need *more* shapeshifters. This faun—that blue mist—"

"I understand," Miss Simone said, "and I'll see if I can gather a few more of us. But right now, these nine children will spread out and keep watch. I could be wrong, but that blue mist didn't seem to affect them. Hal?"

She looked at him, and he felt all eyes turn to him. "Uh, right. She conjured some up and blew it right in my face, and it didn't hurt me."

"How is that possible?" a woman demanded. She frowned and cast her gaze downward. "I mean, I'm glad you weren't hurt, Hal, but . . ." She looked up again, her eyes blazing with anger. "I watched three people I know disintegrate, explode into dust, their ashes floating away on a breeze, and their clothes fluttering in all directions. How did that mist affect them and not you? How can we be sure it won't affect you next time?"

"We'll be careful," Miss Simone assured her. She looked again at Hal and then around at his friends. "*You* will be careful. You'll capture her without going near her."

"How?" Fenton muttered. "I could spit glue on her, but I have to be pretty close."

"My quills didn't do much," Thomas said morosely. "I stuck a few in her, and she just sprang away."

"We'll have to pounce on her and tie her hands," Emily suggested, turning to face them all. "If she conjures blue mist with her hands—"

"So tying her hands will take away her magic powers?" Abigail cut in. "I doubt that."

Emily pouted. "Well, we won't know if we don't try."

"*You* tie her hands, then," Fenton said, "while I spit glue on her."

"And then I can sting her," Thomas added.

Robbie chortled. "And I'll squash her flat, Dewey can stamp on her face, Lauren can tear her apart, Abigail can tickle her to death with her buzzing faerie wings, Darcy can confuse her by being invisible, and Hal can roast her with his fire. Together, we can do this."

His flippant comments sparked a few retorts, but Miss Simone shushed them all and went to talk more directly to what was left of the mob of villagers. The rest, apparently, had fled along with a few goblins. Dealing with a faun was one thing, but a witch-faun who could disintegrate people . . .

"Go home," she told them. "We're tripling the guards all around the village today and all through the night. I'll see if I can muster some of my old shapeshifter friends, but in the meantime, we have an active emergency situation that I'm sure our younger shapeshifters can handle just fine. They're a resourceful bunch."

"And if they can't capture the faun?" a man argued.

"They'll stop her one way or another." Miss Simone cast a look back at Hal. "If there's absolutely no alternative, then they must dispatch the faun for good. She's clearly very dangerous. But I'd prefer her to be captured alive. I want to know what she's doing and how she's doing it. Is this a general faun threat we should be concerned with, or just one individual?"

She left that question hanging and turned back to talk to the shapeshifters. "Go. Stay together, talk it over, form a plan, and split into groups as you see fit. Above all, be careful."

Fenton nudged Thomas and grinned. "So no school until this is over?"

"This isn't funny, moron," Abigail said.

Darcy, who had been very quiet the whole time, said, "Robbie's right, though. I can be invisible. I can sneak up on her." She looked around. "I think we can do this, guys. We just need to be smart." She shot Fenton a glare. "And serious."

"I can be serious." Fenton drew himself up straight and lifted his chin so he looked down on her. It looked for a moment like he was posturing, about to make some wise crack and warn her to watch her mouth. Instead: "What do you have in mind, Darcy? Count me in."

She nodded. "I have some ideas. Gather round, everybody."

In the background, Miss Simone pulled her silky cloak tight around her shoulders and strode off to join the goblins and villagers. They dispersed, apparently satisfied to let the shapeshifters take over the hunt for a while. A few men and a woman lingered, each clutching a weapon of some kind, but Miss Simone firmly ushered them away.

"You have until morning," she called to the children. "Then I'm calling in Molly."

Hal shuddered. Since Molly was a gorgon, calling her in meant one thing only, and that was a quick end to the problem. One instant of eye-to-eye contact and the faun would turn to stone.

"Using Molly sounds good to me," Thomas muttered. "Why should *we* put ourselves at risk?"

Nobody responded. He could be a little selfish and thoughtless at times. Not even Fenton stooped that low. Years of living with manticores in the forest had hardened his heart somewhat.

A minute later, the shapeshifters were alone, just the nine of them to figure out a plan to capture an elusive and dangerous faun.

"Okay," Darcy said as everyone circled her. "So we need to do three things. First, we find her. Second, we sneak up on her. Third, we catch her. I can do the second part. I can be invisible while she's sleeping or distracted, sneak up on her, and maybe use the plants to snag her wrists or ankles."

"Like you did with the soldiers," Abigail exclaimed. She grinned. "Good, yes. And if you can get her pinned down or something, the rest of us can leap in and tie her up."

"Or I can wrap my snake tail around her," Emily offered.

"Or Fenton can glue her," Dewey said.

"And once she's secured, I can carry her upside down into the sky," Lauren chipped in, "and take her off to Carter."

Hal was already warming to the slew of ideas. He grinned. His friends really were cool. "So we just need to find her. That's where I can help. I have a pretty good nose when I'm in dragon form—"

"Yeah, but you're not exactly quiet," Darcy argued. "Sorry, Hal, but if you go crashing through the woods again, we'll never sneak up on her."

Fenton sighed. "So what's the plan? Wait for her to show up again?"

"That could take *forever*," Emily said. Then she frowned. "Unless . . ."

Everyone turned to her. "Unless what?" Abigail prompted. "You have something? Spit it out."

Emily lowered her voice. "What if one or two of us are bait? We hang about, make a campfire, and wait for the faun to come get us. If she's interested, she'll probably watch us for a bit first."

"And that's when I sneak up," Darcy agreed. "Yes! She'll be spying on you, and I'll be spying on her. We don't have to go find her. We just have to wait for her to come to us."

Hal felt this part of the plan was a little optimistic, but he had nothing better to suggest. "Sounds good to me. Let's get into position, then. I guess we'll all just spread out and hide while the bait sets up camp right here?"

His doubt strengthened. What were the chances of the faun coming back to this very spot? What if she suspected a trap? She might even recognize some of the shapeshifters. Everyone in the village knew the faun was out here somewhere, so it would seem mighty suspicious for a couple of ordinary kids to be camping right in the middle of it all.

The bait was Emily and Dewey. "Make noises like you're staying to hunt her down," Hal said quietly to them. "The faun might believe that and be tempted to take you on. But she won't come near if she thinks it's too easy. It would stink like a trap."

"Don't worry," Emily told Dewey. "I'll protect you."

Fenton snorted and laughed at Dewey's reddening face. "Yeah, Dewey, a *girl* will take care of you."

As Darcy and Lauren gathered a few sticks to make a campfire, Emily found a rocky patch on the riverbank. She sat and nodded. "This is dry enough." She raised her voice. "We'll wait right here and keep watch. The rest of you can go on home. Dewey and I can take care of things."

Abigail quickly caught on. "Are you sure, Em? You can handle the faun on your own?"

"No problem. Go home."

With that, the trap was set. But Hal couldn't help thinking it was all a little too easy. If the faun was spying right now and had heard that last exchange, she also would have heard the entire plan beforehand.

Still, what else could they do? It was worth a shot.

Leaving Emily and Dewey behind, the rest of them sauntered away from the riverbank and into the woods, headed for home . . . but they didn't go far. Silently, they slipped behind a huge rotting log and crouched there without saying a word.

"Okay," Darcy whispered after a while, "I'm going back to the river. I'll sit near them and keep quiet. They'll know I'm there, but hopefully the faun won't. You guys stay close but out of sight."

She transformed. Sometimes her shift to dryad form was as simple as turning invisible, but this time Hal caught a glimpse of her strange woodland skin texture, rather like bark, and the curious tree-stump forehead that projected upward. Then she faded from sight. It wasn't exactly invisibility, more of a chameleon-style camouflage that helped her blend in with the surroundings. But what a camouflage! Hal blinked, trying to focus on her. When she stood still, the bush in the background seemed like it was painted across her front. And yet, when one of his other friends looked at her, they saw something else depending on their angle of view.

Only when she moved did she give herself away, though it took a few glances to spot her. Hal blinked again, rubbing his eyes at her blurry shape.

"I love it when a plan comes together," Lauren murmured. "Remember when we were at the Labyrinth of Fire? The plan to rescue Abigail from the dragons?"

Hal sighed. "That was crazy. Fenton dangling his tail down through the hole in the roof . . ."

"What about you and the harpies?" Abigail said, nudging Lauren. "Rescuing a baby from under their noses!"

Lauren laughed softly. "That was mostly Darcy."

"It was your plan, and you did all the talking."

Robbie grinned. "We'll make this work. But we should get closer. We need to see what's going on."

"Easy for me," Abigail said. "I can be small. I'm not sure the rest of you can sneak closer without being seen. An ogre, a dragon, a giant lizard, a manticore—even a harpy! You'll stand out a mile, all of you."

Hal shook his head. "You're wrong. We can all creep closer just fine—in human form."

It was like the idea had never occurred to any of them. They all nodded. "Yeah," Fenton said. "We'll just crawl through the bushes until we're near the riverbank. Then we wait."

"Then we wait," Abigail agreed.

* * *

They waited.

Each of them lay on their belly, spaced a few feet apart, tucked under a bush or behind a tree with a clear view of Emily and Dewey on the riverbank perhaps a stone's throw away.

The two sat face to face, chatting idly around their dwindling campfire. The smoke drifted lazily into the clear afternoon sky. A pile of logs lay to one side, and Dewey occasionally stoked the fire with one. Their conversation seemed to have trailed off a bit, and boredom had set in.

Hal rolled onto his back, groaning. He'd love a walk right about now. Or a good flight above the treetops. "How long have we been here?" he muttered.

Beside him, Abigail sighed. "You asked that ten minutes ago. I told you about two hours."

After a pause, he said, "So two hours and ten minutes, then."

She chuckled. "I guess so."

Hal happened to be on the end of the line of stealthy shapeshifters, so he had no neighbor on his other side. Next to Abigail, Lauren whispered, "Seriously, how long do you think we should keep this up? When do we decide the faun isn't coming back?"

"Two hours is nothing," Abigail scoffed. "We have to be more patient than that. We might be here for the rest of the day and night before she shows. We can't go back and say we got bored after two hours."

Fenton let out a moan. "All day and night? Are you kidding?"

"Shh!" That was Robbie, sounding irritated.

The group lapsed into silence.

Abigail sighed again. "I'm going for a fly-about. Maybe the faun is across the other side of the river spying on Emily and Dewey right now. Who knows? I'll go take a look."

And have a break from lying around, Hal thought with a pang of envy. He watched her shrink down to a mere six inches in height and zip away across the river, staying low to the rushing water.

"I'm hungry," Fenton muttered.

"You're always hungry," Robbie retorted.

"Shut your mouth, beanpole."

After a brief pause, Lauren said, "We *will* need to eat, though. We missed lunch already. I don't want to miss dinner as well. If we're going to be here all night . . ."

"I ate already," Thomas growled from the far end of the hidden shapeshifters.

Fenton laughed. "Yeah, a groundhog."

Lauren made a choking sound. "Eww!"

"Guys," Hal whispered fiercely. "You're getting louder and louder."

Everyone lapsed into silence again. Hal sighed, knowing it wouldn't last. Meanwhile, Emily and Dewey seemed to have given up on conversation, too. They sat by their campfire on the riverbank looking thoroughly bored. There was no sign of Darcy, though she might be sitting right there with them, invisible unless she moved.

"Lauren, do you want to go get us something to eat?" Hal whispered.

She looked at him from the shadows of the bush she lay under. "Why me? Because I'm a girl? That's sexist."

"Because you have wings," Hal explained.

"*You* have wings."

"But I'm more noticeable. And you have hands."

She scowled, then nodded. "I guess. All right. Anything's better than lying around here with you losers." She nudged Robbie and smiled. "Except you, of course."

Robbie grinned. "See you soon."

She wriggled backward out of the bush, turned, and crawled away. Hal listened for the sound of her transforming, the *whump* of her wings springing open, the fluttering of her feathers as she took off . . . but he heard nothing. She'd done well to mask her departure.

Well, that's food taken care of, he thought.

Another half-hour crawled by. Emily lay back on the grass and fell asleep while Dewey—and everyone else—kept watch. Behind his tree, Fenton looked like he was dozing off, too. Hal sighed. He was uncomfortable, bored, and hungry. Being a shapeshifter wasn't all excitement and danger. Sometimes it just plain sucked.

"What do we know about fauns?" Robbie asked in a low voice, breaking the silence.

Hal blinked at him. "They have horns and goat legs."

"Yeah, but what else?"

Thomas chimed in. "I thought fauns were male."

"Fauns are male *and* female, idiot," Robbie said.

"So what's a satyr?"

"That's a male faun."

Thomas laughed. "So a male faun is a satyr *and* a faun?"

Robbie clicked his tongue. "A satyr is the leader of the group, the dominant male. There's usually one for every clan."

Everyone digested that.

"But what I want to know is, are they dangerous?" Robbie went on. "I mean, this one is, but are they *normally* dangerous?"

Nobody answered.

"I guess we don't get many fauns around here," Robbie went on. "Otherwise we'd have seen one before now."

"Did you see how fast she moved?" Hal asked. "How high she jumped?"

"She was gone before I caught up," Fenton muttered.

"Well, she's got a spring in her step. She'll be hard to pin down."

"Yeah," Thomas admitted. "I thought I had her, but she kind of slipped loose and jumped away. My poison quills didn't slow her down at all."

Hal searched the far banks of the river, looking for Abigail. He didn't see her, but he did see a small, shuffling creature with a hideous, screwed-up, wrinkled face and bulging eyes, and orange matted fur. He watched it for a while as it sniffed here and there and moved on. A squonk. They had incredibly low self-esteem. Stare too hard in its direction and it was liable to dissolve into a puddle of tears. What kind of strange world created such a sad and pointless animal?

Another movement caught his eye, and he twisted his neck—and found the horned, goat-legged faun standing right behind Thomas.

"T-Thomas!" Hal croaked, struggling to sit up. "Behind you!"

Thomas rolled over and looked, and his eyes grew big and round as the faun took a step toward him. She started moving her hands in that mysterious way . . .

Everyone moved at once. Fenton transformed right where he lay. Thomas sprang to his hands and knees, apparently mesmerized by the faun's conjuring trick. Robbie yelled out and scrambled sideways, almost bumping into Hal.

Fenton, in his ten-foot solid-black lizard form, with an equally long tail that curled around and around, reared back and sprayed glue-water at the faun. It drenched her face and shoulders, breaking her concentration for a second.

As blue mist seeped from her fingers, Hal switched to his dragon form while Robbie grew to full ogre size. They got in each other's way and jostled briefly, tangled in bushes and pressed up against trees.

Thomas finally shifted, too, and he roared as the blue mist engulfed him.

The faun let out a hiss of rage and backed away, sweeping her hands around and allowing her weird mist to billow forth from the palms of her hands so it quickly masked her whereabouts. But Hal and his friends were used to mist, blue or otherwise, and they plunged through it.

Again, Hal and Robbie bumped against each other, a wing catching a hairy shoulder, and a giant foot stepping on a reptilian paw. Then they emerged on the other side of the mist. Hal spotted the faun darting off, and he went after her.

Thomas shot past, the only one of them fast enough to have a chance of catching up.

Then Dewey came galloping through the trees from the riverbank, his head down. He looked determined, a fierce warrior centaur even though he had no weapon but his hands. Emily sat on his back, in human form, urging him on.

Hal had never felt so useless. Being a dragon just didn't work in the middle of dense woods, especially with a thirty-foot ogre getting in his way. He angrily shoved against Robbie and tried to get into a clear spot. Finding none, he spun around and headed back to the riverbank, almost stepping on Fenton's long tail in the process.

He launched off the grassy bank and climbed into the sky, looking down on the trees. Once more, the faun was on the run. She couldn't get away again!

To his surprise, he actually glimpsed the faun through the canopy of branches below. Right behind her, Dewey galloped with Emily sprawled across his back. They were fast catching up. Any second now—

Seeing a rare opening in the trees ahead, Hal put on a burst of speed and dive-bombed, hurtling toward the ground. Protruding branches snagged at him. His landing was rough and twisted, and he fell heavily, pain shooting up one side.

But he had no time to fret over minor injuries. He spun around just in time to see the faun leaping out of the trees. She hit the ground running, then spotted him and immediately tried to change course— but Dewey galloped through a thicket and rammed into her so hard she went down in a shower of soil and leaves.

Emily launched off his back and staggered to right herself. The faun rolled over, got up on her elbows, then sprang to her hoofed feet in one impossibly agile movement. She pounced on Emily and pushed her down, then sidestepped to avoid Dewey's flailing front legs as he spun around and reared up on his hindquarters.

Blue mist erupted from the faun's palms. She leaned over Emily and waved her hands about, and the mist thickened.

Hal stomped closer, flames licking from his mouth as he prepared to send a roaring inferno her way—if Emily would hurry up and move!

Instead, Emily clambered to her feet. The blue mist crept toward her, and she stood straight with her fists balled, a challenging look on her face. "Yeah? You can't hurt us, faun! We're shapeshifters!"

The faun lunged, shoving her spread hands even closer and causing the mist to billow around Emily's face and shoulders.

"Em!" Dewey shouted, trotting closer. "Just change and wrap her up!"

Yeah, Em—get it done! Hal thought, feeling helpless.

He saw Emily's expression change from angry defiance to sudden fear as the blue mist enveloped her.

And then she exploded into dust.

Chapter Seven
Gone

Hal and Dewey stood perfectly still, rooted to the spot and shaken to the core.

The faun was long gone. They'd barely been aware of her departure.

They stared at the spot Emily had stood moments before, where the blue mist slowly dissipated to reveal her scattered clothing—a silky green dress here, a pair of smart shoes there, and some undergarments that Hal felt he shouldn't be looking at—all thrown about as though a miniature whirlwind had ripped through the woods.

Emily was gone. She'd literally exploded into a cloud of dust.

The image of what had happened was seared into Hal's mind. There had been a moment when her face had frozen solid and cracked down the middle, particles floating loose as though she were a porcelain doll ravaged by a vicious wind. Then she'd erupted in a thick cloud, her clothes flung far and wide. Rather than coat the surrounding area in a fine layer of ash, the cloud had dispersed on an upward draft, her essence lifting skyward while her clothes dropped to the ground.

And at some point during or after, the faun had leapt away.

Hal reverted to human form and, mindful of the remaining puffs of blue mist, dropped to his knees where Emily had last been standing. He clawed at the ground. "No, no, no. Emily!"

Dewey clip-clopped closer, then abruptly shifted and crouched beside Hal. "There's no way," he whispered. "She *can't* be."

Hal pulled the silky dress toward him. Still warm. It had no signs of damage, no rips or tears, not even a drop of blood. He saw no fine ashes or dust particles, nothing to suggest Emily had literally dissolved within the garment.

He watched a faint, blue wisp drift away. How could something so innocuous be so deadly? And why? Why had it affected Emily but not the others?

"She was herself," he whispered. "She was in human form."

Dewey squinted at him. "Huh?"

When Hal thought about it, he realized he and all the others had been in their alternate forms when the mist had confronted them. Thomas had been lucky, barely escaping with his life earlier, transforming at the last second as the faun stood over him. Emily was the *only* one who'd been in human form as the mist had enveloped her.

Hal sighed and gave a nod. "Miss Simone was wrong. Shapeshifters aren't invincible. We're only safe while we're transformed. Otherwise, we're just like everyone else."

Dewey dropped his head and choked out his next words. "But she can't be gone, Hal. She *can't*. Not Em!"

As he fought back tears and let out small gasping noises, Hal gripped Emily's dress and climbed to his feet. He felt strangely empty. Trembling, he searched the woods for the faun, thinking she might be lurking somewhere nearby, watching.

"Where are you?" he yelled in sudden fury.

A voice came to him in the distance. "We're coming!"

He blinked, then remembered his friends, who were probably rushing through the trees in their hurry to catch up. Some of his anger dissipated. Now he was faced with the prospect of telling them Emily was . . . *gone*.

He stood and waited, clenching and unclenching his fists over and over. He called out a few times to guide his friends as they crashed through the undergrowth, drawing closer.

Abigail appeared first, at full size but with faerie wings spread, buzzing into view and zigzagging toward him. Behind her, in human form, Fenton panted as he jogged alongside a casually trotting manticore. And above, Lauren flitted across the treetops carrying a basket, trying to find a way down to the ground.

"What happened?" Abigail called as she zipped closer. "Did you catch the faun? Did she get away?" She sucked in a breath, then whispered, "Why's Dewey crying?"

It was at that moment her gaze fell on the dress gripped in Hal's hands. She stared, frowned, looked up at him, opened her mouth to say something, paused . . . and then the color drained from her face.

"No," she gasped.

Hal shakily held out the silky material. Abigail took it, and it was as though she'd just been handed irrefutable proof. Her face crumpled, and tears welled up.

A scream pierced the air. Hal jumped, jerking around and seeing nobody. But then Darcy fuzzed into view, running toward them ahead of Fenton and Thomas. "Emily! EMILY!"

The next thirty minutes were pure misery. Hal broke down with the rest of them and collapsed around the very spot she'd disappeared, where Emily's clothes sat in a pile. Fenton demanded answers and made accusations. "This is *your* fault, Hal!" he roared at one point. Thomas tore off, eventually returning to sit aloof with his tail curled around and the scorpion stinger thudding gently on the ground as if he were contemplating revenge. Lauren, who had returned from the village with a basket of food, sobbed openly and clung to Darcy. Her basket had turned over, spilling a few wrapped items that nobody paid any attention to. Hal held Abigail, Dewey rocked back and forth with his knees drawn up, and Robbie sat alone with his head in his hands.

All of them dissolved into tears at least once or twice.

Silence fell eventually. Exhausted, they sat huddled together in a circle, saying nothing, doing nothing. Hal told himself over and over it was all his fault, that Fenton was right, he should have stopped the faun, blasted her with fire—or better still, caught her the *first* time. Hal felt like he'd underestimated the creature every step of the way, and now Emily . . . Emily . . .

He squeezed his eyes shut. What were the various stages of grief? He couldn't remember, but he'd definitely been through denial, though it had been quick; it was hard to deny what he'd seen. Right now he felt nothing but anger.

"She's not dead," he blurted.

Darcy visibly jumped at his outburst. She looked up at him from across the circle, peering out from behind her blond hair. "What?"

Hal swallowed and sat up straight. "There's no body," he muttered. "She just . . . vanished."

Dewey shook his head. "She exploded into dust."

"Yeah, but worse things can happen."

Everyone stared at Hal in silence. He sensed a few of them— Fenton, Thomas, maybe even Darcy—held him responsible, and they sent a simmering resentment toward him. Others were just plain miserable, too wrapped up in grief to assign blame.

Hal shifted uncomfortably. "What I mean is . . . well, look at Fenton."

Several gazes shifted his way. Fenton's scowl deepened.

"See," Hal went on, "Fenton was turned to stone by a gorgon. Molly accidentally looked at him without her veil on. Remember?"

Of course they remember, he thought. He could see their tear-stricken scowls turning into thoughtful frowns, so he pressed on.

"Fenton was *dead*—or so we thought. Right? Then a phoenix wiped magic from the land, and he woke up. So when we all thought he was well and truly dead—"

"Stop saying that word!" Lauren snapped.

Hal nodded. "Sorry. But you get my point. This land we live in . . . well, it's magical. The faun is magical. That blue mist is magical. What happened to Emily was magical, too. She might be alive somewhere."

As frowns faded and hope flickered across several of his friends' faces, Hal gently disengaged from Abigail, stood, and rubbed his face vigorously as if to wipe away the misery. Then he stared at his right hand and wiggled his fingers.

"Look at that. Almost back to normal. I had my fingers chewed off by a dragon, and now they've grown back. How many people can say that? I don't know, guys—maybe that blue mist kills ordinary people, but we're special. Or maybe that mist isn't meant to kill at all." He drew himself up. "I'm not giving up on her until I know for sure."

Darcy was the next to leap up. "You really think there's a chance?"

He shrugged. "We can sit around and accept she's . . . *gone*, or we can do something. What if she's still here somewhere? What if she's watching us right now as we just give up and go home, leaving her trapped somewhere?"

Dewey and Abigail slowly stood, followed by Robbie and Lauren.

"If there's any possibility at all," Abigail said, "then we need to get back to work."

"So we split up and look for Emily?" Dewey asked. "But, I mean, she turned to dust, so . . ."

"We look for the faun," Hal said firmly. "We need to catch her— *alive*," he added with a steely glare toward Thomas. "She knows better than anyone what that blue mist does to people and if there's a chance of saving them after they've . . . you know, exploded."

Everyone cast their eyes downward. Hal couldn't help feeling he was grasping at straws, probably going through the next stage of grief. What was it? Bargaining? Or was he back to denial again? Either way, he wasn't ready to give up.

The shapeshifters organized themselves, which meant simply heading out in different directions to trawl the woods yet again. It was like looking for a needle in a haystack, and the faun could strike again at any time. "Stay in pairs," Hal ordered, realizing he had somehow taken the lead despite being the one to blame.

"We need Miss Simone and a bunch of other shifters," Robbie grumbled. "These woods are huge. We'll never find her. It'll be dark before we know it."

"Go home then," Fenton retorted. "I'm staying for as long as it takes."

"You should transform," Hal warned. "The mist can't harm you then."

Fenton grimaced. "Too slow. I'll switch if I see the faun."

The big boy stomped away with Thomas the manticore once more at his side. Lauren climbed onto Robbie's shoulders once he'd grown to full ogre height, and Dewey trotted away with an invisible Darcy astride his back.

Abigail grabbed Emily's dress and smart shoes and stuck with Hal, buzzing up to perch on his neck the moment he was in dragon form. She patted him as he set off. "It's not your fault, Hal. Fenton's just a big mouth. We're all upset, but not with you."

He couldn't answer, so he grunted.

"I think you're right, though," she continued. "I think Emily's okay. We just need to save her."

Doubt crept into her voice during her last few words, and she lapsed into silence.

* * *

They didn't so much search as wander aimlessly for hours, calling Emily's name from time to time. Hal heard his friends in the distance and sometimes up close, and once in a while he crossed paths with one or another. Between them, they probably explored a relatively small area in a random, crisscrossing way. Still, it seemed clear the faun was either long gone or had hidden herself away.

If Miss Simone had organized reinforcements, they were a long time coming. Hal imagined a goblin or two would have to lead the way back to this hidden spot in the forest, which itself would take time.

Who would be best suited for searches? He thought of Miss Simone's old classmates, the previous generation of shapeshifters that had grown up and moved away . . .

Lucas the lycan would be a great ally. His acute wolf senses and fierce nature would serve the team well. Maybe Bo and Astrid, the sphinxes? Canaan the elf, although Hal was pretty sure she was off visiting an elfin clan somewhere at the moment. He doubted Ellie the unicorn or Orson the pegasus would be much help. Though sensitive, they were far too timid.

Charlie the griffin would be a good hunter, but like Hal, he was too big to get around easily. Riley . . . well, he was Blacknail the goblin, and heavy-footed goblins were better at tinkering with machines and launching into battle than stealthy woodland hunting. Blair the phoenix? Maybe he could dive-bomb a rabbit in a field, but what could he do among the trees? Then there was Miss Simone's brother Felipe, otherwise known as Burnflank the dragon—but of course he was a long way off, nestled in the hot lava tubes in the Labyrinth of Fire.

Other than Miss Simone herself, that left one other: Molly the gorgon. And she was the last person the search party needed if they wanted to take the faun alive. Unless of course she turned the faun to stone, then put the statue in a cage and asked Blair to perform his phoenix rebirth trick to nullify the magic and bring her back . . .

Hal shook his head. Nullifying the faun's magic might obliterate any chances of saving Emily.

So, in a nutshell, Hal and his friends were better off on their own. Maybe Miss Simone had come to the same conclusion already.

Abigail chatted from time to time about trivial things just to lighten the mood, but Hal could only muster a few grunts and grumbles in return, and she soon shut down again. He had no interest in small talk right now. He was preoccupied with what had turned out to be a rather obvious fact.

He pondered as he absently crashed through a thicket for perhaps the third time. They'd all been fools. The more he thought about it, the more obvious it seemed. Goblins had entered the faun's cave and walked through puffs of blue mist without harm. A little later on, in dragon form, Hal had got a faceful of the stuff with no ill effects. There had been shapeshifters and goblins present alongside humans in that same skirmish, and the only victims were people from the village: humans. Just recently, quite a few of the shapeshifters had been in close quarters with the faun and her magical mist, and none had been affected. Until Emily, who had not transformed in time.

He abruptly reverted to human form. Abigail let out a squeal and toppled off his back, landing roughly in the dirt along with Emily's clothes. "What the heck!" she exclaimed.

Hal held out his hand and helped her up. "The faun is targeting humans."

She frowned at him as she brushed herself down. "Well, we've only had human victims so far, so I guess—"

"No, I mean she's *really* targeting humans. That blue mist doesn't affect goblins, and it doesn't affect us while we're in our different forms. But she wanted it to. Remember how she tried to get Thomas with it? No, wait, you weren't there. She did, though. He transformed just in time without even realizing that was what saved his bacon. And me! The faun conjured that blue mist right at me while I was a dragon, and she had this look on her face like she was testing it out to see if it would work."

"Testing it out?" she said, picking up Emily's dress and smart shoes again.

"Yeah. She knew we were shapeshifters, and she wasn't sure if her mist would work on us since we're half and half. Well, she got her answer—it doesn't while we're monsters. And then she tested it on Emily while she was human, and it worked. So now she knows."

Abigail looked around at the unnaturally quiet woods. "Okay, so the blue mist only works on humans . . ."

"But don't you see? It's not like that mist is some natural faun defense system. She conjured it. She created a spell that *specifically targets humans*. Why would a faun do that?"

Abigail just stared at him, frowning.

Hal looked skyward. It was getting dark. "It just seems weird to me that a faun would work so hard on a spell that causes only humans to explode into dust. You'd think a spell with a wider reach would be more useful, something to protect her from all kinds of predators and enemies."

"Maybe she just found a spellbook somewhere and doesn't really know what she's doing," Abigail murmured.

But Hal could tell she didn't believe that. "Makes you wonder, though," he whispered. He moved closer, feeling a need to keep his voice down. "Fauns don't normally do magic, but this one does. Where did she get the spellbook and learn how to conjure things? And why? If she's really just targeting humans"—he spread his hands—"again, *why?*"

As if to punctuate his ominous question, thunder rumbled in the distance. Hal looked up. That was why the sky was so dark all of a sudden. "Storm's rolling in," he said. "We *have* to find that faun."

Abigail sighed. "I know, but we won't. Not by wandering aimlessly. We've passed this same spot three times already. The faun is probably laughing at us. We need a better plan."

"Do you have one?"

"No."

Hal huffed with annoyance. "Then we keep looking. We can't go home until we find Emily. Can you imagine facing her parents and telling them she's dead? I can't. I won't. Not until we're sure."

He realized he was choking up again, and Abigail stuffed Emily's clothes under one arm and slipped her other arm around him. "I know. I agree. But we can't traipse around in the woods in the dark, either, especially if it starts raining. It'll be useless. We might as well hide in a cave or something until—"

She broke off, then pulled away and gazed at him.

"That's what we need to do. We need to get everyone together and take shelter in that cave. We'll have to stay the night. Lauren already brought us food."

"She did?" He'd completely forgotten about her basket. And he had to admit he liked the sound of taking shelter a lot better than searching aimlessly even for one more minute. With a pang of guilt, he nodded. "Let's do that." He looked up into the treetops and raised his voice. "We're not going anywhere, Emily. We're sticking around. Just hang in there."

Abigail shot him a funny look but smiled as well. "I really want to believe she's out there somewhere, but—"

"It's not just that. I'm letting the faun know we're staying. I think the only way to find her is for *her to find us.* Like we did before, only this time we'll be prepared."

"We thought we were prepared last time."

"Yeah, well, we weren't," Hal said shortly. "Come on, let's find the others."

* * *

It took far longer than expected to round up the gang despite the seemingly tight circles they'd all made in their endless search. Hal returned to his dragon form and let Abigail yell for the others, making no pretense of their plan. Why bother?

"We're going to spend the night in the cave!" she shouted.

Robbie and Lauren appeared first, carrying the basket between them. To Hal's surprise, they were both in human form, at risk from the faun's blue mist. He guessed they'd grown tired of not being able to talk; ogres weren't good conversationalists. Nor were dragons, for that matter.

"You should transform," Hal insisted. After explaining his suspicions, they agreed and did so. A faun targeting humans was a little more dangerous than one with a quirky spell.

About fifteen minutes later, the four of them eventually came across Dewey clip-clopping around the riverbank. The rushing water had masked Abigail's yelling, so he hadn't heard a thing. On his back, Darcy briefly shimmered into being, then fuzzed out again.

Thomas and Fenton had meandered all the way down the slopes to a mosquito-infested swamp. They stood at the end of a raised pathway. While Thomas allowed the annoying biters to whine around his red-furred face, Fenton constantly slapped at them as they alighted on his hands and neck. "Let's *go*," he insisted.

"Maybe fauns like swamps," Thomas said plaintively in his high, flutey, manticore voice.

"Okay, I'm done with this," Fenton snapped. He dropped out of sight, transforming into his long, black, lizard form. The mosquitoes were unlikely to bother him now.

Hal and the others approached. "We're calling it a night," Abigail called to them. "A storm's coming, and we're going to the cave."

Not even Thomas felt a need to argue. Before they left the swamp, Fenton spent some time guzzling from the green, murky water. The others watched, morbidly fascinated at the amount of liquid he sucked in. Hal knew these still-unnamed lizards had an extra stomach or two to store the water, but even so, that was a *lot* to drink. They all waited patiently, knowing his stored water could be a valuable weapon later.

The group walked in pairs through the woods, exhausted now. Darkness was descending, and so were the first drops of rain. The storm was soon overhead and hammering them hard with rain while lightning flickered and thunder rumbled. They walked at a steady pace, trudging through mud and fast-running rivulets, drenched and shivering and almost dead on their feet by the time they reached the faun's cave.

Naturally, the cave was darker than dark—and full of bats. The group yelled with alarm as a whole swarm of the critters screeched and flapped past them, escaping into the night sky.

After that, once nerves had settled, all but Thomas and Fenton reverted to human form, and Hal was aware that the faun would have easy pickings if she came by while they slept. He lit up the place with blasts of fire from his human throat as the others scavenged for dry wood in the cave. With a collection of twigs and only partially soaked logs, they got a campfire going and collapsed around it.

Lauren uncovered the basket and handed out some of the food she'd brought back—bread rolls, cheese, slabs of ham, and some dense, sticky cake. They all ate in silence for a few minutes. Afterward, Hal smacked his lips, wishing he had some fresh water to wash everything down. Fenton's murky swamp sounded good right now.

Afterward, Abigail laid out Emily's dress and smart shoes to dry. "We should take turns sleeping," she said, then frowned as Fenton's snores rose above the thunder. He remained in lizard form, stretched out long and flat. "Well, I guess Fenton can take over later. Let's keep two on watch for a couple of hours. Volunteers?"

Since Dewey, Robbie, and Darcy appeared a little spaced out, Abigail looked around at the remaining shapeshifters. "Hal? Lauren? Thomas? Volunteers to take first watch?"

Hal really wanted to sit up with Abigail, but not on first shift. He just felt drained. Luckily, Thomas spoke up. "I'll go first. I'm not tired."

"Lauren?" Abigail said, turning to her.

Lauren smiled and rolled her eyes. "I get it. Then you and Hal get to take watch together, right?"

"Well . . ."

"It's okay," Lauren told her. "Go ahead. I might have some more to eat. I'll talk to Thomas for a while. I'm sure it'll be riveting conversation—right, Thomas?"

"I doubt that," the manticore said with a yawn. He sat in his regal, catlike pose with front feet close together and back straight, tail curled around. The ball of quills and stinger for once gave Hal a sense of security. A manticore on first watch? It could be worse.

"Thanks, Thomas," Abigail said. "And Lauren. Wake us in a bit. And, you know, if . . ."

Lauren nodded. "If the faun shows up, right."

Robbie quietly increased his overall size by half and rolled over. He couldn't be full ogre size, but a partial ogre was better than nothing. Dewey, unfortunately, was just too big; a centaur would fill the space and probably stamp on them all, so he remained human. Darcy simply fuzzed out.

As Hal lay back, wishing the fire would heat him from both sides, he turned over to find Abigail gazing at him in the flickering firelight.

"Hey," he said, already sleepy. "Do me a favor?"

"Mm?"

"Be a faerie tonight."

She blinked, then nodded. "Gotcha. What about you?"

"I'll have to be me," he whispered.

It took but a moment for her to shrink down to her diminutive six-inch height. In true faerie form, her eyes had an extra shine to them because of her night vision. He thought maybe her skin had a little glow to it as well, although that might be the firelight playing tricks on him.

But what mattered was that she would go to sleep a faerie and not as a human.

Chapter Eight
Cave of Voices

Hal woke to the sound of voices.

They whispered from afar, echoing in the darkness. He sat up, blinking in the feeble firelight.

Abigail and everyone else remained asleep—everyone except Thomas, who lay stretched out, staring back at him from the opposite side of the campfire with his bright-blue eyes.

"What was that?" Hal whispered.

Thomas shrugged.

"But you heard it, right?"

"Yeah," Thomas agreed. "Whispering. From outside, I think."

Hal peered around at his sleeping friends. "How come nobody else heard?"

"Because everybody else is well out of it. You're not. You've been restless."

A quick check revealed all his friends were present except Darcy.

Thomas saw him looking and murmured, "She's there. I can feel her foot."

Hal realized then that Thomas had one of his paws stretched out. "Okay," Hal whispered. "So what happened to Lauren?"

"She stayed awake for a bit, but she kept fighting it, and in the end just fell asleep. I'm still wide awake."

And I thought cats were the laziest, sleepiest animals in the world, Hal thought as he carefully got up without disturbing the tiny faerie lying next to him. "I'm going outside."

Thomas nodded. "Be a dragon."

"I will."

Hal crept out of the relatively warm and cozy cave into the damp night. The storm had moved on, but the rain was still coming down in a light drizzle. An occasional flicker of lightning lit up the sky in the distance.

Heeding Thomas's warning, he transformed and crouched in the rain, ignoring the cold wetness on his scaly back. He felt safe now. The faun couldn't hurt him one way or another.

Listening hard, he waited.

The whispering came again, and he sucked in a breath. It was distant but definitely the sound of voices. Or one voice. It was hard to tell. If only he could hear what they were saying . . .

It was impossible to discern one word from another. He could get closer, but that would mean leaving his friends. The voices were mysterious, but he had to play it safe.

He reverted to human form and hurried back into the cave.

Wide awake now, he nodded at Thomas. "You and me, then. But if you want to go to sleep, go ahead and I'll wake someone else. You've done your turn."

Thomas sneered, revealing his needle-like teeth. "Ah, I see how it is. You want to wake Abigail. Better company than me, right?"

Hal sighed. "*Anyone's* better company than you when you get all snotty."

In this form, Thomas had a habit of making snide comments and trying to rile people up. It was his nature to spark up a discussion or argument about anything at all. Manticores liked a long conversation before devouring a meal, and usually that meant talking to their victim before killing them. But Thomas was human at heart, and he needed to try harder at curbing his belligerent remarks.

Truthfully, Hal wished Thomas *would* roll over and go to sleep. On the other hand, the manticore was a good watchdog. Or watchcat.

"So what was it?" Thomas asked quietly. "The whispering outside?"

Hal shrugged. "Voices, maybe. In the distance. Weird."

"And you didn't want to check it out?"

There was that challenging tone again. "Yes, Thomas, I did, but I thought it would be better to stay here and keep watch. Okay?"

"Okay."

Thomas's reply was somewhat muted. He knew he'd been put in his place, and he dipped his head to stare at the cave floor.

"Sorry," the manticore said. "I forget who I am sometimes."

The Thomas they all knew and liked had returned. "I know," Hal said in a much kinder tone. "I get it. Six years living with other manticores is a hard habit to break. You'll get there."

They both jumped at the sound of another whisper, this one much louder and sharper—and inside the cave with them. A tiny Abigail jerked awake, as did Robbie and Dewey. Lauren stirred.

"Who's there?" Hal called out.

What kind of faun trickery is this? he wondered, suddenly annoyed. Was she trying to lure them out of the cave? Or perhaps lure *him* out and leave his friends unprotected?

"Listen, faun," he said, raising his voice, "we're sticking together in here, so if you want to show yourself and blast us with your weird blue mist, you just go right ahead. I'll be waiting."

He listened and waited, glancing across the fire at Thomas. He kept his eyes open for blue mist, too. What if the faun hid just outside and let the mist drift into the cave toward them? A silent, swift death for them all.

Heck, what if she were already inside, maybe in the nearby tunnel?

There's no way she'd come back here, he thought, the idea chilling him. The goblins had searched these tunnels earlier and found her lair, but Miss Simone had guessed the faun was long gone, the place abandoned. But what if she'd returned? She was certainly bold enough.

The whisper came again, about the same volume as before and just as sharp. This time, he thought he made out a word: *lost*

"Lost?" Hal repeated loudly. He waited for a response, but nothing came. "What do you mean lost? Who's lost?"

"Emily," Abigail squeaked, sitting up and growing rapidly until she was full human size. She raised her much more familiar voice and spoke to the cave walls. "Do you mean Emily?"

The whisper came again, quieter now, as though it had floated off down a tunnel.

By now, those who hadn't already woken were being prodded and kicked. Soon everyone was sitting upright and alert, listening hard. The whisper rose occasionally like the distant, gentle rise and fall of the tide on a beach.

"Well, that was interesting," Robbie broke in at last, his voice deep. He glanced at his hands and arms as if surprised to find them twice as thick and hairy as usual. "Is it morning yet?"

Lauren swept a hand through her hair. "No, it's still the middle of the night. Did I drop off?" She looked horrified.

"You not only fell asleep," Thomas said in a mocking tone, "but you didn't even bother switching to harpy form. Kinda stupid, Lauren."

From out of nowhere, Darcy sighed and said, "Knock it off, Thomas."

Robbie lay back. "So what time is it?"

"It's two thirty-four in the morning," Abigail said, looking at a non-existent wristwatch. Then she rolled her eyes. "How are we supposed to know, Robbie? We're not Old Earthers. We don't have those *mobile phone* things I heard about."

"Maybe we should," Darcy muttered. "Then we'd be able to call home."

"We used to wear watches," Robbie remarked. "Funny how we stopped."

Lauren leaned over and prodded him. "They tend to get broken when we transform."

"Oh yeah."

Darcy wasn't done with her train of thought. "It seems silly, doesn't it? That we don't have any decent way to communicate in this world? Miss Simone has a hologram thing set up in one of the labs, a combination of magic and science. It's kind of crude, and it only talks to a few other towns—Louis in the north, a place called Garlen's Well in the west . . . But that's about it. There are no standard witch spells for long-distance chats."

"What's wrong with carrier pigeons?" Dewey asked.

"They get picked off by rocs," Thomas said with a chuckle.

"Guys," Hal said, raising his voice above the rising babble. "Did anyone else hear what that whispering was about? Did you make out any words?"

"Just 'lost' or something like that," Abigail said.

Pretty much everyone agreed.

"Who's lost, though?" Hal persisted. "Emily? Or the voice?"

"Maybe the voice *is* Emily," Lauren suggested.

After a long silence, the whole group sat up and looked around at one another in the near darkness. The fire struggled to stay alight; the grey embers barely had any orange glows to them, and just a few meager flames licked at the sides of a log that stuck out rather stubbornly beyond the circle of ash.

Hal tossed a couple of logs into the center of the burnt-out remains, leaned forward, and gave them a startup burst of fire. His flames roared hot and bright, and everyone cringed.

Once the fire was reestablished, Hal warmed his hands and said, "What if the voice *was* Emily? What if she's here, like a ghost?"

"If she's a ghost . . ." Darcy said with wide eyes.

"Well, maybe not a real ghost. Remember, this is New Earth. This is *Elsewhere*, a magical place where magical things happen."

It had been a while since any of his friends had called the world Elsewhere. The name still fit.

"Emily!" Abigail suddenly yelled, making everyone jump. "Are you here? If you can hear us, give us a sign!"

Hal glared at her, ready to scold her if she was trying to be even remotely funny. But she looked earnest, and he let it go.

Abigail tried again. "EMILY! Talk to us!"

Fenton, still in black lizard form, with his red eyes glowing, uncoiled his long tail and edged closer to the fire. His tongue flicked out, and he opened his mouth as if to say something. Then he shook his head and abruptly reverted to his human form. "Seems like everyone heard the ghost, but did anyone else *see* it?"

Several of the friends clamored for him to explain himself.

He frowned and shrugged. "It was like a . . . a glowing smudge, drifting across the ceiling. It went off down that tunnel."

"You actually *saw* it?" Lauren gasped. "Was it . . . Did you recognize . . . ?"

"It was a glowing smudge. It didn't look like anything or anyone."

"How come you saw it and we didn't?" Robbie demanded.

Fenton smirked. "Because I have x-ray vision. Or some kind of vision, anyway." As everyone continued to stare at him, he gave a shrug and looked away. "I saw a little cloud of magic over a faerie patch one time."

"Why did you never mention that?" Abigail asked.

He shrugged again. "Didn't seem important."

"Okay," Darcy said, fuzzing into view, "so you saw a ghostly glow floating through the cave, and we all heard a whispery voice that might have mentioned being lost. What does this mean? Could it be Emily?"

"There were other voices in the woods," Hal said.

"There were other victims," Thomas quickly added.

That caused another thoughtful silence.

"Lost souls," Abigail whispered. Her eyes were wide and gleaming in the firelight. "Could that be it? The faun's victims are floating around as lost souls?"

"But that means they're dead!" Robbie protested.

Hal shook his head. "Not necessarily. Sylphs take souls. They took some of *our* souls back on the beach at Brodon. But we survived."

"Our bodies weren't harmed, though."

"But Robbie, don't you see?" Hal gazed at his friend with excitement. "We don't know what this blue mist does. Maybe it's not exploding people into dust. Maybe it's just transporting them someplace else, or their bodies anyway, and their souls get left behind."

Thomas let out a scoffing sound. "Wow! Talk about grasping at straws." He grinned around at them all. "Sorry, but . . . this is all kind of a leap, isn't it? Maybe Emily is just *dead*."

The collective gasp told the manticore he'd gone too far. Thomas visibly paled even with his red-furred face. He lowered his head and looked sheepish.

Lauren stood up and pointed at him. "Thomas, if you can't find anything useful to say, then shut up. We might be grasping at straws here, but we have to hope for something, and this is the best we can do. And it's no more unbelievable than Fenton being turned to stone and returning to life, or Hal sitting underneath creepy white tentacle plants and 'feeding the brain'!"

"Ah, well," Thomas said, giving her a scornful glare—but he changed his mind and clamped his mouth shut.

Abigail cupped her hands around her mouth. "EMILY!"

They all joined in, shouting as loud as they could. Their noise would either bring the faun to them or chase her away. Hal almost hoped she would come running to attack them. Then they could get this night over with one way or another.

"Emily!" Hal yelled. "If you're here, *talk* to us!"

His voice was drowned out by the others, but they all said pretty much the same thing. All eight of them stood there around the fire, facing each other but looking up at the cave ceiling a few feet above. If Emily's soul happened to drift by, maybe she'd glow strongly enough that they'd all see her.

Hal happened to glance around the circle of faces at that moment, noticing that only three were in some state of transformation, partial or otherwise—Darcy, who kept fuzzing in and out of view; Robbie, who stood a little taller than the rest and with much broader shoulders, his face covered with thick, coarse, brown hair; and Thomas, who remained in manticore form. The rest of them . . .

Too late, Hal saw blue mist rising over the shoulders of those opposite. "Lauren!" he yelled, breaking through the noise. "Robbie! Watch out!"

They spun around and backed up, almost stamping into the campfire. It was already too late, though. Lauren let out a scream as blue mist engulfed her. She spun around again, her feet dangerously close to the fire, and her hands up to her face as though that might protect her from the mist.

It didn't. Her expression glazed over, and her skin took on a faint, bluish hue. She froze.

The mist crept over her shoulders and caressed her neck, reaching around to smother her face. Next to her, Robbie stood still, the mist shrouding him also. Everyone else darted sideways, stumbling to get out of the way.

Lauren's white, porcelain face cracked down the middle.

As Abigail and Darcy screamed, and the boys yelled in terror, Lauren's hardened flesh crumbled apart, and small chunks drifted upward. Then, suddenly, she exploded. Hal felt cold dust particles on his face, and he brushed them away like they were gnats. But he stopped immediately, staring in amazement and horror as Lauren's dress fluttered to the ground and her scattered ashes rose to the ceiling with a faint glow.

Robbie seemed frozen, too, but in shock rather than a physical paralysis. Fenton transformed and dropped to the ground in lizard form. Darcy had already vanished. Abigail bumped roughly against Hal, then shrank, her tiny faerie form zipping away in panic. Dewey pushed past the manticore and ran for the exit.

Hal realized he was the only one left that the mist could harm. He stood plastered against the wall, but the mist seemed to have lost its momentum. It twisted slowly, spiraling upward. It was gone seconds later.

But so was Lauren.

Her clothes lay on the ground. In the shocked silence that followed, Thomas pawed at a silky green dress while Fenton stood perfectly still, his red eyes cast upward.

Abigail zipped by, screaming something in her high-pitched faerie voice.

Hal felt a sense of disbelief mixed with shock and dismay. It had happened yet again. The faun had been here all along. She'd conjured her deadly mist and sent it up the tunnels, and it had found Lauren in human form.

Thomas let out a howl of rage and tore off into the darkness of the nearby tunnel. Hal shook himself, broke free of his paralysis, and hurried after him. He ignored Abigail's shouted warnings and Darcy's cries of horror. Like Thomas, he was driven only by fury.

He lost sight of the manticore. Hal had been down this same dark tunnel before, and he lit the way with bursts of fire. Last time, blue mist had stopped him from going too deep. He'd retreated like a coward, and now Emily and Lauren were gone. It wouldn't happen again. He'd transform the best he could in the cramped space. Maybe a partial change would be enough . . .

"Thomas!" he yelled. His voice echoed ahead, and he let loose with another blast of fire. The tunnel stretched ahead, narrow and straight, its walls tilted to his right, the ceiling low. Transforming here would be dangerous for him. Still, he'd already made it farther than last time.

Spurred on, he sprinted along the tunnel. Behind him, he heard Abigail's distant calls and knew she was probably trailing after him a little more cautiously.

How could the faun have made it so far so quickly? She must have been right there around the corner from the campfire when she'd unleashed her blue mist on them. She hadn't had much of a head start, yet there was no sign of her. She was *fast*. He imagined her bounding, springing, hurtling along on those strong goat legs . . .

He rounded a corner and found steps leading down. Steps! He lit fire again, trying to make sense of it. Yes, rough-hewn steps, wide and shallow, plunging into darkness. His flames didn't reach far enough to illuminate the bottom.

"Thomas!" he called again, more softly this time. He started down the steps, breathing fire until his breath ran out, then sucking in a lungful and letting it rip again. Every time his flames cut off, tiny sparks flickered and danced like fireflies until the next powerful blast lit up the place, so he was never quite in the dark.

Did breathing fire while in human form count as non-human? He doubted it. There had to be a line somewhere, a point at which he stopped being human and became dragon. But where was that line? When he was a quarter formed? Half? It would be good to know.

He scampered down the steps and along another tunnel, amazed at how far it went. What *was* this place? The walls seemed less rocky now and were taking on an earthen texture. He ran a hand over one side. Dirt with rock embedded here and there. Thick tree roots twisted down the walls from the ceiling, and he had to hop over some of them.

The tunnel ended, and he moved out into a dimly illuminated cavern. He had no need to breathe fire because the domed ceiling was alight with hundreds of faintly glowing blue strings or perhaps hanging roots—it was hard to tell what from where he stood. The cavern had to be the width and height of a house and was furnished with a carved wood table and a couple of chairs at one side, a chest of drawers and a cabinet at another, tapestries and furs hanging close by, and an enormous throne on a rocky platform in the center. Naturally, everything was bathed in the same pale blue hue—including Thomas, who stood near the throne.

Hal did a double take. The manticore's tail was arched high as he pawed at something lying at his feet. Some*one*. Hal ran closer, then halted with a cry of astonishment. The faun was down. Thomas had her pinned to the ground.

"Got her," the manticore panted, turning his head to grin. "She thought she'd given me the slip, and she slowed down."

The faun struggled and thrashed, but her movements were feeble, somewhat lethargic. Hal saw five or six needles sticking out of her neck—no, more than that, some broken off where she'd slapped at them. The manticore poison had worked its way into her bloodstream. Though harmless, it acted to slow her down so Thomas could deliver the final deadly blow with his scorpion stinger.

"Don't kill her," Hal said softly.

"I wasn't going to."

They stared down at the squirming faun. Thomas had one of her arms pinned. The other she waved feebly, and blue mist crept from her palm . . . but it drifted aimlessly, dispersing on its way to the ceiling. Hal watched it with trepidation, knowing he was vulnerable.

But then the faun stopped moving. Her head lolled to one side, and she lay there motionless, her chest slowly rising and falling.

"Don't ease up on her," Hal warned. "She might be faking."

Thomas nodded and instead pressed down harder with his front paws, putting his full weight across her midsection.

Hal could hear the sounds of his friends clattering down the steps and an occasional call. He knelt to look closer at the faun. She definitely seemed to be out of it.

"So now what do we do?" Thomas muttered.

Hal thought about rope, maybe vines, to tie her up. Then he had a simpler solution. He stood and waited as his friends emerged one by one into the cavern and looked around in wonder. The last to arrive was the long, black, sinister lizard with the red, glowing eyes.

"Fenton," Hal called to him. "Get over here."

Chapter Nine
The Prisoner

Fenton was more than happy to belch up a deluge of foul-smelling water over the faun. He drenched her from head to toe where she lay unconscious, and then he breathed on her, causing the liquid to solidify into a sticky, glue-like substance, effectively cocooning her, arms tightly pinned.

Only then did the shapeshifters feel safe to revert to human form.

Hal checked that everyone was present. He remembered Dewey had run outside so he could be a centaur, but he was here now. They all were, standing in a somber circle. Fenton was the last to revert and join the group.

Everyone except Emily and Lauren, Hal thought grimly. Her loss was too much to absorb, and he suspected they all felt the same way, that she and Emily just *couldn't* be dead. Not properly dead, anyway.

He gave the faun a swift kick on one of her goat legs. It felt as heavy as a fallen branch, and he vowed not to do it again since he only had smart shoes on. They didn't protect his toes very well. "Wake up," he demanded.

The faun didn't stir.

"What *is* this place?" Darcy whispered. "Look at all the blue light! What's causing that?"

They all looked up and around. Since the cavern roof was too high to reach, they moved closer to the nearest wall where the dome started. There were just as many dangling blue strings there. They hung straight down rather like ultra-thin icicles, except they wobbled at the slightest movement in the air.

"Sap from the tree roots?" Hal wondered aloud.

"Blue sap?" Fenton scoffed.

"They're glow worms," Darcy said, a look of wonder on her bluelit face.

For a moment, the disappearance of Emily and Lauren was forgotten. "Those are *worms*?" Fenton said, sounding doubtful.

Darcy shook her head. "The worms are higher up. See their silk nests? They look like delicate pearl necklaces. And all these hanging threads are to catch prey. They're sticky."

"And they glow why?" Abigail asked, sounding almost suspicious.

"Bioluminescence. You might as well ask why fireflies glow. Or will-o'-wisps. Or faeries, for that matter. What do you think, Robbie?"

Ordinarily, Robbie would have been jumping up and down with excitement. Bugs were his passion. Right now, though, he looked sullen and worried. "It's cool," he muttered. "How about we get back to business and find the girls?"

And so the moment of wonder passed. In its place, misery settled over them all.

"Lauren's gone," Robbie said softly in the silence.

Darcy edged closer and nudged him. "We'll get her back."

"How?"

"I don't know. We just have to keep searching and hoping."

Robbie didn't look convinced. Nor did anybody else.

"Let's check out the place," Hal said.

They quit staring at the display of delicate, wobbling, glowing threads and moved slowly around the cavern like a tour group.

"Okay, so this is the faun's home?" Robbie said. "The goblins said she'd obviously been down here for a while, but we all assumed she'd run off for good."

Abigail scowled. "She was here all the time, right under our noses. Why didn't we explore this place?"

Hal sighed. "Because we were tired and wet after traipsing around the woods."

"I mean why didn't we come here earlier in the day, instead of wandering around the forest? Why did we assume she'd leave all this behind? I mean, this is obviously where she lives. She wouldn't abandon all this forever."

"No, but she knew we were looking for her," Hal argued. "I think she's got a lot of nerve coming back here so soon."

"This is her bed," Robbie said, roughly kicking at a pile of furs on the ground. The makeshift bed was shielded from the rest of the cavern behind a threadbare tapestry that hung from a rough framework of thin branches. "Correction—this is her bedroom, I guess."

Hal couldn't help thinking that fauns lived a lot like humans. But then, so did the naga, centaurs, and especially elves and goblins. Even ogres to some extent. On the table, Hal found a rather fine mug made from hardened clay, and some highly polished clay plates. The faun had metal pots and wooden spoons, though no sign of a hearth or even the remains of a campfire. She probably didn't want to fill the cavern with smoke or disturb the glow worms. She must cook food someplace else—if indeed fauns cooked food.

His tour of the place wound up back where he'd started, standing over the motionless faun. He knelt to study her. She lay on her side, snoozing, a thick layer of glue pinning her arms to her body. She had coppery-brown skin daubed with streaks of gold paint.

Looking closer, he saw that she wasn't as bald as he'd first thought. She had hair; it was plastered flat across the top and sides of her head, caked in the same gold paint. Her twin horns, thick and curved like a goat's, stuck up from her temples.

Other than the horns and the thick, fur-covered legs, she appeared human. He couldn't help staring. Her upper half was that of a slender human, and she didn't have a whole lot of clothing on under the swaths of glue, just a weird leafy fabric covering her chest and belly. Her arms, shoulders, and upper back were bare. Didn't she get cold?

He glanced away when Abigail cleared her throat. He could feel his face heating up. "She, uh, h-has gold paint on her skin," he stammered.

"I noticed that," Abigail murmured. She knelt beside him. "I also see that she's not wearing much."

Hal blinked at her. "Isn't she? Never noticed. Better get her some clothes."

"It kind of looks like she's got furry pajama pants on already, except those are goat legs. Look at those hooves. Definitely not human."

Hal was glad to have something to demand his attention. He cast his gaze over the hooves. "Hmm, yeah, they couldn't be faked. You'd never get human feet down inside those thin lower legs and hooves."

"Especially as her knees bend the wrong way."

The others crowded around. "Wake her up," Fenton growled. "We have some questions to ask."

Hal reached out, grabbed a shoulder, and shook her roughly. Her head rocked back and forth, one horn embedded in the dirt and forcing her face downward. How did fauns sleep with those great big things sticking out?

She didn't stir.

"How long will the poison last?" Hal asked Thomas, carefully plucking the quills from her neck. He pulled six full-length ones and four broken stubs. That was quite a hit she'd taken.

"Not too long," Thomas said, moving closer. "Give her ten minutes."

"Should we chain her up?" Robbie suggested. "I mean, I'm sure your glue will keep her still, Fenton, but I'd feel better with her in chains as well."

Everyone except Fenton muttered their agreement. "Where are you gonna get chains, moron?" he said.

"Well, rope, then. Or vines. There are roots and vines on the walls . . ." Robbie got up and started hunting around.

"We should take her to Miss Simone," Dewey said. "Let's get her outside. You can tie her to my back, and I'll gallop home as fast as I can."

"I can fly her a lot quicker," Hal said. "But we need to find Emily and Lauren first."

Robbie nodded. "Yeah. I'm not going anywhere until we find them, and nor is the faun."

They all stared down at the silent figure. She looked harmless, even shy. How could such a timid and strangely beautiful creature be so cold and merciless?

"Think she can still conjure up some of the blue mist?" Robbie asked.

Half the group took a step back. "Her hands are free," Darcy said. "Her arms are stuck down, but she can bend her wrists and wiggle her hands about. She might be able to do her magic."

"Let her try," Thomas growled.

"Any sign of hocus-pocus," Fenton said, "and I'll soak her some more. I have plenty of that glue-water left in my gut."

At that moment, the eerie whispering started up again, loud and sharp, filling the cavern. They all flinched and ducked at first, then straightened up and looked about.

"Emily?" Darcy called. "Lauren? Are you there?"

As if in answer, the whispering increased in volume. Definitely words, but impossible to discern.

"They're alive," Robbie breathed.

Hal reached for Abigail's hand and gripped it tight, grinning with relief and excitement. She didn't look quite so convinced.

The group listened carefully to the whispering, which came and went as if on an ocean breeze. Hal wondered what, if anything, lost souls saw from their perspective. If indeed they were souls, then shouldn't they be in that special place where the Lady of Light resided, the world of darkness that he'd visited when he'd been turned to stone? But if so, the souls wouldn't be making themselves heard out here in the real world. No, this was something new. Emily and Lauren had exploded into dust, completely disintegrated, and now they roamed the air like clouds of molecules, somehow finding a way to cry for help or just voice their displeasure.

"Lauren sounds annoyed," Robbie said with a choking laugh. He trembled, his eyes gleaming wet as he looked toward the bluelit ceiling.

"Wake up!" Fenton shouted at the faun. He moved closer and pulled back a foot to kick at her.

He froze. She was stirring.

"Watch out, everyone," Abigail warned. "She's awake."

They all took another step back, spreading out and forming a complete circle around her in case she tried to cast a spell. She'd never get them all at once.

The faun's eyes opened wide, a vivid yellow color with black irises. She glanced about, struggled frantically for about ten seconds, then broke off and lay there panting.

"You done?" Fenton said.

"Tell us what you did with our friends," Darcy demanded. "How do we get them back?"

The faun simply stared at her and the others in turn.

"Start talking," Hal warned.

Instead, the faun struggled again, rolling back and forth and straining against the greyish glue that smothered her arms, legs, and body. She paused to stare at the curious substance on one shoulder, almost cross-eyed in her effort to focus on it. She thrashed a bit more, working up a sweat and getting herself dirty as she wriggled about on the ground.

She gave up again, a scowl on her face.

"Talk," Hal said.

The faun hissed at him. It was a cat-like sound, quite unexpected from a creature with a human upper half. He glimpsed stubby fangs, which surprised him. She could probably put a hurt on someone if she managed to clamp those jaws around a wrist or ankle.

She refused to talk, too busy looking about for a way to get loose.

Thomas moved closer and transformed directly in front of her. His red-furred manticore frame filled her vision as he crouched with his claws inches from her nose. His tail arched over his head and dangled over hers, the stinger exposed and a gob of yellow venom oozing out. The single droplet wobbled for a moment, then broke free and splashed onto her shoulder.

She winced and squirmed. Hal remembered a similar feeling the first time he'd come across Thomas in Black Woods back on the island. The manticore had stood over him, and a gob of venom had fallen on his cheek, stinging him quite vividly.

"You'd better talk to us," Fenton said, "or Thomas here will decide you're not worth keeping alive."

If the faun understood what he said, she didn't show it. She stared up at Thomas with wide, frightened eyes but made no attempt to communicate.

Hal muscled in next to Thomas. "What's your name?" he asked, adopting a gentler tone.

She merely glanced at him before returning her gaze to Thomas's stinger.

"Your name?" Hal asked again, firmer this time.

She didn't answer. This was getting tiresome.

"Maybe she doesn't speak our language," Darcy suggested. "The naga don't. Nor do the elves."

"Anyone speak faunish?" Robbie said.

Dacry sighed. "We'll have to take her to Miss Simone. She must know someone who can help translate."

"Not unless there's a shapeshifter we don't know about," Robbie argued. "That's the whole point of us—to translate."

"Well, to act as emissaries," Abigail corrected him. "But you're right. I doubt Miss Simone knows anyone who speaks faunish."

Fenton stepped closer, balling his fists. "How about I beat the truth out of her?"

"Oh, give it a rest, Fenton," Hal complained. He knelt down so he was closer to eye level with the captured faun. She looked at him warily as he held the palms of his hands toward her then wiggled his fingers in an effort to emulate the blue mist. He then pointed around at his friends and finished with a pronounced shrug with his hands spread.

She stared back.

"She thinks you're an idiot," Fenton muttered.

Hal spread his hands again, putting on a fierce expression. "Where are they?"

The faun flexed her wrists and tried to turn her palms upward, but the glue restricted her movements too much. She started wriggling again, straining at the grey stuff and kicking with her goat feet. She pushed her belly upward and lifted herself off the ground, arching her back until she was standing on her hooves at one end and the top of her head at the other, with her horns dug into the ground.

Hal fell back, alarmed, as she somehow inched her hooves all the way back under her body, folded almost double. Then—

She sprang upright, going from a contorted horizontal position to a full stand in one single bound. Everyone yelled out and backed away, but the faun didn't look comfortable, standing there in a stiff, bent-over-sideways position thanks to the gluey cocoon.

Still, she was upright. She stood and swayed for a moment, straining at the glue and failing. Then she hobbled toward the darkest corner of the cavern, which apparently was a hidden exit.

Hal reached out and grabbed her shoulder. "You're not going anywhere."

She immediately lashed out, swinging around and kicking high. Hal felt a tremendous jolt to his chest and flew backward, slamming down with arms and legs akimbo.

Abigail rushed to him. "Are you okay?"

He was aware of Fenton, Thomas, and a half-ogre-sized Robbie scrambling around the faun, Dewey switching to his centaur form, a manticore leaping in with a roar, and Darcy promptly vanishing. The faun hopped from one side to another, trying to get away but hemmed in by the shapeshifters.

Hal groaned and sat up, holding his chest. "I think she broke all fifty ribs."

"You only have twelve pairs," Abigail said, her hands on his shoulders. "Don't get up. Take a second."

"Stand back," Hal told her, grimacing as he climbed to his feet. He was ready to transform—except the cavern wasn't quite big enough for his full-sized adult dragon body while his friends were running about. Feeling useless again, he had to watch as the others surrounded the faun shoulder to shoulder.

She quit hopping and stood panting in a half-bent posture, Fenton's glue still pinning her arms to her sides in awkward positions and contorting her body. "*Leis fei go*," she said.

Everyone did a double take. The faun had spoken! Her voice was clear and melodic.

"What did she say?" Fenton muttered.

"Let me go?" Darcy replied, fuzzing into view. She remained in dryad form, her skin the color and texture of tree bark, and her normally blond hair oddly stiff like it had been carved from a log. She blended into the earthen, root-filled cavern environment. "That's what it sounded like, anyway."

"Ask her what happened to Emily and Lauren," Robbie said in a low, rumbling voice as he towered above the others. "Ask her how we get them back."

Darcy opened her mouth to ask Robbie's questions, then frowned. "Wait, what? *You* ask her. I can't speak faunish any more than you can. You'd realize that if you weren't half ogre."

Thomas barked a laugh. "Yeah, Robbie. Half your brain has turned to mush."

Robbie stomped closer to the faun. "Where did our friends go?"

She shuffled backwards as he leaned over her. But Thomas stood right behind her, and she stopped. "*Leive fei ilae!*" she cried, her wavering voice tinged with anger.

Everyone looked at Darcy.

She spread her hands. "How should I know what she said?"

Hal and Abigail squeezed their way into the circle of shapeshifters. The faun glanced at them both. Her yellow eyes gave Hal the creeps. Lauren's were yellow, too, but a harpy's eyes were clear and bright, almost translucent compared to this dark, ugly, mustard color.

The faun wriggled some more to no avail. Fenton had a look of satisfaction on his face, clearly proud of his handiwork.

She started jabbering, speaking a language that sounded oddly familiar but not quite intelligible, the meaning just out of grasp. Since everyone wore the same puzzled expression, she eventually broke off and rolled her eyes in a very human way, then stood silently for a moment, staring at the ground.

She lifted her head and spoke to Darcy. "*Iri ax yam imqyampim.*" She nodded her head, indicating something to the far side of the cavern. "*Lyia'i id lyi leygi. Yri um i fei.*"

Hal looked over his shoulder to where the faun had nodded, listening to his friends' mumbled comments:

"Huh? What's she wanting?"

"Something over there. Maybe a glass of water?"

"No, something more important than that. She seems pretty frantic about it."

"What's she nodding at? That big throne?"

"Or the table on the far side?"

The faun shuffled that way, and Abigail said, "Wait, let her through. We're not getting anywhere, so let's see what she wants."

"Watch her," Hal warned.

The group trailed after her, flanking her sides and keeping a close eye on her as she hobbled and hopped past the great throne to the table containing a collection of trinkets—random bits of jewelry, small ornaments and shiny treasures, a couple of worn leather-bound journals, and various other things she thought worthy of saving. But saving from where, what, or whom? Hal eyed the collection with suspicion, wondering if these were things she'd picked up off people she'd dispatched with her deadly blue mist.

The faun stopped before the table and stared intently at one thing in particular.

"This?" Darcy said, pointing to the journals.

The faun shook her head, her gaze fixed.

"That stupid necklace," Fenton guessed. "Or the knife! There's a knife there. I bet that's what she wants."

Darcy pointed to each in turn, and the faun shook her head again.

It turned out she was focused on a twisted conch shell as big as Hal's hand. It looked blue, but then, pretty much everything was tinted blue thanks to the glow worms above. Hal peered at it, wondering if it had washed up on a beach, and if so, how the faun had come by it. He couldn't imagine this woodland creature strutting along the beach. More likely, she'd found it among the personal belongings of a traveler.

"You want this?" Darcy confirmed, pointing directly at the shell. "Why?"

The faun mumbled something, her eyes wide. She nodded to Darcy, encouraging her to pick it up.

"Don't," Abigail said. "It might be dangerous."

"It's just a shell!" Thomas exclaimed. "I doubt there's a crab in there. It's not dangerous, but it's no use, either. Let her have it."

Hal reached for it. "It's heavy." He looked at the faun and held up the shell in front of her face. "So what about it?"

She leaned toward him, and he pulled back. Frowning, the faun shook her head and leaned forward again. "Stand still."

Her simple command took them all by surprise. Hal let his hand fall to his side, still clutching the shell. "So you *do* speak our language!"

She rolled her eyes, huffed, and said something unintelligible.

Abigail gently pried the shell from Hal's hand and gave him a smile. "Let me handle this. It's pretty obvious what's going on here."

With the shell once more raised high, the faun put her mouth close to it and spoke quickly. "This shell helps us understand one another. It translates what passes through its chamber."

Everyone let out a gasp.

The faun stood there, tightly cocooned and leaning awkwardly to one side, her arms pinned and legs restricted. She was no threat right now. All that mattered was communication.

"So let's talk," Robbie rumbled.

Chapter Ten
The Faun's Magic

The faun rushed out her words as though her life depended on it. Judging by the threatening look on Fenton's face, maybe it did.

"Please do not worry. I harm nobody. I simply put things right, restore nature's balance. That is my plan, anyway."

She leaned close to Abigail's proffered conch shell, speaking into it. It seemed like her words should emerge translated from the other end, but that didn't appear to be the case. Yet when she backed off from the shell more than a few inches, the translation quit working.

Some of her phrasing seemed a little stilted and odd, like a foreigner with a rudimentary grasp of the language. Whether that was the magical shell's doing or just the way she spoke, at least her meaning was clear.

"Your friends are safe, I assure you. They are simply at a halfway stage. Soon they will have life again, like those in the woods."

"Halfway stage?" Hal frowned at her, bewildered. "What do you mean they will have life again? They're alive *now*, right? Just . . . hidden?"

He thought perhaps she wouldn't understand him since he wasn't standing near the conch, but apparently she did.

"They are without physical body," the faun said. "They are restless souls, a collection of particles. I will give them life very soon—if you let me."

All the shapeshifters shared glances. "We want them back," Darcy said simply.

"And you shall have them back." The faun smiled, showing a neat row of pointed teeth. "Release me, and I shall make it so."

"No way!" Dewey cried, clip-clopping backward in alarm. He'd been reasonably quiet and still until now, but the idea of letting the faun go clearly perturbed him. "Don't let her free. She'll use that blue mist on us!"

The faun smiled again and shook her head. "You are more than just human. The evolution need not apply to you—unless you willfully remain human. I urge you to transcend your human state and be free. Be who you *can* be, not who you are."

Fenton gripped her by the shoulder. "*What* are you going on about?"

"Release me so I may bring your friends back."

The gold-painted creature smiled around at them all, her expression radiating encouragement and friendliness. Hal almost felt compelled to break her free right then and there, except it would take some work to get her out of that glue.

"Not happening," Thomas growled at her, baring his multiple rows of needle teeth.

"Now, hang on a minute," Robbie said, quickly shrinking down to his normal height. "Let's think about this. If we want Emily and Lauren back, we need the faun. Right? And if we don't let her go, she's not likely to help."

"I can make her cooperate," Thomas said, raising his stinger high. The faun's smile faltered.

"Yeah, we have ways," Fenton agreed, bunching his fists. His eyes glowed red for a moment, and water dribbled from the corners of his mouth.

Abigail looked at Hal. "What about you?"

"I, uh . . ." Hal looked from her to Robbie, then to Fenton and Thomas. He rubbed his sore chest before answering. "I don't want to free her *completely*, but I think she can help just as easily if we free her a little bit."

After a pause, Darcy said, "That's smart. Yeah, I'm with Hal on this."

Abigail agreed, too. "Let's cut away the glue from her arms so she has her hands free but can't run off."

"But the blue mist—!" Dewey exclaimed, beginning to clip-clop around in circles again. His tail swished at them as he turned.

"It can't hurt us if we're not human," Abigail said. She addressed everyone together. "Okay?"

Nobody could refute her plan. Hal, though, had a problem. "I can't transform in here. I might fit inside this cavern, but nobody would have room to move. We should go outside."

"It's dark outside," Darcy complained. "It's the middle of the night. How about you stay as you are but keep back out of the way?"

Hal reluctantly agreed. It was either that or miss out.

Thomas set about chewing on the grey, rubbery coating that bound the faun's arms. She stood motionless, a nervous look in her eye as the manticore's teeth came dangerously close to her skin. A perfectly good knife lay on the table, and they all knew it. He was playing with her; the glint in his blue eyes was plain to see.

While he gnawed, Fenton transformed and slid away to the darkest side of the cavern where his glowing red eyes would have the most unnerving effect. Hal remembered the first time they'd all run across a similar and much larger lizard, the so-called Shadow Demon in the Mountain of Whispers.

Robbie grew to half-ogre size again, a slow and smooth morphing process that left no doubt he had full control of his shapeshifting abilities. Abigail remained at human height but buzzed out of reach near the earthen walls. Darcy simply vanished from sight again. And Dewey couldn't keep still, his hooves dancing and causing him to turn in circles so he had to continually twist his neck to keep watching the faun.

Hal took a few more steps back as Thomas finished chewing at the grey glue and yanked an upper section away. The faun stifled a scream as it pulled at her skin.

Now that one arm was free, Thomas moved to the other side.

Abigail stopped him. "That's good enough. I'm sure one arm is fine." She zipped closer to their prisoner and held out the conch. "What's your name?"

The faun peered at her. "I am River."

"River?"

Thomas couldn't help snickering. "Her parents are Ravine and Cliff."

"My parents are dead," the faun said quietly.

"Did they fall in the ravine, over the cliff, or in the river?"

"Thomas!" Darcy snapped out of nowhere. "That's so cruel."

"So what?" Robbie grumbled as the manticore chuckled quietly. "Who cares if we're cruel to this goat thing? She took Emily and Lauren from us! Did you forget?"

Darcy fuzzed into view for a second, and in that moment, Hal could see her storming across the cavern toward Thomas, casting a look toward the hulking half-ogre. "Boys, let's not lower ourselves and resort to cheap insults. We're better than that. Thomas, back away. Abigail's right—you've done enough. River only needs one arm free."

River leaned forward and spoke into the shell Abigail held out. "I need both hands. I must be able to—"

"You'll use one hand," Abigail told her, "or we'll take you back to the village where you'll face a lot of angry people out for your blood. Help us right now, or we're done."

Hal felt proud of her. Of both girls, actually. They'd taken over the show and put the boys in their places. Well, two of the boys, anyway. Hal knew he never would have resorted to insensitive comments the way Thomas had.

River wriggled and stretched. Now that she had a hand free, she pulled at the tough glue on the other arm—but Abigail made a warning sound as though she were scolding a small child. She wagged a finger and shook her head, and the faun scowled.

It had to be hard for River not to make a concerted effort to release herself from the cocoon. She could probably manage it alone given time, but not while everyone was watching, and while Thomas stood nearby threatening her with his stinger.

As if to distract the faun from fiddling with the rubbery substance, Abigail said, "What happened to your parents?"

Her ploy worked. River froze, looked at her with suspicion, then glanced beyond her. Following her gaze, Hal saw nothing but the bed— a pile of furs and the frame with the tapestry draped over it.

Abigail followed the faun to the tapestry. Everyone moved a little closer, peering over her shoulder. Now that he studied it, Hal realized it was quite an intricate piece of art, a mixture of thin pencil lines and daubs of colored paint, including subtle gold highlights. He saw a dozen detailed scenes surrounding a single sprawling oak tree in the center.

"My family," River said softly, pointing to a group of figures at top-left. Two grown-ups and three small children, all with the distinctive goat-legs and horns. They were a little more detailed than stick figures. She tapped the smallest of the children. "This is me."

Silent, the shapeshifters watched as she ran a loving hand over the surface of the tapestry, tracing the gold paint from one scene to the next, all of which showed the same family of fauns, playing and working together. One scene included a centaur, another a griffin. A third showed a naga. All seemed amiable toward the fauns.

"Love and compassion," she whispered into Abigail's conch shell. "My parents taught my brothers and I the true meaning of life. Every day, we daubed our faces in gold to indicate our good nature to every creature in the forest. And every creature in the forest understood."

Her slender finger moved to another scene at bottom-right, what was clearly a mob of humans brandishing pitchforks and spears. Ahead of them, the family of fauns ran for their lives.

"Except for humans," she said bitterly. "Your people have no business in this world. Time and time again, humans cross the line. They do not just claim territory as their own and hunt for food. That would be understandable. No, they go further. They hunt for pleasure, or for small and selfish reasons, for greed and anger. They push too hard. They want too much. They kill for nothing."

Hal didn't need to hear any more to know where this was headed.

"They killed my family," the faun said in a flat, even voice.

Darcy sighed. "I'm sorry."

"I heard the centaurs created a virus," the faun said, glancing at Dewey. "I learned of their plot to exterminate humans for good, how they tested it on the humans in the other world. For a long time, I wished they would unleash the virus here." She sighed. "But I am not that cold. My parents taught me compassion. And I saw a better way forward."

"By blowing people up?" Thomas suddenly blurted, making everyone jump.

The faun shook her head. "It is not that simple."

Thomas snorted. "Looks pretty simple from where I'm standing. Your parents were killed by humans, right? I'm sorry about that. But if you think you can wipe us all out—"

"It is not that simple," River said again. "I have a better way, a *kinder* way. I will prove it."

She hobbled over to the throne, fell into it with her legs still pinned together, and closed her eyes.

Everyone crowded around. It looked like she were suffering a restless nightmare the way she tilted her head back and mumbled silent words while gripping one of the throne's arms with her free hand. Hal kept a close eye on that free hand, expecting blue mist to start pouring out.

"Is this a spell?" Abigail whispered, sidling closer to him.

"Looks like it."

Since the faun's mutterings were absolutely silent, nothing could be heard from anyone for the next minute except for Dewey's fidgety hooves. Hal felt sure she would have plenty of time by now to create a large enough plume of mist to fill the cavern. Outside, she'd conjured small puffs of the stuff in seconds. She had to be working on something else. Hopefully what she'd promised—the safe return of Emily and Lauren.

Yet he felt uneasy. River spoke of humans with scorn. She spoke of being better, suggesting they all switch to their alternate forms and stay there. She spoke of *evolution*. What did she mean by that, exactly?

His skin prickled at the sound of whispering—two voices that rose in volume as they swirled around the room like phantoms. Abigail reached for his hand and gripped it tight, and they both looked skyward toward the hundreds of hanging, wobbling blue threads, seeking any other signs of movement, anything at all. The threads wobbled a little more violently at times as though a breeze were rushing past, but nothing else stood out.

Still, the whispering increased.

"Lauren?" Robbie called in a deep, booming voice.

In answer, one of the whispers grew more frantic, and a distinct word echoed around the place: ". . . *obbie* . . . ?"

Then, chillingly: ". . . *get me out of here* . . ."

All the shapeshifters murmured with astonishment and excitement. If there had been any doubt before that the girls were alive in some form, now there was none. They were right here in some kind of spiritual form. The faun had summoned them.

River remained on the throne, perched upright with her head tilted back, still mumbling to herself.

The whispers clarified further, two different voices:

". . . *want to go home* . . ."

". . . *make her stop* . . ."

Hal suddenly wondered if the faun was hurting the girls right now with her incantations. Make her stop? That had been Emily. But did she mean make her stop exploding people into dust? Or make her stop reciting that spell?

He rushed toward the throne. "Hey—River—stop!"

"Hal?" Abigail said, darting alongside with a loud buzz.

"Emily said make her stop!"

"Yeah, but I thought she meant that generally—to stop the faun."

"What if Emily meant to stop her right now?"

Hal stood before the throne, undecided. Abigail hovered next to him. The others watched with wide-eyed wonder, just as uncertain.

But it was too late to decide anyway. The faun jolted upright and let out an exclamation, a single word in her own language that apparently unleashed the full power of the spell. The whispers cut off, a blast of wind and static energy whipped through the cavern, and two separate clouds of sparkling particles appeared out of nowhere and swarmed like gnats around all those who stood there.

Abruptly, both clouds dive-bombed to the ground and coalesced into two fuzzy, flickering figures. It was like watching an explosion in reverse, an *implosion* of particles that came together into complete, solid, very real people.

Both of them wobbled and staggered before collapsing.

River let out a cry of joy and smiled in the dim light.

Everyone else gasped and stared in amazement.

Hal was the first to break the paralysis that rooted him to the spot. He ran to the girls and threw himself down between them—then recoiled, jumping to his feet and backing away. "What's this?" he yelled, spinning to face the faun. "What have you done?"

River's delighted smile faded, and she said something unintelligible.

Irritated, Hal ran to Abigail, snatched the conch shell from her hand, and practically shoved the thing in the faun's face. "Say that again!" he demanded.

"I have brought them back," River said calmly. "Fear not, they are alive and well. And *better*."

Ordinarily, after a traumatic event involving souls being wrenched from bodies and put back again, "better" would have meant their health had greatly improved, that they were on the road to recovery. But that wasn't what she meant at all.

"They are *evolved*," the faun said with a sense of awe. "Better than they were before. Better than *humans*."

Neither Emily nor Lauren were themselves. One of them carefully stood up, looking down at herself and then at the shapeshifters surrounding her. "Guys?" she said, standing taller and much hairier than almost everyone else.

She was a troll, covered in shaggy hair, long-limbed with huge hands and feet.

The other girl remained crouched on the ground, utterly confused. She let out a whimper. "What's happened?" She looked at the troll. "Lauren?"

Somehow, Emily had come back in the form of a goblin, stout and ugly with gnarly, wrinkled skin, her piglike grimace wet with tears. She huddled in a ball under the pale-blue light.

Hal pulled off his shirt and threw it to her, then turned and stumbled away, feeling sick with anger and worry. *This* was what River had planned for them? This was her idea of *evolution*?

He was dimly aware of his friends starting up with cries of horror and fright, and Thomas letting out a roar of anger, and Fenton hissing from the darkness. Dewey wailed and trotted dangerously about the place. The only calm person was Abigail, and when Hal looked back over his shoulder, she'd helped Emily into his smart shirt, which no doubt expanded to fit her much stouter physique.

He got up and raced to the throne. "What have you—?" he yelled in fury.

Then he stopped and blinked.

The faun was gone.

Glancing around, he knew she must have hopped away through the back exit. He gave a shout and went after her, knowing he was at risk if she happened to be conjuring blue mist as she escaped. But she couldn't have gone far, restricted by glue as she was.

Thomas suddenly shot past him, nearly bowling him over.

Hal was grateful for the help but annoyed that he couldn't bring the faun down himself. *I hate tunnels*, he thought, gritting his teeth as he stumbled in the darkness.

Without the glow worms lighting the way, visibility was down to zero. Thomas could probably see in the dark, but Hal had to breathe fire again. "River!" he yelled.

Ferocious roars ahead sent a stab of fear into his heart. Thomas must have caught up to the faun already.

"Thomas!" Hal shouted. "Don't kill her! We need her!"

He heard galloping behind—Dewey—and heard a girl calling for him. He focused only on what lay ahead. Rounding a corner, he came across Thomas once more standing over the panting faun. In the brief light of his fire, Hal saw fresh claw marks across her shoulder.

"Enough," he said, plunging into darkness as his fire cut off.

"Yeah, I get it," Thomas grumbled. "I'm not stupid."

But sometimes you're too much like a manticore and give in to your urges. Or you just don't stop to think.

Hal kept those thoughts to himself. "Could you do me a favor? Go grab the girls' clothes. They're by our campfire."

"Why *me*?"

"Because you're the fastest. You'll be back in no time."

With a sigh, Thomas trotted away, breaking into a light-footed run.

Hal gave a shiver, suddenly feeling the cold on his bare skin. He breathed fire again, staring down at the faun. She said something, but her words were meaningless. Though she wore a mask of pain, the smile suggested she was pleased with the results of her experiment. Was it her first time fully evolving someone? What about Derek and the other three villagers? Were they still dust, floating around in the woods?

His friends caught up, and in total darkness, Hal told them in no uncertain terms he was done with tunnels. "Drag her outside, Robbie," he told his friend, who ducked low under the rocky ceiling. "Then I'll take her back." He belched up some flames to make sure River still lay on the floor.

"Yeah, hang her upside down from your claws," Fenton said. He'd obviously reverted to human form.

There wasn't much more to be said. With the entire group walking in single file, Hal led the way, followed by Robbie dragging the faun. After them, Dewey, Darcy, Abigail, Lauren, and Emily, the whole team safely back together—except for Thomas, who would be back shortly.

The tunnel finally dumped them outside at the foot of a low cliff. Hal had been here before, though it was hard to see much in the middle of the night. This was where the faun had tried to lure him earlier that day. He hadn't been fooled by her trickery.

He turned to watch as the others emerged one by one from the darkness, his short bursts of fire lighting the way. He felt sick when he saw Lauren in her troll body, and even sicker when Emily waddled out.

"Can you still shift?" he asked them.

The troll frowned at him. Then she gave it a go.

To everyone's surprise, white wings spread open with a *whump!* sound, and Lauren's familiar harpy form stood before them. Everyone let out a gasp, and Lauren cried with joy.

Emily immediately did the same, transforming from a stout, ugly goblin into an impressive serpent wearing Hal's shirt. She smiled around at the group. "Thank goodness! Honestly, I'd much rather be a naga than an awful goblin. I mean, I have nothing against goblins, but . . ."

She broke off, narrowing her eyes as they all stared at her.

Finally, she worked it out. Raising her hands to her face, she let out a moan. "Oh no. I've still got a goblin face, haven't I?"

There was something very strange and off-putting about a naga with anything but a human upper body. Nagas were by nature half human, half serpent. Anything else was just . . . weird.

Lauren reverted to her natural form and quickly checked herself over. She grimaced, her troll face even fiercer than usual. She morphed again. At least her harpy form was familiar to her, and she was a *complete* harpy, not some strange troll-like semblance of one. As far as shapeshifters were concerned, her harpy form was positively normal.

Hal felt sorry for Emily. She couldn't escape her goblin persona no matter what she did. If anything, she was less conspicuous in goblin form. Whoever heard of a naga with a goblin face? She'd not be welcome anywhere.

Thomas emerged from the tunnel, silky clothes and two pairs of smart shoes gripped in his jaws. Panting, he threw them down and sat, curling his tail around. He looked every bit like a proud dog who'd just brought his master a stick.

It took only a minute for Emily and Lauren to dress while everyone faced away. Lauren made a comment about her dress being slimy with Thomas's drool. Then Abigail passed Hal his shirt, and he put it back on, grateful for the warmth.

"Okay, let's go home," Abigail said. "Everyone stand back for Hal."

When a suitable space had been cleared, Hal transformed and filled the entire area with his massive dragon bulk. Turning to face the cowering faun, he gave her an impressive roar just to let off some of his anger and give her something to think about.

He waited impatiently for Abigail, Robbie, and Emily to climb aboard. Lauren could fly alongside, and the rest could make their own way back. Miss Simone had reminded him he could carry more if he was careful, but he wasn't in the mood for that right now.

He clamped a front paw around the faun's goat legs, tipped her upside down, and launched into the night sky.

Chapter Eleven
Evolution

Although the laboratory doors were locked, a few night watchmen and goblin sentries patrolled the place inside and out. Security had been ramped up after scrags had stormed the lab and stolen the secrets to the Shapeshifter Program a few months before.

While Lauren made a detour to fetch Miss Simone from her house, Hal landed on the grass outside the sprawling lab building and pinned his hapless prisoner under one front paw. Robbie and Emily climbed down, and Abigail grew to her normal size to join them.

Emily stood in silence, looking forlorn and somewhat embarrassed, hanging her head in shame at what she'd become. Abigail gave her a nudge and an encouraging smile. "It'll be okay," she murmured.

The lab seemed like the best place to bring the faun. It had once been a modest one-story building of stone and wood, with a number of small barns and shacks out back linked by rickety closed-in timber walkways. In recent months, those shacks had been upgraded and enlarged, and the main building expanded. It was now probably the most modern structure in New Earth. Magic, science—whatever the faun dabbled in, her experiments were best studied here.

"Stay put," Robbie growled at her. He stepped up to the double entrance doors and rapped his knuckles on the glass. "Anyone here?"

A night watchman appeared in the dimly lit corridor within. "Lab is closed," the burly man said, his voice muffled behind the thick glass.

"I see that," Robbie retorted. He pointed back at Hal and the faun. "We have a prisoner. We need to lock her up and interrogate her. Lauren has gone to fetch Miss Simone."

The night watchman stared at him for a moment. Then he nodded and unlocked the door. "If you were any other kid," he said in a much clearer voice as he stepped outside, "I'd tell you to run along home and go to bed." He winked and pushed past Robbie to escort the prisoner inside.

"Watch out," Abigail warned. "If you see any blue mist coming out of her hands . . ."

The guard gave her a quizzical look as he hoisted the faun onto her feet. He grabbed her free hand and went to grab the other before realizing it was pinned to her body under a stiff, rubbery layer of dried glue. Keeping a firm grip, he marched her into the lab. "I'll put her in Observation 4."

Robbie went with him.

Hal at last felt safe to revert to human form. He stretched and spent a moment studying his fingers. They were completely healed. Relief washed over him, and he privately thanked his amazing shapeshifter talents. There were plans afoot to introduce a brand new, council-approved Shapeshifter Program that allowed ordinary people of any age to become a shifter if they so desired, assuming they passed certain tests and were given the green light by the council. The program was a few years away yet, but one day, Carter would be filled with people able to shift into other creatures. And healing would be a part of that talent. Who wouldn't want to be a shifter with a side effect like that? Hal vowed to bestow the gift on future children if he ever had any of his own . . .

He turned to Emily, wishing it were as simple for her. Somehow, he doubted switching back and forth twenty or thirty times would help. But what if it did? When he started to tell her of his idea, she shook her head.

"Tried," she said. "I switched about ten times on the way here and stopped when I nearly slid off your back. No difference at all."

She held up her hands for him to inspect, though her gnarly goblin face was all the proof he needed that shifting hadn't worked.

"We'll figure something out," he assured her.

The three of them walked inside. A goblin sentry had appeared, and he nodded at them as they passed, giving Emily an extra-curious look. *Probably wondering whose goblin kid she is*, Hal thought. *And why she's hanging out with us, pretending to be a shapeshifter with her smart clothes and everything.*

Observation 4 was a room within a room. The first was large but as poorly lit as the corridor, with several chairs facing a glass wall. Behind the glass was the second room, much brighter but smaller, with a bunk on the back wall. Entry to this ten-foot-square space was on the left-hand side of the glass wall through a narrow steel door. It had a small hatch at waist height, presumably so orderlies could pass food and water through.

Hal wondered about its purpose. It couldn't be a prison cell, not in a science lab, but it sure looked like one. Why have seats facing the glass? What could scientists be studying, exactly?

The night watchmen badgered Robbie for a briefing about the faun before leaving the room with his keys jangling. He said to call if anybody needed him.

In the glass-fronted cell, the faun growled something, using her free hand to wrench sections of glue off her shoulder and arm.

Hal, Robbie, Abigail, and Emily the goblin watched the faun in silence. The overhead light spotlighted her in a stark, white glare. She glanced up at the circular fixture once or twice, clearly irritated and perhaps a little afraid. She'd probably never seen anything powered by electricity.

Most of the homes in Carter had some kind of wiring these days, either for lighting or to keep their water nicely heated, all run by magical geo-rocks. The lab was on its way to being fully powered by *actual electricity from Old Earth*. Some "bright spark," as the running joke went, had come up with the idea of running thick electrical cables through one of the black, smoky portals into New Earth and straight into the laboratory building. Geo-rocks were systematically being moved aside to make way for the modern age.

Hal didn't care one way or another, but he had to admit the super-bright light in the cell was perfect for observing the faun and making sure she didn't secretly generate any blue mist. Even better, the larger room Hal and his friends stood in was dark, so she probably couldn't see much of them through the glass.

Abigail held out her hand to Emily. "Give me the shell."

Emily fished in a bulging pocket and extracted the conch shell. She'd held it while Abigail had shrunk to faerie size for the journey home.

Abigail opened the hatch and bent to peer through. "Oh, there's a shelf," she said, sliding the shell inside. When Hal leaned forward and pressed his face to the glass, he could see the shelf she was talking about protruding from the other side of the steel door. "Take it," she said, raising her voice to the faun.

The faun glared at her and shook her head, too busy clawing her way out of the rubber cocoon to worry about talking. She'd freed both arms now, though a large patch of glue still clung to her chest and shoulder and all the way down her furry goat legs. She worked on the tough sheathing below her knees, determined to remedy her limited movement.

"Fenton's glue is pretty amazing," Hal commented.

"He has his uses," Robbie agreed.

They waited until the faun had ripped the glue apart and could stride freely around the cell. Finally, after giving them all a hard stare, she stamped over to the door and picked up the conch from the shelf.

"Let me out," she growled into the shell, "or you will be sorry."

Her voice was muffled behind the glass. Most of the sound came through the small hatch, which Abigail had left open.

"Why will we be sorry?" Hal asked.

"Because only I have the power to evolve you into something worthy. I could just as easily leave you to float around the air like a lost soul."

Hal glanced sideways at his friends. They looked as puzzled as he felt.

"That's assuming you'll get a chance to use your blue mist on us," Abigail said.

"Oh, I will."

The faun's determined and slightly smug expression worried Hal, but he tried not to show it. "Why are you doing this? I mean, I get it, your family was hunted by humans, right? But you can't just—"

"Humans are a scourge," the faun said with a fierce look. "But do not worry, I will evolve you all into something better." She pointed at Emily, and her voice softened. "Look at you now. Are you not happy to be out of that ugly human body? I saved you! And in time, you will thank me."

"Are you kidding?" Emily suddenly yelled, making them all jump. "I'm a goblin! I'm hideous!"

Hal reached out to touch her arm, to tell her to keep her voice down, worried other goblins might be listening. She ignored him.

"Turn me back! I want to be the way I was! You've *ruined* me. Look!" She promptly transformed, and her thick snake coils nearly knocked Abigail off her feet as they spread out across the floor. "I can't even be a naga!" She lowered her voice, clearly trying to control her anger. "A naga can't have a goblin face. They'll shun me. Do you see?

100

I'm a shapeshifter! I'm supposed to act as a liaison between the naga and the humans so that—"

"There will not be any humans by the time I am finished," the faun interrupted, looking her up and down. "So, a goblin naga is better, yes?"

"Argh!" Emily screeched. She turned and raced away, slithering out of the room and disappearing into the darkened corridor beyond.

Still clutching the conch, the faun pressed her face against the glass to watch her go, one of her horns clunking noisily. "She is blessed," she remarked, her voice a little more muffled now that she was away from the open hatch. "A goblin *and* a naga. She gets to choose—and so do you. But everyone else, all other humans? I will choose for them."

Robbie grew a few inches in height and slammed a thick, overly hairy arm against the glass, causing the faun to leap back in alarm. "I'm not marrying a troll!" he yelled.

In the silence that followed, he reddened and shrank back down.

"She is a harpy," the faun said into the shell. "If she does not want to be a troll, she can be a perfect harpy."

"She doesn't want to be a harpy," Robbie growled through gritted teeth. "She wants to be human. Why is that so hard to understand?"

"River, listen to me," Abigail said quietly. Hal blinked. He'd forgotten the faun had a name. "What if we turned you into an elf or a griffin or a squonk? How would you feel about that? You wouldn't like that, would you?"

The faun smiled. "It would be terrible to become a squonk. That is a very primitive and ugly little animal—a precious life, of course, but hardly a suitable alternative for the mind of a faun. Nor a human, for that matter. I would not do that. I loathe humans, but I value life, and I believe each and every soul can be saved if given the chance for a second life in a new body. That body has to be suitable. It has to be equal. An elf, a goblin, a troll—these are all viable alternatives. A griffin is smart but too *different*."

River looked at Hal, narrowing her eyes and looking thoughtful.

"Yet you seem to do well as a dragon. Perhaps a griffin is a suitable alternative after all? Do you think a human could adapt to such a different way of life?"

"No!" Hal and Robbie exclaimed in unison.

"The point is," Hal added, "that we don't want to be anything except what we already are."

The moment he said that, he wondered if that was in fact true. How many people had mentioned to him how lucky he was to be a dragon? Of course, they were talking about being a *shapeshifter* dragon, still human most of the time . . .

"Unfortunately," the faun said, tilting her head to one side, "that is not an option. You all must change. You must be *better*. But I may offer you all the chance to choose what you would like to be."

The audacity of the prisoner was astounding. Hal glanced at Abigail and Robbie. Their mouths hung open in amazement.

"Whatever plan you had," Robbie said in a low voice, "you can forget it. You aren't going anywhere, and you're not turning anyone else into dust. You're going to turn Lauren and Emily back into humans, and then you're going to save the other people in the forest, too—Derek and whoever else you messed with."

River smiled. "No."

And that was that. She put the shell back on the shelf and went to lie on the bunk, her awkward-looking goat legs giving her a twisted, broken appearance like she were the victim of a terrible fall from a cliff. She closed her eyes and steepled her slender, gold-painted fingers on her belly.

Hal clenched and unclenched his fists a few times. He felt like he could easily make her talk with a sound roasting . . . but he also knew that, when it came down to it, he would break first. He couldn't *actually* roast her.

Maybe Miss Simone and her sword-wielding, wrench-carrying goblins might come up with an effective method of persuasion. The Prison of Despair would be a good place to start; the faun could sit in there for a week and wallow for what seemed to her like months. She'd be begging for release in no time.

Even so, a week for Emily and Lauren stuck in their present guises . . .

Hal, Robbie, and Abigail filed along the dark corridors and out of the building, passing several formidable watchmen and stout, grim-faced goblins as they went. Emily sat alone on a tree stump, back in goblin form, hunched over with her head in her hands, thoroughly miserable.

"Why do things happen to *me*?" she complained, looking up as they approached.

Even though he knew she was a goblin, Hal still felt a jolt of shock when he saw her deeply furrowed brow and flared, piglike nostrils. Her voice was only marginally different, which added to the weirdness of it all.

"First Jolie makes me terminally ill," she went on, "and then I was turned to dust and left to float in a breeze in the woods—and now *this*?"

Hal attempted a smile. "Yeah, Jolie made you terminally ill, but you got better. Most terminally ill patients don't get better. That's why they're called terminally ill. So yeah, you're now a goblin—but we'll figure something out."

"Speaking of which," Abigail said, squeezing onto the tree stump next to her, "tell us about that. About floating around in the forest like a cloud of dust."

"What's to tell? One minute I was human, about to turn into a naga and wrap my tail around that faun, and the next . . ." She frowned. "It didn't hurt. I just felt strange when the blue mist puffed up into my face. Everything kind of froze, and then suddenly I was floating upward and spinning, and I guess I blacked out. I woke sometime after, and it was dark. I just started shouting for everyone, wondering where you all were, and I sort of drifted about trying to find you."

"Did you know you were a cloud of dust?" Robbie asked.

Emily shook her head.

Robbie blinked at her. "You didn't know? How could you not know?"

"I just didn't. I felt like I was in a dream, drifting through the trees. Then I remembered the cave and headed back there." Emily frowned as if she'd just recalled something else. "I found Lauren there. I couldn't see her, but I could . . . *hear* her? Sense her? I'm not sure. But she was there, and so were all you guys. I shouted and shouted, but you kind of ignored me."

"We couldn't hear what you were saying," Abigail told her. "Just whispers."

"Next thing I know, I'm sitting on the floor in the faun's cavern with a load of glow worms above my head. It was a wonderful moment—until I realized what I was."

"So it didn't feel like you were gone for long?" Robbie asked.

"Not really. An hour or two, maybe. It felt like a dream, sort of fragmented."

She fell silent.

Abigail gave her a hug. "Well, I'm sure the faun can get you back to normal."

"How? Turn me into dust again?" Tears welled in Emily's eyes as she turned to Abigail, seeking a comforting answer, and those tears broke and ran down her cheeks when Abigail, chewing her lip, looked down at the ground. "Yeah, I figured. So I have to explode again, then float around like a ghost for a bit, then *maybe* turn human again. And will I be the same person I was before? How exactly does that work? Does the faun have the plans for my original body saved somewhere, like a blueprint stuffed in a filing cabinet?"

"I don't know," Abigail whispered.

"And that's assuming she *agrees* to turn me human again! And if she *can*! She seems to have some grand plan to turn every human into something else, but I doubt she made backup plans to turn them back again."

Emily buried her face and sobbed. Abigail could do nothing but hug and comfort her while the two boys stood awkwardly, wishing they were someplace else.

"The others will be here soon," Robbie said, nodding.

"As if that'll help," Emily said, sniffling behind her hands.

"And Miss Simone," Hal offered. "Actually, she really *should* be here soon . . ."

He guessed she would have been if she'd allowed Lauren to carry her, but that was a pretty undignified and dangerous way to travel, so Miss Simone was most likely dashing through the streets with a lantern wiggling from side to side and her silky cloak billowing.

Lauren arrived just a few minutes later. She thudded down, her white-feathered wings catching the wan moonlight. Just for a moment, she looked rather magical and splendid—until she switched to her troll form. Then the spell was broken, and Robbie's face fell.

"She's on her way," Lauren said.

"What did she think when she saw you?" Hal asked.

"Well, I stayed in harpy form until just now."

Robbie's eyebrows shot up. "So she doesn't know you're a troll?"

"Not yet. I just told her we have the faun and Emily's in trouble."

Emily peeked from behind her hands. "But *you* are, too."

"Yeah, but . . . you're worse off than me."

Somehow, this shook Emily from her misery. She rubbed her face, stood up, and went to hug Lauren. "No, I'm not. It's bad for us both. Sorry about all the crying. I'm okay now."

"There she is," Abigail said with a grin, getting to her feet. "There's the Emily we know and love. And look—there's Miss Simone."

Just as Hal imagined, the woman came hurrying around the corner with a lamp swinging from one hand, her knee-length silk dress and light cloak flapping.

"Children!" Miss Simone gasped as she ran across the grass. "What's happening? Are you all right? You—"

She stopped dead and stared at the goblin sitting on the tree stump.

"What exactly did you tell her, Lauren?" Hal murmured.

"I told her Emily was in trouble."

Miss Simone approached, completely forgetting to be winded from the long run. "Is that—Emily? Is that you?" Hal could almost see her brain whirring behind her blue eyes. "The new Shapeshifter Program," she said at last. "You've messed with it, somehow. Or . . . the faun did? I'm confused."

"I'm a goblin now," Emily muttered.

"I see that." Miss Simone glanced at Lauren. "Anyone care to explain what's going on here? Why is Emily now a goblin, and why is a troll—?" She broke off.

Almost as one, both Emily and Lauren transformed. A second or two later, a beautiful harpy stood there with her wings spread and yellow eyes blazing . . . alongside a naga with a goblin's head.

Miss Simone staggered back. "I don't understand. Lauren is a troll? Emily is a goblin?"

Abigail hastened to explain before Robbie could jump in. She started at the beginning, from the moment they had planned to capture the faun, how that plan had gone horribly wrong, and how Emily had ended up exploding into a cloud of dust like Derek and some of the villagers, and then Lauren a little while after. She mentioned the faun's cavern and how the creature had turned both girls into something they weren't.

Miss Simone listened intently the whole time, casting her gaze from Emily to Lauren and back again until the tale was done.

"And the faun is inside," Miss Simone muttered, looking toward the lab building. It wasn't a question, more a statement directed at herself.

Abigail touched Miss Simone's arm. "We need your help. The faun needs to put Emily and Lauren back as they were—but she's refusing."

Miss Simone nodded. "So I need to persuade her. Well, I think I have just the thing."

Chapter Twelve
Witchcraft

"Restrain her," Miss Simone said, pulling the steel door open.

Four goblins filed into Observation 4's glass-fronted inner cell and approached the wary faun, who backed into a corner and crouched. She sprang—but so did the goblins, moving surprisingly fast. They grabbed the faun by her arms and legs, tripped her, threw her down, and sat on her so she lay screeching on her back, wriggling furiously.

Once she was restrained, Miss Simone slid into the room holding a test tube filled with murky water. The faun's eyes widened, and she thrashed harder. But one goblin gripped her horns and held her head still while another clamped strong fingers on her jaw and forced her mouth open. "Drink," he growled.

Miss Simone tipped the murky water down her throat and stepped back. The faun gagged and had no choice but to swallow when the goblin squeezed her nostrils shut.

As soon as that was done, Miss Simone left the cell. The faun lay there after the goblins climbed off and filed out, but she sat up when the last one slammed the door and locked it.

"*Whal lei phan?*" River said, standing up and grimacing at the taste.

Abigail pointed at the conch on the door's inner shelf. It teetered on the edge.

Reluctantly, the faun picked it up and spoke into it. "What was that?"

Miss Simone offered a thin smile. "Something to make you feel like talking."

A truth serum, she'd said earlier. *An old witch's brew.*

Hal and all his friends crowded together in the dimly lit observation room with Miss Simone and the four goblins. While the mermaid scientist had been hunting around on shelves for the truth serum, Dewey had shown up with Darcy on his back, Fenton and Thomas in tow. They'd run, jogged, walked, run again, and were exhausted from the hasty journey. But not too exhausted to miss out on the interrogation.

"I will tell you nothing," the faun snarled.

Miss Simone nodded, looking thoughtful. "I just have a few questions for you. You'll stay in there until you answer me."

River held the conch to her lips and glared at her with yellow eyes. "So ask your questions. I may choose not to answer."

"If you're going to mumble, please stand near the open hatch so we can hear you better."

To Hal's surprise, the faun did as she was told.

"Where did you learn to do magic?" Miss Simone asked.

The faun frowned. "Why is that important?"

"I'm a scientist. I'm just interested. Fauns don't normally do magic. Where did you learn?"

With a shrug, River said, "I sought help from the naga."

Emily spoke up then. "The naga don't do magic either."

Miss Simone put a hand on her shoulder.

"There is a small group of naga that practices magic," the faun said defiantly. "They call themselves the Kallans. I sought them out and found one. Alas, he would not help me. So I found a human witch. Imagine my surprise when she agreed to help."

Hal looked at Miss Simone but saw nothing written on her face. Was the truth serum working?

Despite claiming she would say nothing, the faun smiled and kept on talking. "The irony! One of your own helping me to erase your existence!"

"And she taught you how to turn humans into other creatures?"

"No, she taught me how to turn *creatures* into other creatures," River said. "She was not specific. She had used the spell before. The last time, she had turned a man into a frog." Her gaze drifted. "It was just what I wanted. I asked her to teach me the spell."

"And she did?" Miss Simone demanded. "Just like that? Why?"

"Because she wanted to further my cause," the faun said.

The moment she said that, the side of her face began swelling up and giving her coppery-brown skin a weird blue tinge. She felt it, too. Her eyes widened, and she raised a hand to her face.

"Ha!" Fenton blurted out. He and Thomas chortled openly until receiving a stern look from Miss Simone.

She returned her glare to the faun. "That was a lie. The witch knew nothing of your cause. Why did she teach you the spell?"

River's hand shook. "Wh-what is happening?" she stuttered into the conch shell.

"It will pass the moment you start telling the truth again. Answer my question."

"I . . . I ran errands for the witch."

The puffiness and blue tinge immediately began to fade.

"What sort of errands?"

"Fetching ingredients for numerous other spells the witch liked to dabble in."

"For how long?"

"Five years."

Everyone gasped. "Five years?" Abigail exclaimed. "You worked for the witch for five years just so she could teach you a spell?"

"It took five years for me to learn it," River retorted. "Do you think a spell that powerful can be taught in a day? It takes years just to learn the craft of conjuring basic spells—making bad smells, causing spots to appear on skin, and other minor irritations. But to learn a spell of such magnitude . . ." She trailed off and scowled. "So I fetched and carried for five years, learning while earning my keep."

Miss Simone said nothing for a moment. Then: "Who is this witch?"

"Why should I tell you? You cannot *make* me talk."

"Oh, but I can. You'd be wise to answer these questions." After a moment, she said, "Was it Madame Frost who taught you?"

"No." But the faun's face puffed up again and turned blue. She let out a cry of rage and clutched her cheek. "Yes! Yes!"

"Who's Madame Frost?" Darcy whispered.

Miss Simone answered without taking her eyes off the faun. "One of a few local witches I know of. She's a nasty piece of work." She addressed the faun again. "Is there a cure for the spell? Can you put Emily and Lauren back the way they were before?"

River threw the conch down with such violence it shattered on the hard floor. She slammed a hand against the glass, causing everyone to flinch, and then she danced about the room like a rampaging bull, springing high with her powerful goat legs and occasionally ramming against the wall with her horns. Everyone watched, amazed, as she vented her anger and frustration and caused various dents and scuffs on the walls. Finally, she let out a cry and punched the circular light on the ceiling. The glass flew apart, the bulb broke, and the room plunged into darkness.

"Lights!" one of the goblins yelled, and everyone clearly heard the sound of his heavy footsteps pounding across the room. He hunted around for a light switch while shouting, "Nightwatch! Get me a lantern!"

Though there was very little light in the main room, Hal's eyes soon adjusted well enough to make out his friends' faces. The cell remained in absolute darkness, so the faun was invisible to them. Through the open hatch, Hal could hear her panting.

Miss Simone gave a sigh and tapped on the door. "I still need to know. Is there a cure for Emily and Lauren? I know you can understand me. Tap once for yes, twice for no."

A silence fell. Even the faun's panting subsided. Hal found Abigail's hand slipping into his, and he squeezed it tight.

Come on, Hal thought anxiously. *Give us a single tap.*

A few more seconds stretched by, and then, in the darkness, a mere silhouette of the faun behind the glass reached out.

Tap.

Just for a split second, Hal let out a sigh of relief.

Tap.

He froze.

Emily whimpered, and both Thomas and Fenton cursed. Hal hung his head and turned away. But then he wondered: What if she were lying? Her face might be puffing up right now, and nobody could see it.

"Stand back," he told Abigail and whoever else was nearest. "I'm gonna breathe some fire."

Once everyone had shuffled sideways, he let rip with a generous blast of flame that lit up the glass and the faun that pressed against it from the inside. She flinched, but she kept her hands on the glass—or one of them, anyway. The other was stretched sideways toward the open hatch in the door.

And from the hatch, blue mist crept silently into the room.

Everyone saw it at the same time and started yelling, but for some it was already too late. Hal would have stayed rooted to the spot if Abigail hadn't turned and threw herself at him. He staggered backward, almost fell, and stumbled toward the exit with her. A couple others were right behind them, but Hal had no time to see who. He hoped *all* were on their way out, but he had a horrible feeling one or two would be missing.

A goblin chose that moment to appear in the doorway with a lamp. Pushing past him was like trying to shove a tree trunk aside. Hal bounced off, stumbled again, and heard Abigail yelling at the goblin to move out of the way.

In the corridor, Hal and Abigail turned to see Darcy and Robbie tumbling out after them, then a goblin and a troll—Emily and Lauren—with wisps of blue mist trailing behind.

They skidded to a halt and spun around, and the six of them, alongside a startled goblin, watched the doorway to see who would come next.

Nobody.

Observation 4 remained dark and eerily quiet.

Hal went to march back inside, but Abigail held him. Instead, Darcy morphed into her dryad form and turned partially transparent before entering. Lauren went with her. They stood in the doorway and stared. Then Darcy quietly pulled the door shut.

"They're all gone!" she sobbed, collapsing to her knees.

The troll spread her hands in a hopeless gesture. "Gone."

"Dewey's gone?" Abigail exclaimed. "And Thomas? Fenton?"

"And Miss Simone."

Hal, Abigail, Robbie, and Emily stared at them. Hal couldn't believe it. He had to see for himself and went to open the door . . . but once again, Abigail held him back.

"No," she whispered with a fierce expression. "Don't you dare. I can't lose you, too. We have to stay safe so we can help the others."

"There's no helping them," Hal moaned.

Abigail pummeled his chest with her fists, tears welling up. "Don't talk like that!"

Darcy continued to sob, Lauren and Emily hugged each other, and Robbie swayed from side to side like he was dizzy. The goblin sentry scowled and pushed past them all. "You kids move aside. Let *me* see."

He cracked the door open just a little and peered through the gap. Hal craned his neck to see. The room looked empty except for the shadowy figure within the glass-fronted cell.

After a long pause, the goblin pulled the door shut again. "They're gone."

A couple of night watchmen appeared. "What's happening?" one asked.

The goblin started to explain as Hal stared furiously at the door. He felt like transforming and smashing his way in, throwing fireballs at the faun, then grabbing her and crashing straight up through the ceiling to the clouds high above, and letting her drop.

Fire erupted from his lips rather like a belch, and he felt extreme heat on his nose and eyebrows. The unexpected backfire broke him out of his fury, and he realized he was standing there with fists clenched, trembling and quivering.

Abigail moved into view, her face inches from his. "We're all angry, Hal, but we need to be smart about this."

He blinked at her, then nodded. "I know."

She turned to where Robbie stood with Emily and Lauren. Then she knelt next to Darcy. "Come on, guys, get it together. We haven't lost them for good. We just need to figure this out. We need a plan."

"I need some air," Robbie muttered. He marched off.

"I think we all need some air," Hal said.

He and Abigail pulled Darcy to her feet, and they headed outside with Emily and Lauren trudging along behind.

A goblin shouted after them. "What now?"

Why is he asking me? Hal thought. *I'm just a kid!*

He shouted back, "Don't let anyone in there—and don't let her out!"

* * *

"She got Thomas, Fenton, Dewey, *and* Miss Simone," Darcy said, wiping her eyes again. She squinted at Emily and Lauren in the feeble moonlight. "Not to mention you two."

"We know," Abigail replied, patting her shoulder. "But at least Em and Lauren are with us. That's six shapeshifters against one faun."

"And maybe the faun will bring the others back in some form," Robbie said. "Then they can be with us, too—whatever they are."

Hal shuddered to think what the faun would evolve them into. Ogres? Pixies? "Okay, look, we can't talk to her anymore because she broke the conch shell. And even if we could talk to her, she's not gonna help us. Not willingly."

Robbie huffed and shook his head. "So what do we do, then?"

"We go see the witch."

Everyone stared at Hal. Then Abigail nodded. "Yes. We'll find Madame Frost. She taught River everything, which means she knows more about the spell than the faun does."

"And she's human, one of our kind, so I would think she'll be way more willing to talk," Darcy agreed. She took a step toward the village. "Why didn't we think of this before? Let's go!"

Hal stopped her. "Go where? Do any of you know where this witch lives?" Of course nobody did. "Who might know? Orson? Dr. Kessler?"

"Miss Simone," Emily grumbled.

"Orson's off somewhere again with his pegasus friends," Abigail said. "We could try Dr. Kessler, though."

"Or the soothsayer," Robbie added.

His idea hung in the night air for a moment. Then Abigail smiled. "That's even better. The soothsayer might know a few things about the future. Maybe he's seen what happens next."

"Yeah, he kind of knows stuff," Darcy agreed, frowning. "So where does *he* live?"

Emily spoke up. "He used to be a wandering hermit, but I heard he made a home in the hills outside the village. *That* way, I think. To the south."

Robbie nodded. "I heard that, too. A little shack overlooking the forest."

Forestland surrounded Carter on all sides. The south was a little more hilly, and Hal had a pretty good idea where to start—a craggy ridge protruding from the treetops with the village sprawled below, an almost godlike place for an old man who regularly dreamt of the future and knew things he shouldn't. Hal had seen the old soothsayer in the vicinity of those hills before.

"Yeah, it would be good if he's foreseen things about this faun," Hal said. "Let's go now. He might be able to help."

The fact that it was three o'clock in the morning or thereabouts seemed irrelevant. Nobody said a word about it. In the back of Hal's mind, they had a deadline—because nobody wanted to face their parents in the morning and explain that some of the group had changed beyond recognition and might even be gone forever.

"I can't take everyone with me," Hal said out of habit. Then he checked himself. Lauren didn't need a ride, and Abigail would be weightless in faerie form. That only left Robbie, Emily, and Darcy. "Wait, sure I can. Climb on."

He transformed. Back on the island, when he'd become a dragon for the very first time, he'd been just twenty foot long. He'd conditioned himself to carrying no more than two at a time, three at the most. Now, ever since his encounter with werewolves a few months ago, he was twice the size and able to carry more weight.

When he launched into the sky with three human passengers and a diminutive faerie, he vowed not to underestimate his own strength again. Two, three, four . . . He could barely feel them back there. It wouldn't make a difference if he had all eight of his friends perched on his back, sitting side by side.

He soared high and raced to catch up to Lauren.

Finding an old hermit's home on a clifftop wasn't easy in the middle of the night. The craggy ridge showed itself in the moonlight as a black outline above the treetops, so they flew back and forth along its length, scouring the darkness.

Abigail spotted it first. "There!" she squeaked.

Nobody else saw a thing. Hal had to circle a few times, listening to Abigail's frantic directions and noticing that her voice grew louder by the second as she returned to her full human size.

He couldn't see any small buildings even after he'd landed on a plateau. Although Abigail buzzed down to the ground and headed off toward a stand of trees, he saw nothing that resembled a home, not even for an old hermit.

Once the others had dismounted, he switched to human form and joined the group, squinting in the darkness.

"I just see trees," Robbie muttered.

The plateau was fairly smooth, nothing but hard rock sloping gently upward. Small shrubs sprouted here and there. Trees clustered together on one side of the ridge, at the edge of a drop-off, and a stream trickled through. It made sense for a hermit to live here. He had fresh water and shelter among the trees as well as a fantastic view.

"Oh!" Darcy cried. "I see it!"

Abigail led them straight toward what turned out to be a shack at the edge of the trees. It was so heavily shadowed that only a faerie with night vision could possibly have seen it.

"You realize he's going to be sound asleep," Robbie whispered.

"We can't worry about that," Emily grunted.

Lauren, now back in troll form, strode ahead with her long legs, quickly passing Abigail. "Yeah, we can't wait."

Abigail reached out to grab her. "Hey, let *me* knock and wake him. I'm not sure how he'll react to a troll knocking on his door."

Lauren stopped dead and glanced down at herself. "Oops. I forgot."

They all waited a few yards back as Abigail knocked sharply on the door. She retracted her wings as she waited; they slid easily into the flesh between her shoulder blades and disappeared, and the fabric of her smart dress closed up afterward.

She knocked again.

The third time, she pounded and put her mouth to the door. "Please wake up! We need your help!"

Something fell over inside, perhaps a metal cup or something. "What?" a muffled voice said. Further mumblings came from the room within, along with the sounds of rummaging and a few scrapes. A bolt slid back, and the door creaked open a few inches.

If the tiny shack wasn't dark enough on the outside, the gap in the door was absolutely black. "Who's there?" an old man said in a wavering voice.

"Don't you know?" Robbie demanded. "I thought you knew everything."

Hal nudged him. "Shh!"

Abigail edged closer. "Sorry to bother you, sir. We need your help. Something's happening in the village—a faun using magic and turning people into something they're not—and she won't talk to us and put things right. We need to see the witch who taught her the spell. Do you know Madame Frost? Do you know where she lives?"

The old man was silent for half a minute. Then the door creaked open, and he shuffled out with a cane clacking on the rock.

Hal saw only the outline of a robed man with a slight stoop, bald on the top of his head but with straggly white hair at the back. If the moonlight fell on his face, it would reveal one good eye, the other nothing but a ghastly socket. Hal was happy not to see that right now.

"I had a dream about this," the hermit croaked.

Robbie sighed and whispered, "Of course you did, you crazy old coot."

Hal tensed up. The soothsayer might come across weird and eccentric, but his visions had always come true in some form. He'd seen the Shadow Demon on Whisper Mountain and nine children that would set things right. He'd glimpsed the giant lizard monsters that demolished part of the village. And he'd foretold the village of Carter floating on water, which had turned out to be a result of numerous household geo-rocks exploding and forming portals that opened up over the sea in Old Earth.

"Tell us about it," Abigail said softly.

The old man peered closer at her, then turned and squinted at the others. His gaze skipped over Robbie and Darcy, paused on Emily and Lauren, then stopped on Hal. "You again," he said, nodding. "Yes, yes, it makes sense. My dreams always make sense in the end."

"What did you see?" Hal asked.

The man hobbled a little closer, his cane tapping the ground. Thankfully, his face was still heavily shadowed. "Not much. It was even more vague than usual. I saw a faun, and I saw blue mist, and people screaming, *so* many people . . ." He shuddered, then leaned closer. The moonlight fell upon his empty socket. "And I saw a boy."

"Me?" Hal guessed.

"No, not you. Not any of you. Another boy." He frowned. "A boy and a girl. They are known to you—or *will* be. They are important. They will end this siege once and for all."

Everyone was silent while digesting that information.

The old man nodded, tapped his cane, and spun back around to Abigail. "Madame Frost, you say? Be careful with her. Treacherous old witch. She lives in the Swamps of Misery north of here."

"That sounds *charming!*" Darcy exclaimed, clapping her hands together. She rolled her eyes and let her arms fall to her sides. "Why can't she live in the Springs of Happiness or Waterfalls of Delight? Why does it have to be the Swamps of *Misery?*"

"She's an evil witch," Lauren said.

That seemed to answer the question.

Abigail frowned. "There were some swamps in the woods near the faun's cave. Fenton and Thomas wound up on the bank."

Everyone looked to the old man, and he gave a shrug. "All I know is that the witch lives in the most miserable place in the land."

Chapter Thirteen
Swamps of Misery

They flew to the woods north of the village and touched down where Hal could find a decent clearing. Again, finding their way in the dark promised to be a real chore, even with a few lamps they'd picked up from a helpful goblin sentry on the way over.

"Maybe we should wait until dawn," Lauren said with a sigh as they trudged through the trees.

Hal held his lamp high, looking ahead at the impossibly thick vegetation. They'd have to skirt around. Sooner or later, he hoped to come across something they recognized. Fenton had drunk from the swamp, and that particular bank had to be somewhere close by.

"I'm not going home to bed," Darcy said stiffly. "As tired as I am, I can't imagine crawling into bed and going to sleep, then waking up and telling my parents that you're now a troll and Emily is a goblin, and oh, by the way, some of the others are clouds of dust floating around in the air."

"No, I can't either," Lauren agreed. "Sorry. Just fed up."

They kept walking, saying nothing except for the occasional "This way?" and "Have we been here before?" But, at last, Robbie squelched into something and withdrew a muddy foot.

"The ground is boggy here," he said, sounding pleased. "Could we be close?"

They kept their lamps low after that, trying to avoid sinking into puddles and sticky mud. A much harder and slightly raised trail emerged, and everyone exclaimed with delight, finally recognizing the route. They hurried along, single file, until they ended up at the vaguely familiar bank of a swamp.

"This is it!" Hal said with a grin. "This was exactly where Fenton took his drink."

Robbie grimaced. "Yeah, this is it, mosquitoes and all."

They stood and stared across the swamp, holding their lamps high. There wasn't much to see nearby, and even less out in the shadows.

The swamp water was utterly still, with reeds poking up everywhere and a few willow trees trailing their branches on the surface. In the daytime, with the sun's morning rays and a fine white mist rising off the water, it could almost be tranquil and picturesque . . . except Hal doubted the place could ever be that. It was grim.

The swamp stretched a long way. Trees grew straight out of the water or from numerous muddy islands. Vines hung everywhere, and fluffy white moss dangled in places. The light from the lamps cast weird shadows, giving the place a ghostly vibe.

"We need our raft," Robbie murmured.

Abigail looked at Hal. "I'm best suited for this kind of travel, but I can't take passengers. Maybe you should be a dragon? Just wade through with us on your back."

Hal sighed. "I guess."

He transformed and stepped into the water. It wasn't deep at all, barely coming up to his thick, reptilian ankles. He lowered himself as far as he could, lying flat on the submerged mud while his friends clambered up onto his back and arranged themselves in pairs. At least he wouldn't be bothered by mosquitoes; he could hear Robbie grumbling about it again. Lauren had a thick troll hide, and Emily probably wouldn't care if the biting bugs whined around her gnarly, goblin skin. As for Darcy . . .

"I don't think the mosquitoes know I'm here," she said with a laugh.

"I guess dryads aren't bothered by stuff like that," Abigail agreed, slapping at one. Hal couldn't see or even feel his friends back there, but he could hear everything—every whine and slap.

"That's it, I'm turning ogre," Robbie said.

An annoyed squeal from Darcy suggested she'd been shoved aside by Robbie's sudden transformation.

Their journey was slow but easy. The swamp deepened until it came up to Hal's belly, and then up his sides. It seemed to go on forever, long but relatively narrow. They could have traveled around to one side and followed its crowded mudbanks, but that would have been hard-going. The trees thrived here, even in the water, and the canopy of branches spread thick overhead. Hal guessed the swamp was invisible from above even in the daytime.

"Hope we're going the right way," Emily growled. Hal swore she sounded more like a true goblin every time she opened her mouth. Her general attitude seemed grumpier, too. She had a right to be grumpy, of course, but maybe the natural goblin demeanor was beginning to assert itself. "Ain't got time to mess about."

Yep, Hal thought. *Definitely sounding more like a goblin.*

What did that mean for Lauren? Trolls were pretty hostile creatures at the best of times. It occurred to him that trolls and ogres didn't get along, always scrapping. That didn't bode well for Lauren and Robbie . . .

Hal heard the sound of sniffling and paused to listen. A squonk lay on a nearby mudbank. As large as a pig and much rounder, it had various rolls of wart-riddled fat under its orange fur. Its ears were as pointed and floppy as a hyena's, and its ugly, wrinkled face with bulging eyes reminded Hal of a pug. Tears streamed down its cheeks, and the creature cried harder when everyone paused to watch it.

"What's *wrong* with that thing?" Darcy asked.

"It's just a squonk," Robbie said. "They're always crying."

They watched it for a little longer before realizing there were more—at least six of them spaced out along the banks, barely visible in the feeble light of the lamps. The closest began wailing, and Hal noticed something odd.

"Is it . . . *melting?*" Abigail asked, voicing his own concern.

Robbie sighed. "It's dissolving. They're miserable most of the time, full of guilt and shame, and they dissolve into tears if everyone stares at them too hard."

"Well, why are we staring, then?" Lauren exclaimed. "Look away, everyone! Let's move on, Hal."

He figured it was too late for the poor creature. He couldn't help glancing at it as he sloshed onward through the swamp. The squonk flattened out into a liquid mess, and then it stopped crying and melted away, a puddle of tears pouring into the murky water.

"Maybe this whole swamp is just a load of melted squonks," Robbie said after a while. "That would explain its name."

Swamps of Misery, Hal thought with a shudder. Sure enough, the sounds of sniffling and crying and wailing sounded from all sides now, and he tried his hardest not to turn and stare. What sad and truly pathetic creatures these were.

Thick, green algae covered the water in these parts, and the surface was completely still. The stagnant nature of the swamp made it smell like rotten eggs. Hal saw all manner of critters out of the corner of his eye, shuffling about on the bank or darting across branches. Several very large serpents slid by underwater, though they dared not come near. He suspected the place would be crawling with even more bugs and nasties during the day.

The slow trek depressed Hal. Everything seemed so *hopeless* here, including the entire point of their journey. He felt like turning back, but that would mean trying to explain his feelings, and the last thing he wanted was to wade around in the swamp in human form. He'd be soaked and would probably sink up to his knees, and he'd be crawling with leeches and other nasties within minutes, and . . .

He sighed and fought back tears. Then he shook his head and growled. *Get it together, Franklin.*

Yet he couldn't shake the awful, miserable feeling seeping into his scaly skin. The water had to be infused with some kind of depressing magic. Maybe all those squonks were the cause.

He heard crying. One of the girls—Darcy, maybe.

"Leave me alone," she said when someone evidently reached for her.

And, seconds later, Lauren started crying as well.

"Guys, keep it together," Abigail whispered—and burst into tears,

Hal wanted to stop and comfort her, but he couldn't without bringing everything to a halt. He fought a rising, trembling anger at the realization he was utterly useless to her right now. She was crying, and he couldn't even speak a few reassuring words. What kind of boyfriend was he?

I'm worthless, he thought.

"I see it," Lauren whispered.

"Me too," Robbie said.

Hal shook his head and paid attention. It was like drifting off to sleep and jolting awake at the sound of a sharp noise. Now fully alert, he couldn't understand what he'd been so upset about.

Directly ahead, a soft glow of light emanated from a dark, blocky structure. It had to be a house, and judging by its location, there could be no doubt it belonged to Madame Frost. Nobody in their right mind would live in this awful place but a witch.

Still, why live *here*? Even witches had to travel into the village once in a while. Then Hal remembered why she'd taught the faun how to work a spell. The payment for that coaching was to fetch and carry.

Fauns were forest-dwellers; who better to run errands to and from the village for five years?

He waded onward, noting that the trees were thinning out and the banks receding. The swamp here was bigger and clearer, with the sky above. Hal could see only stars at the moment, but he imagined this spot was far brighter and tranquil during daylight hours than the depressing mess they'd traversed so far. And the clearing in the trees excited him. When they were done with the witch, he'd take to the sky immediately and be back home in no time.

The house revealed itself in the glow of the lamps as they approached. A one-story, stone-walled cottage with a very tall, very pointed slate roof and an equally tall and rickety chimney. All the windows were dark except for one, possibly a living room, where a few candles burned. An iron fence surrounded the cottage, the bars black and pointed. The gate arched high between two stone columns. On top of those columns, two ugly stone figures perched.

Hal trudged out of the swamp, noting that the cottage stood on a raised island in the exact center of the clearing. No pathways led to the gate, but one existed inside the property, leading to the front door.

Robbie was the first to dismount. In hulking ogre form, he stamped over to the gate and fingered the huge latch. He lifted it and shoved, and the gate groaned inward, scraping heavily across the ground.

Emily shuffled closer and pointed. "I could easily fix that, you know. Just needs a wheel."

Hal reverted to human form and joined the group. Robbie, at the front, stepped all the way through the gate.

The moment he did so, a strong gust of wind tore through the trees, buffeted the shapeshifters, and quickly faded. The two stone figures on top of the gatepost columns came to life and leapt down in front of them.

Everyone gasped. This was their first encounter with real, live gargoyles. They were identical in every way except that one had a chunk missing out of its shoulder. The injury didn't seem to affect its range of motion; a flesh-and-blood person would have lost the use of that arm. The creatures crouched, ready to spring at them. Though humanoid, they had long, vicious-looking, club-ended tails and pointed, almost triangular wings. Their faces were fixed scowls, somewhat demonic, with red-glowing eyes.

"Bash 'em, Robbie," Lauren murmured, apparently not quite as impressed as the others.

"No," Abigail said. "That's not very polite." She stepped up past Robbie and raised her voice. "We want to speak to Madame Frost. May we come in?"

The gargoyles shook their heads and advanced, emitting low growls.

"We don't have time for this," Lauren growled back.

Hal edged closer to Abigail and addressed the gargoyles. "Listen, any one of us could get past you without any trouble, and you'd end up in pieces. So just let us through."

One of the stone creatures—the one with the chunk missing—howled and leapt at Hal. He fell back in alarm, but there was no need, because Robbie swung a fist and caught the creature square on the jaw. The thing's entire head cracked and fell apart, the red glow instantly fading from its eyes as the chunks went in different directions. Halted in mid-jump, the gargoyle toppled sideways. But then, headless, it got back on its feet and seemed confused, turning this way and that, finally reaching up to touch the clean break in the neck. Only then did it understand what had happened, and it started scampering about in the mud, feeling for its missing pieces.

The other gargoyle simply watched, its red eyes blazing. Then it let out a hiss and crouched lower, preparing to leap.

"Oh, please," Lauren said, stomping forward to stand alongside the towering ogre. "Try me next. See what you get. I'll dish out a lot more than this oaf." She jerked a thumb in Robbie's direction.

Uh-oh, Hal thought. *She's turning.*

Abruptly, as if hearing a cue, the gargoyle turned and leapt onto the top of the gatepost again. The other creature, still headless, felt its way to the second column and clambered up with surprising agility as though its hands and feet stuck to the walls.

They do, just like Fenton's! That's why we thought he was a gargoyle the first time we saw him hanging off the lighthouse wall.

How long ago that seemed now.

Entry seemed to have been granted, so Abigail headed through the gate and up the path to the front door. Everyone followed—a half-size ogre, a lanky troll, a squat goblin, an almost invisible dryad . . . and Hal.

The door opened before Abigail had a chance to knock. She stood there with her fist raised as the inside of the cottage slowly revealed itself. It looked cozy enough considering a witch lived here, a perfectly normal living room with furniture, bookshelves, framed paintings, a rug, a table, and a few brightly burning candles on wall sconces. The fire in the hearth was nearly out, but it flared up on its own as the group sidled indoors.

The place smelled weird. Not bad, just strange, like chemicals in a lab. A black pot hung on a metal frame in front of the hearth. Clearly, *something* had been cooking. A magical potion, perhaps? It smelled too weird to be soup.

"Hello?" Abigail called.

Silence greeted them. They waited.

"Maybe she's putting her face on," Darcy muttered.

"Well, she opened the door for us," Hal said.

They started wandering about. Hal was interested to see all the small bottles on one of the shelves—dozens of them, each labeled with tiny scrawled handwriting that he couldn't read. Large tomes wedged into the bookcase added to the witch-like setting. All it needed now was a broom and a black cat . . .

He almost laughed aloud when he spotted a wicker broom standing in a corner alongside a mop. Well, to be fair, *everybody* owned a broom.

"Hello?" Abigail called again, louder this time, a little more impatient.

"Come out, come out, wherever you are," Lauren murmured in a sing-song voice.

Hal glanced around and realized Darcy had vanished. He'd seen her on the doorstep but not since; she'd slipped into full-on dryad mode. That was probably wise. Robbie had now shrunk down to his normal size, a little shorter than the long-armed, long-haired Lauren. Emily stood looking grumpy and bored, her face set in a perpetual grimace.

Abigail edged closer to Hal. "Maybe she's getting dressed?"

"We probably woke her," Hal agreed.

A voice came out nowhere. "What do you want with me?"

Everyone jumped. "Who said that?" Robbie exclaimed.

"Obviously Madame Frost," Lauren retorted. "Question is, where is she?"

They looked into every corner and saw no sign of her. Yet she spoke in the same scratchy, coarse voice. "Why are you here?"

Hal answered. "We need to talk to you about a faun. Her name's River, and she told us you taught her how to do a spell. She was with you for five years, fetching and carrying for you in payment for your help."

The witch suddenly appeared in the center of the room, standing very tall and straight despite being very old. Her face was lined, her grey hair long and unkempt. Her robe had seen better days.

"And what will *you* do in payment for my help?" she demanded.

Hal floundered for a second. "Uh . . ."

"You have to help us," Lauren said with a snarl as she approached the witch. As a young troll, she matched the woman's height almost perfectly. "Look at me. I'm supposed to be human. The faun did this to me—and to Emily." She gestured toward the goblin.

Madame Frost didn't seem too surprised, nor concerned. "As you said, the *faun* did that to you. Not my problem."

"You taught her the spell," Lauren growled.

Hal could see the troll's nature was surfacing. "Please help us," he said. "It's not just us she's attacked. She has a plan to wipe out all humans and turn them into something else—and that includes you, Madame Frost."

"Pah!" the witch scoffed. She strode past Lauren and stared down at Emily, then moved on to Abigail with the ease and grace of a much younger person. "Who *are* you kids? Who sent you?"

"We sent ourselves," Abigail said stiffly. "Miss Simone is . . . no longer with us."

"What does that mean?"

"It means she's a cloud of dust floating in the air. The faun did that, too."

Madame Frost glared at her, then continued past, looking thoughtful. Her gaze bore into Robbie's, and then she turned to stare at . . . nothing. At first Hal assumed she was directing her gaze to the opposite wall, or perhaps out a window, but then he saw a slight movement in the air directly in front of the witch. Darcy hadn't fooled Madame Frost at all.

She fuzzed into view, a little red-faced.

Madame Frost gave a nod, then turned to Hal. "You," she said.

Hal blinked. "Me?"

"I watched you approach. You were a dragon. And your mention of Lady Simone . . . I assume you're one of her shapeshifters? You all are, correct?"

"Right," Abigail said.

Madame Frost stared even harder at Hal. "Fetch me something. That will be your payment."

"Payment for what?" Hal asked, confused.

"Payment for my help. I'll tell you what you need to know after you fetch me something."

Lauren started growling again. "We don't have time for this." She advanced on the witch, curling her long fingers as though to grab the woman by the neck and throw her across the room.

The witch simply tilted her head and muttered something, and suddenly a blast of wind came out of nowhere and buffeted Lauren so hard she staggered backward. Nothing else in the room was affected, not even the drapes in the window right behind. Lauren leaned against the wind and put one foot forward as though forging onward during a blizzard. But the wind hit her harder, and though her large feet were planted wide, she actually slid a few inches across the stone floor.

Everyone watched, amazed. Hal moved closer, ready to blast some fire or something. Opposite him, Robbie was growing, his smart shirt expanding and then beginning to reform into an ogre belt. But he paused when he grew so tall his head touched one of the stout beams above.

Abruptly, the wind cut off, and Lauren stumbled a little before righting herself. The witch glared at her, then turned back to Hal. "Do you agree to my terms?"

No way! Hal thought angrily. *We don't have time to fetch stuff for you!*

"Yes," he found himself saying.

Abigail and Robbie both started to protest, but Emily jumped in and said, "Hal can fly there and back. Should be a quick trip—s'long as whatever it is you want is close?" She directed this last part at the witch.

"It's close," Madame Frost agreed. "East of your village. You can fly straight there and land on the side of a steep hill. There's a waterfall and a hidden shelter. That's where you need to go."

"To fetch what?" Hal asked.

"A blue gem. A young dragon guards it. Since you're a dragon yourself, you're perfect for the job. Go fetch that gem."

Hal couldn't believe what he was hearing. "You want me to steal a blue gem? From a *steamer dragon*, by some chance? The same steamer dragon that bit my fingers off?"

He wiggled his fully grown fingers to prove his point, then realized he was proving nothing.

Madame Frost raised her eyebrows at him. "You've encountered this steamer before? Why?"

"Because a kid stole that blue gem, and the steamer came after it, and I had to send her packing."

"You—" For once, the woman lost her cool composure. "So where is the blue gem now?"

"The steamer has it."

"You gave it back?" Madame Frost shook her head. "I've been after that gem for a while. Dragons are unusually resistant to my spells." She looked again at Hal. "Perhaps you'll do better. Bring me that gem, and I'll tell you everything."

"How about you tell us everything right now," Lauren growled.

"Yeah," Robbie said in a booming voice. He didn't elaborate, though; his half-ogre brain didn't quite have the imagination.

Madame Frost rolled her eyes. "I could cast any number of spells on you both. Please desist, or face the consequences." She offered them a smile of blackened teeth. "Don't forget who you're dealing with. If you think the faun is powerful . . . Pah! She knows but a few spells. I know hundreds."

Lauren took a few steps back. "Fine." Bumping into Robbie, she glanced up at him and bared her teeth. "What are you staring at?"

"Huh?"

Abigail leaned closer to Hal. "I think we should go now." She raised her voice and addressed the witch. "We're heading out now to find this gem. When we come back, you'd *better* tell us what we need to know to stop this faun and get our friends back. Deal?"

The witch bowed. "Deal."

"Let's go," Abigail said, dragging Hal toward the door.

"What about us?" Darcy complained. "We should come too."

Abigail shook her head as she continued hustling Hal out the door. "Stay here and talk to Madame Frost."

Her hidden meaning was pretty clear; even the witch understood it judging by the way she raised her eyebrows: *Question her. See if you can find out something useful.*

Robbie, Emily, Lauren, and Darcy remained in the living room with the witch as Abigail pulled the door shut and walked with Hal up the path to the gate. The gargoyles still perched high on either side, one with a missing head.

"I don't think you should come with me," Hal said. "Seriously, these steamer dragons are dangerous. Even the young one—"

"I'm sure you'll look after me." Abigail smiled and stepped to one side, gesturing for him to get on with it.

He sighed and transformed.

Chapter Fourteen
Steamer Dragon Nest

East of the village, Hal thought, recalling Madame Frost's directions. *A waterfall on a steep hill.*

The funny thing was, he knew exactly where she meant. It wasn't a huge waterfall by any means, nor a particularly steep hill, but it was the only location he could think of that fit the bill. Did Miss Simone know the steamer dragons lived there? They must be new in the area. He was pretty sure he'd have encountered them before otherwise.

Why on earth did the witch want a blue gem? He vowed to find out before handing it over.

To his surprise, an orange glow showed on the far eastern horizon as he soared across the treetops. He was both relieved to see daylight approaching and anxious that his friends' parents would be waking in the next hour or so. Heck, the goblins might already have woken them to report the faun's evildoing. He hoped not.

He put on extra speed. They had maybe a couple of hours to find a solution to the problem and restore everyone to their proper human state before panic spread in the village. He couldn't imagine how Mr. and Mrs. Hunter would fare, knowing their daughter had turned into a troll—or the Stantons when they found out they had a goblin in the family. Worse, unless Fenton, Thomas, and Dewey had *evolved* into something else, they were still a collection of dust particles swirling around a room, desperate whispers echoing in a hallway.

Hal grunted with annoyance. Having to seek out a stupid gem for a stupid witch before she would tell him how to reverse the stupid spell— it irked him so much he wanted to turned around and light a fire under her.

The waterfall sparkled in the very first dabs of morning light. It wasn't very impressive from the sky, just a dribble of water running down the slopes. And the shelter Madame Frost had mentioned wasn't so much a cave as a deep recess in a cliff face. The dragons must be there.

"Get down," he told Abigail the moment he landed. The waterfall thundered above, cascading over the jutting rock and falling perhaps thirty feet before hitting the slopes, where it plumed in a faint mist and continued down the hill. He appreciated it much more now that he'd set foot on the grassy hill to one side. It was a nice spot to picnic—or would be if a family of dragons hadn't taken up residence.

She didn't respond to his grunts, so he lowered himself and shook gently until she got the hint. "All right, all right," she said, flying up off his back and zipping around to face him. Hovering a few feet off the ground, she bobbed up and down and wagged a finger at him. "Now, don't do anything silly this time, like turning human and getting your fingers bitten off. Okay?"

He smiled—or tried to—and took off. A short leap and a few beats of his wings landed him on the edge of a shelf of rock under the overhanging cliff face. He had to duck to clear the slanting roof.

As soon as he made it inside, where the noise of the waterfall was greatly reduced, a screech tore out of the shadows. An adult male steamer dragon appeared, stomping forward with wings spread in an obvious display of aggression.

"I just want to talk," Hal said quickly in dragonspeak.

The steamer roared again, taking another couple of stomps toward him, his wings spreading further. *Get away from here!* he demanded. *This is my nest. I claimed it first.*

The 'nest' cut deeper into the hillside than expected. It had to be the size of a house, one cavernous room where the ceiling sloped downward toward the back. He sensed movement in the darkest shadows, but right now the male commanded his attention.

"I don't want your nest," Hal said. "I just want the blue gemstone."

The dragon cocked his head to one side. *Blue gemstone?*

Hal hunkered down and folded his wings, trying to adopt a non-threatening posture. He studied the steamer for a moment. Vibrant greens, long claws, lithe and brawny, and a pronounced and jagged backbone—this was a male dragon with plenty of vigor, standing about the same height as Hal, and a far more experienced fighter.

The only real advantage Hal had was his fire, which would always prevail over steam.

"Your daughter—" Hal paused, trying to think of a more *dragony* word. Maybe offspring? Brood? Hatchling? None of those sounded right.

He continued anyway. "She has a blue gemstone in her collection. I'd like to take it, with your permission?"

Why?

"To put right a wrong," Hal said carefully. "It's very important to me."

What kind of 'wrong' do you refer to?

Hal sighed. "It's hard to explain. But it will save my family—"

And make mine unhappy.

Now it was Hal's turn to ask, "Why?"

Leave this place and return to the plains, the steamer told him. *There is nothing for you here, nor in this forest.*

Hal felt anger stirring. He sat upright, uncurling his wings a little. The steamer saw this and spread his wider, adopting a more aggressive stance.

"I live here," Hal growled. "Not here, but nearby. This is my home. You're new to this area. I was here first." He felt a little childish saying that, but it was true nonetheless. He made an effort to control his irritation and spoke in a softer voice. "Look, the gem can't be worth much, can it? It's just a pretty thing, part of your daughter's collection, right? I can bring you plenty of replacements if you let me take this one."

The dragon allowed a wisp of steam to escape his nostrils. *Part of a collection?* he scoffed. *Do you think us shallow? Do you believe we collect pretty baubles because they sparkle?*

This gave Hal pause. What other reason could a young dragon have? And wasn't it common knowledge that some dragons hoarded treasures?

"Uh . . ." he managed to say.

I would not tolerate such foolish behavior in newly born whelps, let alone fledglings.

"Okay, sorry. I didn't mean to—"

You speak in a foreign tongue, Dragon from the Plains. What is this 'okay' word you use? Never mind. I believe I understand. You are the one with two faces, are you not? A dragon one moment, a human the next. Am I correct?

Hal dipped his head. "I am."

The steamer recoiled in obvious disgust. *You were the one who retrieved the gemstone from other humans before my fledgling got to them. Tell me this: Which of you is the true face, and which is the impostor? Were you born a dragon, or a human?*

"Human," Hal said meekly.

I thought as much. I have no desire to speak with you further. Leave now.

This wasn't going well. Hal opened his mouth to say something, but the steamer had the audacity to turn his back on him and swing his tail a little too close for comfort. The tail might have been an accident, but turning his back . . .

Hal realized his inner-dragon was offended. Normally, such a slight would be grounds for full-scale war. This steamer was openly snubbing him, probably assuming Hal was less than a dragon and no real threat.

The steamer was wrong. Before he could stop himself, Hal blasted the other dragon's rear end with fire.

The roars of pain and fury echoed throughout the cave. The steamer swung around to face him and advanced, and Hal rose up, ready for a retaliation. While his inner-dragon welcomed the challenge, his human self cringed with fear; those claws were awfully long, and the vibrant-green forest dragon wasn't exactly small.

How dare you? the steamer hissed.

"Settle down," Hal said hurriedly. "I really don't want to fight, but if I do, I'll use a lot of fire and burn you. You don't want that. All I want to do—"

The steamer thrust his head forward and released a powerful blast of steam in Hal's face. It was way hotter than he ever could have expected, and he recoiled in pain, shutting his eyes tight. But it felt like his eyelids were melting. He scrambled backward as the steam continued to engulf him, and he suddenly wished he hadn't been so sure of himself. Steam might not be as deadly as fire, but it still *hurt*.

As he backed up, the rock ledge ran out, and his back feet slipped over the edge. He toppled backward, and though he tried to dig his front claws into the rock and arrest his fall, it was impossible to gain purchase on the cold, hard surface. He scrambled and scraped, then tumbled down the hill.

He rolled head over heels a couple of times, his wings flapping ineffectively as he matched the pace of the gushing waterfall. He slashed at the ground, digging into the earth. He was halfway down the grassy hill before he stopped his fall.

"How embarrassing," he told himself as he stood up and shook himself off. His eyes hurt like crazy, and he blinked over and over, trying to clear the redness and blurring. His snout hurt, too, and his face, even his tongue to some extent. How could his tongue hurt from a steaming when he could breathe fire all day long? It didn't make sense.

Abigail buzzed around his face. He could see her movement and hear her wings, but he couldn't focus on her. "Are you all right, Hal?" she shouted over the rushing water.

"Sure," he mumbled.

"Was that a yes or a no? Nod or shake your head."

He opened his mouth to shout, then remembered he was a dragon. He nodded instead.

"Hmm. You don't *look* all right. Your face is all burnt, and your eyelids—eww. They're all gooey and swollen. Hal, can you see?"

Annoyed with himself, and especially with the witch for sending him on this pointless mission, he reverted to human form and went to rub his eyes. But he winced in pain and froze, deciding not to touch. "This is worse," he said. "Hang on."

He transformed again, waited a moment, then turned human.

"Does that look better? It doesn't hurt now." He kept his eyes shut.

Abigail said, "Well, a second ago it looked like someone had thrown acid in your face."

"And now?"

"Now it looks like someone threw acid in your face about a week ago."

He blinked rapidly. "You're saying it looks the same?"

"I'm saying it's the same but more dried out and partially healed. Still bad, though. You'll need to transform a few more times."

Grunting with annoyance, Hal did so over and over until he felt tired. He paused and focused on Abigail. Her face was clear, but the periphery seemed fuzzy.

"That's better," she said. "Now you just look like Robbie punched each of your eyeballs about twenty times."

"Good. I can see now, sort of."

He looked back up at the rocky overhang. He couldn't decide if the greyness was because of his poor vision or just because the morning sun hadn't made it this far yet. Probably both.

"So I guess it didn't go so well?" Abigail said.

He shook his head. "Now I'm going to have to get rough. I really don't want to, and it seems so stupid stealing a gemstone, but we have no choice."

"You have to do what you have to do."

"I won't hurt them, though. I'll try not to, anyway."

"Right—unless they hurt you. Then it's self-defense."

"Yeah, but we're the ones attacking," Hal grumbled. "Man, this is so wrong."

Abigail reached out and touched his face. "Just be firm and strong, but polite and respectful. Show them you mean business."

He warmed to the idea. "Yeah. A show of strength first, and when they're subdued, I'll be nice."

After transforming once more, he headed back up to the overhanging cliff shelter. As before, the moment he flew in and landed, an almighty bellow echoed out of the darkness. The steamer emerged again, clearly much angrier than before.

I warned you! it yelled.

Hal had no time to talk. As the steamer opened his mouth, Hal beat him to it and breathed a long sheet of fire that engulfed his opponent around the neck and caused the dragon to screech and retreat.

Hal cut off his flames and marched forward. His next fiery breath chased away the shadows and spotted two more dragons lying in the farthest corner, both with heads raised, looking at him in alarm.

The bull dragon charged him with a terrible hiss, and Hal had to duck and weave to avoid the cloud of steam. He opened up with more fire, short bursts of it in the steamer's face, just enough to drive him back against the wall.

The other two dragons climbed to their feet and took up defensive positions, the mother nudging the fledgling aside. Hal recognized the younger female and wondered if she remembered him. She'd been there the whole time, hidden in the darkness, so she'd probably overheard her father mention that Hal was the shapeshifter she'd confronted in the village.

"I'm sorry about this," Hal said during a lull in the short but fierce battle. "This is not my choice. I have to take that blue gemstone."

The bull roared and advanced but stopped short of blasting Hal with steam. Instead, hot wisps rose from the corners of his mouth and nostrils. *The gemstones belong to my fledgling,* he snarled. *She cherishes them—and not just because they sparkle.*

So I guessed right, Hal thought. *There's a collection of them.*

He strained his eyes in the darkness. Now that he thought about it, he'd seen an awful lot of glinting reflections in the glow of his fire just now, definitely more than one gemstone's worth.

"So how come a little human girl got hold of one?" he demanded. "That was pretty careless of you. What, she just wandered in here and stole it from under your noses?"

We were out.

"She climbed all the way up here?"

The steamer huffed with impatience and shuffled sideways. *There is a small passage.*

A full picture of what happened slotted into place. The little girl, Sarah, had probably been with her parents at the time, wandering around. She'd found a passage in the hillside leading to the dragon's lair. What a delight it must have been for her to find a pretty blue gemstone. And not just one but . . . how many?

He squinted in the darkness, then gave a quick blast of fire that caused all three steamers to recoil. He saw what he needed to see—a small pile of stones of varying colors. It was a wonder Sarah hadn't taken more.

"She took only one," Hal argued. "I'm surprised you even noticed it missing. What's so important about them?"

After a pause, the steamer said, *Step closer and see.*

Tentatively, Hal approached the two female dragons deeper in the nest. They quietly moved aside for him, casting glances at the bull. Other than a few bones and what looked like a half-eaten bird the size of a dog, there was nothing to see but gemstones standing in a perfectly conical pile where the dragons could crowd around them and stare at them.

But why?

Hal looked closer. The gems differed in color, but they were obviously rather special, most of them clear and glassy but some opaque and dull. They ranged from the size of a chicken's egg to one as big as the chicken itself.

"What are these? Where do they come from?" he asked.

The bull remained where he was. Instead, the daughter eased closer. It was strange meeting her again, this time under much different circumstances. Last time he'd seen her, she'd bitten his fingers off.

That one, she said, lifting a long claw and delicately touching a milky-white stone, *is a toadstone. It comes from the head of a toad and is an antidote to most poisons.*

Hal looked at her. "It comes from the head of a—?"

A toad. And this one— She pointed to a watery-green gem shaped like a teardrop, though it was the size of a human palm. *That is exactly what it looks like, a teardrop, washed up on the beach. There was once a mermaid who fell in love with a ship's captain, and instead of luring his ship onto rocks as mermaids like to do, she warned him off. As a result, she was banished to the depths while others of her kind sank the ship. She still cries glass tears to this day, a reminder to us all of true love.*

Hal was astonished. It wasn't that he didn't believe the stories; it was that a dragon of all creatures should take such an interest in them, and speak so eloquently. These steamers were a lot more intellectually advanced than the battle-ready labyrinth dragons he was used to. He suddenly felt a little ashamed. Why had Miss Simone chosen a rather dumb dragon as part of the Shapeshifter Program? Why not these steamers? Probably because nobody knew they were smart.

The young steamer pointed to a dull-looking stone the size of an apple, with a hole through the middle. It had a rough texture, heavily pockmarked. *This is an adder stone, imbued with the power to protect the wearer against snake bites. It is the hardened saliva of many snakes massing together. They bite into the stone as it solidifies, thus infusing it with venom and giving it special properties.*

The dragon went on to explain a few more—the crystal-clear yellow lyngurium gem formed from lynx urine; the hope diamond, which brought a curse upon those who wore it; a few thunderstones rained down during storms; the vivid red flaming pearl of wisdom and spirituality; and of course the blue gemstone that had brought Hal to the steamers in the first place.

It's a boulder opal. This one came from afar, and on occasion you will see a flash of your past or future life.

"Right," Hal said, unable to keep the skepticism from his voice. Any human listening to the conversation would hear the exact same nonsensical chuffs and growls, but the family of steamers heard his doubt.

Luckily, the young female seemed amused. *The opal is valuable to me. I sometimes see myself in days gone by, and occasionally I see myself in days to come. Why do you want it?*

"I . . . I don't. Someone else does. She's demanding that I fetch it, otherwise she won't help me save my friends."

You are being coerced, the mother broke in, speaking for the first time. She nosed forward. *You have no need for the gemstone yourself. You're not here out of personal gain.*

"No! I just need to . . . to borrow it, I guess." Hal sighed, tired of the discussion. Time was slipping away, and he couldn't take no for an answer. He took a deep breath. "If you don't let me have it, then . . . then I'll have to take it from you!"

The bull grew angry again, and steam rose from his nostrils as he lowered his head and tensed up. He didn't move, though. As affronted as he might feel, Hal's threat hung in the air, and it was something the steamer had to take seriously.

The young female sighed. *You may take it, but only for a short while. I will give you a head start so you may use the gemstone to save your friends.*

Both parents hissed, wings rising and tails thrashing. *We cannot trust this plains dragon, this human interloper, to be true to his word,* the father scorned.

She bared her teeth and focused squarely on Hal. *It doesn't matter. I am attuned to the gemstone. I will come for it as I did before. I will take it back—by force if necessary.*

We all will, her mother snarled.

"Uh, okay, but I'll need time to get it back from the witch after she's told us—"

I suggest you go now and save your friends, the young steamer interrupted. *Then vacate the area before we arrive.*

Hal opened and closed his mouth, not quite sure what to say. To his surprise, the steamer used a claw to knock the blue gemstone out of the pile. It rolled onto the rock floor at Hal's feet.

Despite his uncertainty, his heart soared. "Thank you."

The family of dragons stared at him.

Your head start is slipping away, the bull growled.

"Oh! Well, the thing is . . . I mean, are you going to follow me? How much time will I have?"

The bull sighed with impatience. *My daughter has already informed you she is attuned to the gemstone. She will find it. As for how much time you will have . . . I suggest you fly fast and save your friends quickly.*

Still Hal paused, trying to visualize how it all might play out. Once he gave the gemstone to the witch, he couldn't imagine getting it back off her even with the threat of steamers on their way to reclaim it . . .

But he had to try.

* * *

He left the overhang with the gemstone safely nestled in his mouth, lodged between his bottom lip and teeth. He half expected a vision to pop into his head, something related to a past life. Nothing happened.

Outside, rays of orange daylight spread across the countryside. Abigail waited by the waterfall, sitting on some rocks looking up the hill toward him. She jumped up when he landed.

He gently spat the gemstone onto the grass for Abigail to pick up. She held it between finger and thumb with a grimace on her face, then washed it in the swirling water and held it up again.

"So this is what all the fuss is about? I mean, it's pretty, but . . ."

Hal wanted to tell her everything, but time was slipping by. Dawn had already arrived. Parents would be waking shortly, wondering how their children had fared overnight in the woods looking for the faun, probably going along to the lab to ask Miss Simone if she'd heard anything . . . It wouldn't be long before panic set in.

Plus, he didn't want to waste his head start.

He gestured for Abigail to climb aboard, and they set off into the brightening sky.

Chapter Fifteen
The Blue Gemstone

The sun felt good on Hal's right-hand side as he flew. The warm, cheerful daylight of a new dawn made everything so much better. Well, almost everything. His friends and Miss Simone were still in trouble.

He found his way to the swamp and tried to overcome a sudden feeling of sadness as he landed on the shore by the witch's home. Somehow, the daylight failed to make *this* place better. Being here depressed him.

"I hate this," he said the moment he'd reverted to human form. He fought back tears as he shuffled toward the gate.

Abigail began sobbing. "I know! Why can't we just . . . Oh, Hal!"

She flung her arms around him and cried into his shoulder, and he had to stop and hold her for a moment, wishing the ground would just crack open and swallow them both. The deepest pits of the earth far below couldn't be any worse than this miserable world in which they existed. Truly, what was the point?

"Let's get this done," he muttered, wiping his eyes.

They shuffled together through the gate, ignoring the baleful stares of the motionless gargoyles—or one of them, anyway. The other still had no head. In any case, they didn't move. Either they were only active at night, or they knew this visit was expected. It didn't matter. Nothing mattered anymore.

Once through the gate, Hal frowned and paused, and Abigail disengaged. The immense feeling of depression and sadness lifted. She looked at him, and he looked back. Then he huffed and rolled his eyes. "Next time, remind me to land a little closer, like inside the gate."

"Let's take a moment," she said, pulling him off the path to a narrow tree stump.

"What? We can't. I'm on a deadline."

"Just one minute, okay?"

"Abi—"

But she had already seated herself on the stump. The tree itself lay in neatly chopped sections across the lawn, an axe standing upright on its own with weeds wound around it. She sat and wiped her eyes again. Her face was red.

After glancing up at the sky to look for steamers, Hal squeezed onto the stump with her. "You all right?"

"I think maybe the spell on the swamp affects us a little more than most who come here. We have good reason to feel miserable."

"Yeah."

She dug in her pocket and pulled out the blue gemstone. "Okay, so what's the plan? We give this to Madame Frost, and she hopefully tells us what we need to know. But what if she doesn't? We should hold onto this as long as we can. Should we hide it?"

Hal shrugged. "I'm pretty certain she's watching us right now, wondering why we're sitting out here instead of coming in. She'll see us if we try to hide it. No, we'll hand it over and trust her to tell us how to defeat the faun and get our friends back."

They both stared at the gemstone.

"Do you remember," Abigail said, "when I had that little faerie ball? We sat down with it and stared into it, just like we're doing now."

"We saw our past lives," Hal agreed. "This thing is supposed to show us our past lives, too. Past and future, apparently."

They stared some more.

Hal nudged her. "We don't have much time."

She frowned. "What do you mean?"

"I'll explain later." He stood up. "Come on, let's get this done."

Abigail sighed and tucked the gem back into her pocket. "All right."

Hal jerked in surprise, then grabbed her wrist and stopped her. "Hey."

"What?"

He pointed. Her pocket was glowing brightly.

With a gasp, Abigail fished the gem out and almost threw it aside. A dazzling light shone from it, causing them to squint in the glare. She tossed it from hand to hand as though it were a burning ember, but then she paused and held it still in her palm, where the light pulsed gently, flashing every few seconds almost like the lamp of a lighthouse. "That's weird."

"That *is* weird," Hal said.

"What do you suppose—"

Before she could say anything more, a figure appeared. A ghostly presence had materialized on the witch's unkempt lawn. Hal and Abigail stared in amazement as the phantom gradually solidified—not all the way, but enough to reveal a boy about their age with sandy-colored hair. He hadn't seen them yet; he was facing another direction, nodding, perhaps listening to someone talking.

Then the ghost-boy saw Hal and Abigail, and his eyes widened. He stared for a long time.

"Hello?" Abigail said. "Can you . . . can you see us?"

"Yes," the ghost-boy said. "Wow. This is so weird. I, uh . . . I need your help."

Hal frowned. "You need our help? How come? We've never even met."

The boy looked away, gesturing to someone who wasn't there. The ghost was transposed on the real world so that he appeared to be standing in front of them on the grass—only he wasn't, as evidenced by his faded legs and almost invisible feet. Behind him, very faint smudges of a different reality showed through—definitely a stone wall.

"Come here," the boy was saying to someone. "You have to see this."

A girl appeared. Just as ghostlike as the boy, she had long, dark hair and stood as tall if not taller. "Huh?" she said. "Is that who I think it is?"

"Yep."

Hal and Abigail looked at one another. She still held the gemstone, which glowed brightly on her raised palm. The ghostly boy and girl had to be some kind of projection. But even when she curled her fingers around it, the light continued shining, and the phantoms remained.

"You have to tell us what you did with the potion," the ghost-boy said, looking at Abigail. He then directed his stare at Hal.

It seemed impossible for a projection to be that unerringly accurate. Just to test a theory, Hal sidestepped away from Abigail. The boy's gaze followed him.

This is happening in real-time, he thought.

"What potion?" Abigail asked.

The boy and girl looked at her. "The potion to turn everyone normal," the boy said. "We need it urgently."

When he received no answer, the girl spoke up. "You got a potion from the witch. From Madame Frost. What did you do with it? I know you used some, but there was a bit left over. Where did you put it?"

Hal had never felt so befuddled in all his life. He was fully aware of his mouth hanging open as he turned again to look at Abigail. She looked equally bewildered—but she had another expression, too, one he couldn't fathom.

"You have to help us," the ghost-girl said. "I know this is weird for you—for all of us—but we need that potion. We've asked you a million times already, but you can't remember." She broke off and frowned. "Okay, let me reword that. We've asked the *other* you—the older you. But everything's gone wrong here, so we're asking you instead, the *younger* you. Does that make sense?"

"Who *are* you guys?" Hal finally exclaimed.

The figures started to flicker and fade. They stabilized, but the images seemed weaker now, and when the boy spoke again, his voice was decidedly fainter.

"Uh, we're . . . from the future," the boy said. "The faun is back, and she's worse now. You have to tell us where you left the potion."

Both figures leaned forward, intent looks on their faces as they flickered again. The blinding light from the gemstone was rapidly dimming.

Hal opened and closed his mouth a few times and finally said, "I—I don't know. I mean, we haven't—*What* potion? Look, what are you saying? What do you know about the faun? I don't understand any of this!"

The girl's eyes widened, and she looked sideways at the boy. "They haven't made it that far yet."

The boy nodded. "Okay. Listen, Dad, this is important. When you find the potion, you must make sure to store it safely, maybe in a place that we might find easily? We've looked everywhere, but we can't . . ."

The figures faded, flickered back in, faded again. What the boy said next was unintelligible.

Abigail sat red-faced and tear-stricken as the projection, or whatever it was, died. The blue gemstone in her hand dimmed, and she opened her fingers to find it back to normal, perhaps a little clearer and bluer than before.

She gazed at Hal with glistening eyes. "He called you 'Dad.' Did you hear that?"

Hal's heart thumped. The gemstone clearly had some kind of power, though he couldn't quite put his finger on what had just happened. "Th-they said they were from the future."

Abigail said nothing, just sat with her mouth open, staring into space with a look of wonder on her face.

"Abi, they talked about the faun like . . . like it had already happened for them. They said the faun is *back*." He gasped. "The soothsayer! Do you remember what he said? He said there'd be a boy and a girl that would save us all. Do you think he meant *those* two?"

She focused her watery gaze on him. "As soon as I saw that boy," she murmured in a shaky voice, "I thought he reminded me of you, like he was a cousin or a brother or something."

"I don't have a brother. Or a cousin."

"No, but . . . one day . . ." She gripped his hand so hard he had to refrain from yelling out. "Hal, that was your *son*. Maybe . . . maybe *our* son. He'd *better* be our son, or—"

"Abi, we're running out of time," he interrupted. Shaking his head, he wrenched his hand free and checked the sky again. Still no sign of steamers, but they might not be far behind. "Let's just forget about this for now and do what we came here to do. Our friends are waiting on us."

Catching her hand, he gently pried her fingers open and took the gemstone. Then, ignoring her wide-eyed smile, he marched to the cottage.

The door was wide open. The witch stood there, hands on hips. She backed inside as he approached and swept her hand in a welcoming gesture. "Do come in. I see that you brought me my gift."

"It's not a gift," Hal muttered, stomping inside. Darcy sat in a rocking chair by the fire, and Emily knelt on the floor with an old clock in pieces in front of her. "What's happening? Where are the others?"

As if to answer his question, he heard a thump from out back, and a snarl, then a different kind of growl. He stood and listened, confused. Was that Robbie he could hear?

"What . . . ?" he asked.

Darcy rolled her eyes. "Robbie and Lauren have been scrapping since you left. It's not serious. They're kind of enjoying it, I think. She insults him, he grumbles about it, she insults him more and backhands him, and finally he breaks and punches her—"

"Robbie *punched* Lauren?" Abigail cried, her hands flying to her mouth.

"Yeah, and she laughed and punched him right back, and then they rolled about kicking and kneeing one another, and knocking things

142

over, and in the end Madame Frost sent them outside." Darcy sighed. "It goes quiet for a while, and then they start up again. I checked on them, and they're both fine, just a bit bloody with tufts of hair missing."

This day had started out weird and was getting weirder. Hal rubbed his face, then turned to the witch. But he was distracted. "And what's with Emily?" he asked, pointing at her.

Darcy shrugged. "She's happy enough. Needed something to tinker with."

"This is much worse than I thought," Abigail muttered.

Hal turned again to the witch and held out the gemstone. "All right, here it is." When she went to snatch it, he closed his fingers around the gem and dropped his arm. "*When* you've told us what we need to know."

"Which is?" she inquired, sounding bored. She perched on the edge of a table and inspected her fingernails.

"How do we stop the faun, and how do we turn our friends back to normal?"

The question hung in the air. Even Emily looked up from her tinkering, a tiny cog in one hand and a screwdriver in the other.

Madame Frost pursed her lips. "What did you see out there on the lawn? What did the gemstone show you?"

Hal shook his head. "No. We have a deal. Answer me, or I'll go outside right now and transform, and I'll burn this place to the ground." His heart was thumping hard, and he felt fire in his chest. "Trust me—I am *not* in the mood to be messed with."

Madame Frost sighed. "You can stop the faun however you like— capture her, imprison her, execute her, it doesn't matter. She's just a faun. A wily one, granted, but a faun just the same. Either bag her hands, or cut them off. That'll stop the blue mist. Problem solved."

Hal glared at her. "And . . . ?"

"The other question has a simple answer, too—when you know what it is. The spell I taught her was advanced dark magic, but she advanced it further. My spell was a simple liquid concoction, but creating liquid out of thin air is very difficult, so she turned it into a mist, which is easier to conjure and spread around. I didn't know what her plans were, but I assumed she had a few scores to settle."

"And . . . ?" Hal prompted.

"So she developed her own variation of the spell. It's an old, old transmogrification spell. You've heard tales of witches turning princes into frogs and so on. Well, this is the spell. She mobilized it, advanced it from a simple potion to an invocation. Very bright student."

Hal's heart thudded harder. *Potion?*

"There's an antidote, of course."

"That's it!" Abigail exclaimed. "That's what we need! Where?"

"It's the same potion, actually, just administered in a different way. She may or may not have developed an invocation spell for the antidote, but whether she has or not, the original potion will work. If you can find it."

"You don't have one?" Abigail said. "But you can make us one, right?"

The witch shrugged. "It would take days to find the ingredients." She smiled and revealed her blackened teeth. "However, if you would like to strike a new deal and go fetch me those ingredients along with a few more—"

"Not happening," Hal interrupted. "What does this potion look like? What's it called?"

Madame Frost sighed. "I can't recall. It has a very long name. Let me consult my book."

She ambled over to one of the bookcases, and Hal had to fight the urge to scream at her to hurry. He knew for sure that would only slow her further. He shifted from foot to foot, balling his fists and chewing his lip. Time was running out.

"Darcy," he said quietly. She was still in her chair but perched on the very front. "Please tell Robbie and Lauren to meet at the front of the cottage, outside the gate. Don't forget the lamps."

"Ohh-kay," she said slowly, frowning, obviously suspicious. "What's going on?"

"We're leaving," he said shortly. Glancing at the witch, who was reaching for a heavy tome on the top shelf, he lowered his voice further. "*Outside* the gate. You too. Hurry."

She blurred. He just had time to see her getting up and grabbing one of the lamps they'd brought. Then she disappeared. The next thing he knew, he felt a breeze as she hurried past, and then a back door opening and closing.

Abigail raised her eyebrow at him but said nothing.

Hal knelt by Emily. "Hey. We have to leave. Will you go outside, please?"

She turned her gnarly face to him and scowled. "Why you talking to me like that? I ain't stupid."

"All right, good. Please wait outside the gate. I'll be there in a minute."

She looked down at the clock. "I think I figured out why it don't work. Reckon I can put it together. I'll be right quick—"

"No, Em, you have to go outside. *Now*."

Abigail moved in. "Come on, Em, get up. There are plenty more clocks and machines to fix back home. Let's go."

Grumbling, Emily allowed Abigail to guide her to the front door.

The witch glanced around. "Going so soon?" Putting the book down, she ignored Abigail and Emily as they slipped out but planted herself in front of the door to face Hal. "Trying to sneak out without paying your dues?"

Hal shook his head. "Not at all." He fingered the gemstone. "Listen, I need to return this to—"

She immediately raised a hand and pinched her fingers and thumb together. The effect it had on Hal terrified him: a sudden pressure on his throat, blocking his windpipe. He clutched at his neck, trying to dislodge the invisible iron grip.

He threw the gemstone in a panic, and she snatched it out of the air. Only then did she release her magical grip on his throat, and he gasped and choked.

She stared at the bright-blue boulder opal. "It's said these gems can show you the future."

"Seen it," Hal croaked. He gagged and coughed, then licked his lips. "I've also seen *your* future. It won't go well for you if you keep that thing."

She laughed and moved across to the table, where she picked up a magnifying glass and peered through it. "Wonderful." She glanced sideways at him. "How did you activate it?"

"I didn't. It activated itself. Look, I'm going now."

"Do as you please. Our deal is done."

As Hal headed for the door, he slowed and felt a pang of guilt. He pulled the door wide open and stared out. Daylight greeted him. His friends were already clustered outside the gate, misery painted across their faces. The two gargoyles stared impassively down at them even though one had no head. They looked just as sad.

Hal turned back. "New deal. You put the gemstone down, come with us now, and help. In return, you can work with Miss Simone and learn about the Shapeshifter Program."

Madame Frost placed the gem on the table and the magnifying glass beside it. "My, my. And what gives you the right to speak on Lady Simone's behalf? She's an eminent scientist and practically in charge of the village."

"She would work with you," Hal said, his hands suddenly feeling very sweaty. "Madame Frost, please, put the gemstone down and come outside. Or throw the stone out and stay inside."

She narrowed her eyes. "I smell a rat."

"I smell steamer dragons," Hal cried in desperation. He looked out the door. Sure enough, three winged creatures approached from the sky, flying low over the trees. They would arrive in half a minute at most. "Seriously—I can stop this, but only if you hand that gemstone back right now."

The witch dashed across the room toward him. He barreled out onto the pathway and kept moving as she paused on the threshold and searched the sky. With a cry of rage and fear, she turned and slammed the door—taking the gemstone with her.

"No!" Hal yelled. With a sigh of frustration and fear, he bolted for the gate. Once outside with his friends, he halted and pointed upward. "Dragons on their way. Time for us to go."

Darcy let out a gasp. Robbie, still in full ogre form, moaned and covered his head with his hands. Lauren ran for the swamp, splashing in without pause and beginning to swim arm over arm. Emily grunted something and waddled after her.

Abigail looked at Hal. "Are we safe?"

"Maybe," Hal said, feeling miserable. "They're here for the gemstone."

"Wait—was this *your* idea?" Tears welled up in the corner of Abigail's eyes.

Hal shook his head, lost for words.

He and Abigail backed away as the three dragons swept in with a chorus of screeches and several huffs of steam. They landed almost simultaneously on the cottage roof, severely damaging it; the bull crashed right through, and his wings stuck up through the hole while he stood there roaring.

The witch screamed at them from within, a stream of gibberish that Hal assumed was some kind of spell. Moments later, a sonic blast shattered all the windows and numerous other glass objects inside the cottage. All three dragons recoiled from the noise, and the two on the roof nearly slid off. But the spell only served to anger them further, and they stomped about the place, smashing and ripping.

Again the witch screamed and yelled, and the steamers roared back at her. All three had gained access by now, the youngest squirming her way through the large front window, and the mother ramming a hole directly through the wall. Another spell was cast, this one sending out a ripple of energy that battered the dragons and caused them to recoil and shake their heads—but they paused only for a moment before resuming their rampage.

"They really want that gemstone back," Abigail said with a sniffle beside him.

Hal fought to keep from choking up as he answered. "The daughter's kind of attuned to it. That's how she tracked it to little Sarah in the classroom, and that's how she found her way here so easily. They gave me a head start." He shook with emotion, his heart aching for Sarah and the loss of her prize, then the steamer dragon for the loss of hers, and all of them for the generally miserable situation they found themselves in.

Thoroughly depressed, he and Abigail watched the carnage for a little longer, aware that Robbie stood to one side with his hands still covering his head. Lauren and Emily continued swimming. At least their tears were lost in the lake.

"What did you do, Hal?" Darcy whispered from behind. "I feel awful about this."

He jumped. She was still invisible. *Probably wise.*

"We should go," Hal said, swallowing. "We need to find a potion."

"I guess we go to the faun's cavern and hunt around," Abigail muttered. "Plenty of potions there. But we have no idea what it looks like or what it's called." She broke down and sobbed openly. "This has been a colossal waste of time."

Hal forced a smile, his bottom lip wobbling. "Well, we now know there's a cure. We just need to find it."

He transformed and lay flat so Darcy and Abigail could climb aboard. It took the dimwitted ogre a moment to catch on, and when he did, the girls had to yell at him to shift back to human form before putting all his ample weight on Hal's back.

Hal waded into the water and went after the other two girls. Behind him, the thunderous sounds of three dragons ripping a house to shreds should have been satisfying and well-deserved for such a mean-spirited, selfish witch. Instead, he felt empty.

It's the swamp, he told himself over and over as first Emily and then Lauren climbed aboard. *None of us are thinking straight. We're just wallowing in self-pity.*

He realized as he shot straight upward out of the swamp and into the sky that Lauren could have switched to her harpy form instead of swimming in the murky swamp. Had she forgotten? It seemed that way. What with her fighting Robbie, and Emily tinkering with broken clocks, the faun's plan to *evolve* people was really happening. He dreaded what he'd find back home.

But first—the potion.

Chapter Sixteen
Altered States

Hal landed as close as he could to the faun's lair—in the clearing by the rocky stream. They had good daylight by the time his passengers disembarked. Then again, that meant Emily, in her goblin form, stuck out even more like a sore thumb. Lauren, too, once she'd landed and switched from harpy to troll. It just seemed weird having these two tagging along, like rookie newbies who'd recently joined their shapeshifting gang.

Since Robbie was human again, the urge to scrap with the troll had faded. Lauren showed him no interest at all, and though he cast glances her way every so often, it was hard to make out what he was thinking.

"You think those two are all right?" Hal whispered to Abigail as they all traipsed once more through the woods.

"Obviously Robbie's worried, but Lauren seems to have accepted who she is now."

Darcy was right behind and overheard. "Yeah, and that's a problem. Her and Emily are the same. They're not freaking out anymore, and they're acting less and less like the people we know."

Abigail nodded. "They're turning."

Hal glanced back past Darcy and Robbie. The troll and goblin trailed well behind, yards apart, keeping to themselves as though strangers on a guided tour of the area.

Noises to their left caused everyone to pause and glance that way. Standing perfectly still, they listened and squinted. The noise came again, a hurried rustling sound.

Then it appeared, half-hidden among the bushes—a small, upright figure with two arms and legs. It was too small for a human, too large for a faerie, too flesh-and-blood to be a gargoyle, and not nearly blue enough to pass as an elf. Hal stared, pretty sure he'd come across such a creature in a book. The boy, or perhaps a tiny man, stood no more than three feet tall, had extremely long, pointed ears and a thin, almost snake-like tail that stuck up behind.

"Hey," Abigail called.

But the creature darted away.

After a brief silence, Hal said, "What was that?"

Abigail shrugged. "A pixie, I think."

Darcy nodded. "Definitely a pixie. But so what? Can we get on with this, please?"

Hal found the cave and plunged into the darkness. The campfire had died out. It was hard to believe they'd been sleeping here just hours ago listening to whispers in the night. A lot had happened since then.

"I hate tunnels," Hal muttered as he held up a lamp and led the way into the narrow passage in the corner.

He picked his way deeper into the darkness, glad he had some real light this time. He headed down the rough steps to the cavern. There, the glow worms were as bright as ever. He couldn't help marveling at the peace and tranquility of the place. His friends emerged from the tunnel behind him and spread out, equally silent and awestruck.

"Well," Abigail said with a sigh, "we can't stand here gawking all day. Let's find the potion."

They headed for the table first and started poking around. Hal had expected to find a plethora of bottles clearly labeled with spell names and descriptions. In fact, he'd pinned his hopes on something like: *Transmogrification Spell. To reverse the effects, add five drops to a glass of water and drink. Normality will be restored instantly.*

No such luck. It took about five seconds to realize there were no spells here.

"Maybe she stashed them in drawers," Darcy said, hurrying over to the wooden chest. She yanked drawers open and rummaged around, pulling out all manner of furs and animal skins. But no potions.

The faun kept a lot of stuff, mainly trinkets and small tools, even a number of weighty books written in an old but mostly recognizable dialect. Hal imagined a group of ancient witches and wizards scrawling with their ink-dipped quills and cackling as they recorded their evil spells. He wondered how the faun managed to read such books when she couldn't even speak the language.

That gave him pause. For that matter, how had the witch taught her for five years? Had they used the conch shell all that time? It didn't seem likely. Either the witch had cast a long-lasting translation spell, or one of them had learned a new language.

"There's nothing here," Abigail said at last.

They all stood and looked at one another. Emily seemed a little more engaged right now, but Lauren seemed bored, maybe thinking of all the things she could be doing instead, like loafing around in the woods, or building bridges for travelers and then charging a fortune to cross, or whatever else trolls did.

"So we're screwed," Robbie muttered. "We went to see the witch for nothing. All that time wasted. We have no potion and no way to get our friends back." He looked pointedly at Lauren as he said this.

Abigail frowned. "Hal, what we saw outside the witch's house . . . Do you remember what the boy and girl said? They talked like we *had* found the potion—just not *yet*."

"What?" Darcy said. "What are you talking about? What happened outside the witch's house?"

"Later, Darcy." Abigail stared at Hal. "There has to be one somewhere."

Hal opened his mouth to argue that the weird vision or projection or whatever it was made very little sense—but then a memory clicked into place, and he sucked in a breath. "Wait," he said.

Everyone waited.

"Well?" Robbie demanded. "I can hear your brain clanking away. What gives?"

Hal began shaking with excitement. "There *is* a potion. I'd forgotten all about it. I came across it the first time we were hunting the faun. It was just sitting there out in the woods, jammed into a log."

Abigail gripped his arms. "Can you find it again?"

He smiled . . . then frowned. "Maybe. Sure, I think."

After that, the six of them scrambled to get back outside. Hal pretended to have some clue where to start looking. This was literally the only hope they had right now. He transformed and waited for everyone to climb aboard, and then he began stomping through the trees, marching in what he thought *might* be the right direction.

His nostrils picked up plenty of aromas, but he sought a distinctive chemical smell, something completely foreign to the woods. He remembered that much. It took a while to chance across the faintest hint of such a scent, and when he did, he paused and clung to it, turning his head carefully to pinpoint the direction.

He kept forgetting his friends were on his back and ducked under a few too many low-hanging branches that swept them off. They opted to walk after the third time, and they stayed well back in case he swung his tail at them.

At last, the weird odor strengthened. He crashed through a thicket of brambles, shoved a sapling aside so hard it snapped, and clambered over a mass of dead branches where a tree had fallen. The potion was still there, jammed into the bark near the base.

He gave a throaty roar to indicate he'd found it. Abigail and the others came running, and he could barely contain his jubilance as she plucked it loose and stashed it carefully in her pocket.

She looked up at him with a smile. "Good work, Hal. Now take us home."

Of course, that meant tramping through the woods once more until he found a clearing. He already hated caves and tunnels with a passion. Now he added a new mantra: *I hate the woods.*

* * *

They arrived in Carter right around the time school would be starting on a normal day.

Today was anything but normal, and class was far from their minds. After reverting to human form, Hal and the others dashed inside the science laboratory building past the tired-looking night watchmen and goblin sentries. One tried to stop them, asking "Did you—" . . . but that was as far as he got, because the shapeshifters ran straight past.

The group skidded to a halt in the corridor leading to Observation 4. Six heavily armed goblins stood outside the room along with three white-coated scientists and a very large group of parents.

"Uh-oh," Hal muttered.

The doctors were doing their best to placate the parents. One of the white-coats was Dr. Kessler, a short, curly-headed woman with round spectacles on her nose. "It's too dangerous, Mrs. Bridges. Please trust me."

"You said the faun is secured!"

"The faun is trapped in the cell, yes, but she still might release some of her mist. Just let the goblins secure her properly, and then we'll see what's what."

"This is ridiculous!" a man exclaimed—Dewey's dad, by the sound of his deep Welsh accent.

But just then, someone spotted Hal and the others. He and his friends were suddenly in the spotlight as a sea of faces turned their way and shouts rang out.

"Hal! You're all right!"

"Oh, Abi!"

"Darcy!"

"There's my boy!" Mrs. Strickland finished up with a cry of relief.

The greeting for Lauren and Emily wasn't quite the same, though. A silence fell, and Mrs. Hunter eased closer. Hal would have given anything to be in class with her right now instead of being here for *this*. He'd hoped to avoid this situation, to get back with a cure and put everyone right before all the parents showed up and started freaking out.

"I don't understand," Mrs. Hunter said. "Where's . . . is that . . . is that you, Lauren?"

She must have recognized Lauren's smart clothes. Though the material was largely the same for them all, each wore something slightly different, with variations in color and pattern.

For the moment, Lauren acted perfectly human and threw herself at her mom and dad as they came forward from the crowd. They hugged and cried while others stifled exclamations of horror and grief.

Then Mr. and Mrs. Stanton approached, and Hal dreaded what they'd think of their Emily.

To his surprise, their reaction was exactly the same as the Hunters', and they swept Emily into their arms and held her tight as she poured out her tears.

Hal realized this was what he'd been afraid of. Somehow, the parents finding out what had happened and being so emotional about it kind of cemented the problem, made it a very serious reality. Before now, there had been a desperate sense of *let's-fix-this-before-it's-real*. But that time had passed. Now everyone knew.

"You're still my baby girl," Mr. Stanton said, his voice cracking as he pulled Emily tight.

As the crowd grew louder, and the troll and goblin were smothered by hugging arms, Dr. Kessler fought to approach Hal, Abigail, Robbie, and Darcy. But their own parents came surging forward, their relief plain to see as they crowded around and badgered them with questions. Hal felt ready to leap up through the ceiling and take to the skies to escape the din.

"Enough!" Dr. Kessler yelled.

Her piercing voice cut through the babble and caused a lot of heads to turn her way.

"If you're all *quite finished*," she said sternly, her face red with frustration. "I know you're all very concerned, but nothing is going to get done until we have some order here. And that means you all need to let me get back to work."

She was greeted with a lot of mumbles and grumbles, some of them angry, others in apology for the disruption. With over twenty adults plus a group of goblins and half a dozen shapeshifters, the packed corridor was growing hot, and beads of sweat stood out on Dr. Kessler's face.

"Now," she said a little more calmly as an orderly hush fell, "all those who don't absolutely need to be here, please vacate this corridor. Go home if you can. The rest of you—those whose children need attention—may stay. But you have to give me some space."

The next five minutes gave way to raised voices again as Robbie's and Darcy's parents tried to insist they come home with them out of harm's way. Naturally, Robbie kicked up a stink and refused, and Darcy practically stamped her foot in her insistence to stay.

Hal's mom opened her mouth to say something, but he must have had a certain look on his face, because she clammed up. His dad sighed and put his arm around her. "Come on. He's here to do a job. This is what shapeshifters do." He raised his voice a little. "This is what we signed up for all those years ago."

Other parents heard him, and they looked troubled. But his words had the desired effect, and the parent-child struggle fizzled out. It was true, after all. The only reason any of their parents were here in New Earth, or *Elsewhere*, was because of the deal they'd struck with Miss Simone many years before, a deal that had saved them from the virus that swept across the world. It was why they'd ended up on a secluded foggy island, safe and alive, raising children they wouldn't have had otherwise. The terms of the deal were simply to let the shapeshifters be shapeshifters and allow them to do their job—even if that meant being in harm's way.

Abigail helped things along by producing the potion and giving it to Dr. Kessler. "It's a cure," she said. "We just have to figure out how to use it."

"Which might take some time," Dr. Kessler said firmly to the crowd. "So leave me to get on with it."

In the end, *all* the parents filed out of the corridor. Some went home with a degree of relief, and others went to wait in the much larger conference hall for further news of the cure. Emily and Lauren stayed. They were, after all, likely to be the first test subjects.

"Prepare one of the lab rooms," Dr. Kessler said to the other two white-coated scientists, both women. She handed one of them the potion. "Keep this very, very safe. It's all we have." They headed off, further reducing the number of people in the corridor.

The potion, Hal thought as the invaluable cure left his sight.

"Peace," one of the goblin sentries muttered. The other five chortled and agreed.

Dr. Kessler clapped her hands. "All right. Now, let's get our heads together and figure out what that potion is all about. We can try to identify what's in it, or we can—"

"What about our friends?" Hal cut in. "Are they still . . . dust?"

The doctor shook her head. "I've heard voices. That means one or more have been reintegrated." She took off her glasses for a moment, rubbed the bridge of her nose, then put them back on. "All I know of this strange blue mist and its effects is what Simone explained yesterday and what the night watchmen told me when I was woken at 4 AM and rushed here. I think I have it all straight, but you've seen it with your own eyes, so I'll be guided by what you tell me."

"We want to see our friends," Hal said.

"Yeah," Robbie agreed.

The doctor glanced at the heavily guarded door to Observation 4. "Yes. I haven't yet opened the door. It seems too risky even to take a peek. The room might be filled with the mist. If it spills into the corridor . . . Everyone in there is quarantined for the moment."

"So the faun is still locked in her cell," Darcy said, "and the others are in the viewing room. What about Miss Simone? Have you spoken to her?"

"No. I have to assume she's still *dust*, as you said. I've heard two distinct voices, though they haven't said much at all. One is a deep voice, the other soft and high-pitched."

Hal tried to picture the scene inside the room. Fenton, Thomas, Dewey, and Miss Simone. Two of them had been brought back. He had to assume the deep voice was one of the boys, though that might not necessarily be true.

"I think there's only one thing to do at the moment," Dr. Kessler said. "I'll clear the corridor and send the goblins in. The mist won't harm them, if there's any. They can block the hatch in the door so the faun can't send any more mist through. Once it's clear in there, we can go in and see what's what."

It was a pretty straightforward plan. She spoke to the goblins, and they nodded, one saying, "'Bout time."

"Let's move away from the door, children," Dr. Kessler said, and she ushered them twenty feet down the corridor.

Abigail clung to Hal's arm. Surprisingly, Lauren also clung to Robbie's. It seemed the reunion with emotional parents had shaken the troll loose for the moment. Emily, too, was engaged and alert, one of the gang. The six of them, along with Dr. Kessler, waited patiently while the goblins filed into Observation 4.

At first, all was quiet. Then came some yelling—the faun kicking up a fuss about something. After that, the goblins filed back out and slammed the door.

Dr. Kessler hurried to talk to them. Hal and his friends were hot on her trail.

"Everything all right?" she asked.

"We didn't touch her," a goblin grunted. "Just shut the hatch and bent the pin so the latch won't slide."

"So there's no way for the blue mist to get out? Good. And the room is clear?"

"Yes, ma'am. Just the nasty stink of gnome."

Hal shot Abigail a glance. One of their friends was a *gnome*? He supposed there could be worse things.

Dr. Kessler approached the door. "All right, then. Let's see what we have in here."

She went inside.

Hal followed her in, his friends crowding behind.

The room did seem to have an unpleasant odor to it, rather like smelly feet. Hal noted the table and empty chairs, and the glass-fronted darkened cell with the closed hatch. He found the owner of the smelly feet right away—a short, skinny boy no taller than Hal's chest, with an enormous head and jutting ears. He stood by the opposite wall, twisted around like he'd just turned to face them. As young as his face looked, his deepset eyes had wrinkles at the corners, and the creature's light-brown hair was thick and untidy. He wore smart clothes, which had shrunk to fit.

Hal had come across a gnome on the beach of Brodon. That one had been a woman, but she'd had an equally large head.

The other figure in the room moved into view from the corner—an elf. The petite, blue-skinned boy had white hair and wore snug-fitting smart clothes.

Glad they got dressed, Hal thought. Scanning the room, he found all kinds of garments scattered around, including Miss Simone's dress and cape. One set of boys' clothes remained.

Darcy approached the gnome and said, "How are you doing, Fenton?"

Hal wasn't sure how she knew it was him. Female intuition? Or maybe she just recognized the slight variations in the clothing.

The gnome shrugged, then turned to the wall and banged his head on it.

Darcy ran to him. "Hey, stop that! What are you doing?"

Fenton did it again before turning to her. He had no sign of injury to his forehead. "What's up with you?" he grumbled in a remarkably deep voice.

"I—I just—" Darcy scratched her head. "Please don't bang your head like that. Things will work out okay."

The gnome raised a bushy eyebrow at her. "Things are just fine. Or they will be when I get out of here. Can I go now?"

Hal tore his gaze from Fenton and glanced at Abigail. She shrugged at him. Over in the corner, the elf had his eyes on the door. "Are we free?" he said.

His voice was, as Dr. Kessler had described, soft and high-pitched. He had a snub nose and very long, pointed ears. With pale-blue skin and faint wisps of blue in his short, white hair, he cut a curiously striking figure.

"Not yet," Dr. Kessler said, sidestepping to block his way. She nodded at the goblins outside, and they pulled the door shut. "Don't run out on us yet. We need to talk. And you are . . . ?"

"That's Dewey," Abigail said. She looked around, then ducked to peer under the table and chairs that stood in front of the glass wall. "I guess Thomas and Miss Simone are still missing."

They heard a chortle from inside the glass-fronted cell. The faun had pressed herself to the glass. "*Pheil da um*," she called, her voice muffled.

"Shut up," Abigail growled. She reached for Dewey. "Hey, are you okay?"

Dewey backed up, his deep-blue eyes widening.

Abigail paused. "I'm not going to hurt you. Do you . . . do you know who we are?"

The elf glanced from her to the others. "I don't remember. But I'm sure my family will be missing me. Please let me go."

"Dewey, *we're* your family," Darcy said, moving away from Fenton and joining Abigail. "Are you saying you don't remember us?"

"I'm ready to go home now," the elf said quietly.

Hal swallowed. "And where's your home?"

Dewey looked at him, then toward the door with a slight frown. "The mountains."

Robbie sidled closer to Hal. "Is he remembering Whisper Mountain? Those are the only elves we've visited. Maybe he's confused."

"*Obviously* he's confused," Darcy snapped. She turned back to Fenton. "What about you? Where's your home?"

Fenton shrugged. "Wherever." He promptly banged his head on the wall again.

Hal hurried toward him. "Stop doing that! Why do you keep doing that?"

The gnome looked alarmed at the sight of Hal rushing toward him. He dropped into a defensive posture, fingers curled into claws.

Now that he thought about it, Hal realized the gnome on Brodon's beach had kept banging her head, too. It was apparently something gnomes did, though he had no idea why. "Okay," he said softly. "Bang your head if you want to. Just tell me—what's your name? Do you remember?"

Fenton looked thoughtful. He made a "Fffff" sound like he kind of remembered, but then he trailed off and left it hanging. He shrugged. "Whatever."

"Wherever, whatever," Darcy said. "That's pretty vague."

"They have amnesia," Dr. Kessler said, breaking into the conversation.

"But Emily and Lauren don't," Hal protested. He turned to them both. They stood there looking for all the world like part of the gang, but he had a feeling Lauren was starting to lose her grip again. He could tell by the way her gaze shifted. She was growing bored.

The faun laughed again. "*Pheil da um*," she said again.

"We don't understand what you're saying," Hal said, feeling anger building up. "You broke the conch shell. So just shut up."

The faun pressed herself to the glass so she was visible. "Who needs a conch shell?" she said, sounding smug.

Everybody in the room did a double-take. "But—" Robbie started. "You—"

She smiled through the glass at them.

Chapter Seventeen
Identity Crisis

Hal studied the faun, trying to suppress the feeling he'd been duped. Robbie, Abigail, and Darcy stood alongside, mouths open. Dr. Kessler huffed with annoyance.

"How can you speak our language without the conch shell?" Robbie demanded of the faun.

River continued smiling, her horns pressed to the glass. "The conch shell did nothing. But it was very pretty, was it not?"

Its fragments lay scattered across the floor.

Emily gave a typical goblin snort, and Lauren growled.

"So why . . . ?" Robbie said, spreading his hands. "Why did you pretend . . . ?"

Hal sighed. He'd already suspected she might have learned to speak their language. How else could she spend five years working with a witch? And, although she'd spoken into the conch the whole time, nobody else had, yet she'd understood perfectly.

The faun wagged a finger at them. "Feigning ignorance of another's language is a very good way to listen in on secret conversations. Madame Frost always talked to herself. I learned a lot, far more than she intended."

Abigail snorted. "And what did you learn from us, River?"

River tilted her head to one side and considered. "Your silly plan to trap me on the riverbank, for example."

"You were *supposed* to hear that."

"Only I heard everything else, too. I heard the plan *behind* the plan."

Fenton let out a grunt. When Hal glanced around, he saw the gnome rubbing his head where he'd apparently bumped it a little too hard on the wall. Meanwhile, Dewey the elf fidgeted from side to side, clearly anxious to leave.

Hal stepped up to the glass and glared through it. "We have your potion. The potion you left in the forest, jammed into a fallen tree. Did you know *that*?"

He watched her closely. Her smile faltered just a little bit, and her brow creased.

"That is a worthless spell," she said. "It is why I discarded it."

Hal shook his head. "I don't think so. I think you needed it at first, before coming up with a mist version of the spell. I'll bet you went out to try the mist on a couple of travelers but took the potion along just in case, and you put it down on that log . . . and when the mist worked so well, you just left the potion behind. Right?"

Her smile slipped a little further. "I do not need the potion now."

"I know *you* don't. But we do. We need it to turn our friends back."

River slapped the glass, turned away, and started pacing her cell in the dim light. She returned to the glass almost immediately. "Possessing the potion is pointless if you do not know how to use it."

Hal scowled at her. "That's why you're going to show us."

The faun's smile returned in full force. "No. I will not show you. I will escape from this prison very soon, and then I will continue to evolve humans. My tests have been successful. And I have concluded that an amnesia spell is essential."

"What?" Hal said.

Abigail let out a huff of annoyance. "Escape? How can you even—? Look, you're not going anywhere. You're *done*."

River nodded toward Dewey the elf. "See how he has forgotten his identity? I used an amnesia spell, as I usually do. It helps the subject to move forward, to accept a new role in life instead of clinging to a lost humanity. But I omitted the amnesia spell with the goblin and troll because you had me trapped, and I needed them to know who they were, who *you* were, to prove they were indeed your friends and not strangers. It worked, yes? But I will never omit the amnesia spell again. It is essential. Look at the elf and gnome. They have forgotten their identities, so they are more willing to accept new lives." Her eyes positively gleamed in triumph. "They no longer see themselves as human. Do you understand?"

"Shut up!" Darcy suddenly yelled, rushing forward to pound on the glass. The faun barely flinched. "You're crazy! Do you really think you're going to evolve the entire human race? Are you nuts? All you've done is mess with a few people we care about—and you're going to put things right, or—or—"

River just ignored her. She started pacing. "I have to devise a way to spread my magic across a greater area. That will take some time."

Darcy gave the glass one last slap. "Just stop this! What right do you have to *change* people into something they're not? Look, I know some bad people hurt your family, but it wasn't us. The gang who came after your parents and your brothers . . . yes, they should be punished! But the rest of the world is innocent."

The faun paused. She turned and approached the glass, her expression one of amazement. "*Innocent*? I know things about your world, this place you call Old Earth. The centaurs were wrong to release a deadly virus there, because all life should be cherished, not destroyed—but humans are causing unspeakable damage to the planet, and they must be stopped."

Dr. Kessler spoke quietly to the faun. "I understand you're an environmentalist. You don't like that the people of Old Earth have cut down so many rainforests and hunted endangered species, and—"

"And farming," the faun said. Everyone fell silent. "Yes, farming is a cause, too—not grain and crops, but meat and dairy. Before the virus, did you know that three quarters of all land mammals in Old Earth were humans and livestock?"

"Huh?" Hal blurted.

"Think about that. *Three quarters.* Cows, pigs, and humans. Humans shared the planet with their food. The remaining quarter was *all other mammals* on land."

Dr. Kessler shook her head. "Come, now . . ."

"That is not the way anymore, thanks to the centaurs' virus," the faun said, "but it will be that way again, because humans will not change their ways."

"Are you saying it's wrong to eat meat?" Darcy said incredulously. "Are you saying we should all be vegetarians?"

"It is fine to kill for meat. It is the natural order of things. It is not so natural to raise animals whose purpose in life is to be milked and slaughtered. What kind of existence is that? And now humans are *here*, in this world." She leaned forward and scowled, causing Darcy and Dr. Kessler to back up. "I had good reason to seek vengeance for the loss of my family, yet I chose a higher path, one that would avoid bloodshed and instead convert human life to something better. All souls are precious. Life is life. But now that our beautiful land has been opened up to the humans of Old Earth, I fear what it will become. I dread how much they will take for themselves, and what they will destroy." She slammed her fist on the glass. "*That* is why I must evolve the human race. It is the only way New Earth will survive."

"Because of cows and pigs," Abigail murmured.

"Do not mock me," River snarled. She tapped the side of her head. "I learned your language. I listened, I read, I researched. I visited Old Earth months ago and did not like what I saw. It is my duty to protect my home from becoming the same. I will not stop until humans are *gone*." She gave a sigh. "I will leave now."

As Hal and his friends watched in amazement, the faun began whispering under her breath.

"What's she doing?" he asked, suddenly nervous.

"I don't like this," Dr. Kessler murmured. "I think everyone should leave. *Now*, please. Everybody out."

Dewey didn't need convincing. He was already headed that way. The rest made a halfhearted effort to move toward the door, but curiosity got the better of them, and they paused to watch the faun. She couldn't escape with a spell, could she? And she couldn't turn anyone to dust if her blue mist was trapped in the cell with her.

There was no blue mist, though. She stood with her arms at her side, deeply focused. The incantation sounded familiar . . .

A blast of wind swept through the room. Whispers filled the air—two distinct voices. Dust particles appeared out of nowhere and started to swirl around like a swarm of tiny gnats.

"Oh no," Abigail muttered. "It's Thomas and Miss Simone."

Dr. Kessler began hustling them all from the room. "What's going on?" she demanded. "Come on, let's go."

"She's doing it again!" Darcy cried.

Dr. Kessler had the door open. Dewey had already left. The rest of them crowded that way. Even Fenton stopped banging his head and hurried to join them.

Two separate whirlwinds of dust formed and solidified. They both started out in human form, one taller than the other, almost recognizable as Miss Simone and Thomas. But then they changed, almost like a new set of reassembly instructions had just been issued.

The smaller of the fuzzy figures suddenly expanded, quickly filling the room and changing shape, becoming four-legged and too large to fit under the ceiling. The fuzziness sharpened and clarified, revealing golden fur and feathers, huge claws, and massive wings. The table and all the chairs in the room were shoved violently to one side as the giant swung around. The glass wall fronting the faun's cell shattered when a huge body pressed up against it, the steel door bending inward and flying off its hinges. The walls cracked. And then, in a frenzy, the monster smashed its way out through the ceiling with a terrible screeching roar, its wings bringing down splintered wood beams, lath and plaster, and a deluge of dust and debris.

Coughing and yelling, Hal and his friends scrambled out of the room. The goblins loitering outside the door had already rushed to safety, because whatever had materialized in Observation 4 had smashed against the wall and cracked it, sending more debris into the corridor. Dr. Kessler staggered around, trying to see through the dust.

"Is everyone here?" she shouted.

It took half a minute to establish that everyone was indeed present—all except Dewey. "I saw him take off," Abigail gasped. "He was first out."

"We're all here apart from him," Hal confirmed, seeing Darcy leaning against a wall, Robbie and the troll clinging to each other, Emily seeking the comfort of other goblins, and the large-headed gnome pushing past a crowd of startled doctors who had emerged from adjacent rooms.

"Who *was* that in there? Miss Simone?" Robbie squawked.

"Nope," Abigail groaned. "It was Thomas. Now he's a manticore *and* a griffin."

"So what happened to Miss Simone?" Darcy said. "I hope she wasn't hurt in all that mess!"

Hal was the first to reach the doorway to Observation 4. He rushed through and scoured the carnage—upended chairs, huge chunks of timber and plaster, glass scattered across the floor, dust everywhere, and a gaping hole in the ceiling letting in a fine drizzle of morning rain.

The faun was gone. Thomas was gone. And it appeared Miss Simone was gone, too.

Others crowded in behind him, jostling for a look. "Where is she?" Abigail said.

At that moment, a low hiss sounded from the rubble. They all squinted through the dust cloud. "What *is* that . . . ?" Darcy whispered.

Dr. Kessler suddenly yelled, making them all jump. "Don't look! DON'T LOOK! Get outside NOW!"

A chorus of exclamations filled the air.

"What?"

"Why?"

"I don't see—Oh!"

Hal saw it at the same time, and he hurriedly looked away and turned to race from the room with everyone else. Nobody could get into the corridor fast enough. The sight of a small, six-legged, red-and-yellow lizard filled him with horror. The infamous basilisk was extremely rare and perhaps the deadliest creature in the world.

"Don't look at it!" Dr. Kessler yelled over and over. "Outside now! Shut the door!"

"A *basilisk?*" Abigail exclaimed, wide-eyed. "I didn't see it, but—really?"

"We've all seen pictures," Hal said shakily. "This one's red with yellow stripes and stubby wings, and sometimes they're black with no wings, but it's definitely a basilisk—about the size of my forearm, with six legs, just standing there in the dust." He shuddered. "It was looking right at us, but the dust—I think the dust saved us. If it had focused on us, we'd be dead right now."

Having a resident gorgon shapeshifter named Molly was dangerous enough. She kept a veil on her face at all times, because anyone who looked into her eyes instantly turned to stone. The basilisk was similar except it also spat a terrible venom.

Dr. Kessler barked orders up and down the corridor at startled goblins. "Gloves! Goggles! Hurry! The thing has wings, and it might fly out the hole in the roof! We need it bagged right now!—but *carefully*. That's Simone in there."

"She won't hurt us, then," a goblin commented.

"She will if she's confused about her identity," Dr. Kessler retorted.

A few goblins hurried away, but others crowded closer, armor clanking. If they feared the deadly creature, they didn't show it.

In all the chaos, nobody had thought too much about the faun getting away. Everyone knew it, but her escape plan and distraction had worked perfectly. A large enough monster to demolish the room and the cell's glass wall, giving her the chance to leap out through the ceiling—and a tiny creature guaranteed to have everyone scrambling.

Hal let out a cry of frustration. He and his friends had the transmogrification potion, but nobody knew how to make it work. Or, more specifically, how to make it work *in reverse*.

"We have to go after her," he said to Abigail. "I'm going."

"Me too."

He grabbed her hand and dragged her along the crowded corridor. Robbie opened his mouth as they passed, but Hal simply told him, "We're going after her," and didn't stop long enough to give him the option of coming along. There was no time. She couldn't get away yet again.

His mind whirled. What if he caught up to the faun and had no potion? He'd have to drag her back here before he could make her show him how to use it. No, he needed the potion back, and he needed it *now*.

Seeing a familiar face ahead of them, Hal stopped and said, "Do you have the potion?"

The aged doctor, who had shoulder-length fair hair and a thin face, blinked at him. "What? Yes, I still have it." She absently tapped her coat pocket. "I've just set up some equipment to—"

"I need it," he said, holding out his hand. "Hurry, please—the faun's getting away."

She frowned. "But why would you—"

Abigail snaked out a hand and reached into the woman's coat pocket.

The doctor gasped and slapped her hand away. "Stop that! This potion is too valuable to—"

"We know," Abigail said, and she took off running down the corridor with the woman shouting after her.

Hal raced to catch up. "Did you get it?"

She said nothing but grinned while slipping the bottle of potion into her own pocket as she ran.

"That was some sneaky stuff," he told her. He'd actually had in mind to get a small sampling of it rather than the whole thing, but the faun already had a massive head start; finding her again would be difficult enough without waiting around while the doctor poured a few drops into another bottle.

They burst out of the main doors. Behind them, Hal heard the voices of parents as they rushed to investigate all the noise.

He transformed, and Abigail clambered on board. He was airborne seconds later.

In a way, he was glad to be back in the peace and quiet of the sky rather than the hustle and bustle of the lab building. Too many people and too much noise—not to mention a deadly basilisk on the loose. He was certain the goblins would take care of the problem as long as it didn't fly away, if indeed it could fly. He wasn't sure those tiny wings were meant for that purpose. They looked almost decorative. A basilisk was bad enough, but a *flying* one . . . ?

But it's Miss Simone! he reminded himself. *Even with an amnesia spell, she can't have forgotten everything and everyone. Can she?*

He shuddered.

When it came to hunting the faun from above, he had absolutely no idea where to start. She could literally be anywhere. She could be running amok in the streets of Carter for all he knew, spraying her blue mist at people. But she'd mentioned trying to find a way to spread it more efficiently, so maybe right now she was content with making her escape.

In which case . . .

It made sense for her to head straight for the woods. Hal flew west, scouring the trees, hoping to spot a faun leaping along. No such luck, though. The chances of him finding her from above were remote at best. He had to be smarter than this. What would likely be her next move?

He sucked in a breath. What if she needed the witch's help with the next stage of her plan? That made sense.

He flew hard and low, returning to the Swamps of Misery about three minutes later. Patches of it showed through the trees, a dull-green, completely flat and motionless surface. He followed the occasional reflections north until he found the witch's house, on its island in a clearing.

He gasped when he arrived. The steamer dragons had worked the place over. Much of the roof was missing, and one wall had all but fallen inward. Bits of furniture had been torn asunder and thrown from the house, littering the unkempt lawn along with numerous smaller objects—her ornaments, books, papers, bottles and boxes, even pots and pans.

Madame Frost was there, picking her way through the debris, looking rather lost. Hal circled overhead, almost afraid to approach. What kind of wrath would she unleash on him if he had the nerve to land on her property again?

But he had to try.

"What are you doing, Hal?" Abigail called, sounding nervous.

He couldn't answer effectively, so he said nothing. He flew down and landed on the island just outside the gate, mindful of the gargoyles. One was still headless, but it didn't seem to affect its guard duty. It somehow peered down at him anyway, giving Hal an eerie feeling. The other gargoyle, with glowing red eyes staring right at him, was far less creepy.

"How dare you come here!" Madame Frost hissed from across the yard. She began stalking toward him, and a blast of wind came out of nowhere and whorled around her, causing her robes and long hair to flutter and flap. "Go away!"

Since Hal remained in dragon form, Abigail had to do the talking. "Has the faun come to see you? Or—I guess it's too early yet. If she *does* come to see you, it'll be to ask for your help. She's planning to—"

"I don't care what she's planning," the witch snapped, stopping just inside the gate and glaring at her. "I have no interest in such things. Unless . . ." She narrowed her eyes. "Unless what she's planning directly affects *you*. In which case, I'll be glad to help."

"She's planning to get rid of every last human being on the planet. I doubt that's what you want. Even if she spared you, what kind of life would that be for you? No other humans to talk to, nobody to do business with . . . You'd be the last human on Earth. The naga and elves would turn their backs on you. So would the centaurs. Maybe you'll be okay making conversation with goblins, though?"

Hal smiled to himself. Abigail had a way of getting her point across.

Still, Madame Frost didn't look too bothered. She shrugged. "I live alone for a reason. People annoy me. If the faun shows up here, maybe I'll help her after all, just to spite you."

She narrowed her eyes at Hal as if pondering the possibility of taking him down with a spell. She stroked her chin for a moment, then pointed at him. "Your fire gland—it's extremely valuable. Allow me to take it from you, and I'll join forces with you against the faun."

"Huh?" Hal grunted. Even in dragonspeak, his meaning was clear.

The witch smiled. "I can understand if you don't want to give up your own. But perhaps you could be instrumental in relieving another dragon of his? The benefits would be tremendous. I would be far more powerful—for instance, an attack by a family of steamer dragons would be laughable against the raw energy I could unleash with the help of a fire gland."

"You're not getting a fire gland," Abigail said shortly.

"Are you sure?" The witch's smile turned to a scowl. "Then we have nothing more to talk about. Now leave. I have some spring cleaning to do."

She turned her back and strode toward an area strewn with books. Stooping, she began the process of picking them up, brushing them off, and stacking them neatly on a wooden box.

Hal sighed. He saw no reason to hang around other than to wait in case the faun showed up. And if he waited, he'd better do so incognito. That would mean reverting to human form and hiding in the trees or wallowing in the swamp. He felt misery descending on him just at the thought of it. No wonder the faun had grown so bitter; she'd spent years in this place, darkness eating away at her very soul.

He lifted into the sky.

Farther south, heading back to Carter, he spotted the river they'd spent some time at in an earlier attempt to trap the faun. What a failure *that* had turned out to be. But the faun had swum off downriver, so perhaps there was some place she knew of, a second home or emergency retreat. Miss Simone had gone after her in mermaid form, and the faun had still escaped, probably leaping out of the river on one side or another.

As Hal circled once more, he spotted something odd—a woman dragging herself out of the woods toward the riverbank. He did a double-take, sure he was seeing things. It wasn't a woman but a mermaid, face down as she pulled herself across the grass, obviously struggling with the effort, her back sheathed with sweat.

What the—?

Hal descended. He wasn't sure what to make of this, but something was wrong. He'd literally just been thinking about Miss Simone, and here was a mermaid crawling out of the trees. It obviously wasn't Miss Simone—this mermaid's hair was darker and shorter, for one thing, and anyway, Miss Simone was back at the lab being hunted by goblins

"Are you all right?" Abigail shouted as Hal thumped down.

The mermaid glanced up, her eyes widening. She'd made it to the river's edge, and she looked poised to throw herself into the water.

Abigail buzzed toward her. "Don't be scared. You're from Carter, aren't you? I think the faun must have changed you earlier. She turned you into a mermaid and left you in the middle of the woods, and it's taken you all this time to get to the river. I'm so sorry. But we can help. We can take you back to Carter, and—"

The mermaid launched herself into the river with a splash.

"No!" Abigail yelled. "Come back! Oh, no—we'll never catch up with her now."

The mermaid was already long gone.

With no way to help, they had to leave her be and report back to Dr. Kessler. It troubled Hal to think of the poor woman swimming about with no idea where she'd come from. Then again, the same could be said for the others—three men, if he recalled correctly, with Derek being the first of them. If this woman had been turned, then so had the others. The faun had performed her magic on them long before being captured and taken to the lab.

And then Hal remembered the funny little pixie stumbling about in the woods. Could that have been one of the men? He kicked himself at the realization. A pixie, a mermaid, and what else? Two other men had been changed into—what? Where were they now?

He wanted to talk to Abigail about it, but she'd probably figured it all out already.

He flew over Carter, circled around, and picked a random direction. He had nowhere specific in mind, just *somewhere*. He was tired of the woods. If the faun were in the woods, he had no hope of finding her. And he severely doubted she was anywhere near the village. Perhaps the nearby hills? He gave them a cursory fly-by but saw no sign of her. He tried another range of hills farther north; they were a little craggy and steep, but she was agile enough to scale them if she wanted to. Again, no luck.

He ended up over the plains to the north and started to turn back. She wouldn't be out here. There was nothing this way, nothing but open ground for miles and miles, hard-baked earth where nothing grew, a barren wasteland. Their journey in Blacknail's buggy to the labyrinth had included much of this featureless terrain. Robbie's first encounter with ogres was somewhere out here, too.

"There!" Abigail yelled.

Hal blinked. *What?*

He looked twice, three times. What was she yelling about?

And then he spotted the faun.

Chapter Eighteen
Trapped!

"Get her, Hal!"

Abigail's triumphant shriek was almost swept away by the rush of wind as Hal shot toward the ground with his wings stretched wide. The faun hadn't seen them yet. She ran at a leisurely pace, leaving the woods behind as she headed out into the vast plains.

She leapt over a narrow fissure that stretched a long way in both directions where an earthquake had split the land in two. Quakes had done even more damage farther north on the way to the Labyrinth of Fire. New Earth could be quite volatile.

Once safely on the other side, the faun glanced back over her shoulder at the massive crack in the ground—and caught sight of Hal's shadow. River jerked to a stop, glanced up, and sprang sideways as he descended with claws outstretched.

Hal missed his target and landed heavily on the hard rock. He immediately launched again, leaping toward her as she scrambled to escape. Even an agile faun was no match for a dragon in a wide-open expanse of land, and Hal quickly had her pinned down.

To his surprise, she squirmed loose. One moment he had her under his front right foot, and the next she'd slipped free and sprung back up again. He roared and lunged toward her, but she ducked and sidestepped and ran back the way she'd come.

"No way!" Hal yelled with a throaty dragon bellow. "We are *not* losing you in the forest again. You're mine!"

He half ran, half flew at her, but she vanished right out from under his front paws. He thudded down, straddling the fissure she'd leapt over moments before.

Peering into the crack in the ground, he groaned with annoyance. That was where she'd gone, but he couldn't fit down in dragon form. In a panic, she'd taken a risk and jumped without looking. She'd fallen probably thirty feet to the bottom, not too far but still out of his reach.

It was narrower farther down; the walls closed in tight, and the wedge-shaped fissure had her trapped.

Hal pawed at the edge of the miniature chasm, feeling firm and solid rock. He stuck his snout in the gap, knowing it would be impossible for a full-grown dragon to squeeze inside. The faun hadn't escaped him, but he hadn't exactly caught her, either.

Seeing nowhere for her to go, he reverted to human form and caused Abigail to tumble from his back. He waited for her to pick herself up. She frowned at him as she did so, saying, "I wish you'd give me some warning when you shift like that."

"Sorry. Okay, so what now?"

They both stared down into the heavily shadowed fissure. The faun, wedged tight, glared back with her yellow eyes. She tried to move, but it seemed one of her hooved feet was pretty well stuck, her ankle possibly twisted.

Hal sighed. He couldn't fit his dragon body down there, and he doubted he could tackle the faun in his human form. Nor could Abigail. "Are you stuck?" he yelled.

His voice echoed off the walls. The faun stared back at him, her expression hard to fathom. She looked down, squirmed a bit, and it became clear she really did have her foot stuck. And judging by her grimace, she'd hurt herself pretty badly.

She gazed upward again, a look of pain and anger on her face. "It seems we are at an impasse," she said through gritted teeth.

Abigail gripped Hal's arm and pulled him back away from the edge so they could talk. "We'll have to get help. If we just had a rope, you could drag her out . . . or you could dangle your tail down if it were long enough."

They both took a quick peek into the fissure just to clarify in their minds that Hal's tail was indeed too short to dangle that far.

"And you can't lift her out?" he asked.

She shook her head. "Even if her foot wasn't stuck, I don't think I could."

"She's smaller than me. Or thinner, anyway."

"Her legs are stronger, probably much heavier. And she's got those horns."

"Well, what about yanking on her just enough to get her free? Then she could probably leap up on her own."

"What, with a twisted ankle?" Abigail pursed her lips. "Do fauns have ankles? Anyway, you know what I mean."

They took another peek. Could Abigail hover in place and drag the faun free? And if she were a human-sized faerie, would there even be room to spread her wings, which spread as wide as her arms?

And if she pulled River free, could the faun then leap up a sheer wall with a bad ankle?

"We need a rope," Hal admitted.

"Or we could just leave her," Abigail said loudly, leaning over the edge so her voice carried down into the fissure. "Should we do that, River? Just leave you there?"

The faun failed to react with fear. Instead, she remained calm, perhaps even determined. "Do what you must."

Abigail sighed. "Okay, let's head back for a rope."

But Hal was reluctant to leave. He just knew the faun would be long gone by the time they got back. He knelt by the edge and studied the steep walls. There was absolutely nothing to hold onto. The gap was about right to 'wall walk' down by placing his hands on one side and feet on the other and simply exerting force as he eased himself down . . . but the idea of that gave him the heebie-jeebies. One slip and . . .

What if Abigail carried him down? She could manage short lifts. But then what?

He sighed. What a silly predicament! After everything he and his shapeshifter friends had been through together, he couldn't even navigate a little crack in the ground?

Okay, a thirty-foot-deep crack, he told himself.

The very bottom of the narrowing fissure wasn't all the way closed. He saw blackness through a gap as thick as his arm. He couldn't possibly slide through, but still, there might be hundreds of feet of *emptiness* down there.

"Are you done?" Abigail asked with a smile on her face. "You've weighed all the odds and come to the same conclusion I did ages ago?"

"Yeah, I guess. Rope it is, then." He raised his voice. "We're going to get a rope. You'll have to wait on us to get back."

She narrowed her eyes.

Hal withdrew from the edge. "Well, let's go. I don't think she's—"

"Wait," the faun called.

They both peered down again. She looked almost pitiful, firmly wedged in place, her hands flat against the back wall as she craned her neck to look up.

"Perhaps . . ." She trailed off.

"What?" Hal prompted.

"Perhaps a spell might help."

He shared a glance with Abigail.

"What kind of spell?" she asked.

"A spell that will enable you to come down here and help me."

Hal huffed a laugh and shook his head. "Uh, that's a big fat no. You can keep your spells to yourself."

"I may free myself while you are gone," she warned. "I have a number of spells I could try. But the safest, and with the most certain outcome, would be if you allowed me to evolve you."

Hal's mouth fell open. "You—you want to—you—"

"You want to *change* him?" Abigail exclaimed, equally astonished. "You actually want us to agree to this? Are you completely nuts?"

The faun retained her earnest expression as she stared up at Hal. "Think about it. As a dragon, you are magnificent—but no good in this situation. As a human, you are useless. What if I evolved you into something more suited to climbing? Another troll like your friend, for instance? You could climb down and release me, perhaps even carry me out. There would be no need for you to fetch a rope."

"Oh!" Hal scoffed. "Oh, well then. That sounds great. So I get to become a troll just to save your butt?"

"Only for a while," River said. "There would be a truce between us. I evolve you, you save me, and then, if you like, I will change you back."

A long silence followed. Hal felt like time had temporarily paused while he digested the faun's suggestion. As much as he scorned the idea of allowing himself to be *evolved*, he suddenly realized that the reward could be huge. If she changed him back, then he would learn how to change the *others* back as well.

"No, Hal," Abigail whispered. She was staring at him.

"Just . . . think about it," he whispered back. "I don't want to be evolved, obviously, but if it means she has to turn me back, then we'll see how it's done, and that means—"

"She's a liar. She won't change you back. You'll rescue her, and then she'll be off."

"Not if we plan this right."

He started pacing, his mind whirling. The critical moment would be after he pulled her loose. Once free, there would be very little to stop her escaping. She might not be able to leap about very well, but it didn't matter. What if she simply refused to turn him back? What could he do about that?

And if he were something like a troll, would he even care about becoming human again if he forgot who he was supposed to be?

He nodded to himself. He saw through her plan. "... *And then, if you like, I will change you back.*" Those were her words. She knew he would forget who he was and be quite happy to remain a troll afterward.

He could insist she omit the amnesia spell, but how on earth could he enforce that? No, he and Abigail needed another card to play once she was free, some serious leverage to make sure she followed through with her end of the bargain.

Threatening physical harm wouldn't work. She knew that. Even if he allowed Abigail to be evolved in his place so he could stand over the faun in a threatening fire-breathing manner until she put things right, she still probably wouldn't be swayed. And anyway, he would never let Abigail take his place.

Blackmail? They had nothing to blackmail her with.

Bribes? Rewards of some kind? Very doubtful.

It had to be something immediate, a no-way-out situation for her unless she complied.

Abigail leaned over the edge. "Turn it on yourself! Evolve yourself into something smaller and with wings so you can escape. Maybe a faerie?"

Hal had to admit her idea was genius. It would solve all their problems.

The faun gave a shrug. "I considered that. Unfortunately, I cannot evolve myself."

"Show us how to do the spell, and we'll do it for you," Abigail said. "We have the potion." She patted her pocket.

The faun shook her head. "The transmogrification spell takes years to perfect. It is not possible for you to perform it on me."

"All we want is to be able to turn our friends back to normal. Are you saying we can't learn the spell unless we study for years?"

"I mean you cannot evolve me into something else."

Abigail sighed. "Well, there's nothing you can offer us, then. If our friends will be stuck as they are for years, then you have nothing to bargain with."

The faun shook her head again. "You misunderstand. It is very difficult to perform the transmogrification spell. It is *not* difficult to reverse it. There is no spell required for that. The potion does all the work."

Hal felt like punching the air. They were close to an answer.

"How?" he demanded.

River said nothing for a moment. "I feel we are circling each other. Help me first, and I will help you."

"Do we just drink a bit of the potion?" Abigail persisted.

The faun clammed up.

Hal thought for a second. "We could try that," he whispered. "I mean, not *us*, but Emily and Lauren and the others. They could take a sip and—"

"That is not advisable," the faun called.

Wow, good hearing.

"What happens if they take a sip?"

"Try it and see." The faun sounded tired now.

Still, Hal felt they were close. "What if we just go find Madame Frost and—" He stopped, thinking of the steamer dragons demolishing her home. "What if we find some other witch and ask how the potion works?"

Abigail nodded. "I like that idea. We can leave the faun here and take our chances with another witch. Let's go."

"I cannot keep my end of the bargain if you do not release me first," River said. "If I could show you how to reverse the spell, I would do so. But I have no way to show you unless you allow yourself to be evolved and save me from this predicament."

They were back to that again. Hal sighed heavily. "*Trust* you, you mean," he said in a sour tone.

"Trust each other."

"But we'd have to trust you *more*," Abigail muttered. "Come on, Hal, let's go. It won't take long to go find a rope and come back for her."

"All right," he admitted.

But the moment he transformed and waited for Abigail to climb up, they both heard the faun's voice, low and mumbling, a continuous stream of unintelligible words. Hal paused to listen. Then he sighed in annoyance. She was invoking some kind of spell.

He stomped to the edge of the fissure and peered down. River had her eyes closed and her hands raised, palms up as if testing for rain. As she mumbled her spell, a deep, ominous rumbling started up deep underground. Trickles of dust ran down the steep rock walls. Hal felt a steady vibration under his paws. The noise rose, slow and steady, and the tremors increased. The faun raised her voice as though trying to be heard.

"What's she doing?" Abigail shouted from her perch behind his head.

Hal could only shrug. He watched with interest as the steep walls began visibly shaking and more dust and tiny rocks ran down.

Then, all at once, the narrow gap right under the faun's hooves widened. She let out a cry of pain as the fissure finally let her go—but instead of springing loose with her usual gusto, she dropped into the blackness, her elbows slamming into the opposing wall to arrest her fall. There, she clung awkwardly as the fissure continued to widen.

She'd quit her spell already, but it seemed the magic wanted to carry on. The ground shook and shuddered, and Hal spread his feet wide and planted his tail to avoid stumbling one way or another. The crack in the ground rumbled open another few inches, and suddenly the faun looked desperate as she scrambled on the rock and tried to get a hold—and failed.

She slipped and fell into the widening abyss, neatly disappearing without a sound. The moment she was gone, the rumbling abated, and the tremors faded.

Silence fell. Hal stared down at the empty space where the faun had been trapped. She was no more.

"If she was just trying to free her foot," Abigail said, breaking the silence, "then her magic worked way better than she expected. Look at the hole she opened up!" She buzzed down to hover over the fissure. "That's unfortunate. I really didn't want to see her die, but how could she have survived that? The crack in the ground could be miles deep."

She might have landed on a ledge or something, Hal thought. Unwilling to assume she was just *gone* so easily, he gave a grunt and leaned over the edge, stretching his neck. There was still no way he could fit down in the gap, but Abigail could.

She had the same notion. "Stay here. I'll take a look."

"Be careful," Hal growled.

She flew down. When she reached the pitch-black crack along the bottom of the v-shaped fissure, she hovered there for a moment and then shrank to her tiny faerie size before zipping down into the darkness. Hal felt a pang of anxiety as she vanished from sight. What if the faun was just below?

To his relief, Abigail zipped back into view again. She flew up toward him and grew to full human size. "It's not very deep at all, maybe just another ten feet. But the crack is miles long, and I saw River hobbling off in *that* direction."

She pointed toward the east, and Hal ran his gaze along the jagged fissure, almost expecting to see her spring out in a single bound.

"So she's not getting away from us," Abigail went on, "but we can't really get at her, either. Or *you* can't. I can."

Hal frantically shook his head.

Abigail rolled her eyes. "I know, I know, I'm just a faerie. What can we do, though? How about I follow her while you get help? We need . . ." She pursed her lips. "Lauren would be handy. She could climb down there and carry her back up. Or Robbie if he's at half size."

But Hal had another idea. He gave a grunt, briefly shook his head, then nodded at her, trying to indicate she should go after the faun at a safe distance while he explored the fissure farther along.

She raised an eyebrow at him. "Yeah, that made no sense. Where are you going?"

He started trotting along one edge of the fissure, heading east. Glancing back, he saw Abigail shrug and dive back into the narrow space, disappearing from view again.

The fissure went on and on. It wasn't all v-shaped; in fact, the walls were completely vertical most of the way. The crack along the bottom opened wider in places, and Hal slowed to investigate, wondering if he could slide down in dragon form . . .

It wasn't long before he came across a gap large enough to halt him in his tracks. Would he fit? He leaned into the fissure, studying the smooth, sloping walls. Maybe if he folded his wings really tight, he could ease down and squeeze through the gap in the bottom. Then he could simply wait for the faun.

He gave it a try, turning sideways and carefully placing one rear foot over the edge. His claws snagged on something, giving him a foothold, so he swung his tail out, lowered himself onto the edge, and reached for—

His back foot slipped, and he tipped sideways. In sudden panic, he scrabbled for a new grip but found nothing. He ended up sliding into the rapidly narrowing fissure to the bottom, where he discovered very quickly that the open gap at the base was nowhere near big enough to fit through.

He jammed tight, one of his wings wedged so hard it hurt. His tail flopped down into the gap, and he felt solid ground just below. That was good.

Taking a deep breath, he reverted to human form as slowly as he could. As his dragon body morphed and shrank, he suddenly popped free and tumbled deeper, falling through the gap just as the faun had. He yelled in fright, then let out an "Oomph!" when he landed flat on his back.

Winded, he lay there until he could breathe normally. Then he climbed to his feet.

It was like being in a long, long tunnel with an open roof stretching for miles, an endless crack in the ceiling where daylight flooded in. The tunnel he stood in had to be twice as wide as the v-shaped fissure above, but the ceiling wasn't high enough for him to be a dragon even if he pushed his wings straight up through the opening.

He sighed. "Nicely done, moron," he muttered.

Turning to the west, he waited in silence, listening. Neither the faun nor Abigail knew he was down here. Hopefully, River would keep on coming toward him, and he'd stand his ground and confront her when she arrived. He could breathe fire, after all. She couldn't get past him.

He moved to one side where he'd be partially obscured by a jutting section of the rock wall.

As tunnels went, this wasn't such a bad one. It had plenty of room and natural daylight, though the sides were heavily shadowed. The ground could be flatter; it was all lumps and bumps, slabs of uneven rock. He couldn't imagine traveling such awkward terrain with a broken ankle.

The faun appeared about ten minutes later, heading his way. Hal heard her panting and talking to herself as she hobbled along, scrambling over the rocky floor. Every time she climbed onto a slab, she glanced upward, looking for a way out.

Hal waited.

When she was within ten feet, he stepped out in front of her. She didn't see him straight away; she kept looking upward, then down at her feet to see where she was walking, then up again. It was almost by accident that she glanced forward.

She halted, her eyes widening.

"Hey," Hal said. "Going somewhere?"

River gave a sigh and lowered herself onto a natural rocky seat at the edge of the shaft of daylight. "I cannot."

Her ankle was definitely broken. Her right hoof angled outward in a disturbingly unnatural way, the break badly swollen.

"That's right," Hal agreed, edging toward her. "So, here's the deal. Tell us what we need to know, and I'll get you out of here."

She glanced at him, scowling. Then she surveyed the walls, and her scowl turned distinctly smug. "You are trapped, too. You cannot be a dragon down here, and therefore you cannot fly us out."

"Abigail can."

"A faerie?" the faun scoffed.

"A human-sized faerie. She's carried me before. She can carry you, too."

"Then why did she not do so when I was trapped?"

"Because your foot was wedged. She's not that strong." Hal huffed with impatience. "Never mind. Tell us what we need to know, and we'll get you out of here."

River folded her arms, tilted her head back, and looked down her nose at him. "I would rather take my chances alone. I will find a way out of this place before long."

"With a broken ankle? Good luck with that."

They both stood in silence, glaring at each other.

Then Hal heard a faint buzz in the distance. It quickly grew in volume, and Abigail came into sight, her wings catching the rays of light from above. Her face lit up when she spotted Hal and the faun. She buzzed over River's head and landed by Hal's side. Her wings stilled, and he felt them nudging at him as she moved closer.

"I told River you could lift her out of here," Hal said, "but only when she tells us how to use the potion."

Abigail looked at him, then at the faun, then up at the steep walls. "Sure," she said, a hint of doubt in her voice.

The faun smiled at Hal. "I do not believe your faerie friend shares your confidence. I suggest we do this my way. I will evolve you into something with wings—larger than a faerie but smaller than a dragon—and you will carry me out of here. Then I will reverse the spell if you so wish."

They were going around in circles again. Hal's patience was at an end. "Let's go, Abi. Leave her here. We'll figure out some other way to help the others."

"Yeah," Abigail said.

Her wings buzzed into action. She stepped behind Hal, threaded her arms under his, locked her fingers across his chest, and lifted off with a great deal of heavy breathing. Hal knew he was a deadweight and wished he could do something to help instead of just hanging there.

He couldn't fathom the faun's expression as he rose. If she cared about being left behind, she didn't show it.

Abigail began groaning about halfway up, and Hal suddenly feared she would give out and drop him. He could end up breaking an ankle himself—or worse. But the walls were just far enough apart that he could *maybe* transform safely . . . if he remembered to keep his wings tucked in . . .

"I can't!" she gasped.

They began dropping. It was a controlled fall, and Hal remained still while she brought them safely down to the ground close to where they'd started. He avoided the faun's gaze; she was probably laughing, or at least grinning smugly.

He turned to give Abigail a hug. Red-faced, with beads of sweat on her forehead, she slumped on his shoulder and said, "I'm sorry."

"It's okay," he assured her. "I guess I'm heavier than I was a few months ago. No big deal."

It was true he'd gained an inch in height and put on a little more muscle.

"Except now we're all stuck down here," she muttered.

"*You're* not. You can still go get help."

She nodded. But then she froze, cocking her head and listening.

A second later, Hal heard it, too—growling and snarling, the sound of a pack of dogs on the hunt. He and Abigail turned to peer east along the endless fissure with its smooth but occasionally jutting walls and uneven floor. Something was coming.

"I don't like this," Abigail whispered.

Hal reached for her hand. He could breathe fire at whatever was on its way, so he felt confident he could protect them both. Fairly confident, anyway. Unless there was a lot of them, in which case one or two might slip through. And how long could he stand there breathing fire?

He blinked and squinted. In the distance, he saw movement—and what looked like fire. Yes, definitely fire. Flames and black smoke licked up. The fast-moving animals appeared to be escaping an equally fast-moving fire. It had to be right behind them judging by the way the flames seemed to be pouring off their backs . . .

Hal felt a sinking sensation in his stomach. These animals weren't escaping a fire. They were bringing it with them. They *loved* fire. They would roll around in the flames if they could.

They were hellhounds.

Chapter Nineteen
Fire and Smoke

The pack of hellhounds raged closer. Fire and smoke rose from their coal-black bodies as a dozen of the creatures leapt over boulders and slabs of rock. From this distance, they appeared to flow like a volcanic mass of fiery oil along the fissure.

Where had they come from? Was this the kind of thing that spewed from the depths of the planet when a quake split the ground open? Were they trapped down here? He hoped so!—except he was trapped, too.

The faun hobbled closer. "There is very little time," she urged. "We must do this."

Hal saw fear on her face. He opened his mouth to argue, then closed it again. What was there to say? Abigail couldn't lift either one of them out of the chasm, and certainly wouldn't have the strength to come back for the other. Hal couldn't hold off the hellhounds with his fire. And he had no room to transform.

"Get out of here," he told Abigail. "You know those things are hot. Don't get close to them, or they'll melt your wings."

"I'm not leaving you," she said, her eyes widening.

"The faun needs to do her thing," he said stiffly. "There's no time. Go!" He grabbed her arm. "But don't go far. We need the potion. Okay?"

Before she could protest any further, he spun around to face the faun. Behind him, the snarling of the distant hellhounds rose in pitch, becoming more urgent as if they'd just spotted the three of them.

"Do it," Hal told the faun. "But no amnesia spell!"

River had already started conjuring, her eyes rolled upward. Blue mist leaked from her hands even though her arms hung stiffly at her sides. As her whispering rose in volume and urgency, she lifted her hands toward him, palms out.

"Go!" Hal told Abigail.

With a cry, she shot straight upward out of the fissure.

Hal glanced over his shoulder and shuddered. They were so close. He figured he had half a minute, if that. He heard their hungry panting and the clicks of their claws on the rock.

Looking back at the faun, he just had time to see the palms of her hands close to his face before thick blue mist engulfed him. Then something strange happened—a feeling of time pausing, everything going cold and still, sound shutting out. He stared ahead, seeing the faun and her raised hands, and the mist itself, but all was motionless.

Then his world shattered. Everything fell apart, disintegrating before his very eyes, though he knew it was actually *him* scattering to the wind.

After that, a moment of peace and emptiness, a smudge of darkness.

The next thing he knew, he blinked awake.

"Hurry!" the faun hissed.

The snarling had risen to a deafening level, and Hal spun around in horror. The entire pack had more than halved the distance by now, and they hurtled toward him, a mass of red eyes and deep-black coats and flickering flames—and a tremendous heat.

"Get us out of here!" the faun shrieked.

"Hurry, Hal!" another voice screamed from somewhere above.

The faun leapt at him, throwing her arms around his neck so hard that he staggered backward. He realized at that moment that his feet weren't his own. He felt different all over, though he couldn't quite figure out—

"NOW!"

As the lead hellhound pounced and flew toward him, Hal instinctively leapt away, springing as high as he could and flapping his arms despite the weight hanging off his neck. To his surprise, he continued rising, and it was then he realized his arms were in fact wings—leathery appendages, mostly orange with red tips. Gasping, he kept flapping as the hellhounds tore over the rocky ground he'd just vacated, a dozen black, fiery bodies scrambling and fighting, leaping and snapping at his feet. Waves of heat rolled upward, scorching his tail.

His tail?

Beating his wings hard, he focused for a second on his dangling reptilian claws. Though very much like a dragon's, they definitely weren't his own. They were slender, and much smaller.

"Watch where you're going!" the faun warned.

He glanced up, sucked in a breath, and veered to the right a split second before he crashed into a solid wall. Then he was out, clearing the fissure and rising into the open world above.

Thumping down on the expanse of flat, hard-baked dirt, he tried to clear his mind. A dark-haired girl stood there. She had large insectoid wings spreading wide from her back, but otherwise she looked human. The faun clinging to his neck eventually let go and stepped away—no, *hobbled* away, trying to avoid putting weight on her broken ankle.

The snapping and howling of frustrated hellhounds continued to fill the air, and a blast of heat radiated from the fissure. Hal wanted to leave this place and go home, but he couldn't exactly remember where 'home' was.

"What—" he said. His voice emerged as a far lighter growl than his own. What *was* this? He was a *dragon*. Or was he? "What's going on?" he asked. "Where am I?"

The faun said nothing, but the dark-haired human approached. "Hal? Are you in there?"

Hal . . .

Yes, that was his name, though it seemed a little silly, hardly fitting for a . . . for a . . .

He craned his neck to study his wings, his lithe, brightly scaled body, and the long tail with the vicious barb on the end. He was orange with blue patches here and there, and his wings had red tips.

A wyvern, he thought, suddenly remembering. *Funny how I'd forgotten that. I feel like I just woke from a bad dream. Weird—I thought I was a different kind of dragon.*

The memory lingered: dark-green scales, a huge club-ended tail, visions of stomping through the woods and smashing bushes flat . . . He remembered these details as if they were real. But apparently not! He wasn't anywhere near that big. Wyverns weren't much bigger than this human girl. And his coloring was much brighter than the dull greens of an ordinary dragon.

"Hal?" the girl said, moving closer. She had some nerve. "If you can understand me, please nod your head."

He leaned toward her and growled. "Stay back, girl-with-wings."

She halted.

Then she turned to the faun and held up a small glass bottle. "Change him back right now."

The faun stared at her, then at Hal, then back at the girl. She smiled. "I think not. He is much better in this form, is he not? A small dragon, *and* a large dragon if he so desires."

"Change him back!" the girl screamed, so angry that Hal flinched. "You promised!"

An argument ensued between the two, one shouting and waving the small bottle in the air, and the other smiling and shaking her head. Hal only half listened. He was preoccupied with his own muddled thoughts. What was he doing here? Why couldn't he remember the last few hours? Maybe he'd lost *days*—it was impossible to tell. The last thing he remembered was . . .

He stared into space, tuning out the squabbling females. The last thing he remembered was . . . what? He felt as though a thin, gauzy veil had dropped over his memory. He knew his mind was intact, could *almost* see everything just beyond the haze, yet the details remained out of reach. The dark-haired winged girl was someone he knew, though probably not anyone of great importance. And he had no affinity to the faun at all.

So why was he here?

The winged girl suddenly buzzed into the air, and he reared back, startled. The faun made a leap for her, but it was a poor, one-legged effort, and she dropped to the ground with a cry of pain.

"Yeah, try that again!" the winged girl shouted, still angry. She gripped the tiny bottle in one fist and shook it. "I'm giving you one last chance, River. Turn Hal back, or I swear—" She broke off, trembling with fury.

The faun, on one knee and clutching her broken ankle, peered up at and sneered. "Go home, little human girl. Warn your friends and family. I am coming for you all. Prepare for a storm. Prepare to be *evolved.*"

Hal watched the buzzing girl for a moment, amused by the sheer indignation and astonishment on her face. But as the faun started to hobble away—heading nowhere in particular that he could see—he lost interest and shook his head, trying to shake loose some useful memories.

The last thing he remembered was . . .

Annoyingly, he still couldn't put his claw on it. He couldn't recall anything from an hour ago, or earlier that morning, or yesterday, or anytime last week, perhaps even in the past month. His mind was blank.

Worried, he looked into the distance. One thing he knew for sure was that he had a nest somewhere. Did he have a brood waiting for him back home? A vague memory surfaced: a shadowy cave, a young dragon, a pile of shining gems. He struggled to clarify the image in his head, but it kept slipping sideways every time he focused on it. It had to mean something, though.

All he had right now was a powerful urge to find family, to be in the company of his own kind. He spread his wings, sniffing the air. Which way? To the south?

"Hal, don't fly away without me!" the winged girl called, buzzing closer. "We can fix this. We don't need the faun. We'll just find another witch. Will you let me climb onto your back?"

Ignoring her, Hal launched off the ground and beat his wings hard, reaching for the sky. The rush of wind on his face felt good. Yes, this was where he was he supposed to be: flying high, gazing down on the vast expanse of land and the distant horizons. He altered his course, allowing instinct to take over. The dragon in the cave was *this* way, he was sure.

It's not a wyvern, a small voice told him.

He frowned. Somehow, he knew that to be true. The dragon in the cave was *not* a wyvern. Then again, any kind of dragon was a step closer to family than these squabbling humans and fauns.

He glanced back. The little winged girl was far behind, waving her arms at him. A curious creature, he decided. Her insectoid wings, rather like a dragonfly's, made her look like a faerie—but faeries were tiny, and this girl was not.

A forest lay directly ahead. Rain clouds hung low, dark and ominous, and he saw the fuzzy mist of a downpour. But no lightning, so all was good. Rain didn't matter. He sped on, feeling the first few drops on his snout as he neared the forest.

Something made him glance to the right. He spotted rooftops—the telltale sign of a human settlement. Yes, that place lurked in his veiled memory. He'd been there before, though he had no idea why.

Abigail.

A fleeting word caught his attention. A name, perhaps? If so, it was as silly as his own name. And now that he thought about it, he couldn't be certain 'Hal' was in fact his real name. Maybe humans had just named him for their own convenience or amusement. But if his name wasn't Hal, then what was it?

He flew over a waterfall and jerked in surprise. This was the place! He'd been here recently. Circling around, he scoured the hillside and fast-flowing water for something familiar, something that looked like . . .

A cave! There, behind the falls. He made a dive for it, certain the dragon who lived there would be able to shed some light on his memory loss.

The moment he flew in and landed, a terrible roar sounded from his left. He spun and tried to focus in the sudden darkness as a shape lurched toward him.

"I—" was all Hal managed to spit out.

The dragon—much bigger than he'd remembered—rammed into him with jaws snapping and claws slashing. The teeth latched onto his neck, and the weight of the creature pushed him down and pinned him to the cold rock floor. Pain shot through his neck as the dragon bit harder and thrashed from side to side, trying to rip out a chunk of flesh.

Suddenly terrified, Hal wriggled and squirmed, completely overwhelmed by the size and brute force of his adversary. Wyverns had always been small and puny compared to other dragons. Still, he had a barbed tail . . .

He lashed out, swinging it as hard as he could. His aim was good; the barb smacked viciously into the dragon's face and sliced a clean gash through the hard scales. The dragon shook his head, and droplets of blood flew out.

Hal lashed out again, this time catching the dragon on his neck. Once more, a fine gash opened up. He felt a moment of triumph. Wyverns weren't big and strong, but they could flay just about anything to ribbons. His barb had poison in it, too, though he doubted it would affect a dragon. It was more effective on smaller creatures.

With the dragon momentarily distracted, Hal squirmed and slipped free, then snuck under the monster's belly and tore into it. His own teeth were much sharper than the dragon's, and he had no trouble biting through its scales and ripping its flesh open.

But then he realized the awful truth—that this monster wasn't alone.

The creature he'd seen in his vision had been smaller. This one was an adult male, and an adult female was now on his tail, opening her mouth and blasting him with a cloud of scalding steam.

He screeched in pain and scrambled free of the male's iron grip. But he was cornered. And in the few seconds he had to take stock of his surroundings, he knew there was no way out for him. He'd blundered into a nest of steamer dragons, and they'd rightly attacked him. What had he been thinking? Now he was trapped. The two adults pressed together side by side, facing him, pushing him back into an ever-decreasing space.

"I just wanted to ask you something!" he yelled, stopping with his back pressed against the slanted ceiling. He couldn't retreat any farther.

The male, with blood dripping from his face, neck, and belly, snarled and advanced. *Finish him*, he muttered to his mate.

They both opened their mouths wide, and Hal could almost hear the steam building deep down in their throats, about to blast loose.

If only I were bigger, he moaned to himself. *If only—*

Suddenly, the ceiling pressed harder into his back, squashing his wings low. Gasping, he inched forward, trying to squeeze out from under the oppressive weight. It felt like the ceiling had just come loose and was resting on his spine!

The steamer dragons paused, then closed their mouths and took a step back almost in unison. Both looked shocked and confused, staring at him.

Hal realized something had happened, something inexplicable. Even in the darkness, he could see that his wings were no longer orange and red, and when he looked down at his chest, he saw dark green rather than orange with blue patches. Something was wrong.

What is the meaning of this? the male steamer demanded.

Why did you come here and attack us? the female added.

Hal edged forward a little more, grunting and groaning at the effort of squeezing out from under the slanted ceiling. "I didn't mean to attack you," he managed at last. "Wait—I *didn't* attack you. You attacked *me*."

You trespassed, the male steamer said.

Fair enough, Hal thought. "I'm sorry. I wasn't thinking straight." He frowned. "I'm still not sure why I came here. I just . . . I . . ."

He was finally able to stand up straight. Amazed, he now looked *down* on the steamer dragons.

Are you here to burn us out? the female asked in a trembling, whispering voice.

"What? I couldn't even if I wanted to!" But even as Hal said it, a memory slotted into place. He had fire-breath. He *could* burn them out. "What I mean is . . ."

A silence fell, broken only by the low growls and heavy breathing of the two deeply worried steamers.

Then, a new voice from behind them: *You are not yourself.*

A third steamer wove into view, poking her head between the adults to peer at him. *This* was the dragon Hal had seen in his fuzzy memory, along with her collection of shiny stones—her gems.

Memories were sharpening by the second. "Something happened to me," Hal agreed. "I don't know what."

You were a dragon-human, the young steamer said. *Now you are a dragon-wyvern. Are you still human, too?*

"Human?" Hal exclaimed. He scoffed at the idea of such a thing, but then he frowned and blinked, trying to latch onto the fleeting remnants of his scattered recollection. Earlier, he'd dreamed he was a different kind of dragon, and he hadn't quite got that straight in his head yet. Was there some truth there? Was he a small, orange, lithe wyvern? Or a huge, dark-green monster from the labyrinth?

The labyrinth . . .

Another vision flashed in his mind: lava tubes in the cliff face, home to dozens of dragons just like him. He *was* a fire-breathing labyrinth dragon. At least, he was now.

So why had he been a wyvern a few moments before?

He shook his head, trying to clear it. And if he wasn't confused enough, these steamers were suggesting he might actually be *human*, too?

"What do you mean, human?" he asked.

Leave here, the male demanded. *We have our gemstone back. We are done. Go now.*

"Gemstone? I don't remember . . ."

Pah! The dragon shuffled backward, nudging the others aside. The three of them cleared a space, moving to the other side of the cave— actually more of a wedge-shaped shelter in the hillside, shrouded in darkness. *The half-dragon has become a half-wit. Give him room so he may leave.*

With three steamers staring at Hal and waiting, he sighed and stomped to the entrance where the ceiling was much higher. He stood looking out over the hillside, watching the waterfall, a new memory struggling to make itself known.

Abigail.

He imagined the dark-haired winged girl sitting on the rocks down by the water. He'd talked to her there. He'd talked to her lots of times in many different places. Though just a human—or an oversized faerie—it seemed she meant more to him than he'd supposed. Why else would he keep thinking about her?

Hal wondered about himself, too. Wyvern . . . dragon . . . human . . . What *was* he?

He launched from the ledge and had a moment of shock when he fell heavier than expected. Beating his massive green wings and swooping down over the hillside, he yearned for the lightweight wyvern form he'd arrived in. Much better for flying than this oversized, monstrous body. Then again, once he'd climbed into the air and leveled out, cruising was easy, and he cut through the gusts of wind instead of being buffeted by them. *Pros and cons,* he thought.

The human village lay nearby. He had half a mind to fly over and see if it sparked any more memories, but he felt the winged girl might prove more useful. *Abigail.* She'd tried to talk to him earlier, but he'd ignored her. Now he wanted nothing more than for her to explain what was going on, what had happened to him, and why he couldn't remember anything.

As he flew over the forest toward the plains, he glanced sideways at his giant right-hand wing. Then, with a bit of concentration, he morphed into the wyvern form, and his wing shrank, the dark green brightening to orange, the tips turning red. He immediately felt lighter, his body a fraction of the size. He twisted his neck downward and peered at his belly, seeing his long, thin tail stretched out behind.

Wyvern . . . and dragon. I'm both.

Still, his memory had huge gaps in it. The steamer had said he was human, too. That didn't make any sense whatsoever.

He spotted a tiny figure in the distance, the winged girl flying low to the ground, buzzing along at what he guessed was her fastest speed. She hadn't made it out of the plains to the forest yet. He veered toward her, angling down and gliding. For a moment, he felt an urge to snatch her out of the air as he would any prey. He had to fight the urge. Now was the time for answers, not a hearty meal.

She saw him coming and paused in mid-air, the wide-eyed look on her face hard to read. Was she terrified? Surprised? Hopeful? He hurtled toward her and thumped down, leaving his orange wings spread wide for a moment longer than necessary. *Check out my colors,* he thought with a surge of pride. *See that red? That's the sign of a true warrior. And the blue across my chest? That shows intelligence and wisdom.*

All male wyverns had similar markings, but his were enviable by any standards. Females were a brighter orange, more in the realms of yellow, with swaths of green. Some had red wingtips, but Hal preferred those with a softer side, the tips more purple than red, signifying kindness and loyalty, perhaps even romance . . .

Arghh! Stop this!

He switched to his other form, expanding in size and causing Abigail to buzz backward a few yards. But then she smiled and approached again. "That's better!"

The coloring of his body faded into insignificance, and he scoffed. As if it mattered how much red or blue marked his body! All that mattered was size and strength—and how much fire he could breathe.

"I have your clothes," the girl said. She patted some tightly folded garments tucked under her arm. "I had to wait for the hellhounds to go, and it took ages to find one of your shoes . . ." She trailed off, then sighed. "Hal, do you know what's going on? Do you know what happened to you?"

He focused on her. She hovered before him, her wings a buzzing blur. "No," he growled, shaking his head so she could understand him.

"Okay, well, listen up. You're human. And you're a dragon. You're a human-dragon shapeshifter. You're *not* a wyvern. Do you hear me?"

After a moment, he nodded. He heard her just fine, and he understood what she was saying. Believing her was another matter.

"We have to go after the faun," Abigail said. "I have the potion. We have to make it work, to put you back the way you were. She used an amnesia spell on you when she turned you into a wyvern, so you don't remember much." She frowned, studying him. "I can't imagine how confusing things must be for you, but trust me, okay? Everything will be all right. You'll be human again soon."

He shrugged. What she'd said made sense, and for some reason he trusted her. He felt he knew her from old. But he didn't fully believe what she was saying. There was no way he could be human. A shapeshifter, yes—he'd already proved that to himself. But a wyvern-dragon shapeshifter, not a *human*.

He shuddered. What a horrible thought.

"Are you ready?" Abigail asked.

He shrugged again. He'd go along for the ride and see what happened. All he wanted was for his foggy memory to clear. If this potion she mentioned could help with that, then he was game.

"You need to put these on," the girl said, unfolding the bundle of clothes. Two thin shoes fell loose as the shiny green material hung loose from her hands.

Hal scoffed noisily.

"Yes, I know, they won't fit over your wings. But . . . let me try something . . ."

He stood there in stunned disbelief as she approached and started to wrap one piece of clothing around him. It seemed to alter its shape the moment it touched his scaly hide, thinning and lengthening so it was more like a strap. He jerked away from the unnatural garment, appalled at both the darkness of the magic and the girl's overfamiliarity. The indignity of it!

She gave him a stern look. "Stop being a baby. When you turn human again, you'll be glad you're wearing these. Now, hold still before I get annoyed."

Chapter Twenty
The Potion

"She can't have gone far," Abigail called from her perch on his shoulders.

It felt weird letting her ride on his back, especially now that she'd draped those weird garments around his neck and tied them off. He'd drawn the line at the shoes, and she'd stuffed them into her pocket.

He hoped other dragons didn't see him. He'd never live it down. Plus, they might shun him, treat him like a human-lover, a traitor to his own kind. Oddly, though, he had the feeling she'd ridden on his back many times, and that he'd never had a problem with it before. Clearly he'd lost his way over time. In that sense, maybe his loss of memory was a good thing; it shone a light on who he really was.

One time only, he promised himself. *I'll take this girl to the faun, we'll sort out what needs to be done, and that'll be the end of it.*

He couldn't help thinking of the labyrinth in the north as they flew low across the plains looking for the faun. He recalled his visit there, running afoul of several angry dragons, meeting the emperor, known as the 'Old One,' and—and what? Other aspects of the visit were not so clear. He felt sure he'd been with humans and other creatures, but everything seemed foggy.

All he knew was that he yearned to recover his memory and, even more importantly, return to the labyrinth. Forget his alternate wyvern form. Who'd choose *that* over a fire-breathing dragon? Pathetic. And forget those steamers. They weren't his kind.

Anger stirred in him when he spotted the faun hopping along. He couldn't wait for this business to be over. She'd better not mess with him.

He flew overhead, turned, and thumped down just yards away from her, sending up a cloud of dust. She stopped dead and hissed, fear evident in her eyes. Sweat beaded her forehead, and she appeared to be in a lot of pain from her broken ankle. He couldn't imagine where she was headed; there was nothing but open ground for miles all around, except for the forest behind her to the south.

Abigail buzzed off his back and flew into view, hovering out of reach of the faun. "There's nowhere for you to go. It's time to put things right."

The faun made a scoffing sound. "I *am* putting things right. Stand aside and leave me be."

"There's literally nothing out here!" Abigail exclaimed, spinning around and making a sweeping gesture. "Are you planning to hop all the way to the horizon? Just stop. Help me with this potion, put Hal back the way he was, and then we'll help you."

"I will not."

The faun began hopping again, keeping her right leg lifted the whole time. It had to take an enormous amount of effort and strength to balance and hop for such a long way.

She veered around Hal, but he lazily moved his tail and flicked the heavy clubbed end in her direction, making it sway like the head of a giant cobra. She paused, eyeing it with unease.

"You will not harm me," she said, lifting her gaze to Hal's.

It wasn't so much a command as a statement of fact. *That's what you think*, Hal thought. He snarled and pushed his snout toward her, opening his mouth slightly to let out a sampling of the heat building in his chest. She recoiled.

"You're forgetting, River," Abigail said, "that Hal is no longer Hal. You wiped his memory and made him into a wyvern, which means he has the instinct and mindset of—well, not one dragon but two. That's the point, isn't it? To make people forget who and what they are so they feel a need to go join their own kind. That's what you did to Fenton and Dewey. They couldn't wait to get out of that lab room and back to the gnomes and elves."

The faun scowled, then grimaced, reaching down to clutch her ankle.

"So Hal is nothing but a dragon right now," Abigail went on. "I doubt there's anything stopping him from burning you where you stand."

"Do it," River panted. "Your threats hold no weight, girl. Either do it, or get out of my way."

Abigail was silent for a moment. She bobbed up and down, her wings a blur where they poked through the back of her green, silky dress.

"What can I offer you in return?" she said at last.

The faun's scowl faded, and her heavy breathing subsided. She took on a calculating look, her yellow eyes narrowing. "Take me where I need to go and leave me there. I will then turn Hal back to his *human* form." Her voice dripped with disdain.

"But I have to watch you do it," Abigail countered.

The faun sneered at her. "Because you want to see how the potion works. All right—but you do not get the potion back. That is the deal I offer. I put your friend back the way he was, and you get to watch, but you do not take the potion away."

After a pause, Abigail nodded. "Deal."

River stared at her. "I know you will not leave it at that. You will seek to steal the potion from me the moment your friend is restored."

"You're right," Abigail said simply. "Do we still have a deal?"

For a moment, the faun looked like she might shake her head and try to hobble past Hal. But she gave a barely perceptible nod. "I respect your honesty. Let me climb up."

Hal waited as patiently as he could while the faun struggled to clamber up his tail and onto his back. He fought mounting indignation and anger. Only the possibility of regaining his memory kept him from throwing her off and burning her. He tamped down the fire in his chest and struggled to control his trembling rage.

The faun and the girl dared to make deals in front of him—*about him*—as if he wasn't there. Well, he had plans of his own. They argued over who would get to keep the potion afterward as if that were the most important thing, but they would have no such concerns when they were going up in flames where they stood. The very moment Hal's memory returned, he would turn both females to charred lumps of meat and feast on them before heading off to the labyrinth.

Enough with this nonsense, he thought with simmering anger.

When the faun and winged girl were seated, he took off as violently as he pleased and reveled in the yelps of fright as he bucked his body and rolled into his turns. Let them hang on for dear life as he soared high in the sky. Wings or not, he doubted the girl named *Abigail* was equipped for such altitudes. And the faun would drop like a stone if she fell.

But then I'll never get my memory back, he told himself. That was a sobering thought. He grudgingly steadied his flight and vowed to go easy for the moment.

"To the right," the faun yelled over the rushing wind.

He veered that way.

"Begin your descent!"

Already? Hal grunted and headed back down to the ground. Seeing nothing of interest, he could only keep a straight course and listen for instructions as he swooped lower. Even though it had been a very short flight, he'd covered a lot of ground, far more than she could have managed hopping on one leg.

"Fly low," the faun called. "Angle left just a little bit—there, like that. Stay straight. We are close."

Curious, Hal focused ahead. He still saw nothing but open plains for miles around.

"Slower!"

Hal did his best to slow his flight, but it was hard without dropping to the ground. The hard-baked earth rushed by twenty feet below.

"Land!"

He threw up his wings and thudded down, skidding a little. Once the faun had climbed off, he stood tall and glared at her. What kind of trickery was this? The location was no different from before—nothing to see, nowhere to hide, not even a crack in the ground to slide into.

"What *is* this?" Abigail asked as she buzzed around in a circle. "Why are we here?"

River said nothing but started hopping again. Hal and Abigail watched her in silence, mystified.

And then she vanished.

One moment she was there, the next—gone. Hal blinked in amazement. Abigail gasped, then rushed to follow. A second later, she vanished, too.

Hal was alone. He had no choice but to stomp closer and see what had happened. When he did so, his vision blurred, and he stopped and blinked.

Refocusing, he found himself staring at a single tree—the thickest, oldest oak he'd ever seen, with gnarled bark and twisted limbs. It wasn't tall, just stout. Fine grass grew all around its trunk, thinning a few yards out. The soil looked rich under the knotted roots, and a few bees buzzed around a couple of small, flowered shrubs.

Forgetting himself, forgetting everything for the moment, Hal eased closer, looking up and around. The branches were full and green, vibrant with life. The tree existed within a cocoon, perhaps a perfect dome encompassing every last leaf and reaching to the ground right about where the grass petered out.

Hal glanced backward. His rear end stood quite still in the plains. He had only encroached into the magical realm up to his shoulders. He could see the plains stretching for miles, and the forest in the far distance, the sun beating down. Only his head and neck were inside the cocoon, where the air was notably cooler and a little moist.

Abigail dropped lightly onto the grass and stilled her wings. She padded over to the tree, reaching out to touch the bark.

The faun, resting with her back to the trunk, watched her for a moment and then said, "This is a place of tranquility. It is mine."

"Where—" Abigail started. "How did you *find* this tree? What's it doing here? How does it survive out here in the plains?"

River said nothing.

"What kind of faun *are* you?" Abigail asked. "I thought you guys never left the woods."

"That would be a very limited existence. Besides, this *is* the woods."

"Yes, but . . . how?"

The faun gestured for Hal to move closer. For some reason, his back legs ached all of a sudden. "Let us get this over with," she said. "For this to work, it is probably necessary for you to be in your wyvern form."

"*Probably* necessary?" Abigail demanded.

"I have not dealt with a shapeshifter before. Let us assume just to be on the safe side."

When Abigail looked across at Hal, he let out a deep, rumbling sigh of agreement. He morphed, shrinking down to his wyvern form so that he stood on the edge of the grass just under the canopy of branches. He folded his wings and stomped closer to the faun and Abigail. He still had aches in his legs, maybe even a little cramp.

"That is better," River said. "I do not expect it is safe to straddle both realms at once for too long. As you can see, it is dusk already."

Hal and Abigail immediately looked out across the plains. The sun was indeed descending, the sky reddening.

"What's happening?" Abigail exclaimed.

The faun shrugged. "Every faun has a tree. I have never questioned the existence of this tranquil place. It just is." She looked at Hal. "Do you ache?"

He glanced at her with suspicion and nodded.

She smiled. "While we have been standing inside this realm for the last minute, your rear end has stood outside. The remainder of the day has passed out there, perhaps six hours? It is no wonder you ache. I killed a snake one time. It came down from a branch with the intent to bite me. I snapped its neck and tossed it down. Its head and nearly half its body lay inside the tranquil realm, the tail end outside. The tail end decomposed very quickly; the head did not. By the time the head end started gathering flies, the rest had turned to mush, only its bones left."

Abigail covered her mouth with one hand, her eyes wide. Hal had no such squeamishness, but he did find the story interesting.

"This tree was once part of the forest," the faun murmured, gazing up into the branches. "The forest covered this entire region, stretching far into the north. But something happened. The rain stopped coming, and the forest dried up. The land baked and cracked. This tree remained, protected by magic."

"What happened?" Abigail asked.

But the faun didn't answer. "We will finish this," she said, climbing to her feet—or rather one of them. She leaned against the tree and kept the other foot lifted. The bones would need setting; her cloven hoof hung at a strange angle. "Give me the potion."

Abigail shook her head. "You do the spell, I'll handle the potion."

"That was not the deal."

"When Hal is back to normal, you can have the potion. *That* was the deal. Anyway, you can always make more, right?"

River stared at her, then sighed. "The issue is not whether I can make more. The issue is that I do not want *you* to have it."

"Hmm. Well, at least you're honest."

The two stared at each other.

Hal let out a growl. He was growing tired of standing around while the two of them bickered. He was tempted to fly away and leave them. Previous thoughts of heading to the labyrinth were abandoned; he had fellow wyverns to find, not dimwitted fire-breathers.

"I think I can resolve this," the faun said, letting go of the tree and standing upright on one foot. "Pour most of the potion away. You only need a few drops."

"I'm not pouring it away!"

Hal growled again, louder this time. *I just want my memory back.*

River let out a screech of sudden rage, startling him. "You are an infuriating human!" she yelled.

Abigail smiled. "I know. Now, let's get this done."

The faun clenched her fists. "Put one drop in each of your friend's eyes."

"And then?"

"Then nothing."

After a long pause, Abigail shook her head. "But you said there's a spell—"

"I did not. *You* said that. Now, do as I say, and then begone from my place of tranquility."

"A drop in each—" Abigail repeated.

Hal gave a roar and advanced on her. He lowered himself onto the grass and spread his wings wide, thrusting his face toward her. He gave another snarl just for good measure.

Taken aback, she muttered, "All right, all right, keep your hair on." She uncorked the thin-necked bottle, peered into it, sniffed at it, then looked again at the faun. "So just one drop in each eye?"

The faun gave a curt nod.

Abigail raised the bottle over Hal's head, then leaned closer, aiming carefully. Hal tilted his head to one side, staring straight up at the teetering droplet. It fell and splashed right on target, and he closed both eyes, making sure the liquid didn't get away. When he opened his eyes again, Abigail was ready for the next drop, and he tilted his head the other way.

The second droplet fell, and the task was done.

"Now what?" Abigail said, turning to the faun.

"Now nothing. The potion will unveil your friend's view on life, and soon he will see himself for what he is—a mere human. There is no spell. This is a simple reversion. On its own, it cannot work in any other way except to restore what is natural. Coupled with powerful magic, however, the potion can pervert the natural order and turn a creature into what he is not."

"Like you did with your mist," Abigail muttered, staring at Hal.

He lay there waiting for something to happen, peering around through a watery gaze. He felt no different. His memory had certainly not returned. Anger flared in his chest, and he rose, preparing to flick his barbed tail at both females and leave them with an open wound full of poison. He was done with this nonsense.

"The potion," River said quietly, holding out her hand.

Abigail corked it and closed her hand tightly around the glass bottle. "Nothing has happened yet."

"But when it does, you must honor your end of the deal."

"Why? I have other friends to save."

"We made a deal."

"Only because I had no choice!" Abigail snapped. "I'll save my friends, and I'll save Miss Simone, and I'll save Derek and the other people you turned. Then, and *only* then, can you have the potion back. Or, since you don't need it, I'll promise to pour it out."

The faun scoffed and sneered, turning away. "If my ankle wasn't broken . . ." She hopped around to the far side of the thick tree. "Do not disturb me while I rest." She paused a second, giving Abigail a strange look. "I will be gone for some time."

As she vanished from sight, Abigail tucked the potion into her pocket and called after her. "How long will this take?"

She received no answer.

Hal turned to leave also. Night had fallen across the plains, though it seemed daylight continued to flood the tree realm. When he stepped off the grass and onto hard ground, the air cooled considerably, and a breeze sprang out of nowhere. Turning, he was startled to find no trace of the tree at all.

He spread his wings—but before he could take off, Abigail buzzed into view. "Don't leave me behind! Hal, wait, please. Take me with you."

Snarling, he raised his barbed tail to give her a whack.

She zipped out of range but didn't go far. "Hal, I know you're not yourself right now, but if the potion works—if the faun was telling the truth—then everything will be all right in just a minute. You'll see. Please wait. Don't leave me here. It'll take me *ages* to get home on my own."

He snarled again, advancing on her. This winged human had driven his patience to the edge.

Yet still she evaded him, zipping around just out of range. "Hal, if you let me ride on your back, I'll tell you everything you need to know about yourself. I'll remind you of all the things you've forgotten. Maybe jogging your memory will help turn you back."

Hal paused. She could jog his memory? It was true that she knew him; that much was obvious. How a human knew a wyvern so well was beyond him, but learning of their history together would almost certainly help. *Then* he could dispatch her. He could simply turn upside down mid-flight and drop her.

Grunting, he bowed his head, then lowered himself to the ground. Abigail buzzed closer, gripped his neck, and straddled his shoulders. Unlike the monstrous dragon form, he felt every ounce of her weight as she hung off his back with her arms around his neck and legs halfway around his midsection. He growled. Hoisting a faun out of a chasm with hellhounds pouncing at him was quite a bit different to carrying a human long-distance across the plains.

He lifted off into the night sky. The moon hid behind clouds, but he could see enough. Besides, it looked like dawn was approaching judging by the orange-tinted sky in the east. Could it really be morning already? The sun had only just gone down! The better part of twenty-four hours had passed sitting under that ridiculous tree of tranquility.

"So, where do I start?" Abigail said from his back, her voice raised above the wind. "We grew up together on a foggy island. Do you remember that? One day, we all started changing. I grew these wings, and Robbie turned into an ogre. You transformed into a dragon. All our friends were there, experiencing some kind of weirdness . . ."

She went on like that for a while, talking about how they all kept their secrets quiet until, one day, they gathered together at the lighthouse and showed off their transformation powers, some more proudly than others. Hal listened, interested but nonplussed by the whole thing. She spoke as though this had actually happened to *him*, like he'd been a part of it, one of these human children living together on an island—and yet he was a wyvern, and the idea of being even remotely human *for a second* made him shudder.

None of what she said helped his memory. And the eye-drops hadn't done anything, either.

The girl on his back started talking about the labyrinth of dragons. Her story somehow fit with what little he recalled—he remembered the emperor dragon and the tunnels of lava, and he knew humans had been there with him—but he'd been a dragon the whole time, which went against what she was claiming.

Growing angry again, he decided enough was enough. Abruptly, he lurched to one side and dumped her off his back.

She screamed as she fell, and he felt a pang of regret, a feeling that he really did know her well, that she was special to him . . . He considered diving and catching her before she hit the ground. That would be the kind thing to do.

But even as he thought it, she sprouted those weird little faerie wings. He couldn't hear their buzz from this distance, but he knew they were working overtime to arrest her fall. She spun fast all the way down but gradually got that under control and, at the last second, came out of her plummet and dropped lightly onto her feet.

Then she jumped up and down, waving her hands around, her screeching voice too distant to make sense of. He guessed she wasn't saying anything very nice.

Happy she was safe, and glad to be rid of her once and for all, he resumed his journey south. Now, where would he most likely find a family of wyverns—

He suddenly morphed, losing his wings and bright orange scales, losing the power of flight. He let out a yelp as he dropped out of the sky.

The wind rushed past as he flapped his utterly useless human arms. His smart clothes rippled wildly, and he felt the hair on his head tugging at his scalp as it whipped about. He toppled head over heels, spinning and yelling in terror. He was *human*, and he was going to die!

Wait a minute.

He broke off from his yelling. Everything clarified in an instant. As the ground rushed toward him, he shifted to dragon form and swooped out of the dive. Letting out a sigh of relief, he circled around to find Abigail.

Poor Abi! What have I done?

She stood quite still, watching him, a lonely figure in the vast, empty plains. The morning sunlight hadn't reached this far yet, but it was close. Hal landed in front of her. She said nothing, just watched him silently, hands on hips, her face expressionless. He grunted, trying to tell her to climb aboard so they could be on their way. Still she said nothing, just stood there and stared at him.

Finally, he reverted to human form. It took him a second to realize he had no shoes on—but he *was* wearing the rest of his smart clothes thanks to her insistence that she wrap them around his neck earlier. His thin, flexible shoes were stuffed in her pocket.

He approached. "Sorry about that," he said. "I can't believe I—"

She punched his shoulder *really* hard. "You threw me off!" she yelled. "You could have killed me!"

"That wasn't me!" Hal protested. "I mean, it *was*, but I—Look, you know I wouldn't normally—I just wasn't thinking straight, and . . ." He trailed off as she folded her arms and pouted.

"The wedding's off," she said.

"Th-the *what?*"

She gazed off toward the rising sun. "I can't marry someone who thinks it's okay to drop me from a great height."

Hal blinked at her, his mouth opening and closing. But then he saw a telltale twinkle in her eye, the curl of a tiny smile, and he let out a long sigh. "You're messing with me." He rubbed his shoulder. "That really hurt."

She narrowed her eyes and put on a stern expression. "You deserved it. But I forgive you. Now, shall we get back home and save our friends?"

He grinned. "Now you're talking."

Chapter Twenty-One
A Drop in Each Eye

Hal landed outside Miss Simone's laboratory building as dawn broke across Carter. He was hungry, though not as hungry as he should be considering he'd been gone almost a day in real time. His legs still felt a little achy from straddling the wrong side of the faun's tranquil place as the day had whizzed by.

"Where have you been?" Dr. Kessler exclaimed, almost bumping into Hal and Abigail as they strode along the corridor. "We'd lost hope! Did you find the faun? Do you still have the potion?"

"We have it," Abigail said, fishing the bottle out of her pocket. "And we know how to use it. One drop in each eye."

"One drop in—?" the woman repeated. "All right. Hand it over so I can get things moving."

As the scientist stalked away with the potion, Abigail muttered, "You're welcome."

Hal shook his head and smiled. "I guess she got tired of waiting for us. We've been gone a day, remember."

"Yeah, and what has everyone else done while we've been putting ourselves in danger?"

Hal took her hand and walked with her along the corridor, following the fast-moving scientist as she headed toward the front of the building. "It doesn't matter as long as the potion works."

To their surprise, Dr. Kessler hurried straight out the main doors.

Hal hurried to catch up. "Where are you going?"

The doctor glanced at him. "To deal with the problem. We'll go to young Dewey's first."

"So they're not in the lab?"

"Of course not! What, you think everyone is going to hang around the lab building all night waiting for you to show up? No, I sent everyone home."

"But they're confused," Abigail protested. "They don't think home is really home."

"I know. I have their parents keeping a close eye on them. Nobody gets to wander off."

The three of them kept up a quick pace through the streets. Dr. Kessler looked flustered and rather grim. When they asked her what was wrong, she spoke in short, terse sentences.

"Simone is missing. Imagine a basilisk on the loose in the village. *That's* what wrong."

"She got away?" Abigail said.

"She escaped the observation room through the ceiling, same way Thomas did. The goblins never did catch her. But they have her cornered at least."

"Cornered where?"

"As for Thomas . . ." Dr. Kessler went on, picking up her speed. "He's been spotted lurking in a quarry south of here. Scared, maybe."

Hal understood. He'd already forgotten most of his stint as a wyvern, but he recalled the urge to be with others of his kind. It seemed crazy now; to think he had wanted to shun humankind and go live with other wyverns. And when in dragon form, he'd felt a need to travel north to the labyrinth. Funny how his human side kept him in check. Without that, he was . . . well, an animal.

He guessed Miss Simone, as a basilisk, was so primitive in nature that she probably didn't even know she could transform into a mermaid. If she could, she'd be much easier to rescue. If Thomas remembered he was a manticore, he might head for the woods and be hard to find among others of his kind. In fact, he'd feel right at home with them as he had for the last six years of his life.

Fenton and Dewey should be easy to put right compared to Miss Simone and Thomas. And not forgetting Emily and Lauren!

When they arrived at Dewey Morgan's house, his stern father opened the door and stepped out. He was huge and bearded. "News?" he asked with his Welsh accent.

Dr. Kessler held out the potion. "I have it."

The man nodded and sighed. "Then come in. He's in his room."

Dewey's mom was standing outside the bedroom, her forehead pressed to the door. She spun around as the visitors walked in. "I've been trying to talk to him, but he's stopped responding. And when I open the door, he throws things at me."

"I had to board up the window," Mr. Morgan rumbled. "Wily things, these elves."

Dr. Kessler swallowed as she took out the potion. "Hold him down for me. I need to put a drop in each eye."

Mr. Morgan was the first to enter the room. Hal followed close behind.

Dewey, in elf form, was hunched into a ball in the corner. When the door opened, he leapt up and flew at the window, which had indeed been boarded up from the outside. Broken glass lay across the floor and chest of drawers. He hammered at the boards, then spun and darted onto the bed, ran the length of it, and tried to hurdle his dad in an effort to escape the room.

Mr. Morgan easily grabbed him in both arms and hugged him tight, then half threw him down onto the bed. "Easy, son."

Hal and Abigail put all their weight on Dewey while Mr. Morgan gripped the elf's head in both hands. Three people to hold a wily elf still!

Only when he was secured, and panting heavily, did Dr. Kessler approach with the precious bottle. One by one, she carefully pried Dewey's eyelids open and applied a drop in each. Then everyone retreated as the elf scampered to the corner and wiped his eyes with an angry mewling sound.

"Never seen such an *angry* elf," Abigail murmured.

"Better than an angry centaur," Hal said. "What if he'd remembered he could shift? He could have galloped off somewhere ages ago."

The delay for the potion to work proved to be an anxious wait. Not much was said, but clearly Mr. and Mrs. Morgan had their doubts judging by the way they kept looking at each other and then across at Dr. Kessler. Hal had doubts of his own. It had worked on *him*, but what if the faun had tricked them? What if the potion did nothing, and she'd simply whispered a spell that had caused him to revert back?

What would be the point, though? he asked himself. *It'll work. Just be patient . . .*

And, finally, it did. Abruptly, the elf sat up straight with a wide-eyed look, then morphed, his blue-tinted skin fading to normal human flesh tones, and his curiously white hair darkening. He grew a little in size; even Dewey was bigger than the average elf.

When the change stopped, he blinked and looked confused. "Wh-what happened?"

His mom let out a cry and ran to him, her feet crunching on glass. His dad sighed with relief and hung his head, then clamped a hand on Hal's shoulder and nodded at Abigail. He said nothing, but he didn't need to.

"One down, five to go," Hal said as they traipsed from the room.

"Don't forget the others," Abigail reminded him. "It's not just Thomas, Fenton, Emily, Lauren, and Miss Simone. There's Derek and a few more, too. We'll have to track them all down."

The success of the potion struck home once they all got outside. Hal and Abigail hugged, and Dr. Kessler looked like she might cry. "I honestly thought—" she started. She shook her head. "Never mind what I thought. Let's work on Fenton next."

Fenton Bridges hadn't been locked in his bedroom. He lay in the tiny, fenced-in backyard in his sleek lizard form, basking in the sun, his eyes closed. Hal looked around. The vertical slats in the fence had small gaps between each, and a padlock hung on the narrow gate's latch. At first glance, there was no way out. But Fenton wasn't a child. Even a large-headed gnome could clamber up and over. In his oily-black reptilian form, he could scale walls with ease. A fence would pose no problem.

"He seems happy to lie there and sleep," Mrs. Bridges said. "We locked him in his room at first, but he needed a bathroom break, and he walked straight past the bathroom and headed outside, so we let him go out for a moment. He peed in the corner, paced about, banged his head a few times, then sat down and grinned at us. He seems . . . *happy*. Maybe he just likes being out in the backyard."

"He's been digging in the dirt," Mr. Bridges said. "He dug a hole by the fence a while ago. Got down to bedrock and stopped. He would have tunneled his way out otherwise."

"Why did he switch forms?" Abigail asked.

Mrs. Bridges shrugged. "Don't know. He just did it out of the blue. I thought maybe I could talk to him then, as I've talked to him many times while he's slithered up walls—but he didn't respond."

Losing his human side, Hal thought.

Dr. Kessler produced the potion. This time, rather than pounce on Fenton and risk getting throttled by his long tail or spat at with sticky glue-water, his mom approached and began stroking his head while everyone else edged closer and knelt on both sides.

Fenton woke from his sleep but seemed too lethargic to react. His eyes glowed red as he opened them, but they became slits again as he started to doze off.

Dr. Kessler gently pried an eyelid open.

"Uh," Hal warned, "he should probably be in gnome form before you do that."

She paused and eyed him. "Why?"

After Hal explained what the faun had said, she considered for a moment, then recorked the bottle. "Well, let's get him into gnome form, then."

It meant waking him up and talking to him awhile, trying to make him understand, persuading him to become a gnome. Fenton seemed a little slow on the uptake, but he eventually obliged when Abigail knelt on the ground and began digging a hole.

Fenton, with a gnomish grin on his face, joined her.

Then everyone pounced on him—a sort of slow, gentle ambush that resulted in him laid out on his back, struggling to be freed.

It was over in seconds. With the second drop applied, everyone retreated, and Fenton sprang to his feet and ran for the fence. He scaled it with surprising ease and threw himself over in a sideways motion. Then he was gone.

Before Mr. and Mrs. Bridges could run after him, Dr. Kessler took them both by the elbows and said, "He'll be fine. He'll be Fenton again in a few minutes, and then he'll come wandering home."

Sure enough, fifteen minutes later, he walked into the house looking sheepish. "Sorry," he muttered.

His mom laughed. "What are you sorry for?"

The big boy shrugged. "Running off." He rubbed his stomach and scowled. "Is it lunchtime?"

Both parents laughed this time. "How about breakfast?" Mr. Bridges said.

With the two relatively easy patients dealt with, the shapeshifters braced themselves to face Thomas the griffin and then, later, Simone the basilisk. Those two would be tough. The others would seem like a walk in the park afterward.

"We need the whole team," Abigail said. "Dewey, Fenton, Robbie, Darcy, Emily, and Lauren—we need everyone together before we tackle a griffin."

Hal agreed. "We can deal with Emily and Lauren pretty easily first, and turn them human again. *Then* we'll have a team." He turned to Dr. Kessler. "The quarry, right? Is that the one with the big treadmill crane?"

She nodded. "It's quite a trek. I wonder if perhaps you could deal with this on your own while we track down some of the missing people from the village? If we divide and conquer . . ."

"Yeah, then deal with Miss Simone last," Hal agreed. "You'll find a mermaid in the river, and a pixie somewhere in the woods. Don't know about the other two."

"Thanks," Dr. Kessler said dryly. "That narrows it down." She started walking. "Let's split this potion in half so we each have a bottle. Safer that way."

Hal thought about the griffin stamping around and knocking everyone flying, and the glass bottle shattering in someone's pocket and leaking the last of the potion everywhere. *Yeah, splitting it into two would be smart.*

* * *

The team assembled outside Emily's house.

Robbie, in ogre form, had brought along his feisty troll, an oversized arm clamped around Lauren's neck while she struggled to get free. Darcy, Fenton, and Dewey hung a safe distance back.

Mr. and Mrs. Stanton allowed Emily to join the group without too much fuss. As a goblin, Emily had no real desire to head off to greener pastures; there were plenty of her kind in the village. In fact, she grumbled about having to leave the house, saying she'd been busy trying to repair the leaking kitchen sink.

"Can we get those drops now?" Darcy complained. "As funny as it is seeing Robbie and Lauren scuffling about, I'd rather we were all back to normal."

Hal laughed. "Abi, how about it?"

She turned and uncorked the potion. It was a much smaller bottle than before, a vial no bigger than a finger, with just a scant amount of magical liquid, way less than half. "Robbie, bring her here."

Robbie mumbled something and tried to wrestle Lauren into a kneeling position so Abigail could reach her face. Lauren resisted, lashing out and clubbing the ogre in the face. The skirmish got worse until the troll ended up flat on her back with Robbie, Hal, Darcy, and Fenton holding her down on the dusty road.

Abigail deftly applied the eyedrops. Then everyone sprang up, and Lauren rolled and climbed to her feet, snarling angrily and blinking the gunk away from her eyes.

"Your turn, Em!" Abigail said, swinging around to face the bemused goblin.

Everyone pounced before Emily had a chance to react. Still standing, she struggled somewhat feebly as Fenton roughly yanked on her thick, dark hair and tilted her head back. Abigail leaned in, and seconds later put the vial away in her pocket.

"Done!" she announced.

"So let's get going," Hal said. "South—to the quarry. I can take you all on my back."

Robbie shrank down to human size and gestured toward Lauren, who still looked pretty steamed and begging for a fight. He looked pretty ticked himself. "Can't we wait a second? If you'd given her the drops earlier, she would have been back to normal by now!"

"Yeah, but then we'd have missed all the fun," Hal murmured.

Fenton chortled, and Abigail covered her mouth.

They didn't have long to wait. Both Lauren and Emily reverted to normal shortly after, one at a time, a minute apart and almost exactly twelve minutes after they'd received the drops.

"It's pretty consistent," Hal commented as the girls exclaimed in wonder and clutched at their faces. "Twelve minutes, and boom!"

"It's not going to be so easy with Thomas," Abigail said, looking thoughtful.

Hal finally took off in dragon form with all his friends on his back—all except Lauren, who soared into the sky as though she'd forgotten she could do such a thing. She whooped and squealed, laughing as she tore back and forth in front of Hal.

The journey to the quarry was uneventful, mainly because Hal was a gigantic dragon; a passing fleet of rocs eyed them warily and stayed well clear. This might have been the exact same fleet of rocs that had attacked them months ago when the shapeshifters had taken to the air in Blacknail the goblin's airship, *CloudDrifter*, on their way to the Mountain of Whispers. Hal looked for telltale burnt feathers, but he didn't get a good enough look.

The quarry was a little farther than he remembered. When it came into view, he saw the ancient timber treadmill crane standing over something resembling a giant well shaft.

At first, the quarry seemed empty apart from the dusty crane and numerous ropes lying about the place. But on second glance, it became obvious Hal and his friends were not alone. A griffin snoozed in a sheltered spot under a low cliff on the north side.

Thomas!

Hal's passengers had been jabbering away throughout the journey, but now they clammed up. A hush fell as Hal circled the quarry. What should he do? Land in front of it and use the element of surprise to pounce and somehow pin it down? Or perhaps come down softly and approach on tiptoes?

Not an it, Hal told himself. *That's Thomas.*

He landed, and everyone slid off his back as quickly as possible. Lauren touched down at his side, her white wings gleaming in the sun.

Hal remained a dragon, not quite sure what to expect. Robbie became an ogre, and Dewey clip-clopped around in his centaur form with Darcy on his back. Emily, Fenton, and Abigail stayed well clear.

We could use ropes, Hal thought. *Maybe tie him down while he's sleeping . . .*

To his surprise, that idea seemed like it might actually work. The griffin never stirred, just lay on his side, completely relaxed, his chest rising and falling. He was pretty magnificent and formidable, a golden lion monster with the head, shoulders, front feet, and wings of an eagle. But he was much bigger than both, probably three times the size of a lion, and a far more dazzling gold color from the feathers at the front to the fur at the rear.

Not as big as Charlie Duggan, Hal thought, remembering their visit to the town of Louis in the north. *But still pretty impressive. And dangerous.*

Hal trotted over to some of the lengths of rope lying about the place. They were thick and heavy. They had once been wrapped around the giant wheel of the treadmill crane, but someone had unraveled them—probably a bunch of ogres. That was Robbie's doing. He'd led a gang of ogres to this spot to help erect the fallen crane and heave a giant lizard monster out of the well shaft. No doubt the ogres had resorted to a fun tug of war once all the hard work was done.

Hal gripped a length in his jaws and dragged it toward the sleeping griffin. Robbie came lumbering over to help, and he soon took over the task, his fat fingers more dexterous than Hal's clawed paws.

But he didn't get far.

Robbie had barely fed the rope around the sleeping monster's hind feet before he woke with a snort and a roar. The griffin struggled to his feet, his wings spreading wide.

Hal leapt on him, throwing all his weight into the fray. As big as the griffin was, Hal was bigger. Still, he faced very sharp claws and a terrible pointed beak that quickly tore into his shoulder. He swung his tail around and clubbed the griffin across the face, making him fall back with a gasp and moan.

Robbie worked quickly to tie the rear lion feet before moving on to the talons at the front. Hal watched anxiously, thinking it would all be pretty pointless if the griffin took off into the sky! The dim-witted ogre hadn't thought of that.

Abigail moved quickly, sprouting her wings and buzzing up above the griffin's head. The monster seemed woozy from the knock on the head, but he opened his eyes at the sound of the incessant buzzing.

"Hit him again!" Fenton yelled.

Hal didn't like to, but he felt it necessary when the snapping beak came within inches of snagging Abigail's foot. He swung again, and his club-ended tail smacked hard against the griffin's head. *Too* hard. Thomas fell back, tongue lolling.

"Do it!" Darcy said.

"Quick, while he's asleep!"

Abigail didn't need to be told twice, or even once. She buzzed closer, landed lightly on the griffin's shoulders, and reached over to drag an eyelid open. The first drop was easy. The second proved a challenge, because the griffin's head needed to be rolled to face the other way, which in turn meant rolling the entire body.

Robbie heaved, and the lion-like monster flopped over. Then Abigail was able to get to the other eyelid. She applied the second drop and buzzed away, grinning as she popped the vial back in her pocket.

Relieved, everyone stood well back as Robbie checked the ropes. The griffin might be groggy, but he might suddenly spring up and attack.

"I hope a drop in each eye is enough," Abigail said as she landed on Hal's back.

"We'll soon find out," Hal mumbled in his gruff dragon voice.

They waited.

And waited.

"It's been twelve minutes by now, right?" Abigail muttered.

Hal had to agree. More like twenty. Maybe two small drops hadn't been enough after all . . .

The griffin woke and blinked. Then he reared up with a screech and spread his wings wide.

"Come on, Thomas, *change!*" Darcy shouted.

"I'm worried he's going to fly up into the air," Abigail said. "What if he changes high off the ground? He'll fall!"

"I'll catch him," Lauren called from just above where she flapped about. "Or Hal will. But we'd better be ready."

Thomas bit the rope into pieces and shrugged them off all too easily. Then he stalked toward the shapeshifters, screeching and hollering, obviously furious at being mistreated while sleeping—not to mention waking to find his eyes all gummed up. He flapped and snapped, clawed and thumped, and generally made a lot of noise in their direction.

But, seeing Hal, the griffin gave a final shriek and took off into the air.

Both Hal and Lauren went after him. The griffin shot them a furious glance and put on a burst of speed. Hal matched him easily until the golden-furred monster started climbing directly upward. Thomas's strength and agility was astounding. Hal ascended as fast as he could but couldn't keep up. In seconds, the griffin was a speck in the sky, heading for the stars.

Lauren fared a little better with the rapid climb, but she grew tired and lagged behind.

This is bad, Hal thought, watching the griffin disappearing way above. *When he changes back . . .*

Hal had climbed high before. The altitude itself wasn't the problem. He just couldn't match the griffin's incredible speed. So he continued a steady climb while keeping a close eye above. Lauren apparently had the same idea.

It's like throwing a ball in the air and waiting for it to come down, Hal thought. *Gotta stay under it.*

The ball in this case was a fearsome, monstrous predator—but soon the monster would turn into a helpless red-haired boy. Then the desperate chase to catch him would be on.

It seemed the griffin was triumphant judging by the tone of its distant, high-altitude screeches. The winged creature leveled off and eased into a gentle cruise above the clouds, disappearing once in a while, then popping out into a clear patch of blue sky.

Hal and Lauren slowly but surely continued rising, keeping the griffin in their sights.

And then, all at once, the golden beast let out an odd squawk—and promptly vanished.

Or so it seemed.

The massive eagle-headed, lion-bodied monster had just shrunk to a pitiful size, barely visible at such a distance. Hal's heart thumped with terror at the thought of Thomas plummeting so fast, but there was no point rising to meet him; he'd just have to wait for his friend to fall and, hopefully, catch him.

Thomas started screaming as he flailed and twisted through the air, dropping like a rock.

We have one chance, Hal thought.

Lauren flapped like crazy, and it became evident she was nowhere near close enough to reach for Thomas as he spun past. Hal found himself in a better position, and he veered right. But if his friend simply smashed down on a dragon's hard, scaly back at such a colossal speed, the impact would kill him just as easily as smashing into the ground.

Hal let out a roar and began a steep dive. Matching Thomas's rate of descent was the only way this was going to work.

The flailing, red-haired, and completely naked boy rocketed past Lauren, way out of her range. She let out a shriek, her chance lost forever. But by this time, Hal was plummeting pretty fast himself, beating his wings hard, angled straight down and picking up speed. He veered this way and that, making slight adjustments that would bring him closer to Thomas.

Seconds later, the two of them were almost side by side, falling together. Thomas overtook him, and Hal had to adjust his wings back and streamline himself just a little more. At the same time, Thomas windmilled his arms as he twisted and turned. Those slight adjustments brought Hal back in line with his friend, and they fell together once more, their speeds perfectly matched.

The ground rushed up toward them.

In a panic, Hal made another hasty adjustment with his wings and angled toward Thomas a little faster than planned. His friend yelled, then let out an "oomph!" as the two collided. Hal barely felt the impact.

He twisted his neck and glanced all over, frantically looking for the red-haired boy. He couldn't find him anywhere. But then he heard the familiar roar of a manticore, and when he turned his head again, he spotted red fur and an arcing tail somewhere low on his reptilian back. Thomas had somehow clamped on.

Pulling out of the dive, Hal tore low across sparse fields and barely had time to rise again before some low hills appeared in front of him. He banked hard and swooped around, then let out a cry of relief as he skidded down on ugly scrubland.

He lay there panting awhile, watching dust and dry grass puffing up in front of his flaring nostrils. A minute later, he felt slight movement on his back as Thomas jumped down.

The manticore trotted around from one side and stood before him, trembling, his tongue hanging out.

"Th-that was some ride," Thomas croaked.

Chapter Twenty-Two
Basilisk

Hal glanced back, wishing he could twist his neck enough to see his friends sitting astride his back as he and Lauren flew toward Carter. It had to be a weird sight—two human girls, one tiny faerie, three human boys . . . and a manticore. Thomas had dug his claws in tight, holding on while Hal approached the village.

Despite a moment where Thomas had seemed eternally grateful for the daring rescue, he'd quickly reverted to his usual self and shrugged off the incident as a minor annoyance. He even scoffed a little at Lauren's terrible judgment in the air. "You always were useless at catch," he'd said.

But everyone knew he was simply hiding the sheer terror he'd felt on the way down.

Hal landed once more outside the science lab where he assumed Dr. Kessler could be found. His friends clambered off his back just as Lauren touched down. Together, and most of them human once more, they marched into the lab.

"Go find some smart clothes," Darcy told Thomas.

The manticore wandered off along the corridor, and everyone trailed behind. It didn't take him long to steal some from one of the rooms put aside for the Shapeshifter Program. He reappeared fully dressed and in human form.

Dr. Kessler was not around, but Dr. Porter was. "Hey, Mom," Abigail said, walking up to her. "What are you doing?"

The small woman looked a lot like Abigail, though far more highly strung. "Oh, *there* you are," she exclaimed, spinning around and giving her daughter a hug. "I was worried about you, being gone for so long. Poor Hal's mother, too. She doesn't like to make a fuss, but—"

"Yeah, I know," Abigail interrupted in her usual polite but firm manner. "What are you doing here? Do you know where Dr. Kessler is? We have a basilisk to catch."

Dr. Porter closed her eyes and muttered something, then glared at Abigail. "You stay well away. Dr. Kessler and the goblins have the thing cornered. They'll get it."

"But—it's Miss Simone!"

"Yes, yes, I know, but . . . right now it's a nasty, deadly little critter." Dr. Porter looked so aghast that Hal fought to cover his smile. "Go home, my dear. You too, Hal, and everyone else. You've done plenty enough already. Just let the adults handle this situation."

If Hal had a smirk on his face, her comment wiped it clean away. "Let the *adults* . . . ?" he repeated. Behind him, he heard Fenton mutter something rude, and Lauren clicked her tongue.

Abigail stepped back from her mom as if slapped. "Mom! We're shapeshifters. This is our job."

"Not with a basilisk on the loose," her mom insisted. "Now, all of you—"

Abigail shook her head and called out to a goblin as he stalked along the corridor toward the main entrance she and the others had just walked in. "Where's the basilisk?"

The goblin offered her a curt glance. "Stonemason's."

That was all he said. He stomped through the crowd of shapeshifters and shoved the door open wide, marching out into the sunlight.

"Abigail," her mom warned, reaching for her. "Please stay away. One glance from that little monster and—"

"I know, Mom, I know. But we still have to help."

Dr. Porter clung to her daughter's arm with one hand and Hal's with the other. They stared back, and gradually her stern, defiant expression weakened and crumbled. She let her hands drop to her sides.

"If you only knew," she mumbled. "One day, you'll have kids and will know what it is to worry. I'll bet you won't let your child anywhere near a basilisk."

"Mom!" Abigail complained. She took Hal's arm and spun him around. "Let's go. We'll be careful, Mom—as always."

Still, Dr. Porter followed them all, staying ten paces behind as the shapeshifters entered the village. There were quite a few stonemasons around the village, but Hal and Abigail assumed the goblin had meant the one who lived closest to the lab, a man named Gilbert Coin. That was where they headed.

Large crowds blocked the streets near a narrow crossroads. Cottages gave way to small shop windows. It never got as busy as the market here, but the smell of baking bread from one doorway tended to draw customers from the very moment the rotund owner opened up in the morning.

As Hal slowed, Robbie shouldered past, growing larger so he could plow a path through the mass of jostling bodies. Everyone followed in his supersized footsteps.

"Excuse me," Darcy said, sidestepping a surprised woman. She raised her voice. "Shapeshifters coming through!"

The crowds parted, and Robbie led the way straight to the stonemason's door with the others right behind. Somehow, Hal had ended up near the back, but he jostled his way to the front as they arrived at the open doorway.

At least a dozen heavily armored goblins stood outside. Instead of brandishing their usual swords, they wore gloves and held large nets on thick sticks. When one glanced sideways, Hal was startled to see black-tinted round goggles strapped to his head, his eyes completely masked. Hal saw himself in the stark reflection.

More goblins stood inside the stonemason's, blocking the doorway.

"Do those things work against a basilisk?" he asked the goblin, pointing at his face.

The goblin shrugged. "Ain't never seen no basilisk before."

Considering the number of men, women, shapeshifters, and goblins crowded into the tight crossroads, it was surprisingly quiet, just a few low mutterings here and there. Inside the stone building, a woman's voice floated out the doorway.

"It's me, Simone. Just me. If you can hear what I'm saying and understand, please come on out."

Fenton wrestled his way between Hal and the goblin. "Why's this taking so long? If you're all geared up with goggles, gloves, and nets, why don't you just go in there and grab her?"

The goblin scowled behind his goggles. "She's a spitter."

"A *spitter*?" Fenton scoffed and shook his head. "She's not the only one who can spit. Gimme those goggles and gloves. I'll catch her."

"Fenton," Abigail warned.

To Hal's surprise, the goblin seemed quite willing to hand over his protective gear and net. But as soon as he'd done so, he turned and shoved his way through the crowd, apparently relieved of duty. As

Fenton donned the goggles, other goblins began removing theirs and handing them to the shapeshifters.

"Uh," Hal said as a set was shoved into his hands. "Thanks?"

One by one, goblins slipped away—nine in total, wiping sweat from their foreheads. The rest stayed put, stoic and solid, like statues.

"I'm not sure I, er . . ." Emily mumbled, staring at the gear in her hands.

Thomas simply let his goggles, gloves, and net fall to the ground. He said nothing, but he brushed his hands, stuck them in his pockets, and eased backward into the crowd, his message perfectly clear.

Fenton, on the other hand, finished gearing up and brandished his net. "Let's do this," he growled. The goggles looked even weirder on him, black and bulbous. He looked like a giant bug, a somewhat pudgy fly.

"Wait up, Fent," Darcy said, sliding her goggles in place. "Just let me get these gloves on."

Hal sighed. "I guess *we're* doing this," he whispered to Abigail.

She shrugged. "Of course we are. This is the kind of thing we have to deal with as shapeshifters." She swallowed. "Right?"

Fenton pushed his way into the building. Darcy followed.

"I've been here plenty of times," Robbie announced, falling in step behind her—as if his part-time job helping the stonemasons build cottages would somehow help the situation.

Darcy fuzzed out as soon as she passed through the doorway. Her goggles and gloves vanished too. Her net did not, though part of her stick seemed a little vague where she gripped it. Maybe she didn't need goggles. If the basilisk couldn't see her, then—

Or, what if the deadly magic was more about looking *at* the basilisk, looking directly into its eyes rather than the other way around? Invisibility wouldn't help her then. Nor would the goggles— unless they were so dark they rendered the wearer blind.

Hal pulled his on. He could see fine through them, though the world was suddenly plunged into the darkest of nights.

"How do these help?" he asked the nearest remaining goblin.

The sour-faced fellow shrugged. "Mirrors."

He didn't sound very sure.

Another half-dozen goblins were crowded inside the stonemason's lobby. There wasn't much to see from where Hal stood—basically an empty room with a dark-wood counter set diagonally across one corner.

It was freestanding with solid sides, like a desk but taller. Huge sheets of paper were draped across the top. House plans, maybe? There'd been a lot of construction in the village lately. A closed door stood beyond.

"She's under the counter," Dr Kessler said, suddenly appearing by Hal's side and placing a hand on Fenton's arm to stop him from approaching. She, too, wore the black goggles and gloves. "She hasn't moved all morning. We tried to knock her out with a sleep gas, but it agitated her, and she started spitting. She's not responding to my voice at all. We may have to take her by force."

Fenton drew himself up. "I'm on it."

"Fenton!" Darcy hissed, reaching out to grab his shirt collar. "Hold up! Don't be an idiot. Have you forgotten what it's like to be turned to stone?"

Goblins moved aside, seemingly happy to relinquish their roles and let the shapeshifters take over. Hal and his friends suddenly found themselves alone in the lobby. Even Dr. Kessler had slipped through to the rear of the group. "Be very careful," she warned.

At a loss, Hal looked around. He was pleasantly surprised to see Thomas had joined them after all, complete with goggles and gloves.

"Ideas?" Hal said.

Robbie, a foot taller than normal and very broad in the shoulders, grew another few inches. "I could rip the counter out. Mr. Coin doesn't like it there anyway. He wants to install a stone slab. He said a wooden counter belongs in a carpenter's workshop."

"Shut up, beanpole," Fenton growled over his shoulder. "Nobody cares about your part-time job tossing stone blocks around."

"I don't *toss* them. I place them *carefully*. I build walls."

"Shh," Abigail whispered. "Just—pull the counter away so we can— so we can see behind it. But do it fast."

"I'll blast her with glue," Fenton said, already drooling down his chin. He started belching and stretching his neck like a cat trying to bring up a furball.

"Gross," Darcy muttered.

Hal took another look around to see how ready his friends were. All were geared up and shuffling anxiously. Lauren and Dewey hung the farthest back, perhaps the least able to help in a situation like this.

Emily was busy transforming. She rose up high on her thick, serpentine body and slithered forward. "Before you do that, Robbie, let me see if I can distract her. She might understand snake-talk."

"Why? She's a basilisk, not a snake."

But Emily didn't answer. She slid across the flagstones and lowered her head as she approached one side of the large, sturdy wooden counter. She began whispering in a weird voice.

As she did so, Robbie tiptoed to the opposite end, reaching for it with increasingly hairy hands as he grew a little more. His shirt had stopped trying to stretch around his bulging frame and now split wide, beginning to morph into an ogre belt.

Hal gently pushed Abigail backward as he stepped in front. He wasn't sure what he intended to do. He couldn't transform in such a tight space, and breathing fire would only cause harm to everyone present. He certainly didn't want to burn Miss Simone.

"We need a box," he whispered.

"There's one right there," Darcy said from beside him.

He jumped, squinting in an effort to see her. But sure enough, a rectangular metal box about three feet long stood on the floor, obviously brought in by one of the goblins. The sides had lots of small breathing holes punched through.

Hal hurried over to it. It had a metal door at one end, wide open, facing the counter. It was ready to go—if they could just herd the creature inside.

A sudden crash startled him as Robbie violently yanked on the counter and dragged it in an arc across the room. He didn't stop until the entire piece was facing the other way—revealing the basilisk.

Dewey and Lauren both let out shrieks. Thomas cursed. Abigail gasped. The fear in the room was palpable. Emily zipped to safety behind the front of the counter, which now faced the corner.

Of all the things Hal had met and dealt with—dragons, trolls, rocs, werewolves, even the so-called giant Shadow Demon—the six-legged, vivid-yellow basilisk filled him with the most dread. Like his friends, he just wanted to run from the room. Even Molly the gorgon paled against this creature, because she was in control of her faculties and had no desire to harm anyone, whereas this thing, this primitive reptilian critter, probably just wanted to escape into the wild. And like any cornered animal, it would likely fight its way out.

For the moment, it was too busy seeking refuge and not finding it. Like a frightened rat, it scuttled along the inside of the counter, hemmed in by the two end panels and not willing to emerge into the open room. Not yet, anyway.

Fenton leapt forward and belched up a long stream of greyish liquid. The water drenched the red-and-yellow striped creature, and it threw up its wings and started screeching, sounding rather like a banshee. When a banshee wailed, it meant somebody was about to die. The same probably held true for a basilisk.

It started flapping, and it hopped and scuttled out from the counter across the flagstones . . . but Fenton's glue dried just enough to gum up the wings. The basilisk flopped about, screeching and hissing.

"Hal, the box!" Abigail yelled at him.

Hal shoved the metal box across the floor toward the flailing basilisk, which immediately stopped thrashing and spun to face him.

Hal sucked in a breath as he caught sight of the thing's gaze. It locked onto him, and he stared back, feeling a terrible sense of dread very similar to when he'd looked into Molly's eyes and turned to stone.

After a second, the basilisk opened its mouth wide and hissed, revealing neat rows of tiny, pointed teeth.

Hal had a moment of relief. The deadly gaze hadn't killed him! The goggles worked!

But then the basilisk spat at him.

Searing yellow droplets spattered his gloved hands and bare forearms. The smoldering venom was as hot as lava. He fell back in horror as smoke poured from his wounds. His friends began yelling and screaming, and he felt hands grabbing him to pull him away.

The basilisk tried to fly toward him, but instead it skittered and skidded on its six legs. Hal ended up on his back as the creature leapt onto his chest. He stared into its eyes again, saw the mouth open wide—and then Robbie's enormous hairy foot swung in and kicked the basilisk across the room.

It flew in an arc, hit the wall, and slid down. Momentarily stunned, it gave Hal the chance to stagger to his feet, his forearms still smoldering and smoking, the pain almost too much to bear. He just wanted to flee, but his friends surrounded him, inadvertently standing in his way.

"We have to get it *now*!" Fenton shouted, taking a few steps toward the basilisk but faltering.

A fuzzy shape flitted across the room—an invisible Darcy with her net raised high.

Hal didn't even know where his own net was. He'd dropped it when the basilisk had come at him. He watched with mounting terror as the almost-invisible shapeshifter crept over. Abruptly, she threw her net aside and fell upon the yellow-and-red reptile, *actually wrestling with it.*

Hal watched in amazement. They all did. Darcy picked the thing up, struggling with its weight, holding its face away from her and toward the wall as she grunted and swayed. "Some help here!" she gasped.

Fenton rushed in at last and, after a moment of fumbling, took the struggling, shrieking creature and held it against his chest, tail-end first, gripping its middle set of legs. It twisted and squirmed but couldn't get loose, so it started spitting again, spraying a wide arc of yellow droplets across the back end of the room. Those droplets sizzled and smoked as they hit the stone floor and wall.

Hal moaned, trembling with shock and pain. He felt pretty useless, and he'd failed at his job with the metal box.

"The box!" Fenton yelled as though reading his mind. "Bring it here!"

Robbie stamped over to get it, his blundering ogre form almost too tall for the wood-beamed ceiling. He picked up the metal box and headed toward Fenton.

Fenton, looking over his shoulder with his black goggles, reversed toward it.

"Don't turn around!" Lauren urged.

Fenton clicked his tongue. "I know that."

But then he gasped and yelled out as the basilisk managed to twist just enough to spatter him with venom. The droplets sizzled through Fenton's shirt sleeves, and he involuntarily jerked away—releasing the squirming creature.

Everyone yelled and scattered. The basilisk dropped to the floor and turned toward them all. If they hadn't been wearing mirrored goggles, they'd all be dead by now.

Mirrors, Hal thought wildly, remembering the effect reflections had on gorgons. *Mirrors send the death-gaze back!*

But not in this case. Basilisks were not gorgons, and apparently the sight of its own gaze didn't bother it one bit.

It ran at them, hissing and spitting. Its aim was wild and thinly scattered, and probably every shapeshifter in the room suffered a sizzle or two. Its range wasn't good, just a few feet, so they could run around to escape—but they kept jostling and bumping one another, and then heels and ankles got sprayed, and smoke poured off their legs, and everyone yelled and screamed in panic and sheer agony.

Then Hal's chance presented itself. The basilisk scuttled past with its sights on Dewey and Emily. It was literally an arm's length away.

He threw himself at it, arms wide, and landed directly on top. Clamping his arms around the thing's head and body, he balled himself up and used his knees to prevent it from squirming backwards. Sweating and trembling, he hugged the basilisk so tight it couldn't move other than twist its neck half an inch one way or another.

He felt the wings trying to flap, the six legs kicking, the short tail whipping about. The jaws snapped, venom spat and dribbled, and the creature went into a frenzy trying to escape.

Hal hugged it tighter still, gritting his teeth and moaning, desperate to win the battle—because if he let go, he would likely get sprayed all over, and so would his friends.

"I'm here," Abigail said, kneeling by his side well away from the basilisk's front end.

Hal felt like his muscles were about to snap. "Hurry," he groaned.

She produced the potion. Deftly, she leaned over the basilisk's head and dared it to look up at her—which it did, hissing louder than ever.

Shakily, Abigail shook drops of the potion loose, splashing it in the tiny, evil little eyes.

"Keep holding on," she said, recorking the small bottle and stashing it away.

Hal closed his eyes and concentrated on one thing only, ignoring his aching muscles and burns. He was aware of his friends crowding around behind him, of hands on his back and shoulders. They couldn't do anything to help, because any kind of fumbling and repositioning would set the thing loose again. So he held on, and he drew strength and reassurance from the touch of his friends.

"Twelve minutes," he groaned.

Yeah, that's not gonna work. I can't hold on that long.

He eyed the box and immediately rejected the idea. When Miss Simone eventually reverted to her normal self . . . He shuddered.

Then he felt gloved hands on his. Fenton's, Thomas's, Robbie's—all of them snaked their way in around his arms and found a place to hold the basilisk down. It was all done calmly and smoothly, and Hal watched as they found a leg, a wing, the tail, something to hold onto and relieve some of his load.

He eased off bit by bit. His muscles screamed as they relaxed, but then he felt immense relief as he gradually slipped out from the tangle of limbs. His friends pressed in on the struggling creature, then blocked his view, and he wound up lying on his back, breathing hard, hurting all over.

The minutes passed at a snail's pace.

Emily vanished through the doorway at the back of the room. She returned a minute later with a blanket, which she carefully draped over the basilisk and the hands holding it down. The three boys looked up at her with puzzled frowns, and then Fenton's eyebrows shot up.

"Oh yeah—she hasn't got any clothes on."

One at a time, they withdrew their hands from under the blanket and repositioned them above. The blanket seemed to calm the basilisk, too; Hal could see from where he lay that it stopped wriggling so much.

And then, finally, an agonizing twelve minutes after the potion had been administered, Miss Simone woke.

Chapter Twenty-Three
A Place of Tranquility

Miss Simone sat up, clutching the blanket around her. She peered at the shapeshifters, noting the oddly positioned counter and the dozens of weird pockmarks across the floor and on the walls where drops of venom had splashed. The huge plans that were once draped across the counter now littered the floor, charred and smoldering.

Slowly, her memory returned. Hal could see it on her face as everything came back to her. Absently, she pulled her blanket tighter. "What have I done?" she whispered.

"Nothing, Miss Simone," Abigail said with a cheerful smile. "Nobody got hurt. Well, not seriously, anyway."

It was then Miss Simone noticed the same pockmarks on all their clothes and on their skin. Her eyes widened. "Are those . . . burns?"

Everyone started brushing at their injuries as if to wipe them away. Hal had it the worst across his forearms—a mess of burns and ugly welts that stung when he touched them.

"The gloves worked, though," Robbie said.

Like most of the others, Hal had already pulled his off and found his hands to be unmarked. It seemed the gloves were lined with something impenetrable, maybe an ultra-thin metal, like a delicate chainmail woven into the fabric . . . All he knew for sure was that the gloves had worked like a charm, as had the goggles.

"And the safety glasses?" Miss Simone asked. She shook her head. "Obviously they worked, or you'd all be stone by now."

"They're kind of dark, though," Lauren said. "Hard to see. It's like nighttime."

"Well, maybe one day we'll get some of those night-vision goggles from Old Earth. I've tried them. Amazing." She climbed to her feet, still clutching the blanket around her. "Go outside and transform a few times. Clean up those wounds. Then we can have a briefing."

After wearing heavily tinted goggles in a dingy room, taking them off and stepping outside into daylight caused a lot of blinking and eye-shielding. Gradually, Hal was able to take a good look around. To his surprise, the streets were just as crowded as before, only much quieter. Both Dr. Kessler and Dr. Porter stood at the front, a legion of goblins to their sides, and villagers amassed behind.

"Abigail!" her mom exclaimed.

"Everyone all right?" Dr. Kessler asked, eyeing them as they filed out.

When Miss Simone emerged in the doorway, a cheer went up. Dr. Kessler closed her eyes for a moment, a smile on her lips, then nodded with approval at Hal and his friends. "Well done. Well done."

Dr. Porter hugged Abigail, then gave her a good talking to. Hal couldn't help grinning behind their backs.

Robbie approached a man in the crowd. "Sorry about the mess, Mr. Coin."

The old, wiry stonemason removed his round spectacles and rubbed them on his shirt, then replaced them and shook his head. "Don't fret over it, boy."

Miss Simone called from the doorway. "Can somebody please get me some clothes?"

* * *

The shapeshifters found a space among the nearby streets to transform back and forth. It reminded Hal of taking a cleansing shower, washing away the dirt. Their wounds almost seemed to melt away, the welts smoothing out and the redness fading.

But their job wasn't yet done.

They returned to find Miss Simone and Dr. Kessler in deep conversation, with Abigail's mom loitering nearby.

"What can we do?" Darcy asked. "Do we know where the rest of the faun's victims are?"

Miss Simone waved a hand in a vague manner. "One is a mermaid in the river. I can deal with her. Another is a dryad, probably wandering around in the woods. He'll take a while to find. The other two have been taken to the lab. One's a naga, the other a pixie."

"Which one is Derek?" Emily asked.

"The dryad. Matilda is already out searching for him."

"We'll split up and find them," Darcy offered. "At least none of them are dangerous."

Miss Simone gave a nod and pulled at her new shirt, which was thick and manly, way too big for her. Her pants were baggy, too, rolled up so that they didn't drag in the dirt. Her feet were bare.

She looked at Hal. "While we're searching for mermaids and dryads, I need you and Abigail to find the faun. It's very important you bring her back."

Hal took Abigail's hand. "No problem. We know where she is."

They departed immediately, leaving the crowded streets behind. Their friends and Miss Simone could find the missing dryad and mermaid while Dr. Kessler used the potion on the naga and pixie in the lab. Hal felt a little envious. He'd have liked to see them all returned to normal. Maybe he still could if the faun wasn't too hard to find.

He flew out north of the village, over the forestland, and toward the plains. Abigail was again perched on his back, raising her voice above the wind.

"We need to be *careful*, Hal. I do *not* want her turning you into a frog or anything. I don't think a simple kiss from a princess will work." She patted his back, though he barely felt it. "The princess is me, by the way."

As he cruised across the open plains, he started to fear they'd never find the hidden tree. How could they? It was *hidden*. Literally invisible. He spotted the fissure easily enough and followed its length looking for the place he'd slipped down through the crack. It took a little while, but he circled what he thought was the right spot and was gratified to hear Abigail agree.

Then it was a case of heading north from that point as they'd done before. He flew for a short while, then came down again—not quite landing but hop-hovering as he called it, bouncing along in leaps as he tried to identify something familiar about the terrain.

"Quit hopping!" Abigail shouted. "Put me down. I'm having a hard time staying on."

But she didn't need to be put down. She simply buzzed off his back and started zigzagging about, shielding her eyes and scouring the area.

Hal landed and turned in a slow circle, taking in all the nearest scents. There wasn't much, this far out in the plains. He detected a dead thing somewhere, but he ignored it, trying to find the musky scent of faun instead.

He found nothing.

They searched and searched, growing more and more frustrated.

Except . . .

No, he'd imagined it.

Or had he?

He sniffed, nostrils flaring, lifting his chin to the air. It was perhaps the very faintest whiff of . . . grass? The fresh smell of nature! He studied the landscape ahead, seeing nothing but dusty, hard-baked plains. There was only one place grass grew around here, and that was the faun's place of tranquility.

He stomped forward, making a beeline for nothing in particular.

"Did you find something?" Abigail called, buzzing closer. She zipped off ahead, zigzagging back and forth. It appeared her strategy was simple: fly until she chanced upon the hidden realm.

It was a perfectly good tactic. Suddenly, without warning, she vanished. Hal blinked, pausing. Then she re-appeared, beaming. "It's right here!"

"Wait!" he said before she could vanish again. "Just hold on there. I need to do something."

She paused, bobbing up and down in the air.

He spent five minutes walking backward around the hidden realm while breathing fire directly onto the ground at his feet. The hard-baked earth and bare rocky patches blackened considerably, and he made sure the burn-line was at least a foot thick. Abigail guided him, plunging in and out of the realm to give him a clue as to its scope. He felt quite proud of his work when he managed to reverse all the way around and meet his starting point with pinpoint accuracy. He'd drawn a very nice circle maybe fifty feet in diameter, probably one that could be seen from space.

Well, maybe not. But it was pretty well defined, at least until the rain washed the scorched earth away and scoured the rock clean.

"Okay, are you finished?" Abigail demanded at last. "Come *on*, Hal!"

She darted out of sight again.

Hal reverted to human form, then moved toward the center of the circle. The tree appeared in front of him, and the grass tickled his feet as he strode toward the thick, gnarled trunk. *This* was what he'd smelled—the natural scents of the forest.

Abigail gestured for him to hurry. "The clock is ticking now."

He shielded his eyes against the sun, wondering if he'd see it move across the sky. Sure enough, time slipped by outside the place of tranquility at a much faster pace, and after a few seconds of squinting, the sun shifted a discernible distance. He guessed an hour had passed out there. For every minute he stood inside the realm . . .

"Come see what I spotted while you were burning the ground," Abigail said, breaking his concentration.

She circled the tree to the far side. Hal followed, remembering how the faun had done the same thing just before they'd left her last time. To his surprise, the trunk was split, forming a cavelike opening, maybe shoulder-width at the bottom and tapering to a point several feet up. The bark had long since grown around the split like an old scar, so the opening had a smooth frame. This was a natural, ancient deformity.

"I haven't been in yet," Abigail said, leaning closer. "But it's bigger than it looks. Come on."

Darkness enveloped her, and she disappeared, swallowed up inside the great tree.

Hal hurried after her, stooping low.

A moment of panic set in as he fumbled in the blackness. "Abi," he called.

"Here," she said, sounding like she might be ten or twenty paces ahead.

Hal felt bark and knotted roots all around, moist earth at his feet, and a slight downhill slope. He hurried to catch up. This place was bigger than it should be.

Her voice floated out of the darkness, much closer now. "I see something."

"Well, I don't have faerie vision like you," he complained.

"Light up with some fire, then."

He did so, just a short burst that left him an image of what lay at her feet—a makeshift bed made from a thick fur, and a dust-covered lamp. A few neatly carved sticks lay there, too, along with lengths of knotted roots formed to make thin rope.

"She rested here," Abigail said after Hal's fire cut off. "This is some kind of hidey-hole. I think she made a splint for her broken ankle."

As much as they wanted to get out of that place as fast as possible, they couldn't leave without a thorough search. The inside of the tree, while unnaturally spacious, didn't stretch too far. Hal's flames picked out every nook and cranny, and it became clear the faun was long gone.

Hal grunted with annoyance. "Let's get out of here."

They returned again to the entrance and stepped outside. The sky above the plains was dark-grey, the clouds low and ominous. The plains had been warm and dry before. Now, a blast of ice-cold air hit them, and a fine white coating of snow surrounded them for miles.

Hal gasped. *Snow?* How was that even possible?

But something else drew his attention. "What the—?"

Abigail sucked in a breath.

They stared out of the hidden realm at a fence surrounding the tree. It was a simple picket fence, nothing fancy. It wouldn't keep people out, nor small animals. It certainly wouldn't keep the faun imprisoned, if that was its purpose.

Abigail let out a strangled noise. "Wh-where did *that* come from?"

"It's built on top of my circle," Hal whispered.

It was as though the fence had grown overnight from his charred marker.

"How long were we gone?" Abigail said with a shiver. She nudged closer to him.

"I don't know. But time passed *way* quicker while we were inside the tree."

Abigail turned to him, her eyes widening. "Last time, we lost a *whole day* just by standing *next* to the tree. But look at that fence! Someone built that while we were inside the tree just now. We've been gone *weeks*!"

That was a harrowing thought.

"So everyone's probably searching for us, right?" Abigail went on. She started pacing. "They've already been here. They know it's easy to lose time, so I guess they all stayed well back. Maybe Miss Simone came in alone. She probably tested things, lost a day or two while the goblins built the fence . . . and probably tested the tree, too."

"Yeah, but she's smarter than us," Hal grumbled. "She probably didn't hang around in there the way we did."

Determined not to lose another second of time, he dragged Abigail out of the hidden realm and across to the snow-covered picket fence. His breath steamed up before his face as the chill swept through him. Abigail was already rubbing her hands vigorously.

"Isn't it beautiful?" she said. "I mean, it's cold as heck, but still . . ."

Hal twisted around. The tree had vanished again. The circular fence seemed so random and bizarre now, a perimeter around nothing—but it left no doubt where the faun's lair was.

They navigated the inside of the fence to where a gate stood slightly ajar. Stepping outside, Hal and Abigail studied the snow together. It was pure and white, untouched since the last snowfall.

"Nobody's been here in a while," Abigail said, voicing his exact thoughts. "No footprints."

Hal sighed. "Let's go home."

As he transformed and waited for Abigail to climb on, he remembered the last time they'd seen the faun, when she'd hobbled around the tree, given them a rather odd look, and said, *"I will be gone for some time."*

His mind whirled with possibilities as he headed for Carter. Trails of smoke rose from chimneys. How was it the dead of winter? It had been late summer when they'd entered the tree. Now it had to be December or January—not weeks later, but *months*. Either that or the world had suffered a dramatic climate change.

And if he and Abigail had lost months after a quick trip through the tree, how much time had the faun lost after a long rest?

The fact that they hadn't crossed paths with River bothered him, too. If she'd entered the tree first and rested for a few hours, she would have lost years in the outside world. But that meant she was still in there right now . . . only she wasn't.

Hal shook his head, completely befuddled.

When he landed outside the laboratory building, a scream pierced the air. Hal swung around to see a woman running away. She glanced back once or twice, staring at him in horror. Goblins spilled out of the main entrance, panic on their faces as they raised short swords toward him. They spread out, forming a line.

"What are you doing?" Abigail shouted at them.

The goblins tore their gazes from Hal and noticed her for the first time as she buzzed down to the ground before them. And then they frowned. One by one, recognition flickered over their faces. "Hey," one growled, nudging another. "Isn't that whatsername?"

Hal decided it was time to be human again, so he reverted to his normal self and immediately felt the icy cold temperature cutting through his thin smart clothes.

"It *is* them," another goblin exclaimed. All their swords lowered. "Get Simone."

Abigail let out an exasperated sigh. She took Hal's hand, and together they marched toward the lab entrance. "It's too cold to stand out here while you figure out who we are. Is Miss Simone inside?"

She didn't wait for an answer. Hal followed her into the lobby, where the temperature was far more bearable. They stood together and shivered, stamping the snow off their icy feet.

"Maybe they think we're dead," Hal muttered as goblins rushed off along the corridor.

Abigail's eyes widened. "Because we were gone so long?"

"Last seen flying off to find the faun. Maybe everyone thought we'd been turned to dust, then maybe transmogrified into elves or gnomes."

Abigail frowned. "Surely someone would have checked the local elf and gnome communities, though."

"Well, the faun could have turned us into frogs or gnats."

They stared at each other. The enormity of the situation was hitting home. Everyone thought them dead—or if not dead, living a life as something entirely different, their human pasts forgotten, eradicated. Their friends had mourned their loss. Hal's mom and dad, and Dr. Porter—

He felt weak at the knees. "This is bad, Abi. They probably had a funeral for us!"

"Oh!" a female voice rang out.

Miss Simone stood there, hands on her face, an expression of shock on her face. That shock turned to delight after a moment, and she rushed forward with her arms wide.

"You're here! You're alive!"

She hugged them both tight, then clasped each of their faces with a hand. Her touch on Hal's cheek was delightfully warm.

"We just went to the faun's tree," Abigail said, sounding a little shaky. "We literally flew out there, found her tree, snuck inside, followed a passage in the darkness, and found where River had rested and fixed up her ankle. But she wasn't there, so we came back out. And there was a fence, and snow everywhere."

Miss Simone took everything in and accepted it without question. "You've been gone four months. We looked for you, of course, and eventually found the faun's tree. The idea of searching the plains for an invisible tree seemed daunting, but *somebody* left us a helpful burn mark . . ."

Hal grinned. "I literally just finished marking that out a little while ago."

The smile faded from Miss Simone's face, and she looked thoughtful. "I dare say you're right. Yet we found it months ago—actually two days after you left."

Hal and Abigail exchanged a glance. How mind-boggling was *that*? His throat still burned a little from all the fire he'd generated.

"I just realized I missed my birthday," Abigail mused.

A pang of guilt struck Hal. "You know, I never did get a chance—" *Deal with that later.* He turned back to Miss Simone. "So does everyone think we're dead?"

"*Lost,*" Miss Simone corrected him. "Nobody gave up on you. We found the tree and assumed you'd gone inside. I went in myself to find you—just flashed a lantern around, then back out again. In that moment, I'd lost a week. It was incredible, and very frightening. So we had a dilemma. Should we go in after you and risk losing months of our own time . . . or just wait for you to come out?"

She shook her head, a familiar awestruck expression on her face.

"As remarkable as that faun's tree is, we decided to wait it out. We just didn't know how long for. I had some goblins erect the fence in case a herd of unicorns unwittingly galloped smack into an invisible tree trunk. Plus, your scorch mark was fading."

"So everyone knows we're okay?" Hal asked.

"Everyone *assumes* and *hopes* you are. Because the alternative . . ."

"Alternative?" Abigail asked.

"Well, what if the faun had ambushed you? What if she'd turned you both?"

Abigail's shoulders slumped. "Yeah, I know."

"What if we'd spent weeks or months waiting for you to come home when all the time you'd wandered off to some remote elf or naga village, your memories wiped?"

"Was that something my mom considered?" Abigail muttered.

Miss Simone placed her hands on her shoulder. "We all did. But we hoped for the best." She smiled. "And you're here now. Your parents must know right away. And your friends."

"We never did find the faun, though," Hal said. "Did you?"

Miss Simone shook her head.

Hal sighed. "So she could be anywhere. Any*when*. She might attack us again one day."

"She might. And in the meantime, Dr. Kessler has the potion. She's been studying it, but it's not making any scientific sense, so I'm going to track down a few witches and talk to them."

Hal scoffed under his breath. "Avoid Madame Frost."

Abigail fished the tiny glass bottle from her pocket. "I have this drop left, too."

"Keep it," Miss Simone said.

The moment she said that, Hal felt his heart stutter at the memory of what the blue gemstone had shown him and Abigail. The faun *would* strike again—twenty years from now. That was where she was right now—in the future. She'd rested her ankle, maybe slept a bit, and finally emerged.

And now she was ready for the next phase of her plan.

We need to hide that potion somewhere, Hal thought.

* * *

Reuniting with their friends and family was a heartbreaking affair, at least for Hal and Abigail. While their parents and all the shapeshifters were amazed and delighted to see them back, the two of them couldn't bear to be the cause of so many tears.

Hal thought his mom and dad looked worn down with worry and grief despite their happy smiles and joyful laughs. "Four months!" his dad kept saying in an almost accusatory tone. "Four months of not knowing where you were!"

"I *knew* you were alive somewhere," his mom told Hal, squeezing him tight. "I felt it in my bones. Alive—hopefully just a few weeks ahead of us, or maybe living a different life somewhere—but alive all the same." She broke down again, and Hal had to fight back tears of his own.

When it was Emily's turn to hug Hal, she said, "I searched all the naga villages looking for anyone who might have shown up confused or lost. But . . . nothing. What exactly happened?"

Abigail went into a little more detail, and the entire crowd fell silent during that minute. She told how Hal had scorched the black circle, and then they'd stepped inside the tree, searched the darkness, and emerged to a snowy landscape. And then came home. Somehow, the simplicity of her story made things worse. Everyone expected *more*.

Robbie punched Hal on the shoulder. "What the heck? We thought you'd been in *actual trouble*."

"Huh?" Hal said. "Should I be sorry, then?"

"Yeah! You had us all worried, thinking you were lost in the future, or dead, or wandering about with severe memory loss. Instead, you visited that faun's tree, climbed inside . . . and came straight home again. No danger at all!"

Hal couldn't help smiling. "But that's good, right?"

"No, it's not." Robbie glanced from Hal to Abigail and back again. "You didn't *think*. You both lost a whole day the first time you went to that tree. You should have known you'd lose more time if you went there again."

"Well, we *did* know that," Abigail said, "but we figured we'd just lose another day or so—not four months. We had no choice. We had to find the faun."

"And did you?" Robbie demanded. Despite his raised voice and angry tone, Hal saw immense relief in his friend's eyes.

"No," Hal said with a sigh. "River's long gone."

It was funny how life could so quickly take an unexpected turn. He and Abigail had popped away for just a minute. Now the entire village regarded them as ghosts.

He asked about Derek and the other three missing faun victims and was told they were all back to normal. That, Thomas grumbled, was old news. It was *all* old news.

Hal's parents insisted he went home for something to eat. They seemed convinced he should be hungry after four months without food. Really what they wanted was for him to just be there with them. They'd missed him, after all. He agreed and said goodbye to everyone.

"Happy birthday, teenager," Hal whispered to Abigail. He fished in his pocket, relieved to find the wooden dragon pendant still wrapped in a cloth. He pressed it into her hands. "Belated birthday present. Don't say I never give you anything."

She rolled her eyes. "Only four months late." Unwrapping the gift and peeking inside, a smile crept across her face. "Hal, that's lovely!" She fingered the tiny wooden dragon. "Kinda looks like you, too."

Hal watched as she slipped the pendant over her head. "Suits you."

"A dragon suits me? Well, I think so, too." She suddenly grew very serious and studied him so hard that he felt like squirming. "Hal . . ."

I know what you're gonna say.

"That boy and girl we saw . . ."

He swallowed. "I don't know what to make of that."

"The boy called you 'Dad' and said he was from the future." Abigail gazed at him, eyes wide. "What if the faun rested inside the tree long enough that a couple of decades passed? I mean, that boy looked about our age, and if you're his dad—"

"What are we supposed to do?" Hal said quietly. "The only way we can help is to go back inside that tree and wait, then step out twenty years from now."

She frowned. "But then you wouldn't be that boy's dad . . ."

"Exactly. You'll drive yourself nuts thinking about it."

But something told him she'd think about very little else from now on.

It looked like the adults were ready to leave. "I'll see you tomorrow," he whispered.

"Count on it," she replied, leaning in for a hug.

Miss Simone organized a thick coat for them both, then put her own on. She walked with Hal and his parents out of the warm lab building and into the snow-covered streets. The biting cold startled Hal, and he pulled his coat tight, wishing he had thicker pants and some heavy boots as well. He'd gone from warm late-summer temperatures to frigid icy air in one afternoon.

"I'm glad you're back, Hal," Miss Simone said as they walked. "I have something lined up for you all."

His parents glanced at each other. "Uh-oh," his dad said. "Another mission?"

"Not so soon," his mom said rather shortly to Miss Simone. "I want him home for a while. It's been *four months*! I need my boy home for a while."

Miss Simone held up her hands and smiled. "Yes, of course, I understand. And it's not a mission, more of a vacation. I just wanted to get him thinking about it, that's all."

"Thinking about what?" Hal asked, intrigued.

She patted his shoulder. "A journey. A *voyage*."

Both Hal's parents stopped and turned to her, eyes narrowed. "To where?" his dad demanded. "He just got home, and already you want to send him off to the other side of the planet?"

Miss Simone shook her head. "Not exactly, no."

Hal sensed something in her voice. He studied her, and she gave him a wink.

"Just to the edge of the world."

Coming Next

Hal and his friends take a ride on the back of a gigantic turtle on a quest to find the fabled edge of the world. They discover the legend is true, that Earth really does end at the horizon, and ships really can sail over the edge. But it's not all death and destruction. Instead, the shapeshifters find something quite breathtaking and are sorely tempted to stay forever . . .

Meanwhile, Twenty Years Later

"Lady Simone!" A small, agile nine-year-old ran toward them. He was a recognizable face around the town, one of many messengers. "The council needs you! There's something coming—something really weird, a storm on the horizon."

"A *storm*?" Miss Simone repeated. "So we need to fetch umbrellas?"

The boy halted in front of her, his face flushed from running but his breathing regular. "It's not that kind of storm. It's like dust, only it's blue. The council said you need to check it out. They're getting word about other towns north of here."

"What about them?"

"They're gone," the boy said with wide eyes. "Completely swallowed up."

While the statement sent a chill down Travis's spine and caused Melinda to suck in a breath, Miss Simone simply raised an eyebrow. "Swallowed up? Really? And I presume those towns miraculously reappeared once the storm had moved on?"

The messenger looked off to the side, his brow creasing. "Um . . . well, I don't know, exactly. The council just said they've been swallowed up. By a weird blue dust storm."

Miss Simone turned to Travis and Melinda. "It's going to be one of those days."

* * *

The faun returns in **Death Storm**, Book 5 of the Island of Fog Legacies spin-off series, set twenty years later and featuring a new generation of shapeshifters. You can jump straight into that series and follow the faun's dastardly plot without needing to read the previous books in the Legacies series. *Forest of Souls* and *Death Storm* can be enjoyed independently or as a pair, and in any order.

Or you can start at the beginning with *Unicorn Hunters*.

Visit **UnearthlyTales.com** for up-to-date information about this series and other books by Keith Robinson.

Did you enjoy *Forest of Souls*? If so, please consider posting a review. Reviews and ratings help sell books. Thank you!

Made in the USA
San Bernardino, CA
29 November 2018